BOOK I

A SAGA OF BLOOD & OIL

D.W. LAYTON

LESLIE BOOKS
SINCE 1910

Otello's Oil: A Saga of Blood & Oil (Book 1)
© Duane Layton
Published by Leslie Books, LLC
Cover design by BookBaby

This book is a work of fiction. Names, characters, businesses, organizations, events, and incidents either are the product of the author's imagination or are used fictionally. Any resemblance to events or actual persons, living or dead, is entirely coincidental.

ISBN: 979-8-35095-430-2

"At present, oil is the weak point of our Empire's national strength and fighting power... As time passes, our capacity to carry on war will decline, and our Empire will become powerless militarily." (Japanese military briefing materials for meetings with Emperor Hirohito, September 5–6, 1941)

Chapter One

(Saturday, October 25, 2031)

Neither they nor the Lyft driver knew exactly where to catch the ferry to Winslow. Seattle's waterfront, at the best of times, was difficult to navigate. Now it was practically impossible. Following the destruction of the Alaskan Way Viaduct, which had cast an ugly shadow over the city's waterfront for more than sixty years, and the opening of the Route 99 tunnel, the city was giving its waterfront a complete makeover. One city official described it as a "kaleidoscope" of new shops, restaurants, attractions, and pedestrian walkways. For now, though, the kaleidoscope was a tortuous maze of construction equipment, traffic cones, detours, and lane closures.

"Just drop us off here," Rachel Jones told the driver. "We'll find it. It can't be far."

Rachel and her dad got out of the car. It was a magnificent day. The sun was out and the *mountain* was *out*.

"Isn't it beautiful, Dad? Look at Mount Rainer. Is that incredible or what?"

At 14,410 feet, Mount Rainer is the fifth tallest peak in the continental United States. It sits only 85 miles southeast of Seattle and only 55 miles southeast of Tacoma. However, on most days, it is covered in clouds—a common feature of the weather in the Pacific Northwest. Clouds and rain. Constant rain. But on those rare and beautiful occasions when the clouds are gone, the sun shines, and it feels as though you can almost reach out and touch Mount Rainer, the locals refer to the "mountain" as "out."

"And the Olympics," she said, pointing west across Elliott Bay. "I've never seen them so clear before. We lucked out on the weather. Especially for the last weekend in October. I wish Mom was here."

Elliot Jones was indeed lucky. Not only was it a gorgeous day, but he was having a great weekend with his daughter.

Rachel was a freshman at the University of Washington (UW). Except for a brief tour of the campus during her junior year of high school, she'd never been to Seattle before. The Pacific Northwest was all new to her.

They had toured Pike Place Market, where Elliot tossed a sockeye salmon to the hoots and hollers of onlookers. Rachel had taken her dad to the Ballard Locks, where they watched coho salmon swim up the fish ladder. And now they were riding one of Washington's iconic green-and-white ferries.

"You know, we have perfect days in DC," Elliot said. "Not often, but we do. But I can't remember a day in DC as beautiful as this. The air here is so crisp and clear. Smell that." He took a deep breath. "Thank God I brought my sunglasses. I almost didn't given Seattle's reputation for lousy weather."

Winslow was a charming little town of about 25,000 on Bainbridge Island. Getting there by ferry would take under an hour. Getting there by car would take over two. In late October the ferries ran every hour. The next one was scheduled to depart at 9:35 a.m. Rachel thought her dad would enjoy riding on the ferries. They could walk around Winslow a little, maybe shop, eat lunch, and then catch one of the afternoon ferries back to Seattle.

It turned out to be a short walk to the Colman Terminal at Pier 52. After they bought their tickets they waited with the other passengers traveling on foot in a small terminal on the second floor. Once the attendants announced boarding Rachel and her dad passed through the turnstiles and made their way up and over the footbridge that connected to the ferry. Below them they could see the cars and trucks as they began the boarding process.

Elliot had never ridden on a ferry this large before. When Rachel was little, he had taken her and her mother on the ferry that crossed the Tred Avon River between Oxford and Saint Michael's, Maryland. But that was a small ferry that strained to carry nine cars. This was one of the largest ferries in the world, what Washington State called a "Jumbo Mark II."

The MV *Chehalis* was 460 feet long and 90 feet wide with propellers on both ends. It could carry over 200 cars and 2,500 passengers at over 20 knots. Its double-end design allowed cars and passengers to board on one end and get off on the other.

Elliot and his daughter didn't know it, but this would be one of the *Chehalis'* last runs for a while. It would soon undergo a major conversion to hybrid-electric propulsion. Its sister ship, the MV *Wenatchee*, had already been converted. The *Chehalis* was next, to be followed by the MV *Puyallup* and the MV *Tacoma*.

Once on board, they passed within a few feet of vehicles taking their place on the ferry. The smell of gasoline and exhaust fumes was strong as they walked up the narrow stairs to the second level. The indoor areas were sterile and spartan. The one on the second level was huge, complete with restrooms, two snack bars, and plenty of seating. However, Elliot wanted to watch the boarding process. Besides, it was a beautiful day, so he headed outside. Rachel followed.

Since they were two of the first to board, they had no problem finding a place standing next to the railing, which was painted emerald green, at the back of the ferry on the second level. Leaning on it, they could see the entirety of Seattle before them—from T-Mobile Park and Lumen Field on their right to the Space Needle on their left. They also had a bird's-eye view of the boarding process.

Passengers traveling by foot continued to board to their left across the footbridge. Below and in front, cars and trucks in a seemingly endless line rumbled over the steel plates and on to the deck of the ferry. As they did, the large plates rattled and clanked. Elliot was fascinated. Rachel? Not so much.

"Dad, I'm going inside. I want to get a cup of tea and maybe a donut. You want anything?"

"No, but thanks. I'll join you in a bit."

"I'll probably sit up front. I want to check out the Olympics."

"Okay, honey."

* * *

As the line of cars waiting to board the ferry shrank, an old Porsche came into view. Elliot loved old cars. He had a 1949 Porsche 356 Speedster in his garage back home. This looked like a '54 Speedster because it had a bent (or curved) windshield. Elliot's Porsche had a split windshield. In any event, the top of this one was down and a well-dressed Hispanic guy wearing aviator sunglasses was behind the wheel. One of the last to board, he maneuvered the car gently over the steel plates. Only the driver of an older, white Chevy "box" van, the kind many painters and contractors used, pulled in behind him.

Elliot couldn't help but stare at the Porsche. It was light green with a black interior. It looked to be in mint condition. The driver got out and grabbed a leather flight jacket from behind his seat before heading inside. He didn't bother to lock it.

Directly behind him the driver of the van got out. He was light-skinned, probably in his early thirties, with an unruly beard. He was a big guy, but in good shape. He wore a dark baseball cap and a light brown denim jacket.

As he got out of the van he tucked a handgun in his belt. The sight of a gun startled Elliot. But then he recalled that Washington State, unlike his home state of Virginia, allowed open carry. This was the Wild West, after all. Maybe it was normal and nothing to worry about.

Before closing the door, the driver of the van tilted his seat forward and reached back into the dark interior. Ten seconds later he slammed his seat back down and closed the door. As he took keys out to lock it, he quickly looked around. Elliot and the man locked eyes. Instinctively, Elliot redirected his gaze out across the water to his right.

Just then shouting erupted down on the deck to Elliot's left. A woman getting out of her car had scraped the door of another. Despite an immediate apology, the aggrieved driver, also a woman, was furious. Two male deckhands tried their best to calm them.

"Looks like a cat fight," a guy standing next to Elliot blurted. "My money's on the brunette," he said with a laugh. "She looks pretty buff."

Elliot feigned agreement just to appease the man. When Elliot looked back in the direction of the van, its driver was gone.

For the first time since he had been out there, Elliot let go of the railing. The show was over. How long had he been there? He should go find Rachel, maybe check out the other end of the ferry. He certainly wanted to put some distance between himself and the guy next to him.

However, as he turned to go more shouting erupted on the deck below. This time it was to his right. A young woman pushing a baby stroller, with two toddlers holding on to her light blue skirt, was yelling at a twentysomething male deckhand left alone by the guys who went to settle the argument on the other side of the ferry.

"Get out of my way. Let me off!" she shouted.

"Ma'am, please," the young man said, holding up both hands in an attempt to stop her.

"I have a doctor's appointment in Seattle. My baby is sick."

"Please."

"Look. I was in the bathroom changing her diaper when we arrived. As you can see, I also have two other little ones. I tried to take the elevator, but it was full. So I came down those damn stairs as quickly as I could!"

"I'm sorry, ma'am. But once boarding starts, we're not supposed to let anyone off."

"I don't care. I am not going back to Winslow," the lady said over the cries of her two toddlers. "Get out of my way!"

The woman pushed her stroller forward. The young man looked for help. None was forthcoming.

As the woman moved forward, her stroller got stuck in a grate. She jerked the stroller back and forth to free it. Now the baby in the stroller was crying, the toddlers were screaming, and the mother was cussing up a storm. Elliot's first instinct was to go down and help.

Just then a man came out from amongst the cars below. "Here, ma'am, let me help you."

In an instant the woman and her kids, together with the man, were off the ferry. In another instant the last line was freed and the ferry's massive engines roared to life. The ferry's distinctive horn bellowed, announcing its departure. It was so loud that it startled Elliot.

The ferry began to pull away from the dock. Seagulls from all directions fell in behind the vessel, hoping to catch a french fry or other morsel tossed in the air by a passenger.

As deckhands strung heavy netting across the back of the ferry and the seagulls danced in the sky waiting for their next meal, Elliot concentrated on the man walking away from the ferry. Elliot couldn't see the man's face and he wasn't wearing a jacket, but he wore a dark baseball cap and he had the same build as the driver of the van. Moreover, the mother didn't seem to know him. Indeed, Elliot never saw her acknowledge him or even talk to him. She was intent on keeping her kids together and getting to wherever she was going.

At that moment, though, Elliot saw the man look to his right in the direction of a small boat about 250 yards off the port side of the ferry. Elliot thought he could make out the words "Boston Whaler" on the side of the boat.

At least two people were on board. The person at the helm appeared to be a man. The person standing at the back appeared to be a woman. She held what looked like binoculars and focused her gaze on the pier.

Elliot looked back at the pier just in time to see the man give the small boat some sort of wave or signal. When he did, the boat immediately turned and headed south toward the Duwamish River inlet. But in that moment, Elliot caught a glimpse of the man's face. He had the same unruly beard as the driver of the van!

Chapter Two

Elliot's mind raced. Was the man on the pier the driver of the van? Or was he the husband or friend of the woman with the kids? It sure didn't seem so. If he *was* the driver of the van, this could be bad, very bad.

In that instant Elliot made a decision. He spun around and raced down the stairs to the car deck. It was a short distance to the van. Because the car deck was open on both ends, the wind slapped Elliot in the face as he approached the van.

First Elliot tried opening the driver's door. Then he tried the passenger and back doors. All were locked. He tried looking inside the van. He pressed his face against the glass. He cupped his hands around his face to cut down on the glare from the sun. He couldn't see anything. The back of the van was dark and the front seats were, for the most part, empty.

He turned and yelled at the first deckhand he saw. "Is a security officer on board?"

"I'm sorry?" the young deckhand asked.

In an even louder voice Elliot yelled, "Do you have a cop or some type of security officer on this ferry?"

"Yes, sir. I believe a VATS officer is on board. What's the matter?"

"Well, get him. Now!!"

"Sir, please, lower your voice. Is this your van?"

By now the two other deckhands were standing next to Elliot.

"No, goddamn it!"

As Elliot showed the deckhands his Diplomatic Security Service (DSS) badge, he said, "My name is Elliot Jones. I'm a senior agent with the US Diplomatic Security Service in Washington, DC. I'm out here for the weekend visiting my daughter. I believe the man who drove this van on board is the same man who left at the last minute with that lady and the screaming kids. The doors are locked. The inside of the van is dark."

As Elliot spoke, the two deckhands next to him tried to open the van's doors. One of them peered into the van the same way Elliot had. They looked at each other without saying a word. Seconds passed.

Then the older of the two deckhands pulled a radio from a leather holster attached to his belt. As he looked the third deckhand in the eyes, he pressed one of the buttons on the side of the radio. Elliot heard the squawk that a radio typically makes.

"Officer Romano? This is Pete Langlie. I'm a deckhand on the *Chehalis*. I'm on the aft deck with a man who claims to be some sort of federal agent from Washington, DC. He believes the driver of a van back here got off before castoff. The van seems to be locked and we can't see inside. Can you get down here right away?"

"Thanks," Elliot said.

"Sure," Langlie replied. "Now what agency did you say you're with?"

"I'm with the Diplomatic Security Service. You ever heard of the Secret Service?"

"Of course."

"Well, we're essentially the same thing, except we protect the US secretary of state 24/7, foreign dignitaries and diplomats when they're in the United States, and our ambassadors and other embassy personnel overseas."

"Oh, gotcha."

At that moment a rather large and imposing Washington State Vessel & Terminal Safety (VATS) officer approached. His uniform was mainly black, except for the top third of his shirt, which was royal blue. Over his shirt he wore a black ballistic vest with his name on it. His belt and vest carried sundry items such as mace, a flashlight, and handcuffs. A Glock .40 caliber pistol hung at his side. Next to him, on a leash, was a black Labrador retriever named Molly.

Langlie spoke first. "Officer Romano, this is Elliot Jones. As I said, he's from Washington and—"

Before he could finish, Elliot, looking briefly at Langlie and then the officer, spoke. "I'm sorry to interrupt, but we may have only minutes or seconds here." Elliot once again displayed his badge.

Speaking quickly, Elliot said, "Officer Romano, I've been in federal law enforcement for over 30 years. I investigated the bombing of our embassies in Kenya and Tanzania in 1998."

Turning and pointing to the railing on the second level above and behind them, Elliot said, "I stood up there and watched the boarding process. I watched the driver of this van get out, place a handgun in his belt, lock the door, and leave. However, before he left he spent about 10 seconds doing something in the back of the van. Then there was a commotion over here."

Elliot pointed to the port side of the ferry. "A mother with three screaming kids insisted on getting off. I believe the man who drove this van got off with that lady and her kids."

Romano listened intently. "So you think there may be explosives in this van?"

"Well, sir, I don't know. But I do believe the man who parked this van got off the ferry. He may have also had accomplices—two people on a small boat a couple of hundred yards over there," Elliot said, pointing south. "When the driver got off he gave them some sort of signal. They immediately turned and headed that way."

The officer stood for a second in silence, thinking. The vessel's large engines rumbled beneath his feet. He looked at Pier 52 as it grew smaller and smaller. The ferry's wake was as determined as its engines. He had made the run between Seattle and Winslow on the *Chehalis* or its sister ferry, the *Tacoma*, many times. He figured they were now about a half mile from the pier with eight and a half miles to go, and about 15 minutes until they were in the middle of the shipping channel used by some of the largest container ships and tankers in the world. In parts of the channel the water's depth was over 800 feet.

By now two couples who had been sitting in their cars came over to see what all the commotion was about. Above them about a dozen passengers lined the rail on the second deck, watching the drama below. More arrived every minute, each asking essentially the same question as the one before: "What's happening? What's going on?"

Without saying anything more, the officer spoke quietly into the radio clipped to his shirt between his collar and his left shoulder.

"Captain Magnuson? This is Officer Romano. We've got a situation down here on the aft car deck. A box van at the end of the line is locked and we believe the driver may have gotten off prior to departure. I know. Yes. It shouldn't have happened. We're going to investigate. I've got K9 support. Hopefully this is a false alarm, so I wouldn't make any announcements that might scare the passengers. I would, though, try to get as many passengers as possible inside and away from glass, especially here at the back. Yes, sir. Thank you. I will, sir."

Officer Romano released the button on his radio and looked at Elliot and the deckhands. At the same time the four onlookers spoke quietly among themselves before racing up the stairs, where they were interrogated by the passengers along the rail. Within minutes all but a handful of them had disappeared.

"Okay," Romano said to no one in particular. "Let's see what we got here."

Romano asked Elliot and the others to step back. Then he gently jerked on Molly's leash. He wanted her full attention.

Looking her squarely in the eyes, he said, "Okay, Molly. Are you ready?"

Romano knew the answer. The dog was shaking with anticipation. "Go seek!"

Without hesitating, Molly moved with purpose. First she moved around the Porsche, her nose constantly working. Then she headed for the van. Romano followed. The dog's nose moved quickly up and down and from side to side. She focused her attention along the bottom edge of the driver's side door. In an instant she stopped and sat on her haunches. She looked intently at the van and back at Romano.

"Good girl, Molly!" With his free hand Romano gave her a small treat.

Conditions were not ideal. The wind was whipping through the cavity of the ferry. But by sitting the way she did, Molly had given Romano a positive sign that explosives were present.

Romano had trained for this moment. Nonetheless, his heart was racing. What should he do next? Did he have probable cause to search the van? The clock was ticking. He wanted to see if Molly would repeat the signal. He led her away from the van, upwind. He then turned to the starboard side of the ferry and approached the van from the passenger side. No reaction from Molly at the passenger door. She worked her way down the side of the van. Again her nose was constantly moving up and down and from side to side. Elliot and the deckhands watched in silence. As Romano rounded the back corner of the van Molly grew more agitated. Her nose was moving across the bottom of the rear doors. In an instant she sat. That was it! That was probable cause.

"Good girl, Molly. Good girl!" He gave the dog another treat.

Romano returned to the front of the van where Elliot and the deckhands were standing. "I have a Slim Jim, but it's in my squad car at the other end of the ferry. Not enough time."

He pulled a small emergency hammer from his belt. "I'm gonna break the glass. Get back."

As they began to step back, one of the younger deckhands whispered into Langlie's ear, "What's a Slim Jim?"

All of Langlie's attention was on Romano and the white van. He didn't want to be distracted. His reply was abrupt. "It's a long piece of metal with hooks on the end. You can unlock a car with it. Now get back!"

Romano spread his feet and rapped the driver's side window once very hard in the corner with a backhand motion. The sharp, conical stainless steel head shattered the glass. He put the hammer back in his belt and grabbed his flashlight. Using the butt end, he proceeded to smash the shards of glass over and over again until he could reach inside.

Once he had the door open he tilted the seat forward and pulled aside the black sheet that concealed the van's cargo. His flashlight confirmed his suspicions. Eight blue plastic barrels filled the back of the van. Two nylon straps held them in place. The smell of diesel was faint but noticeable. Romano suspected half the barrels were filled with diesel and the other half with high-nitrogen fertilizer. On top of each barrel appeared to be about half a pound of C-4 explosive, each with wires running from a fuse to two different master fuses. A single timer ran between the master fuses. The timer's red numbers glowed in the dark—12:02 and counting.

Without saying a word, Romano turned toward Elliot. Romano's silence spoke volumes.

What should he do? A second opinion might help him decide. He handed Elliot his flashlight. "Take a look." The deckhands looked at each other in silence. They were all thinking the same thing—*Should we run?*

After peering inside the van for a few seconds, Elliot spoke to Romano in a whisper. "That's enough to blow the ass off this ferry."

"That's what I thought," Romano said.

"Can you disarm it?" Elliot asked. "I've investigated my fair share of bombings over the years, but I'm not an explosives expert. We have highly trained specialists for that."

"I could try. If that's C-4 on top of the barrels, that's pretty stable stuff. But they've connected each charge to a master fuse, and there are two masters connected to a single timer. Whoever built this wanted some redundancy in case one fuse failed. That tells me these guys knew what they were doing. If I start cutting wires or trying to remove fuses, well—"

Romano did not finish his thought. He didn't need to. Elliot knew exactly what he meant.

Elliot thought for a second, then he said, "What if we just push it off the back?"

Romano stared at Elliot, his eyes wide and unmoving. In the time it would take ink to dry, Romano went from thinking *Are you nuts?* to *What other choice do we have?*

Romano turned to the deckhands, who to their credit or stupidity were still standing there. Raising his voice in order to be heard over the wind and the rumble of the engines, he said, "We don't have much time."

Pointing to Langlie, Romano said, "Get the captain on the radio. Tell him the van is loaded with explosives and we're going to try to push it off the back. If we can get it off, he needs to accelerate as much as possible. The more distance we put between ourselves and the van, the better. He should also notify the Coast Guard. They need to alert all nearby vessels."

Romano pointed up at the passengers looking down from above. "Get those passengers out of here. Everyone should move to the middle of the ferry!"

Finally, pointing at the temporary barrier across the back of the ferry, he told one of the other deckhands, "Get that netting down and out of the way."

Speaking to Elliot and the remaining deckhand, Romano said, "Let's see if we can move this thing." He handed Elliot Molly's leash and got in the van without sweeping off the shards of glass that remained on the seat. There wasn't time. His heart was racing. His palms were sweaty on the wheel. The wind echoed in his ears and inside the van.

He put his right foot on the brake pedal. He released the parking brake by pulling on the handle located between the steering column and the door. As he did, it popped and made a loud *CLUNK* sound. The gearshift was on the right side of the steering column. The van was an automatic. He tried to put it in neutral, but without the van being turned on, the gearshift refused to budge. The timer was down to 9:57.

He frantically jiggled the shifter. "COME ON, COME ON DAMMIT!"

He took his foot off the brake and tried rocking the van back and forth like a child on a schoolyard swing. As he did, he could feel the glass cut his pants and probably his skin. With the van's wheels moving slightly back and forth, he pushed the gearshift arm even harder. "COME ON!"

This time the gearbox relented. It popped into neutral.

Romano jumped out of the van and closed the door. Molly excitedly jumped on his legs. He took her leash from Elliot. Then he yelled, "Come on, PUSH! We're running out of time!!"

Elliot, Romano, and the deckhand strained. The van moved a few feet backward. Molly barked at all the excitement. They had about seventeen feet to go. They pushed even harder. Langlie, who was still on the radio with the captain, helped. The van started to pick up momentum. It was now six feet from the edge. The deckhand who had removed the safety netting also came rushing over to help. All five were now pushing as hard as they could.

The back wheels dropped off the deck with a hard THUNK. Elliot feared the van might get stuck on the edge of the deck. Straining, he yelled, "PUSHHH!"

Luckily, the van had built up enough momentum by the time it reached the edge that it continued to roll and then scraped over the side of the ferry. As the frame and undercarriage passed over the edge, the metal on metal gave a loud screech like nails on a chalkboard. The last part of the vehicle to make contact with the ferry was the front bumper, which caught the deck hard, as if slugged by a boxer with an uppercut.

The instant the front wheels passed over the back edge of the ferry, Romano yelled at Langlie. "Full throttle… NOW!!" Next, he shouted at everyone to "GET BACK. GET DOWN!"

Elliot never saw exactly where the deckhands went. They quickly disappeared into the sea of vehicles parked on the *Chehalis*. He and Romano ran down separate aisles between the cars. They hit the deck at roughly the same time, alongside a pickup truck. At first they both faced the bow. But their curiosity quickly got the best of them and they slid around on the deck in the hopes of spotting the van in the water.

Meanwhile, Molly thought all the running around and lying on the deck was a game meant solely for her entertainment. She barked and tried to lick Romano's face. Romano pulled down on the dog's leash in a vain attempt to calm her and get her to lie down.

At first the van floated, only partly submerged in the water. They both thought the same thing—*SINK, DAMN IT, SINK!* But with the driver's side window open the vehicle soon filled with water and plunged. At a distance of about 400 yards the C-4 detonated together with the diesel and fertilizer.

The concussion caused Elliot and Romano to slam their faces down on the deck. It also caused the windows at the back of the ferry to rattle. The surface of the water heaved violently upward as if pushed by an underwater volcano.

The energy released by the explosion was so great it caused a thirteen-foot wave to pass under the giant ferry. This caused the alarms on dozens of vehicles to go off. Molly responded the only way she knew how—by barking.

After the wave passed and the ferry started to settle, Elliot and Romano looked at each other. Their faces framed by the undercarriage of the pickup and the ferry's deck. Was it over?

They slowly got to their feet. Romano swept the glass off his pants. They looked around. They couldn't believe it. With the exception of four panels that had shattered, the large glass windows across the back of the ferry on the second level remained intact.

"You believe that?" Romano said to Elliot with a mix of astonishment and relief.

"Yeah. We did it. Damn, that was close."

Elliot was in good shape, especially for his age. He worked out three times a week most weeks and tried to go for long walks in his neighborhood the days he didn't go to the gym. Nonetheless, between the stress of the situation and straining to push the van, he was exhausted. He wanted to rest, but he needed to find Rachel.

"Listen, I've got to find my daughter, make sure she's alright. She's up front somewhere. I should also try to clean up a little."

"Understood," Romano said. "I've got to call this in to my headquarters. We'll need a statement from you and help with a description of the driver and the people on the Boston Whaler."

Standing on the deck with the wind howling in his face and car alarms competing with the growl of the ferry's engines, he strained to hear Romano.

"What'd you say?" Elliot cupped his right hand behind his ear.

Romano raised his voice and leaned forward to be heard. "I said we'll need a statement from you and help with a description of the driver and the people on the Boston Whaler. Hopefully we have the driver on video, either on the ferry or the pier. Can you meet me up near the pilot house before you get off? You should meet the captain. I'm sure he'll want to meet you."

"Sure," Elliot shouted. "But I promised my daughter I'd have lunch with her and walk around Winslow. I'd like to keep that promise. I can also talk to you on the ride back if you want. I think I heard her say we were going to try to catch the one heading back at three o'clock. Oh, and here's my card. You can always reach me at that number and e-mail address. I'm taking the red-eye back to Washington tomorrow night."

Romano ignored the irony. To locals like himself, "Washington" meant the state of Washington. Romano extended his hand. "Okay, thanks." They shook. His grip was firm. His eyes said what he was thinking—*Mister, you probably saved my life!*

* * *

Elliot made his way up to the front of the ferry. The Olympic Mountains were on full display. Winslow was fast approaching. They would be there in 10 minutes.

Finding Rachel was not difficult. She was seated in the middle, staring at her phone as if in a trance. White earphones tuned out the rest of the world. An empty paper cup and donut wrapper sat on the bench. He pushed them aside and sat down next to her.

She yanked her earphones out. "There you are. I was wondering what happened to you. What have you been up to? And what's with the grease stains on your pants?"

"I don't know. I must have brushed up against something."

"Did you feel that wave a few minutes ago? That was wild. Must have been the wake from one of those large container ships or tankers. There are some huge ones out here."

"Yeah, that was wild." If she only knew.

They got up to leave. Rachel threw her garbage in a nearby trash can. As they reached the stairs leading down to the auto deck, they heard a voice from behind.

"Mr. Jones, excuse me. Can I have a word with you?"

Rachel and her dad turned to see Captain Magnuson, Officer Romano, and six members of the crew approach. Passengers who were heading downstairs also stopped. Some were speaking in hushed tones and pointing at Elliot. The captain extended his hand to Elliot.

"Mr. Jones, good morning. I'm Captain Magnuson. On behalf of myself and the entire crew of the *Chehalis*, I want to thank you for what you did today. Officer Romano has told me. Everyone on board this vessel owes you their life. Thank you!"

Elliot shook the captain's hand. By now about three dozen passengers stood listening. As soon as the captain finished they burst into applause. Rachel stood speechless with her mouth open, looking at her dad.

As they made their way down the stairs Rachel struggled to process what she had just heard. When they reached the car deck, she whispered in Elliot's ear, "What the hell, Dad?"

"I'll explain later."

Chapter Three

(Four Weeks Earlier)

The Kennedy Center for the Performing Arts sits alone in Washington, DC. Like a medieval castle protected from marauders by a moat and drawbridge, the Kennedy Center is surrounded by parkways, bridges, freeway ramps, and the Potomac River. Not far from Georgetown, it has only two distant neighbors: the Watergate—made famous by President Nixon and his "Plumbers"—and the embassy of the Kingdom of Saudi Arabia.

Completed in 1971, the Kennedy Center is not one venue, but many. The south end of the building is dominated by the 2,465-seat Concert Hall, home to the National Symphony Orchestra (NSO). The north end is home to the Eisenhower Theater—a 1,161-seat stage that hosts plays, musicals, and smaller ballet performances. In the middle is the giant Opera House. Bathed in red fabrics from head to toe and crowned by a majestic Lobmeyr crystal chandelier that was a gift from Austria, the Opera House is the most well known of the Kennedy Center stages. In addition to the Concert Hall, the Eisenhower Theater, and the Opera House, the Kennedy Center houses the Millennium Stage, the River Pavilion, the Skylight Pavilion, the Family

Theater, the Terrace Theater, the Theater Lab, and numerous meeting and rehearsal rooms, including Studios F and J.

Visitors to the Kennedy Center enter via one of two ways. They either enter through the Entrance Plaza, having taken a taxi or rideshare, or walked from the Foggy Bottom–GWU subway stop, or they park their cars underneath the Center and take elevators to the Hall of Nations or the Hall of States.

Each hall has ceilings 63 feet high and provides stunning views from one side of the venue to the other. Both connect to the Grand Foyer—with its 16 handblown Orrefors crystal chandeliers, a gift from Sweden—that faces the Potomac. At 63 feet high and 630 feet long, the Grand Foyer is one of the largest rooms in the world. Its centerpiece is an eight-foot-high, 3,000-pound bronze bust of President John F. Kennedy, after whom the Center is named. Circling the outside of the Kennedy Center like a halo is an expansive rooftop terrace that provides visitors with a 360-degree view of the city and northern Virginia across the Potomac.

* * *

The Washington Opera Company tries to feature at least one *grand* opera each season. Often this means an opera by Giuseppe Verdi, widely regarded as Italy's premier composer. Since 1999 Washington Opera has performed almost 150 operas, with 20 by Verdi, including *Aida*, *Don Carlos*, *La Traviata*, and *Rigoletto*.

Every year, including this one, the opera season begins in the fall as the golden leaves of autumn begin to turn, the temperature starts to bite the skin, and the days grow shorter. Once again an opera by Verdi would launch the 2031-32 Washington Opera season on Saturday, October 25.

Based on William Shakespeare's play *Othello*, *Otello* was one of Verdi's last operas. It premiered at Teatro alla Scala in Milan on February 2, 1887, to critical acclaim. It is a story of love, treachery, and unimaginable grief told in four acts: timeless <u>love</u> between the governor of Cyprus,

General Otello, and his devoted young wife, Desdemona; <u>treachery</u> on the part of Iago, Otello's ensign, who convinces his master that Desdemona is having an affair with Cassio; and, unimaginable <u>grief</u> when Otello, aflame with jealousy, kills his wife and then stabs himself to death when he discovers her innocence.

One week before rehearsals for *Otello* were set to begin, the supernumerary (aka "super") cast as the captain of the guards broke his ankle playing softball on the mall—the grassy expanse between the US Capitol and the Washington Monument. In Act I, as the opening curtain ascends high over the Opera House stage, he was supposed to sprint across the stage and lead his men up the stairs of the castle to see if Otello and his ships were approaching. A broken ankle made this impossible. A last-minute replacement was needed.

* * *

The black Mercedes S580 with diplomatic plates and tinted windows dropped him off in front. He had never been to the Kennedy Center before. He felt small in its cavernous hallways and spaces. He was also struck by how quiet and empty it was inside. At lunchtime on a Thursday afternoon in late September, the crowds were gone, replaced by a few security guards and janitors.

He approached a man pushing a vacuum cleaner back and forth over the blood-red carpet. His movements were rhythmic, as if he were dancing. His name tag read "Craig."

"Excuse me," the man shouted over the roar of the vacuum. At first the janitor did not respond. He was wearing earphones, probably listening to music.

"Excuse me," the man repeated as he tapped the janitor's shoulder. The vacuum stopped and one earpiece was removed. The janitor looked up.

"Sorry, but I'm looking for the stage door to the Opera House."

"It's off the Hall of Nations. This is the Hall of States." With that Craig turned his vacuum back on and resumed his dance.

The man walked back to the Entrance Plaza and over to the Hall of Nations. He soon found a plain, white, unassuming metal door labeled "OPERA HOUSE."

As he entered he was greeted by a guard wearing a gray uniform and a black tie. A two-way radio and notepad lay on the guard's desk. A pen was in his shirt pocket. There was no sign of a weapon.

"Can I help you?"

"Yes, I'm looking for Ms. Treadwell. I believe she is in charge of casting extras for the opera."

"You mean *supers*," the guard replied. "She's on the third floor. Take that elevator over there."

The elevator was large with an oily smell, not the kind of elevator he was used to. He pressed the button marked "3." Where he came from that would have taken him to the fourth floor.

After a short ride the elevator doors opened and immediately the man was confronted by a young woman holding an e-tablet. She had curly, brown hair and thick glasses. She looked up at him.

"You a super or singer?" she asked without introduction or any kind of greeting.

For a moment the man was confused. Then he remembered what the guard had said. "Super."

"What's your name?"

"Raouf, I mean Ralph."

"Well, which is it?"

"Sorry. Ralph. Ralph Allen." He tried to cover his tracks with a small laugh. "Raouf is what my mom calls me. I just got off the phone with her."

As she typed something on her tablet, she motioned her head in the direction of a nearby hallway. "Okay, Ralph Allen. Go down that hallway, last door on the right."

No point in talking to her, he thought. He simply said "thanks" as he turned and started down the hall.

Unlike downstairs, which was cavernous and monastic, the man now found himself in a collection of rooms teeming with people buzzing about like bees determined to pollenate a jasmine bush before nightfall.

As he passed one large room he saw twenty ballet dancers moving in unison to recorded music as a man he could not see counted loudly: "3, 4, 5." In another room were two dozen men and women, with roughly half over in one corner arguing about something and the other half singing as if the others did not exist. Even though the floors were covered in an industrial-grade linoleum, a dusty, slightly musty smell hovered in the air. The janitors who seemed ubiquitous downstairs were probably strangers to this floor.

In any event, no one seemed to notice the man. They were busy going about their business and he didn't matter.

Chapter Four

E milia Treadwell grew up loving opera. Her earliest memories were of a home filled with Caruso, Pavarotti, Price, Domingo, and other greats of opera. She was, in fact, named after Emilia, the tragic wife of Iago and the maid of Desdemona in *Otello*.

"Emmy," as she was known to most, never seemed aware of her beauty. She had auburn hair that hung below her shoulders, green eyes that sparkled like freshly fallen snow, and cheeks that were lightly flushed even though she rarely wore makeup.

Emmy began taking classical singing lessons when she was six. By the time she was 16 it was evident to her—and, eventually, to her mother too—that she lacked the vocal range and pitch to be an opera principal. For a time she held out hope of singing in the chorus of an opera company somewhere, but after several auditions in Baltimore, Philadelphia, and Washington, even that dream ended.

Emmy received her bachelor's degree in political science from Georgetown and then a master's degree in international relations from American University (AU) in Washington, which is where she met Alain Bonnet. Alain's parents were from a small town in the south of

France—Eygalières. He was proud of his French heritage. Even though he was raised in Gaithersburg, Maryland, and had never been to France, he made a point of pronouncing his last name with a distinctly French accent—*Bonay*.

Alain was delightfully eccentric. Whenever the weather in Washington permitted, and sometimes even when it didn't, he wore a scarf around his neck. He loved scarves. His closet was full of them.

Alain was also obsessed with opera. He seemed to know everything about it. He could listen to a recording and within minutes, if not seconds, identify the singer, the song or aria, and the opera.

Alain worked as an assistant director in the AU library. This was both bad news and good news. It was bad news in that after paying for rent, utilities, food, and miscellaneous items, his salary did not leave much room for discretionary expenses such as tickets to the opera. The good news was that his job was 9–5 and Monday through Friday, which meant he had plenty of time to volunteer as a super. Indeed, by the time he met Emmy in the AU library, Alain was a regular fixture at the Kennedy Center.

Alain was seven years older than Emmy. He had a boyfriend named Alan and lived in a two-bedroom apartment off of Massachusetts Avenue in northwest Washington. He could walk to work and occasionally did when the weather was perfect, but more often than not he took the bus, which made numerous stops on Mass Avenue and two on the AU campus.

After graduating from AU Emmy got a job with the Center for Democracy and Civic Education (CDCE), a nonprofit that worked with various think tanks and schools around the world promoting democratic principles. She couldn't afford a car, so she got a one-bedroom apartment on Capitol Hill that was near the South Capitol subway stop and a fifteen-minute walk to work. For a while she dated a guy she met in her global security class at AU. He was cute, but he never wanted to do anything. After a year she stopped seeing him.

Emmy had stayed in touch with Alain after graduating. She enjoyed his company. He and Alan were fun to be with. She often met them for pizza or other cheap eats after work. Occasionally they splurged on tickets to the Sage Theatre or the Arena Stage in southwest Washington.

Like Alain, Emmy could rarely afford the luxury of tickets to the opera. When Alain encouraged her to be a super in Verdi's *Macbeth* at the Kennedy Center, she jumped at the chance. In the fifteen years since, she had appeared in over twenty operas, playing everything from a barmaid in *Falstaff* to a nun in *Dialogues of the Carmelites*.

Being a super was time-consuming. Usually it meant three weeks of rehearsals, followed by six or seven performances over a two-week period. And for this, a super was paid nothing. For most it was a labor of love. As a result, attendance at rehearsals could be and often was a problem.

Emmy, on the other hand, was always there and always on time. Leadership of the Washington Opera Company soon noticed her enthusiasm and dedication. Hence, when the director of supers moved to Missoula with her husband so he could teach creative writing at the University of Montana, Washington Opera offered the job to Emmy. It was only a part-time job that she would need to coordinate with her full-time job, but she was determined to make it work, even if it meant cutting back her hours at the CDCE.

* * *

"Are you Ms. Treadwell?" he asked. She looked up from her desk. His hair was as dark as a raven's. His large, brown eyes complemented his sun-tanned skin, which seemed to glow under a white, linen long-sleeved shirt that was loose around his muscular neck. A five-o'clock shadow graced his face perfectly. She quickly composed herself.

"Yes. Are you here to replace Rudy?"

"Who?"

"Are you here for *Otello* or something else?" she asked with a tinge of impatience.

"A friend said someone got hurt and you needed a replacement."

"Right," Emmy said. "That was Rudy Vargas. He was supposed to be my captain of the guards. Rehearsals for *Otello* start in four days."

He looked Middle Eastern, but he had no accent. She resisted the temptation to ask where he was from. "What's your name?"

"Ralph Allen."

"How tall are you?"

"About six one."

"Have you ever been in an opera before?"

"No, but it sounds interesting and fun."

"Who told you that? Who's your friend?" Emmy inquired.

Allen needed to be careful. The less said the better. "My girlfriend mentioned the other day that a guy she works with used to be in some operas here as an extra—sorry, *super*—and he heard you might need someone because a guy got hurt."

It was silly to be disappointed at the mention of a girlfriend, but Emmy was. Although she was dying to ask him more questions, she was busy and she didn't want to hear anything that might disqualify him. She needed a replacement.

"Okay, but first you need to understand the time commitment. We rehearse every evening, except Sundays, for three weeks, followed by seven evening performances over two weeks. Can you commit to that? This won't work if you decide not to show up for a rehearsal or performance."

Without hesitating Allen said, "Absolutely."

Emmy noticed a tattoo on the inside of his right arm at the wrist. She pointed at it. "What's that? Can I see it?"

He pulled up his sleeve, revealing an ancient Coptic Christian symbol. "It's an Ethiopian Coptic cross."

"Are you Ethiopian? You don't look Ethiopian."

He reflexively snickered, but quickly caught himself. He didn't want to embarrass or insult her. "No. I'm a Coptic Christian. My family is from Egypt."

"Oh, I see. Well, the guards in *Otello* wear uniforms that resemble the ones worn by the gorillas in the original *Planet of the Apes*: black vests, black boots, and thick gray collars over dark tops and pants. Did you ever see that movie?" Emmy asked.

"No, but I'm fine wearing whatever."

"I mention it," Emmy explained, "because I don't think the sleeves will completely cover that tattoo. Makeup will have to cover it up. Nothing permanent. Something you can wash off after each performance. You okay with that?"

"Sure, no problem."

"Okay. Then take that elevator over there down to two and ask for Carl. He's a white guy in his late fifties. You can't miss him. Gray hair usually pulled back in a ponytail. Lots of jewelry. A bit of a hippie, if you know what I mean. Anyway, he's in charge of costumes. He may have something you can try on. If not, you may need to meet him at our annex across the river. In the meantime, here's my card. If you change your mind or if anything at all comes up, let me know right away. I'm counting on you." She looked him in the eyes to emphasize her point.

He returned her glare with a mere glance and a brief "Thanks. I understand." Then he turned and headed for the elevator.

She couldn't help it. She watched him walk away. If ever the expression *tall, dark, and handsome* fit, this was it, she thought. Then fearing others might notice her gaze, she lowered her head as if suddenly caught in a lie. She pretended to get back to work.

* * *

Allen went to every rehearsal. In the beginning the rehearsals were all upstairs in one of the third-floor rooms. At the end of the first week the director told the supers and chorus members that Monday's rehearsal would be on the Opera House stage. That was the first time they saw Otello's castle.

Otello's guards, led by Allen, practiced running across the front of the stage and up the castle's steps. The first two times they did it without rifles. Prior to the third time, two stagehands opened a large, plastic crate and handed each guard a rifle. Although they looked real, they were in fact made of wood and simply painted to look like rifles.

Monday's rehearsal went late. By the time it ended it was close to 10:00 p.m. Allen was one of the last to leave.

It was unusually cool in Washington that day. A touch of fall was in the air. As a result, he wore a light coat without attracting unwanted attention. With most everyone gone and the houselights down, it was easy for Allen to wrap his coat around one of the rifles and walk out with it under his arm. No one said a thing.

The last Wednesday before opening night was set aside for the first of two dress rehearsals. The second one was on Thursday. Since Allen appeared only in Acts I and II, he spent most of the time both nights relaxing in orchestra-level seats with some of the other supers and the small, invitation-only audience comprised mainly of cast members' family and friends.

They first appeared on Wednesday with dogs and electronic devices designed to detect explosives and other hazardous materials. More came on Thursday, and they were ubiquitous on Friday and Saturday.

Many in the cast thought they were FBI agents or members of the US Secret Service. They speculated that the president would attend opening night. In fact, the vast majority were members of the DSS advance team tasked with securing the Kennedy Center. With more than 2,000 special agents and 40,000 professionals assigned to 275 foreign missions in more than 175 countries, the DSS was the largest law enforcement agency most people had never heard of.

Allen made a point of avoiding them. That was not hard. What *was* hard was returning a real rifle made to look and feel like one of the props to the Opera House stage.

Chapter Five

Lynne Palentine had attended Oberlin College, where she majored in political science. James Farnsworth had attended the University of Massachusetts–Amherst, where he pursued a double major: political science and finance. They met in Florence, Italy, during college.

Like many American students whose parents could afford it, they spent the spring of their junior year attending classes abroad and most of the following summer traveling around Europe on Eurail passes before returning home in time for the start of classes in the fall.

They instantly connected. Many warm nights were spent with friends at the Piazza Santa Croce drinking Valpolicella or sipping espresso. But what Lynne really liked was to sit on the stairs of the Piazzale Michelangelo and watch the long rays of the setting sun illuminate the terracotta roofs of Florence.

They were married in a small chapel near the Oberlin campus on June 23, 1983. They both attended law school at the University of Indiana, where Lynne graduated first in her class. Jim dropped out after his first year. He convinced himself rather quickly that law was not the career for him.

For a while he worked as a broker at Merrill Lynch. Then a friend of his who was a consultant at McKinsey & Company encouraged him to leave Merrill and join McKinsey. It was there that he met Jeffrey Skilling.

Skilling's biggest client was Enron. Among other things, Skilling helped Enron create an industry-leading natural gas trading business. Skilling soon impressed the CEO of Enron, Kenneth Lay. In 1990 Lay hired Skilling as the chairman and CEO of the Enron Finance Corporation. In 1991 Skilling became the chairman of the Enron Gas Services Corporation. Not long thereafter he was named CEO and managing director of Enron Capital and Trade Resources, the subsidiary responsible for energy trading and marketing.

Although Jim had limited experience with energy futures, Skilling hired him as his VP in charge of energy trading. Soon Jim was making serious money and jetting all over the world.

When Enron failed in 2001, Jim lost his job but not his freedom. Whereas Skilling and others went to jail, Jim and a couple of his buddies from McKinsey and Enron established *Energy Plus*, an energy start-up with offices in Houston that specialized in trading oil and natural gas.

The first few years were unquestionably tough, but they managed to survive. Jim came close to closing Energy Plus during the economic downturns of 2008 and 2016. All that began to change, however, in 2020 with the outbreak of the Covid-19 pandemic. Covid-19, followed by the imposition of new Western sanctions on Russia over its invasion of Ukraine, led to tremendous volatility in the oil and gas markets. Uncertainty and price volatility were the lifeblood of energy trading and Energy Plus was well positioned to capitalize on those developments.

After law school Lynne had her pick of jobs. Every top law firm in Chicago wanted her. So did many of the big New York firms like Cravath and Skadden. To the surprise of many, she accepted a position in Washington with Senator Richard Lugar—a Republican from Indiana. Jim was not keen to move to Washington, but he did for the sake of his marriage. After renting a two-bedroom rowhouse on Capitol Hill for five years, the Farnsworths bought a four-bedroom colonial off of Foxhall Road in northwest Washington.

Lynne served on Lugar's personal staff for two years. In 1985, when Lugar became the chairman of the Senate Foreign Relations Committee, she moved over to the committee. During the next 19 years, as the chairmanship of the committee switched between Democrats and Republicans, Lynne became a force to be reckon with in Washington on foreign policy and national security matters. She regularly met with the country's foreign policy and national security elites, including Colin Powell, Bob Gates, and Madeline Albright.

She played key roles in Washington during the First and Second Gulf Wars, the collapse of the Soviet Union and Yugoslavia, the Chinese crackdown in Tiananmen Square, and the conflict in Somalia. During her time on the Hill she was also the principal author of numerous reports and legislation, including the Iraq Liberation Act of 1998 and the Afghanistan Freedom Support Act of 2002. In 2003 Senator Lugar reclaimed the chairman's gavel. The next year George W. Bush was reelected president.

Lynne had always dreamed of working at the State Department or the White House. Now was her chance. With the strong support of Chairman Lugar, President Bush asked Lynne to serve as his Special Assistant for Foreign Affairs and National Security.

Then in June 2006, when Bob Zoellick informed the president he would be stepping down later that summer as the deputy secretary of state, President Bush asked Lynne to assume those responsibilities. Given her deep and long-standing ties in the Senate, her confirmation hearings were for the most part *pro forma*. Her nomination passed out of committee on a 16-to-1 vote. The following week the full Senate confirmed Lynne's nomination on a voice vote.

* * *

By her fiftieth birthday Lynne Farnsworth had spent twenty-five years in government: twenty-one on the Hill and four in the White House and at the State Department. The Democrats now controlled the White House and she did not want to go back to the Hill, even as the Minority Staff Director. So when Mike McArthur and Madeline Albright called to see if she was free for lunch, she hung up the phone and smiled.

Mike McArthur had worked for both Democrat and Republican presidents in various roles, including as the White House Chief of Staff (CoS). When he left the government for the last time in 1999, he formed McArthur & Associates (MA), one of the premier lobbying shops in Washington, with Henry Kissinger. Former secretary of state Madeline Albright joined MA in 2004.

They met at La Chaumière in Georgetown. They sat in the back at a private table. The undiminished light of Washington's summer solstice shone through the front window. Over lunch they discussed the growth of MA and Lynne's next career move. After an hour they made their move. Mike said he thought MA would be a good fit for Lynne. They needed someone with her *fresh* connections in the Middle East, especially in Kuwait and Qatar. Secretary Albright concurred. She also stressed that Lynne could engage in public speaking and publish articles using her own voice without the constraints imposed on federal civil servants. It was not a difficult decision, particularly when MA would pay her five times what she made as the deputy secretary of state.

In 2017 Secretary Albright nominated Lynne to join the Council on Foreign Relations (CFR). Her nomination was seconded by General Powell, Senator John McCain, and former secretary of defense Ashton Carter. The CFR was the premier think tank in Washington, focusing on the foreign policy issues facing the United States and other countries. Its membership list was a Who's Who of Washington's elite. Its flagship publication, *Foreign Affairs*, was, according to the CFR website, the "preeminent journal of international affairs and US foreign policy."

During her time in government Lynne had become increasingly concerned about the threat China's rise as a nuclear power posed to America's security and that of its allies. In a bipolar world, where only the United States and the Soviet Union (and later Russia) possessed significant nuclear arsenals, the United States could maintain parity with the Russians. This symmetry meant both countries were less likely to use their nuclear weapons because neither enjoyed a significant advantage over the other. But in a tripolar world, the United States and Russia could not maintain parity with each other *and* China without starting a new, open-ended arms race. Now that she was in the private sector, Lynne wanted to express *her* views on this subject.

Her article appeared in *Foreign Affairs* three months before the first presidential debate. She called for massive increases in US defense spending, especially modernization of America's nuclear *triad* (*i.e.*, land-based ballistic missiles, submarine-launched ballistic missiles, and long-range bombers). Her article was very popular in certain conservative circles. In fact, the ranking member on the Senate Foreign Relations Committee, a Republican from Idaho, had the article entered into the *Congressional Record*. Even the Republican presidential candidate, Walter Hansen, praised the article during the first presidential debate held in Charleston.

Hansen was elected president of the United States by a surprisingly wide margin. He ran on a platform that emphasized law and order, lower taxes, increased drilling for oil and gas, trade agreements that focused on workers and not lower tariffs on goods, and increased spending on defense, especially modernization of America's nuclear arsenal. His demonization of China and Russia was widely popular with voters.

President-elect Hansen asked his transition team to present him with three names for each cabinet post. Lynne Farnsworth was the first and only name seriously considered for the position of secretary of state. Because she had served as the deputy secretary of state, her background check was merely updated. No issues were identified. The Senate confirmed Lynne as the US secretary of state on a bipartisan basis.

Her swearing-in ceremony was held in the diplomatic reception rooms on the seventh and eighth floors of the State Department. Rarely seen by the public, these forty-two ornate rooms are home to one of the finest collections of American paintings, furnishings, and decorative objects from 1740 to 1840. Among the more than 5,000 museum-quality items in the collection are Chippendale carved mahogany side chairs belonging to Francis Scott Key, who penned "The Star Spangled Banner" in 1814, and the table on which Benjamin Franklin and John Adams signed the Treaty of Paris in 1783, formally ending America's Revolutionary War with Great Britain.

The actual swearing-in was a private affair in the Thomas Jefferson Room on the eighth floor. The vice president administered the oath of office. Lynne placed her hand on the Bible next to a table that belonged to Thomas Jefferson, the first secretary of state. Lynne's sister, Ruthie, who flew in from Chicago, and her brother, Edgar, who flew in from Ann Arbor, attended. Jim was supposed to attend, but his flight from Bagdad was delayed.

Afterward everyone went to a reception with hors d'oeuvres and refreshments in the lavish Benjamin Franklin State Dining Room. The Franklin Dining Room is the largest of all the rooms on the top two floors at State. Its walls are flanked by Corinthian columns and its ceiling is adorned with eight cut-glass chandeliers. Both the plush carpet and the ceiling feature the Great Seal of the United States.

When Lynne entered the room she was stunned to see so many people. Hundreds of officials from State, the White House, and the Hill, including at least half the Senate, were in attendance. The event was closed to the press; however, the White House photographer and the State Department's official photographer were there to capture the evening's events.

The reception lasted two hours. Lynne did her best to greet everyone. Several times she found herself glancing at the main entrance to the room in the hope that Jim might make a last-minute appearance. He did not.

Chapter Six

(Opening Night)

From her kitchen window Emmy had a partial view of the Capitol Dome. She loved living on Capitol Hill: lots of young professionals, red-brick sidewalks, decent restaurants, and more and more shops as the area continued to gentrify.

On Saturdays she liked to stroll through Eastern Market—a tumultuous blend of smells, sounds, and colors. On the way home she often picked up a croissant or pain au chocolate from the French couple who ran a small bakery on the corner of C and 6th Streets SE.

This Saturday would be different. It was opening night. She needed to be at the Kennedy Center by 1:00 p.m. As she finished her first cup of coffee her phone rang.

"Hello? Daddy, how are you? You're up early this morning."

Emmy's relationship with her dad had grown in the years since her mom died. He was seventy-four and lived in a modest rowhouse in Baltimore. She didn't see him as often as she liked. She wished they could be closer.

"Any plans for today?" she asked. "You should get out. The weather is supposed to be beautiful today. High of only 73."

"Yeah, I was thinking about taking the bus down to the Inner Harbor. Mom loved it down there this time of year. What are you up to?"

"Just having some coffee. Slow morning. Taking it easy. But I need to start getting ready. I need to be at the Kennedy Center by one. It's opening night. We're doing *Otello*."

"*Otello*? I love that opera, but it's very sad. You know it was one of Verdi's last."

"I know. Say, you should come down and see it. Stay at my place. I can get you tickets. It would be a cheap few days and fun. We could even go to Ben's Chili Bowl on U Street. I know how much you like their half-smokes."

"Thanks, sweetie. Okay, maybe I will. Send me the performance schedule. Let me see if I have any doctor appointments or other conflicts."

She knew her dad. That was code for *I probably won't*. "Okay, but don't wait too long. We're only doing seven performances. It closes two weeks from today. I'd love to see you. I love you, Daddy."

"I love you too, sweetheart. Goodbye."

"Bye, bye." She pursed her lips and gently blew him a kiss he could not see or feel.

Chapter Seven

Secretary Farnsworth sat before her makeup mirror in only her bra and underwear. She was not in shape. Age and gravity were catching up with her. Nonetheless, she did not want to let go of the desire to be appealing, to be attractive.

When they married, Lynne and Jim had only one checking account and one savings account, both at the Senate Federal Credit Union. But as time passed and their wealth grew, they added multiple brokerage and retirement accounts. Energy Plus had its own accounts, which were kept separate.

Her travel plans and activities were often classified. Nonetheless, she did her best to coordinate their schedules whenever possible. Time together in Washington was rare. So too were the few occasions when they were both in a foreign capital at the same time. As much as she tried to make their marriage work, she had to admit that after more than forty-five years, she had few insights into Jim's wealth or activities and, to be honest, he into hers. Tonight was no different. She had no idea where her husband was or what he was doing.

To make matters worse, they had not been intimate in over fifteen years. Thinking about it hurt. Was it her fault or his? Would their marriage have been different if they had had kids? She wasn't sure. What she was sure of is that she wanted to feel love again. She was only seventy-two. With luck she would live another fifteen years. She wanted to live those years with someone who loved her, who wanted to be with her, someone to laugh with, to cry with, to drink a margarita or Aperol Spritz with on a beach in Italy!

For now, though, these thoughts had to take a back seat to work and the moment. A suitcase lay open on her bed. Her flight to Canberra would leave in the morning. She would spend half a day there. Then it was on to Jakarta, where she would represent the United States at the Asia-Pacific Climate Week (APCW). A few items had already been thrown on the bed. She would finish packing later that night or in the morning, if necessary.

The house was quiet. The only noise came from a lawnmower four doors down. The warmth of a late October day had ebbed. The sun over Washington would set in about two hours and the curtain at the Kennedy Center would rise in about three.

Outside, her four-man close security detail from DSS' Protective Division waited in two heavily armored, black Chevy Suburbans. In the driveway, waiting in a bulletproof and blast-resistant highly modified Cadillac limousine, were two more DSS agents. And on each end of her block were two District of Columbia (DC) Metropolitan Police cruisers with their motors running and officers inside.

She was looking forward to tonight. She loved the opera and she always enjoyed spending time with her friend Mohammad Al-Mutairi. The emir had appointed Mutairi Kuwait's oil minister in 2027. Mutairi was 63-years old and married with three sons. He was not a politician, at least not in the traditional sense. He came from an important family, but he was not a member of the Al-Sabah dynasty that had ruled Kuwait for over 270 years. Mutairi was part of the new breed of highly educated technocrats that help govern many countries in the Middle East.

He moved with the measured grace displayed by many royals and ministers around the world. In his perfectly pressed white *thawb* and gold-trimmed, black *Hasawi bisht*, he looked like an actor on a movie set. Despite his stature, he was remarkably down to earth. People liked Mutairi. At Lawrence Academy in Groton, Massachusetts, he had played baseball and was voted class president his senior year. When he returned to Kuwait after high school he joined the army. His commission as a lieutenant was finalized on June 20, 1990. Six weeks later, on August 2, 1990, one hundred thousand Iraqi troops invaded Kuwait.

The emir of Kuwait, his family, and other government officials had little choice. They fled. Many went to Riyadh. Others went to the western Saudi mountain city of Taif. Given his fluency in English and time spent in the United States, Mutairi was tasked with coordinating public messaging by the Kuwaiti government, especially the army, with the US Central Command led by General Norman Schwarzkopf. It was heady stuff for a twenty-two-year old lieutenant. Mutairi regularly met with Schwarzkopf, his CoS General Robert Johnston, and other senior US government and military officials. He respected the integrity and professionalism of the US military. It contrasted sharply with his own military. The Americans were also friendly and approachable.

Mutairi still recalled with fondness his time with the Americans during the First Gulf War. In fact, in his office at Kuwait Petroleum Corporation in Kuwait City, one of his most-prized possessions was a photograph in which Schwarzkopf had his arm around Mutairi's shoulder.

After the war Mutairi returned to the United States. He attended the University of Richmond, where he studied chemistry, graduating in 1999. General Schwarzkopf, by then retired, served as the commencement speaker at the University of Richmond that year. The press led people to believe that Schwarzkopf did so because he had helped establish the Jepson

School of Leadership at the university in the early 1990s. Schwarzkopf's family and close friends knew the real reason—Mutairi asked him to.

As much as he liked chemistry, Mutairi could see the handwriting on the wall. Kuwait was the tenth largest producer of oil in the world. It was struggling to produce three million barrels per day. It needed to produce four or five million. In other countries the government could invite foreign multinational oil producers like Exxon or BP to assist with exploration and new techniques for such things as seismic mapping and deepwater drilling. However, that was difficult, if not impossible, in Kuwait because the constitution did not allow foreign companies to own Kuwait's natural resources. Without an ownership interest, the large multinationals were reluctant to make the substantial investments Kuwait needed. Kuwait would have to do this on its own. Thus, at the urging of the crown prince, Mutairi attended Colorado School of Mines, where he received his master's degree in geology in 2002.

In the years immediately after the Gulf War, Kuwait thrived. Then, beginning around 2006, political infighting and corruption began to take its toll on every aspect of Kuwaiti society, including the energy sector. Despite Kuwait having one of the world's largest oil reserves and a strong fiscal and external balance sheet, turmoil between Kuwait's parliament and executive stalled much-needed investments and reforms. Social services like healthcare and education started to decay due to continuous rifts between elected lawmakers and cabinet members put in place by the ruling Al-Sabah family. Indeed, shortly before Mutairi left Kuwait on his most recent trip abroad, the emir announced that Kuwait's prime minister would be forming his sixth government of the past eleven months. The rapid turnover had given successive ministers little opportunity to push through reforms, with the cycle of disruption delaying economic diversification and deterring foreign investment. It had also fueled Kuwaitis' sentiment that their country was lacking direction and failing to progress.

Mutairi was a trusted advisor to the new crown prince, Sabah Al-Ahmad Al-Sabah. And as much as he loved his country, Mutairi believed significant change was needed.

"We must take steps to regain the trust of the people," he told the prince. Privately, Mutairi saw a looming crisis that could not be resolved unless the state's authoritarian, nondemocratic approach was changed and the sheikhdom's current mentality abandoned.

In an interview with the *Kuwaiti Times* back in August, he let his true feelings bubble to the surface: "Kuwait's malaise needs more than a good person here and there. A total revamp is needed. That requires transformative leadership and bold change."

* * *

One of Mutairi's favorite restaurants in Washington was Fiola Mare in Georgetown. He loved the seafood. Thus, when Lynne had extended an invitation to the opera on the margins of a conference organized by the Organization for Economic Co-operation and Development (OECD) in Paris back in July, Mutairi had half-jokingly said, "on the condition that we eat beforehand at Fiola Mare."

She had not forgotten. They had a light dinner at the restaurant before heading to the opera. When interviewed later by special agents of the DSS, staff and patrons said their discussion seemed intense.

They left the restaurant at 7:55 p.m. Lynne rode alone in the back of her limousine. Her close protection detail rode in the two Suburbans—one in front of the secretary and one behind. The Suburbans were in turn escorted by numerous units of the DC Police Department.

Mutairi, who rode in a black Maybach, had his own escort; however, his motorcade was limited to one Suburban containing two heavily armed DSS agents and a single police cruiser with lights flashing. Their motorcades arrived at the Kennedy Center's Entrance Plaza at 8:05 p.m. They were in their front-row seats by 8:15 p.m.

Chapter Eight

They stood in the dark, immediately behind the curtain. A twentysomething female stage assistant wearing a headset and microphone that stopped in front of her mouth stood next to Allen, pointing a small flashlight at the floor. At exactly 8:00 p.m. she whispered, "Get ready—3, 2, 1, go!"

The curtain jumped skyward with volcanic fury as the orchestra exploded into Verdi's opening *Esultate* in C-sharp major. Otello and his ships approached Cyprus. But first they had to battle the storm and its raging seas.

With a rifle over his shoulder, Allen led the other guards at a full sprint across the front of the stage and up the stairs of the castle. At the top they spread along the ramparts with Allen stopping in front, nearest the audience. As the guards pretended to gaze across the ocean looking for Otello's ships, Allen snuck a peek at the front row. His rifle had a round in the chamber. At this distance, it would be like shooting fish in a barrel. However, the seat was empty. His target was late.

When Allen came off the stage, Emmy was there to greet him. She put her hand on his shoulder and leaned in. Her lips were close to his ear.

"Good job," she whispered. "That looked great, but don't look at the audience. You're there to look for Otello's ships."

"Sorry, it won't happen again."

* * *

Allen and his guards would not appear again until the beginning of Act II and then for only fifteen minutes. As he waited to go back on, Allen tried to keep to himself with his rifle nearby. Emmy noticed.

In Act II Allen and his men, still carrying their rifles, guarded Otello as he entered the castle and confronted Iago and Desdemona. The bright lights hitting the stage made it hard for Allen to see the audience in the dark house. And, unlike during Act I, Allen was never near the front of the stage in Act II. He went off without a shot being fired.

Allen moved through the darkness backstage. As Otello roared his rage at Iago for telling him about Desdemona and Cassio's alleged affair, believing he would never enjoy peace again ("*Ora a per sempre addio*"), Allen placed his rifle in a nearby corner instead of in the box with the others. Before heading up to the men's dressing room to change, he ducked into a nearby restroom to relieve himself. As he came out Emmy confronted him. She held one of the rifles in her hand.

"What's this?" she hissed.

"What do you mean?" replied Allen calmly. "It's one of the rifles."

"I know. This is yours! I saw you carry it off, but instead of putting it in the crate, you tried to hide it in a corner. It's heavier than the others. I think it's real. Who are you? What are you up to? I need to report this."

As she turned to walk away Allen jerked her head back hard as he covered her mouth with his hand. He quickly opened the bathroom door and forced her inside. No one saw them. She struggled to get free, but he overpowered her. The rifle made a loud clanking sound as it fell on the hard tile floor. He dragged her down to the last stall. He slammed her against the wall and down on the toilet so hard that her head snapped back against the porcelain tile, making a sickly hollow sound. As a result, she may have been unconscious when he thrust a 4-inch knife turned sideways into her chest a quarter inch below her fourth rib and to the right of her sternum. The blade, angled slightly to the left, severed the right and left ventricles in a single stroke. She died within seconds.

At one of the sinks Allen cleaned the knife and washed some blood off his hands. As he did so, he surveyed the room. It was quiet and with the exception of Emmy's feet, which dangled just below the closed stall door, the room looked empty. Allen picked up the rifle and left without looking back.

* * *

Allen swiftly made his way up to the men's dressing room on the second floor. Before getting on the elevator, he placed the rifle in the first dark corner he came to backstage. Things had not gone according to plan. He was tempted to leave, but this was his first job for a major client. He couldn't fail. He still had a few options. After changing clothes and washing the makeup off his arm, he headed down to the lobby with his knife tethered around his left calf and a small dose of poison in a ring on his finger.

The Hall of Nations was surprisingly quiet for an opening night. He walked as quickly as he could without attracting undue attention. He knew he did not have much time. Emmy would soon be discovered and his target was likely to visit the lobby during intermission.

The Grand Foyer was bustling with activity. A steady stream of patrons made their way to the restrooms. Others went looking for refreshments or simply a place to stretch their legs. Security was ubiquitous. Allen was certain there was more he could not see.

Once past the giant bust of Kennedy, he made his way over to a coffee stand and snack bar called "Coffee Virtuoso." A young woman named Ally, which was short for Aaliyah, operated it. During three weeks of rehearsals he had become one of her best customers.

"Hi, how are you?" he said.

"I'm fine, thanks. But my assistant picked a fine time to get sick. Opening night!"

"Let me know if I can help."

"Thanks, but I can manage."

Intermission began at 9:45 p.m. Within ten minutes the line for coffee was twenty-feet deep. Murmurs of frustration could be heard. "You sure I can't help?" Allen asked.

Their eyes briefly met. A look of panic was beginning to cross her face. She relented.

"Okay, thanks. Put on that apron over there. You can start by getting more milk, 2 percent and skim, from the cooler behind me."

As she turned her head to greet the next customer, Ally instinctively asked, "Hi, what can I get you?" In an instant she recognized her customer.

President Hansen had made a priority of extending the Abraham Accords (by which Israel normalized its relations with Morocco, the United Arab Emirates, Bahrain, and Sudan) to other Arab or Muslim-majority nations. As a result, Secretary Farnsworth was a frequent guest on CNN and the nightly news discussing America's enduring support for Israel and the need for greater stability throughout the region. This was code for abandoning the policies of Obama and Biden, who had expressed support for regime change and greater democracy throughout the Middle East and North Africa after the Arab Spring in 2011–12, all of which was quite unsettling to the emir of Kuwait and the other hereditary leaders in the region.

Standing alongside Secretary Farnsworth was a man Ally did not recognize. He was Arab—that was obvious from his attire—but beyond that she had no clue. Secretary Farnsworth and her guest were surrounded by security agents in dark suits and earpieces.

Lynne ordered a cappuccino for Mutairi and a small, skim latte for herself. Allen stood a few feet back. He thought about striking with the knife strapped to his leg, but he doubted he could grab it quickly enough; besides, the coffee cart was in his way.

Ally finished the drinks and placed them on the front ledge of her cart. As she started to attach the lids, Mutairi couldn't help himself. "Where are you from? Your name tag says Aaliyah. That's a common name in my part of the world."

She was flattered that he bothered to inquire. "My family emigrated to the US from Lebanon in 1964. I grew up in Alexandria, Virginia."

She resumed placing a lid on his drink; however, as she reached forward, other customers, sensing the presence of someone important, started snapping photos on their phones. A flash caused Ally to spill a small amount of coffee.

Allen stepped forward. "Here, let me help." Allen wiped the spill with a napkin. He then removed the old lid. "These things never work," he grunted. He turned to toss the lid and napkin in a trash container behind him.

It happened quickly. No one noticed. Everyone was listening to Ally and Mutairi. Allen attached a new lid and then swung back around, handing the drink to Mutairi. As he did so, Mutairi thanked Ally and Allen in French. "*Merci, mademoiselle et monsieur.*" His French accent was nearly perfect.

"*Bienvenue, monsieur,*" Ally replied with a wide smile.

As they had many times before, Mutairi's grace and charm impressed Lynne. Together they turned and headed for the steps leading back into the Opera House. The gentle gong announcing the end of intermission sounded.

They stopped at the top of the stairs to finish their drinks. Mutairi said something that made Lynne laugh. Then, after a few quick gulps, they handed their empty cups to the DSS agents at their side, who tossed them into shiny, brass receptacles at the top of the Opera House steps. Allen watched with satisfaction from behind the coffee cart.

Chapter Nine

As Act III began, Iago continued to fan the flames of Otello's passion. He told Otello he had further proof of the affair between Desdemona and Cassio. Otello insulted his wife, calling her a whore ("meretrix").

Just as Otello finished his rant, Lynne felt Mutairi slump. She turned to look at him. His chin had dropped to his chest. His eyes were closed and a small curdle of white foam oozed from the left corner of his mouth. She whispered his name and gently nudged him with her elbow. He did not respond. Then she noticed the blood. At first it was only a small circle in the center of his chest. Soon his white *thawb* was drenched in it.

Lynne turned her head further to the right. She made eye contact with the head of her security detail, DSS agent Roger Payne. He was seated on the aisle one row behind her. He knew that look. She needed help. Roger spoke into the transmitter on his wrist. Within seconds four DSS agents who had been standing in the aisles along the walls carried Mutairi out through an emergency exit a few feet away.

Lynne followed, surrounded by Payne and the other members of her close protection detail. The performance continued. The houselights remained low. No announcement was made. Most in the audience were oblivious to what had happened.

The motorcade raced off in the direction of George Washington University Hospital, only a few blocks away. As it turned on to F Street NW, it passed within a few hundred feet of the Saudi embassy. It also passed a black Audi A8L with diplomatic plates turning quickly on to F Street from 25th Street NW. The inside of the car was dark. Allen was the only passenger. He did not speak to the driver. As the large sedan sliced through the night up Rock Creek Parkway, Allen pulled out his phone. Using a special version of Signal, a double-encrypted messaging platform, he texted a single word: "MUSTABEAD."

In Kuwait City, 6,540 miles away, Major General Sheikh Nawar Al-Ahmad, head of Kuwait's National Guard, was at home having his first cup of tea of the day. His phone vibrated on the table beside him. Nawar recognized the number. He read the message. His face betrayed no reaction or emotion. He picked up another phone. On the other end was his driver. He ordered him to ready his car. After a quick shower, Nawar dressed and left.

It was a short ride to Al-Seif Palace. His driver spoke briefly to the guards at the gate. They peered in the back. The massive metal gates opened slowly. As he walked up the steps of the palace, the morning call to prayer echoed throughout the courtyard before being subdued by the heat already doing battle with the sea breeze coming off the Persian Gulf.

Inside the palace the stone floors helped beat back the heat outside. He walked down the center hallway behind two soldiers dressed in light green ceremonial uniforms with gold epaulettes and belts. At their sides hung brightly polished scimitars. They walked in unison, never looking back. Their footsteps reverberated off the walls of the cavernous chamber. At the end of the hallway Nawar was directed to an anterior room bathed in Persian rugs and upholstered chairs trimmed in gold. He had barely settled into a soft, deep chair when a very slight, dark-skinned man in a neatly pressed white *thawb* appeared from behind a partition. He offered Nawar coffee, which Nawar declined. In an instant the man disappeared.

Heavy double doors made of Lebanese cedar stood sentry outside the crown prince's office. Behind the doors His Highness was signing papers as two male assistants, one on each side of him, managed the flow of paperwork across his desk. He finished and directed the aides to leave.

His office was only slightly smaller than a basketball gymnasium. It regularly hosted foreign delegations in excess of one-hundred people. In fact, the previous evening a congressional delegation (CODEL) from Washington led by Senator Jack Watson, the chairman of the Senate Armed Services Committee, met with the crown prince. The CODEL included senators Anne Waters from New Hampshire and Dorothy Holmquist from New York. While Waters and Holmquist brought with them business leaders from New Hampshire and New York, respectively, most members of the delegation were business leaders from Watson's home state of Rhode Island.

At eighty-three years of age, the prince took a minute to rise and reach the doors. As the doors began to open, Nawar snapped up from his seat. "Your Highness, good morning. I hope you are well."

"Nawar, my old friend, how are you? Come in." They walked to a suite of four upholstered chairs near the doors organized around a low wooden table. Beneath their feet were handmade Isfahan Persian rugs.

As the prince sat down, he asked. "So tell me, Nawar, do you bring news?"

"Yes, Your Highness. Our agent in Washington reports success. Mutairi has been stopped."

The crown prince expressed approval, but he cautioned Nawar. "We must be certain of this news before further steps are taken. You must also maintain the upmost secrecy. You know what happened to Riyadh after Khashoggi."

"Yes, Your Highness. No one in my ministry knows. I am the only one communicating with our agent in Washington."

"Good. Thank you, Nawar. You have done a good job. I knew I could count on you."

"It is my honor to serve you, Your Highness." With that, Nawar rose and left through the same double doors he had entered.

* * *

Emmy's disappearance that evening was soon noticed by members of the cast and staff of the opera company, who began a search even before Act III finished. No one thought to look in a men's room. Those who used the one backstage that evening later told US Park Police that they were either in a hurry and didn't notice anything or they had assumed the guy in the last stall was just taking a shit.

It was Craig's turn that week to work the night shift. His crew started at midnight and finished at 7:00 a.m. if they did not take a lunch break or 8:00 a.m. if they did. By the time he reached the men's room backstage it was 1:45 a.m. He thought it strange that someone would still be in there. With Tina Turner's "We Don't Need Another Hero" booming in his ears, he rapped hard on the stall door. "Hey, whatcha doin' in there?"

Emmy Treadwell was only thirty-seven years old.

Chapter Ten

For over 8,000 years the Nile River has slowly moved through Egypt on its steady march north to the Mediterranean Sea. The Greek historian Herodotus called Egypt "the Nile's gift to the world."

On this day, like on so many in the past, the Nile's water was churned by a hot afternoon breeze that blew across Cairo. Boats of all shapes and sizes bobbed up and down in the river's chop. In the middle of the river was Gezirah Island. For centuries it was largely uninhabited. That began to change in 1830 when Mehmet Ali, the founder of modern Egypt, decided the north end of the island would be a good place for a palace. Today the Sofitel Hotel sits on the south end of the island, promising its guests spectacular views of Cairo from its 433 rooms.

On this Sunday afternoon in late October the hotel's aptly named outdoor venue, the Sunny Bar, was nearly empty. Most guests would wait until the sun set over the desert to the west to fill its tables and chairs. Notwithstanding the sweltering heat, two men sat by themselves talking in the shade of an olive tree at the far end of the bar. They lowered their voices whenever a waiter came by. When they did speak, it was in Italian.

Although they were seated, they made an odd-looking pair. The Russian was tall, very tall. The American was short, very short. The juxtaposition of the two was reminiscent of Robin Hood and Friar Tuck or Prince Hal and Falstaff.

A keen eye could tell the Russian was not a man of means. It wasn't his cheap suit that gave him away. It was his shoes. As the German philosopher Heidegger once said, "Shoes tell us all we need to know about the person who walks in them." The American, on the other hand, was dressed in perfectly pressed slacks and a Brioni sport coat. His brown Ferragamo loafers matched his belt perfectly.

The two men discussed a new oil field discovered in one of Iraq's western provinces. Many believed it was larger than the Ghawar Field in Saudi Arabia—the largest onshore oil field in the world, larger than all existing US oil fields put together. In nine days Bagdad was expected to auction off parcels accounting for approximately eighty percent of the field.

The American complained that a company controlled by Kuwait's oil minister and his family was expected to win several of the larger concessions in a joint venture with someone in the United States. "The Kuwaitis are really pursuing this. Their efforts to expand domestic production have stalled. Winning this bid would be huge for them. I've heard they are spreading money all over Bagdad. We can't compete with that."

"I've heard similar things," the Russian said. "But don't be so pessimistic. The key isn't how much you spend, but where you spend it. Rusoil knows what it's doing. What still amazes me is that you can't find out who the Kuwaitis are working with in the United States. I thought your connections were good."

The American was indignant and didn't try to hide it. "My 'connections' as you call them, are unmatched! As you know, they reach the highest levels of the US government. But people just aren't talking. Trust me, I want to know. We need to win as many of these concessions as possible. *I need to win*—"

"Well, I don't think you have to worry anymore about the Kuwaitis," the Russian said.

"What do you mean?"

"The oil minister, Mutairi—"

"Yeah?"

"He's dead," the Russian said very plainly.

"What?"

"Yes, he died last night in Washington."

"I heard he was in the hospital, but dead? How do you know that?"

"It doesn't matter. I just know. Now how soon can you be ready to go to Bagdad?"

Chapter Eleven

Russia's invasion of Ukraine did not begin in 2021. It actually started in November 2013 when Russian forces without insignia seized Crimea. This was followed by similar actions in the Donbas region of Ukraine in spring 2014.

The reactions of the West to the Russian incursions of 2013 and 2014 were long on speeches and short on actions. President Obama did essentially nothing in 2013 and 2014 except give an impassioned speech in Warsaw that urged the West not to "accept Russia's occupation of Crimea or its violations of Ukraine's sovereignty."

Nonetheless, in March 2014 Russia formally annexed Crimea. And many believed President Trump all but invited President Putin to invade Ukraine when he could be heard on tape in July 2019 telling the president-elect of Ukraine, Volodymyr Zelenskyy, that he would withhold congressionally authorized military assistance to Ukraine unless he helped find dirt on Trump's principal political rival at the time—Joe Biden. Later Trump was famously quoted as praising President Putin as savvy when Russia recognized Donbas' independence.

It was therefore understandable that Putin might have thought a larger incursion into Ukraine would not face a particularly robust response from the West. Thus, on the morning of February 24, 2022, over 100,000 Russian troops, supported by hundreds of tanks and other armored vehicles, invaded Ukraine. This time Russia's target was not an obscure province in the eastern part of the country, but Kiev itself. Putin and his generals thought the war, or "special military operation" as they called it, would be over in a few days. They miscalculated.

Zelenskyy did not flee Kiev. Ukrainian forces did not cut and run. Instead, they stood and fought. And Europe, which had not seen conflict on its soil in over seventy years, woke up. Unlike in 2013 and 2014, this time Europe (a) imposed harsh new economic sanctions on Russia and (b) provided Ukraine with extensive military hardware, including ammunition and weapons systems. The measures the European Union (EU) took were aligned with those adopted by the Group of Seven (G7) nations, including the United States.

Given the timing of the economic sanctions imposed by the West on Russia, they did not take hold until the beginning of 2023. In the first half of that year Russia's revenues from oil and gas fell by forty-seven percent compared to the same period in 2022. They continued to fall between 2024 and 2028. So did Russia's gross domestic product (GDP). Indeed, according to the OECD, Russia's GDP fell by over ten percent between 2021 and 2028. At the same time that revenues and GDP were declining, interest rates and inflation soared. According to an internal report by the Russian Ministry of the Economy, inflation more than doubled between 2020 and 2028. Russia's Ministry of Energy estimated that it would take Russia approximately a decade to get its oil and gas industry back to where it was before the 2021 invasion of Ukraine.

* * *

The disintegration of the Soviet Union in 1991 resulted in the collapse of the most powerful and feared security organization in the world—the

Soviet Committee of State Security (KGB). In the years immediately following the end of the Soviet Union, the KGB morphed into the Federal Counterintelligence Service (FSK), which itself eventually broke into three main parts.

The main successor to the FSK is the infamous Federal Security Service (FSB). The FSB is the principal security agency of Russia, tasked primarily with internal security and counterintelligence. The KGB's foreign military functions have become the responsibility of the Main Intelligence Directorate (GRU). The third and final successor to the KGB is the Foreign Intelligence Service (SVR). Unlike the FSB, the SVR is tasked with intelligence and espionage activities *outside* the Russian Federation. When it comes to foreign intelligence, the SVR is the civilian counterpart to the GRU.

Army General Mikhail Bortaikov was the director of Russia's SVR. He was a short, fat man with the demeanor of a mafia boss. He angered quickly and was known to carry a grudge. Bortaikov once had a reporter killed for something he had written about Bortaikov's wife five years earlier.

On this Monday afternoon Bortaikov was running late. He left the SVR's headquarters in the Yasenevo District of Moscow and got into a black, armored Mercedes S600. As it pulled away SVR agents in black Mercedes G-Class *gelikis* took up positions in front and behind, with the latter swerving back and forth to keep anyone from trying to pass.

Yasenevo was located in the southwest corner of Moscow, just inside the second ring road. It would take at least ninety minutes to get downtown. Bortaikov used part of the time to call the president's CoS.

"Aleksander? This is Mikhail. Do you have a minute?"

"Certainly," President Putin's CoS replied.

"Thanks. I'm on my way to a meeting at the Ministry of Energy. Sergei has invited Rosneft, Gazprom, Rusoil, and most of the other big oil and gas companies in to discuss new investments in production and refining, and a resumption of exports to Europe. The auction next week in Iraq may come up. Therefore, I wanted to compare notes with you on the Mutairi matter. Except for the fact that our agent in Washington reports success, we've heard nothing. All the relevant players in Washington, including the White House, CIA, and State Department, know that he was killed. However, no statements have been made and no actions have been taken. Even the Kuwaitis have said nothing, which is odd. What have you heard?"

"We've heard nothing as well. Is your agent still with the secretary?"

"Yes. They're now in Jakarta. Farnsworth is attending a UN regional climate conference. He is scheduled to accompany her back to Washington on Wednesday or Thursday."

"How about your other agent—the one with the secretary's husband?"

"They've been in Cairo for the past several days, but now they're headed to Bagdad. Mr. Farnsworth thinks our agent works for Rusoil and he'll be paid millions if one of Rusoil's bids is accepted. Our agents believe he'll do basically anything to get his hands on that money."

"Excellent job, Mikhail. I'll be sure to brief the president on your work."

"Thank you, Aleksander. *Do svidaniya.*"

* * *

The meeting took place in the main conference room of the Ministry of Energy on Ulitsa Shchepkina in Moscow. The ministry was housed in a building faithful to the post–World War II rules of modernism embraced by the Soviet Union – straight lines, rectangles, and most of all, minimalism. Inside, the conference room was lined with windows down one side and across one end. In the center of the room was a large, plain table, approximately thirty feet in length and six feet in width. Chairs lined the walls, as did portraits of past Russian ministers of energy and, of course, President Putin.

The CEO of every major Russian oil and gas company attended, along with many of their assistants. Bortaikov was the last to arrive. His status dwarfed that of everyone else in the room, but he wanted to appear gracious. So he headed straight for Sergei Petrov, the energy minister. As he did, everyone in the room watched. They wondered what the head of the SVR was doing there. Fear was an emotion shared by many.

"Sergei, I'm sorry I am late. Please accept my apologies."

Petrov wasn't about to chastise the head of the SVR for being a few minutes late to a meeting. That would not be good for his health.

"Not at all, Mikhail. We were just getting coffee and finding our places around the table. Here, I've saved you a seat next to me."

"Thank you."

"Everyone, please take a seat. Let's get started. I know most of you, but for the new faces in the room, my name is Sergei Petrov. I am the energy minister. With me today is Mikhail Bortaikov. General Bortaikov is the director of the SVR."

Bortaikov nodded to the group. "Good morning."

Petrov continued. "It's been a while since we've met with you as a group. So we thought we should get together to discuss a few matters. First, I want to thank those of you who were able to join me on my recent trip to Suriname. Things are moving along nicely there. Indeed we are ahead of schedule. Next, you don't need me to tell you that the sanctions imposed by the West have hurt our oil and gas industries. We've done what we can to mitigate those affects. For example, we've tried to replace lost sales in Europe with increased sales in India and China. We've also increased our sales in a number of markets, including North Korea, Iran, Belarus, and Cuba. But we need to do more. Tax revenues from oil and gas sales account for roughly forty-seven percent of the federal budget. Therefore, later this week the president will be announcing a set of incentives designed to encourage increased exploration and drilling for both oil and gas. And, as you know, our refineries are in desperate need of repairs and refurbishment, so he will also be announcing plans to build two new refineries in Kemerovo and Tyumen, in addition to the retrofitting of three refineries in Komsomolsk, Achinsk, and Yaroslavl. That's all I can say for now about these measures. Further details will be forthcoming from the president's office and my ministry. Any questions?"

Vladim Rublev was the CEO and president of Rosneft, Russia's largest state-owned oil company. "Good afternoon, Your Excellency. I suspect I speak not only for Rosneft, but also for the other companies in this room, when I express my gratitude for these measures and your concern for the well-being of our companies and our workers. The past few years have indeed been difficult."

"Thank you, Vladim. General, is there anything you would like to add?"

"No, Sergei. Please continue," Bortaikov said with a slight wave of his hand.

"Okay. The third thing we wanted to discuss with you is the resumption of sales into Europe, particularly gas, via the Nord Stream 1 and 2 pipelines. We have reached out to our counterparts in Warsaw, Berlin, and some of the Baltics. They have signaled that if the conflict in Ukraine shows signs of slowing, they might be willing to lobby Brussels and the other members of the EU to lift at least some of the sanctions imposed on us. Washington will obviously oppose such efforts, but Germany and some of the countries in Eastern Europe want these pipelines to run again. So we need to be ready should this happen. Therefore, we need Gazprom and the other suppliers of gas to consult among themselves. Make sure these pipelines are in good working order. And be ready to act should some or all of the sanctions be lifted. Any questions or comments?"

Anatoly Khachanov was the CEO and president of Gazprom, Russia's largest producer of natural gas. "Your Excellency, Gazprom will speak to Novatek and the other companies involved in the supply of gas and LNG to Europe. We will be ready if and when the pipelines reopen."

"Thank you, Anatoly. General Bortaikov, please, is there anything you would like to say?"

"No, Sergei. Thank you. Please continue."

"Then that brings me to the last subject we would like to discuss with you—the upcoming auction in Iraq. Russia has always been self-sufficient when it comes to meeting domestic demand for oil and gas. But this could change. Over the next decade we could see increased demand for oil and petroleum products as Russia recovers from the burdens of the war and the sanctions. The Center for Strategic Research predicts demand for energy will increase by fifteen percent between now and the end of the decade. And the CSR predicts that by 2040 energy use in Russia will exceed 2020 levels by thirty percent. We're concerned that this increase in demand could occur at the very same time that our production and refining facilities are partially or fully offline for repairs and refurbishment. This explains, in part, why the president will soon announce new incentives for exploration and drilling. But it also explains why we are attaching tremendous importance to the auction in Iraq. For those of you who are not familiar with this auction—Iraq has discovered a new oil field in its Anbar Province. And this isn't just any oil field. We and many others believe it is the largest oil field in history. Bigger than even the Ghawar Field in Saudi Arabia. An auction is being held next week in Bagdad for the production rights to at least eighty percent of the field, maybe more. All the major players are expected to submit bids. Total and the French are fully engaged. So too are Shell and the Dutch. We also expect BP and the British to submit bids. And, of course, most of the majors in the United States, such as Exxon and Chevron, are expected to participate. Now, we sat down with Rosneft and Lukoil many months ago to discuss the auction. We concluded that global politics being what they are meant that only one Russian company had a chance—Rusoil. I asked Rusoil's CEO to join us today. Evgeni? Where are you? There you are. Please raise your hand."

A fair-skinned man in his early sixties at the opposite end of the table raised his hand. He was not asked to say anything.

"As you all know, Rusoil is a relatively new company. It is neither owned nor controlled by the government. Moreover, no Russian subject to Western sanctions sits on the board of Rusoil or is an owner of Rusoil. Thus, to date, Rusoil has managed to avoid the kind of sanctions imposed on Rosneft, Lukoil, Gazprom, and many other companies represented around this table."

"Sergei, may I add something?"

"Yes, of course, General."

"Thank you. The SVR has been working very closely with the Office of the President and the Ministry of Energy on this. At first we were skeptical. We didn't think *any* Russian company stood a chance given the widespread condemnation of Russia's special military operation in Ukraine. However, over the past several months, following confidential discussions with the Iraqis and others, we've come to the conclusion that if Rusoil submits a competitive bid, it has a chance. It could win one or more leases. At the urging of the president we have also been working with our friends at KyrgyzOil in Bishkek. I suspect many of you around this table know Dmitri Volkov and his leadership team at KZO. In any event, we have been helping KZO prepare a tender. We view KZO as a kind of insurance policy for Russia in case Rusoil is not successful."

Everyone around the table knew KyrgyzOil (or KZO) was owned by the Republic of Kyrgyzstan. It was the main producer of oil and gas in Kyrgyzstan. Kyrgyzstan had very close ties with Russia dating back to its time as a Soviet Republic. In 2023 the United States and its allies began imposing sanctions on Kyrgyzstan-based companies for allegedly transferring controlled electronic components and other "dual-use" technology to Russia in violation of the sanctions imposed on Russia following its full-scale invasion of Ukraine in 2021. To date, the West had not imposed sanctions on KZO or other members of Kyrgyzstan's oil and gas sector.

Rublev asked, "General Bortaikov, what about Kuwait? We've heard the Kuwaitis are likely to secure most of the concessions."

"Well, it is true that Kuwait and Kuwait Petroleum Corporation have been engaged on this from the beginning. Kuwait has also taken steps in recent years to improve its relationship with Iraq. However, recently, Kuwait's chances of success have suffered a major setback. If you haven't already, you will soon hear that Kuwait's oil minister was killed last Saturday during a visit to Washington."

A quick gasp could be heard around the table. "Moreover, we believe he was the Kuwaiti official most responsible for preparing and presenting Kuwait's bids next week in Bagdad."

"This news is—how shall I say?—very interesting." Rublev tried his best to be diplomatic and not revel in Mutairi's demise.

"What happened to him?"

"We believe he was shot while attending the opera."

"Shot? Do they know who did it? Has anyone been arrested?"

With the calmness of a mafia boss and not the slightest hint of guilt in his voice, Bortaikov said, "No, not that we know of."

Chapter Twelve

At 8:45 a.m. on Monday, October 27, Elliot Jones turned his dark blue 2025 Lexus ES with Virginia plates into the underground parking garage below DSS headquarters in Rosslyn, Virginia. He turned off the radio and lowered his window as he greeted the two armed guards stationed at the entrance to the garage. They immediately recognized Elliot and waved him forward. The heavy steel barrier blocking the driveway slowly sank into the ground.

Once inside he took one of the elevators in the garage up to the lobby. In the lobby he fumbled for the castle key he kept in his wallet. He needed it to pass through the lobby's turnstiles. A woman waited impatiently behind him. She kept her key on the end of a lanyard around her neck. She probably thought he was an idiot for not doing the same. He tried not to swear out loud.

After passing through one of the lobby's stainless steel turnstiles, he took the third elevator on the right up to the eighth floor. Normally, he would have headed for his office on the seventh floor; however, this morning was different. Russell Adams, the director of investigations, had sent him a text Sunday evening asking him to stop by his office first thing Monday morning.

Adams and Elliot had both started at DSS in the fall of 1997. Adams was 63 and Elliot was 62. They were friends, but not the kind of friends who took vacations together or the kind who got together on weekends for family barbecues. They were more the kind of friends who would grab a coffee or a quick lunch together downstairs at the buffet on the corner.

Adams still had kids at home. His oldest was about to head off to college. His youngest was still a sophomore in high school. Elliot and his wife had only one child—their daughter, Rachel, who was out in Seattle. Being alone in the house was a new experience for them. They had officially joined the ranks of the *empty-nesters*.

Adams respected Elliot. He thought he was a brilliant investigator. Indeed he often thought that had it not been for Elliot's three-year fling with a private security firm from 2005 to 2007, it would have been Elliot who was named director.

"How was Seattle?" Adams asked. "Did you take the red-eye?"

Elliot plopped himself down in one of the leather chairs Adams kept in his office. "Yeah, it was fine. I used some miles to upgrade to first. I thought it might be easier to sleep up there, but it wasn't. The damn seats don't recline enough."

"How's Rachel doing? Is she at the University of Washington or—?"

"Yeah. She's a Husky. She's good. She seems to like it. She's in a dorm, but she's thinking about joining a sorority. I just think she's in for a shock when winter comes. It's beautiful there now."

"Why'd she pick Washington? She's a good student. I'm sure she could have gotten into Mason, Tech, or some of the other good schools around here."

"She said it was for the fisheries program, but I think she just wanted to get as far away from her mother and me as possible. Karen's kind of upset about it. Me? Not so much. Being so far away from home might do her some good. Besides, I don't mind visiting Seattle once in a while. As long as it's in the summer or early fall like now. That place is frigging depressing in the winter. Cold. Wet. And the days are short. The damn sun doesn't come up until about 8:00 in the morning and it sets around 4:00. No, thanks. So what's cookin'? Why'd you want to see me?"

"Have you heard what happened to Kuwait's oil minister?"

"Just what the press is reporting. That he's been hospitalized for something. Otherwise, no. What happened?"

"He was killed Saturday night at the Kennedy Center. He was attending the opera with Secretary Farnsworth. The agents on duty said he seemed fine. They had dinner together in Georgetown before the performance. Then all of a sudden, in the third act, he checked out right in his seat."

"What happened?" Elliot asked. "Did our agents see anything?"

Adams handed Elliot the preliminary autopsy and ballistic reports. "We just got these."

Elliot opened the autopsy report and started to skim the executive summary.

Adams continued. "They're running tests on the slug. But preliminarily they think it's Russian. Maybe even Soviet."

"Soviet? What the—?"

"And you ready for this?" Adams asked rhetorically.

"There's more?"

"They also found poison in his system. Again, this is all preliminary, but it looks like batrachotoxin."

Elliot put the report down and looked at Adams. "Somebody really wanted this guy dead. Did anyone get a visual on the shooter?"

"Nope. And no one heard anything either."

Elliot was incredulous. "Wait a minute. A gun goes off inside a crowded theater and no one hears anything? Are operas that loud?"

"Well, I'm no expert, but I'm told they can be. Except all the witnesses said it was pretty quiet when he slumped over."

"Do we have the gun?"

"Nope," Adams grunted. "Forensics found a loaded rifle backstage. It was almost identical to a dozen props found backstage in a crate. But it hadn't been fired. They're checking it now for prints."

Adams handed Elliot the DSS forensics team's report. "Here's their report. In addition to the rifle, I was struck by one other thing."

"What's that?"

"The minister was taken to GW around 10:25 p.m. on Saturday, where he was pronounced dead on arrival. But forensics was not notified of his death until 10:00 a.m. on Sunday."

"Why the delay?"

"Well, the Kuwaitis have been very tight-lipped about this. They still haven't made any sort of announcement and he's been dead for nearly two days."

"But we notified them, right?"

"Of course. In fact, State woke the Kuwaiti ambassador up at around 2:00 a.m. Sunday to tell him."

"And they've done and said nothing since then?" Elliot asked with a hint of suspicion in his voice.

"Nope. Nothing."

"Doesn't that strike you as a little odd? One of their most senior ministers dies in a foreign capital and they're not pounding on the table asking for answers?"

"It strikes me as damn odd!" Adams exclaimed. "So Kuwait is silent, State and the White House aren't saying anything, and *we* certainly don't want to be making any announcements. Bottom line? It's been a bit of a clusterfuck."

"Got it."

"Well, I'm not sure you do. The problem is this—by the time forensics was on scene Sunday around noon, the Kennedy Center cleaning crews had already scrubbed the place. Now, they didn't touch his seat, thank God. The Center's security made sure of that. But everything else, including all trash cans, was cleaned and emptied Saturday night."

"Shit."

"Yup, you got it," Adams sighed.

Adams got up from his desk. He walked over to the window and looked out. He had a partial view of the Potomac River and Georgetown from his office. Elliot had a view of another building from his office.

Without turning around Adams told Elliot, "I'm putting you in charge of the investigation. This is your highest priority. In fact, it's your only priority. You can have whatever resources you want."

Elliot began to rise from his seat. As he did he gathered up the reports on the table next to him.

"Look," Adams said, "we can't keep the press in the dark much longer. And when this gets out, and it definitely will, the White House and State will run for cover like scared rabbits and I don't want DSS to be their frigging roadkill. Oh, and one more thing. The Kuwaiti minister wasn't the only person killed at the Kennedy Center that night."

"What?"

"Yeah. They found a young woman who worked for the opera company stabbed to death in a men's room backstage. Park Police are handling the investigation. A buddy of mine has been assigned to the case. He sent me a copy of the autopsy report. You ready for this? A four-inch blade turned sideways a quarter inch below her fourth rib."

"Classic close quarters technique. Whoever killed her was a pro."

"Yup. But why does a professional kill a meaningless young woman? It must have something to do with the minister's death. You should keep in touch with my friend handling her investigation. His name is Cleveland. Detective Carter Cleveland."

"Oh. I know Cleveland. He's a good guy." Elliot headed for the door with the three reports under his arm. As he reached the door he turned to Adams. "Who was on the secretary's detail that night?"

"I was waiting for you to ask. Roger Payne, Vincent Faber, Wally Condon, and Steve Abramovich."

"I know Payne, Faber, and Condon. But who's Abramovich? Never heard of him. You know him?"

"Abramovich came over to DSS ten years ago from the CIA. He spent some time in Moscow. Consistently good reviews throughout his career. The secretary seems to like him. In fact, she asked for him specifically following her appointment in 2028. Apparently she met him in Moscow and they also worked together on the Hill."

"I'll need full personnel files on the four DSS agents."

"They're already on their way to your office."

"I'll also need to interview each separately and at some point the secretary as well."

"I'm afraid you may have to wait to do that," Adams said.

"Why's that?"

"Because the secretary is in Jakarta, along with her detail, for a regional conference on climate change hosted by the UN. She's not scheduled to return to Washington until the middle of next week. Oh, and one more thing. I got a message on my phone yesterday. I haven't returned it yet. I think he said his name was Kowalski, Captain Kowalski. With the Washington State Patrol. Do you know what that's about? You didn't get yourself in trouble out there, did you?"

"No, no, of course not. I don't know this guy, but I'm sure he's calling about some explosives found in a van on one of the Washington State ferries Saturday. Rachel and I just happened to be on that ferry. I helped a State Patrol officer deal with the situation."

"What? Are you serious? What'd you do?"

"We pushed the van off the back of the ferry. It made quite a splash when it blew."

"Jesus! Are you serious?"

"Yeah, probably four pounds of C-4 and eight barrels of diesel and fertilizer in a Chevy box van. I just happened to see the driver slip off the ferry at the last minute."

"And Rachel was there? Was she scared?"

"Honestly? No. She was sitting up front. She and most of the other passengers were oblivious—too busy looking at their phones or the scenery. The local press ran a few stories on it yesterday. I suspect the national media will pick it up today. If you google it you'll see some coverage. I'm afraid my name is mentioned in one or two places. Nothing much I can do about that except try not to talk to them. Obviously, if anyone in the office gets a call regarding this, they should not comment."

"Of course. I'll send an e-mail around the office giving everyone a heads-up. Well, good to have you back in one piece."

"Thanks."

Chapter Thirteen

The Situation Room is actually several rooms beneath the West Wing of the White House. The main conference room is dominated by a mahogany table fourteen-feet long and four-feet wide and slightly tapered at each end. Thirteen black leather chairs surround three sides of it. At one end of the table is a chair bearing the seal of the president. In front of each chair is a black leather conference table pad.

Black leather chairs line the walls of the room. On each side of the room are two 48-inch flat panel displays. On the wall opposite the president is an assortment of flat panel displays that can connect to different sites around the world simultaneously. On both sides of those monitors is a flag in a brass stand: the American flag in one and the Great Seal of the United States in the other. Finally, a 15-inch monitor in the right front corner of the room indicates whether the microphones in the room are on or off. In front of the president is a small control panel that lets him, among other things, turn the room's microphones on and off.

On this Monday morning the room was full. The smell of new carpeting was inescapable. The president's CoS, his energy secretary, national security advisor, the secretaries of homeland security and defense, and senior deputies from the Central Intelligence Agency (CIA) and Council of Economic Advisers (CEA) were among those seated around the table. Assistants and staff lined the walls. The conference table was strewn with paper tablets, pens, paper coffee cups, and bottles of water. Personal electronic devices, including cell phones, were not allowed in the Sit Room. Persons entering the room were expected to deposit these devices in small, keyed lockers outside.

At 9:35 a.m. President Hansen entered the room. In an instant the cacophony of voices ceased. The president sat down in his chair, one of the few empty chairs in the room.

"Hey, I like the new blue carpeting. That old carpeting was looking pretty ragged. Okay, enough about interior design," Hansen said with a slight smile on his face. "Let's get started. Do we have anyone on remote video or audio?"

The Sit Room was typically staffed by thirty people 24/7. They were divided into five watch teams, each having at least one communications officer. The comms officer that morning was Sergeant Isaac Winston. From an adjacent room, Winston said, "Secretary Farnsworth, Mr. President."

"Lynne, where are you?"

"Good morning, Mr. President. Earlier today I was in Canberra. Now I'm in Jakarta."

"Jakarta, whatcha doin' there?"

"I'm here for the Asia-Pacific Climate Week organized by the UN."

"You're not going to agree to anything, are you?" Hansen said with a smile. "Obama and Biden already tried to give away the store."

"No, Mr. President. This is one of four regional Climate Weeks the UN is holding around the world. The others are in Lima, Lagos, and Amman. While we expect some of the Pacific Island nations to push aggressively on methane emissions and coal, most of the discussion will focus on preparations for the global Climate Change Conference to be held in Doha next year. I want to make sure the agenda for that meeting doesn't go off the rails."

"Good. The last thing I need before the election is to have my base up in arms over the environment."

"Yes, sir. I understand. I might also mention that while I'm here I plan to meet with President Waskito. As you know, Indonesia's posture regarding the South China Sea has grown increasingly ambiguous. Virtually everyone in the region has supported our tough stance against China. We are trying to script a meeting of ASEAN next month in Bangkok where the strongest statement yet against China's actions will be issued. I don't want Indonesia to say or do anything in the meantime that will undercut that message."

"Alright. Safe travels, Lynne." The president turned to his CoS. "Okay, Bob, who's going to kick things off?"

Bob Salter had worked on Hansen's first campaign for the Senate. He was his CoS on the Hill and now at the White House. He knew how Hansen thought and how he liked to handle things. As a result, he was comfortable chairing these kinds of meetings for his boss.

"Mr. President, we thought we would hear first from DOE, then CEA, and perhaps conclude with DOD or CIA."

"Alright. That sounds good. Let's get started. But I have to be over to the Chamber by 12:15 p.m. and I promised them I wouldn't be late."

"Okay, Energy, you're up. Larry?" Salter looked at Larry Middleton, the secretary of energy. Salter didn't like Middleton. He thought he was lazy. However, he was popular in Louisiana and close to the oil and gas industry, having served as the state's governor for three terms. Besides, the president liked him. They were golfing buddies.

"Thanks, Bob," Middleton said with his thick Cajun accent. "Mr. President, I've asked Rick Atwater, who heads up our oil and gas bureau, to brief y'all today. Rick?"

Atwater was the assistant secretary for fossil fuels and carbon management. This was his first time in the Sit Room and only the second time he had briefed the president. He spoke nervously from one of the chairs next to Middleton.

"Good morning, Mr. President. Demand for oil is increasing at a rapid pace. After global recessions in 2008–09 resulting from the financial crisis and in 2020–21 resulting from the Covid pandemic, the economies of China and India are finally healthy and growing at the same time that the economies in Europe, Japan, Korea, and the United States are robust. In the midst of the pandemic global demand for oil stood at roughly 92 million barrels per day. By the end of this year we believe global demand will reach 120 million barrels per day. At the same time that demand is growing, supply is not. In fact, global supply is contracting. Several factors explain this. First is one you spoke about often during the campaign: Obama and Biden attacked the oil and gas industries every chance they got. Their demagoguery played well with their political bases, but it caused the industry to retrench, to not invest in new production."

"You got that right," Hansen grunted.

"Yes, sir. Second, Russia's invasion of Ukraine led to sanctions that disrupted supply, particularly into Europe. Also, pervasive corruption in major oil-producing countries such as Kuwait and Venezuela has caused production in those countries to steadily decline over the past five years. And the Houthis, as you well know, have stepped up their attacks on Saudi Arabia. In 2026 and 2027 these attacks did significant damage to the Shaybah super-field in the northern edge of the Empty Quarter. At the end of the last decade the Shaybah field was producing one million barrels of oil per day. Now it barely produces one-third of that amount. Finally, hurricanes in each of the past three years have wreaked havoc on our oil platforms, refineries, and other facilities in the Gulf of Mexico. In sum, Mr. President, we face a massive supply-demand imbalance that is growing quickly. As recently as 2022 the United States was a net exporter of petroleum. By the end of this year the US will be a net importer and by the end of this decade we expect the US will need to import as much as twenty percent of its total petroleum needs. Mr. President, we can drill all we want. We can expand our drilling of shale oil and fracking. We can expand the extent to which we drill offshore. And even if we could do these things overnight, which we cannot, they would not put a dent in the problem we face. Thus, we expect the price of West Texas intermediate crude to reach $175 a barrel by the end of next year and to steadily go up from there. Where it will stop is anybody's guess. Thank you, Mr. President. I'm happy to answer any questions you may have."

"Does anyone have any questions for Rick?" Salter asked.

"Yes, I do," Hansen said. "What about the SPR? Could we remedy some of the imbalance by releasing more oil from the SPR?"

"Yes, sir, but we caution against it. As you know, we have already released 250 million barrels from the SPR over the past 24 months. It is now at the lowest level in history. Going any lower would put at risk its use in the event of a real emergency."

"Well, it seems to me we face a real emergency now!"

Atwater regretted his choice of words. He was trying to draw a distinction between exogenous oil supply shocks, like a hurricane that destroys oil platforms in the Gulf, as opposed to the current shortage the US faced due to systemic supply-demand conditions. In any event, he wasn't about to get into a debate with the president of the United States over the meaning of the word "emergency."

The room was silent. Awkwardly so. Salter rescued Atwater. "Okay, anyone else have a question for Rick? If not, Steve, why don't you go next?"

"Good morning, Mr. President. My name is Steve Taylor. I'm the deputy director of the CEA. Working with Energy we have modeled the impact on the US economy of oil at $150, $175, and $200 per barrel. Using various econometric models, we can say with a fairly high degree of certainty that if WTI hits $175, inflation would soar to above 14 percent. GDP would turn negative; indeed we would not be surprised if it exceeded the negative 11.6 rate reached in 1946. The real unemployment rate would exceed 22 percent and might well exceed the 25.6 percent rate experienced in 1933. And our current account deficit would swell to over $1 trillion. Suffice it to say that these impacts would be less at $150 and greater at $200. Happy to answer any questions you may have."

"Thanks, Steve," Salter said. "Any questions for Steve? No? Then let's hear from the CIA. I don't know that we will have time for anyone else. Sharon?"

Sharon Holcumb was the deputy director of the CIA. She was a career civil servant, having been at the CIA for over thirty years. Her hair was gray and her glasses were thick. She'd lost track of how many times she had been in the Sit Room.

"Thanks, Bob. Good morning, Mr. President. I'll just take a minute to summarize the Agency's conclusions, which are explained in greater detail in your briefing materials. Essentially, after the First and Second Gulf Wars, the United States expected to secure preferential access to oil and gas supplies in Iraq, Kuwait, and Saudi Arabia. For various reasons, those expectations were never fully realized. Today we are competing for dwindling supplies in those and other countries. Kuwait, in particular, is underperforming. It barely produces two-and-a-half million barrels per day. Were it not for incompetence and corruption, it could easily produce four or even five million barrels per day. Saudi Arabia, as you just heard, is witnessing a dramatic decrease in its output. Publicly, we like to place much of the blame for the Houthi attacks on Iran. In fact, as you know from your daily intelligence briefings, Mr. President, the Houthis, unlike Hezbollah in Lebanon and Hamas in Gaza, are not puppets tightly controlled by Tehran. Since 2023 the Houthis have become a formidable military force and we expect them to continue to be a destabilizing factor in the Arabian peninsula for the foreseeable future. Finally, Iraq is unique. While it too battles corruption and incompetence, it has recently discovered a large oil field in its Anbar Province. In fact, we believe this field may be larger than the Ghawar Field in Saudi Arabia, which as you may know, is the largest oil field in the world. Whoever gains control of this new field in Iraq will have a competitive advantage over other countries that could last well into the next century."

Chapter Fourteen

S pecial Agent Victor Young enlisted in the Marine Corps right after high school. He loved the Marines—the discipline, the accountability, and especially the *esprit de corps*. Initially he was stationed at Camp Lejeune in North Carolina. He was about to be sent to Okinawa in Japan when he was informed that his application to the Marine Corps Police Academy at Fort Leonard Wood in Missouri had been accepted.

The DSS liked applicants with military backgrounds, especially if it included law enforcement. They tended to be patriotic, disciplined, hard-working, and on time. Young had been with DSS for five years. His evals were consistently excellent. He was a rising star.

Around 9:30 a.m. Monday he was lacing up his dress shoes at the YMCA in Alexandria, Virginia. He tried to work out at the gym at least three times a week. On his off days he ran. He liked to run down by the Potomac River on the bike path. Some days, when time permitted, he would run down to George Washington's estate at Mount Vernon and back—a total of 22 miles. On others he would run north up the river to Potomac Overlook Park and back—a total of 21 miles.

His phone rang on the locker room bench next to him. He didn't catch the caller's name, only that she worked for the director of investigations and Young was expected in Senior Agent Elliot Jones' office by 10:15 a.m.

Normally he would have taken the subway to Rosslyn and walked to DSS HQ, but time was short, so he jumped in a cab. With more people working from home on Mondays, traffic was light. He reached DSS HQ by 10:05 and entered Elliot's office by 10:15.

Sitting in one of Elliot's guest chairs was a thirtysomething brunette in a crisp white blouse, tight black skirt, and black high heels with red soles. Around her right ankle was a thin gold bracelet.

"Hi, I'm Vic Young. I was told to be here at 10:15."

The woman rose from her chair. In heels she was almost as tall as Young. She extended her hand. "Hello, I'm Alice Lake. I was also told to be here."

Before she could say another word Elliot walked in. "Please, have a seat. I'm Elliot Jones. You guys know each other?"

Young spoke first. "No, we just met."

"Well, you're gonna be working with me on a high-priority murder investigation. What do you know about batrachotoxin?"

Young had no clue, but before he could confess ignorance Lake offered that "batrachotoxin, or BTX, is one of the most toxic of the four steroidal alkaloids extracted from the skin of the Colombian arrow frog. If ingested by a human it kills within minutes. There is no known antidote."

Elliot's smirk spoke volumes. He was impressed.

"Huh. You just became my new toxicology expert." He also couldn't help but think to himself, *Damn, and smart too.*

Young was instantly jealous of her. He wondered how she knew that.

Elliot continued. "Kuwait's oil minister, a guy named Mutairi, was killed Saturday night at the Kennedy Center. He was there with Secretary

Farnsworth attending the opera. In front of you are preliminary ballistic, forensic, and autopsy reports. Study them. You'll see that he was shot in the chest *and* poisoned. Likely BTX. Vic, I'd like you to bird-dog the ballistic and forensic reports. The sooner we get our hands on the final versions, the better. Alice, please do the same for the autopsy report. And, Vic, I'm extremely interested in the identity of the slug found in Mutairi's body. Preliminarily it looks to be Russian. We need confirmation ASAP."

"Understood. I'm on it," Young said with the determination of a Marine.

"I want to get over to the Kennedy Center before lunch." Elliot picked up his phone. He asked his secretary to call the Kennedy Center. "Tell them we'll be over there in an hour. I want to meet with the general manager, the head of security, and any security personnel on duty Saturday night."

They took one of the agency's black Chevy Suburbans with the white "US government official use only" plates. It was a short drive to the Kennedy Center. Rather than park underneath, they parked in front on the Entrance Plaza.

As they got out a guard approached. "You can't park there."

Without breaking stride Elliot flashed the guard his identification badge and walked past him mumbling, "Official police business." The guard backed off.

They entered through the Center's main doors. A young man surrounded by a dozen men and women was there to greet them. Elliot could not help but notice that he was exceedingly thin and stood very erect. He wore a tight-fitting light gray suit with a salmon-colored dress shirt underneath. His pants stopped two inches above his light brown shoes. He was not wearing socks. His black tie was also thin.

As Elliot, Young, and Lake approached, the young man took a single step forward with his right arm and hand extended straight at Elliot. A bright smile spread across his face. "Hi, I'm Jesse Dawson. I'm the assistant general manager of the Kennedy Center." Sadly for Jesse Dawson, things went downhill from there.

"Hello, Jesse. My name is Elliot Jones. I am a senior agent with the US Diplomatic Security Service. I will be leading the federal investigation into the death of Kuwait's oil minister, Mohammad Al-Mutairi, at the Kennedy Center Saturday night. With me this morning are DSS Special Agents Alice Lake and Victor Young. Where's your boss? I want to meet with the general manager. I believe my office informed you that we wanted to meet with the Center's general manager."

"I'm sorry, but he's not here today. It's his day off," Jesse said with the same smile.

Elliot was not smiling. "Mr. Dawson," Elliot barked through clenched teeth, "a high-ranking official of a key US ally was murdered here two nights ago within a foot of the US secretary of state. Another young woman who worked for the Washington Opera Company was found stabbed to death in a men's room backstage. I don't care if your boss is having a baby. I want his ass down here now! And if he's too busy raking leaves or whatever the fuck he's doing, I'll send the police to pick him up and escort him down here. Do you understand me?"

Young and Lake shot quick glances at each other. They did not utter a word, but their wide eyes said the same thing. Elliot's reputation for being tough and no-nonsense was justified.

Elliot immediately turned to the gray-haired man standing to Dawson's right. "Are you Henry Culbertson?"

The man shook Elliot's hand. "Yes, sir. I'm the director of safety and security at the Kennedy Center. And please call me Hank. With me are the security personnel on duty Saturday night."

"Thank you. Can you show us the Opera House?"

With that, the three DSS agents headed down the Hall of Nations with Culbertson and his team. Jesse Dawson, now completely deflated and standing alone, shuffled back to his office.

Except for some tour groups and a kids play in the Family Theater that day, the Kennedy Center was quiet. Cleaning crews were hard at work giving the bust of President Kennedy its semiannual cleaning. Police tape stretched across the entrance to the Opera House. Two security guards were stationed behind the tape.

It had been years since Elliot had been in the Kennedy Center. He had forgotten how big it was, how plush the red carpeting was, how shiny all the metal, including the hand rails and brass trash receptacles, was. Before heading up the steps and into the Opera House he huddled with Culbertson and his team.

"Most of you were interviewed by DSS agents yesterday. We have those statements. Thank you. Nonetheless, Agents Young and Lake will be in touch with some of you to schedule follow-up interviews. We would appreciate your full cooperation. We also want to obtain copies of all video that recorded the comings and goings Saturday night. Hank, can you help with that?"

"Yes, of course," Culbertson said. "We cooperated fully with the DSS advance team and we will do the same with you and your team."

"Speaking of which, where is your security office? I'd like to see it and understand your video recording and storage protocols."

"Certainly. Would you like to go there now?"

"Yes, but first—" Elliot turned to Young and Lake. "While I go with Hank, I'd like you to check out the inside of the Opera House, including backstage. As you do so, pay particular attention to the areas that align with the angle of bullet entry suggested in the preliminary autopsy report. I'll meet you there in about 45 minutes."

Elliot headed off with Culbertson and a member of his team. As they walked Culbertson introduced his colleague.

"Agent Jones, this is Eric Seastrum. Eric is my deputy. Among other things, he is in charge of our electronic monitoring and security systems. Eric, why don't you give Agent Jones an overview?"

"Sure," Seastrum said. "Well, first I would like to point out the location of some of our cameras. A few of them are above us now and over there behind the pillar. In all, we have over 125 cameras throughout the Center, including six inside the Opera House. In fact, there are cameras in every open area such as our lobbies and performance venues. We also have cameras in the loading docks, cafeteria, employee lounge, and parking garage. Around 50 can transmit and record audio."

In the Center's security office Elliot looked at video recordings from inside the Opera House Saturday night. Two cameras in particular captured Mutairi and Secretary Farnsworth near the middle of the first row. One included audio. Elliot put on headphones. Even with the audio turned up, he didn't hear anything unusual when Mutairi's head dropped or the blood first appeared.

He then watched video of the lobby. Four cameras were trained on this area. He fast-forwarded through each, stopping only to examine the fifteen minutes during intermission. The angle of three cameras was not particularly helpful or revealing; however, one was trained perfectly on the coffee cart. Elliot watched intently. He paused, reversed, and paused again the roughly ninety seconds when Mutairi and Lynne bought their coffee. He stopped the tape at the moment Allen reached for Mutairi's cup. He saw a tattoo on Allen's right arm at the wrist. Some kind of cross. He made a note of it.

Elliot then watched in slow motion as Allen turned away from Mutairi and Lynne. As he studied the video, his back straightened. His nose was only a few inches from the screen.

"Look. See right there," Elliot said to no one in particular. "He drops something in the coffee before turning back to Farnsworth and Mutairi."

Culbertson bent over Elliot's shoulder to look. "Let me see. Can you play that back?"

"Sure," Elliot said.

"That's a poison ring," Culbertson observed while he pointed at the screen.

"A what?"

"A poison ring. They're also called pillbox or locket rings. They were very popular in Western Europe during the Middle Ages. People stored teeth, hair, and the bones of their deceased loved ones in them. But their most famous use was as a way to slip poison into an enemy's food or drink or to commit suicide."

"Huh. I didn't know that."

"Yeah. In fact, in Giuseppe Verdi's opera *Il trovatore*, Lady Leonora commits suicide in Act IV by ingesting poison from her poison ring rather than giving herself to the evil Count di Luna."

"How do you know so much about poison rings?" Elliot asked.

"I don't really. But I studied music history and literature in college before my dad convinced me to switch to criminal justice."

Elliot liked Culbertson. Very straightforward. No bullshit. "Where'd you go to college?"

"Cal State Fullerton. I got a BA in music history and literature there. Then I went to Michigan, where I got my MA in criminal justice."

"Interesting." Elliot looked at Seastrum. "Your boss is quite the Renaissance man."

Culbertson laughed at the suggestion. "I don't know about that."

Elliot refocused. "Okay, we're going to need to send these videos off for further examination. Agent Young or Lake will coordinate with you on that. In the meantime, I need you to place two armed guards outside the door to this office 24/7."

"Certainly," Culbertson said. "Right away."

"Thanks. We'll also need to interview the two people working the coffee cart that night. What are their names?"

"The girl's first name is Aaliyah, but everyone calls her Ally. I don't know her last name. I believe she owns the cart. She sets up in the lobby outside the Opera House for every performance. She's been doing that for the past four or five years, I'd say. She often does the same when there are performances, particularly large ones, at the Eisenhower Theater and the Concert Hall. I don't know the guy. He's new. Ally usually has a girl help her. Eric, do you know her name?"

"Sorry, no. I don't drink coffee or tea," Seastrum said.

"What about the guy? Do you know him?" Culbertson asked.

"No. Like you said, he's new. I've seen him around a lot during rehearsals for *Otello*. He may be a super or in the chorus," Seastrum offered.

"Okay," Elliot said. "Thanks. Well, if you think of anything else about these guys or that evening, please let one of us know. Here's my card. My secretary, Cindy, can always track me down. Same for Agents Young and Lake."

Elliot started to leave, but at the door he stopped. "Oh, one more thing. What happens to the garbage in the brass receptacles at the top of the Opera House stairs in the lobby after it is collected?"

"It's held in dumpsters down at the loading dock," Culbertson explained. "We used to have a contract with Waste Pro. Now it's with Waste Management. I believe they collect every Monday and Thursday."

With a sense of urgency in his voice Elliot asked, "Monday? What time on Monday?"

Culbertson looked at his watch. With his head still down, he said, "Well, anytime between now and four."

"Then please get two of your guys down there NOW! Don't let anyone touch the dumpsters. I'll get forensics to come back and search them. Hopefully they can find Mutairi's cup."

Just then Elliot's cell phone rang. "Hello."

"Sir, this is Vic. We've found something backstage that you need to see."

"Okay. I'm coming now." Elliot looked at Culbertson. "They found something. You should come with me."

Chapter Fifteen

At 11:15 a.m. President Hansen closed his notebook. "Alright, everyone, this has been helpful. Thank you." He slipped into an adjacent room to freshen up his coffee.

Bob Salter told everyone as they rose to watch their e-mails. "We're going to try to meet again on this next Monday, probably same time."

Small talk once again filled the room. Empty paper cups were tossed in the trash. Some tossed empty plastic water bottles in the blue government-issued recycle bin in the corner.

Salter raised his voice above the din. "Sharon, could you please stay for a minute?" He also asked the president's national security advisor, director of national intelligence, secretary of homeland security, and secretary of defense to stay.

As he waited for the room to clear, Salter asked for all microphones to be turned off. He watched the video display in the corner of the room switch from "ON" to "OFF."

Hansen reentered the room. A member of the watch team closed the door behind him. Once everyone was seated, the president turned to Sharon Holcumb.

"What's the story with Mutairi? How's he doing? I heard he's in the hospital."

"I'm afraid he's dead, Mr. President," Holcumb said.

"Dead? What happened?"

"He was assassinated Saturday night, although Kuwait just released a statement saying he died of an apparent heart attack. We're not sure what's behind that. We're checking."

"Assassinated? Do we know by whom?" Hansen asked.

"Not yet. DSS is investigating."

"How was he killed?"

"Looks like he was shot. Someone may have also tried to poison him."

"Geez. I heard this happened at the Kennedy Center. Is that right?"

"Yes, sir."

"And Lynne was there?"

"Yes, sir. She was sitting right next to him."

"Was she ever in danger? How's she doing?"

"She seems to be doing fine. You saw her just now. She seems fine. Apparently she didn't see or hear anything. At least that's what she's saying. Unfortunately, no one has been able to really interview her yet. She left the next morning for the Pacific."

"Okay." The president then asked no one in particular. "So what does this do to our plans?"

The room was silent.

Finally Holcumb spoke up. "I think it destroys them. I know you don't want to hear that, but Mutairi was the key. He believed he had allies in the ministry who would set fire to a few marginal wells in the Ratqa and Abdal Fields in the north. They would make it look like drone attacks. Mutairi was confident that after Iran's drone attacks on the Saudi oil-processing facilities at Abqaiq and Khurais in 2019, the Kuwait News Agency would be quick to blame Iran for the fires. The current emir is weak. So is the crown prince. Mutairi was hopeful that he could get them to declare a state of emergency and invite the US in to help protect Kuwait from further perceived attacks. If they refused, Mutairi was prepared to take further steps until they did. Once in, Chevron, Exxon, ConocoPhillips, and others would soon follow. Even if our troops stayed only a few years, our companies would be able to increase Kuwait's oil production and our access to it."

"Can anyone else in Kuwait take Mutairi's place?" the president asked.

"Potentially, but it will take many months, if not years, to get us back to where we were before Saturday," Holcumb stated.

"Anyone else have a question or want to say anything? Because if not, I need to get over to the Chamber."

For the first time that day Bob Salter heard the gentle whoosh of the air-conditioning system in the Sit Room. Standing up, he said, "Then we're adjourned. Thanks, everybody. Thank you, Mr. President."

Chapter Sixteen

Elliot pulled open one of the thick padded doors at the back of the Opera House. Culbertson followed him. In every direction he was surrounded by red carpeting and red padded walls. It was dark. As he moved toward the light the low ceiling of the hallway gave way to the heavenly ceiling of the Opera House. They walked down one of the two center aisles toward the stage. Elliot was awestruck by the vast and majestic space.

Young and Lake were at the back of the stage. Young was standing on the third rung of an eight-foot aluminum ladder. Lake and some of the Center's security personnel were standing around him, looking up at one of the gargoyles on Otello's castle.

As Elliot approached Young said to him, "You need to see this." He stepped down from the ladder.

Elliot asked, "What is it?"

"Behind the bottom part of that gargoyle is a small handgun braced on an equally small mount. The barrel aligns with the mouth of the gargoyle. I'm not familiar with the pistol, but I have some thoughts on the mount." Young paused.

"Go ahead," Elliot said.

"Well, it seems to have some sort of scope and antenna on it. I saw similar devices when I was in the Marines. The Corps was constantly trying to develop weapons that could be controlled remotely and sent in to high-risk environments in Iraq and Syria. By the time I left the Corps they were trying to simplify these systems so a soldier could even control them with a cell phone. If that's what we're looking at here, the shooter could have been anywhere, including in the audience."

Several members of the Center's security team gasped. Elliot showed no reaction. Instead he climbed the ladder. The light at the back of the stage was low, so he used the flashlight on his phone to illuminate the gun.

After a few moments, Elliot said, "I've never actually seen one of these in person, but I think this may be a PSS or PSS-2, which would explain why no one heard anything and why the slug was thought to be Russian."

"A PSS?" Young asked. "What's that?"

Lake saw her chance to speak. "May I?"

"Of course." Elliot gave a slight wave of his left hand as if to signal it was fine.

Oh no, Young thought to himself.

"The Soviets developed the PSS during the late 1970s and early 1980s," Lake began. "Sometimes it is referred to as the *Vul.* The Soviet Army and the KGB adopted it in 1983. The PSS has a special design that slows down the slide on the final stages of movement in order not to clang. This was a big improvement over the older PB silenced pistol with suppressor, which had significant sound reduction but generated a significant amount of noise by the clank of the slide. The PSS is chambered for a special 7.62 x 42 mm SP-4 bullet. The cartridge has an integrated silencing feature. It has a gas-sealing piston that pushes the bullet. Once the bullet is away all powder gasses are locked within the strengthened case. As a result, the PSS is much quieter than most conventional pistols with sound suppressors. This ammunition is, however, of limited power. Its effective range is only 80 to 100 feet. Then, around 2011, the FSB developed a new PSS-2 silenced pistol. It is based on the original PSS, but with some new features and improvements. It fires SP-16 noiseless 7.62 x 43 mm ammunition, which is more powerful than the original 7.62 x 42 mm cartridge. Finally, it's been rumored that a PSS-3 may be in the works, but the specs on that, if it exists, are not known."

For the love of God, Young said under his breath.

"Thanks, Alice." Elliot couldn't help but smile. "In addition to being my toxicology expert, you're also my ballistics expert. Now what puzzles me is how DSS forensics missed this on Sunday. I mean, if you guys could find it within an hour, how is it that an entire forensics team could not find it over the course of an entire day?"

Young held a piece of black molded plastic about the size and shape of the back of a human skull in his hand. "Well, I obviously don't know how large the DSS forensics team was or how long they were here yesterday, but in fairness to them, this molded cover was lying on the floor of the stage when we arrived. It looks like it was designed to fit across the back of the gun and mount. These seem to be screw holes here and here, although both are damaged," Young said, pointing to two holes. "In any event, if this piece was attached and secure behind the gargoyle, the investigators could have easily thought it was all just part of the castle."

Before Young finished Lake put on light blue latex gloves and pulled an evidence bag from a large purse over her shoulder. Elliot nodded approval. He told them to get the gun and mount over to the lab as soon as they got back to DSS.

"I doubt they'll find much, though. Whoever did this is not stupid or careless enough to leave prints. But it would be good to get confirmation on the make of the gun."

Elliot looked at his watch. They had been there a little over two-and-a-half hours. Elliot needed to get back to his office for a meeting at 3:30 p.m. He turned to Culbertson.

As he shook his hand, Elliot said, "Thanks, Hank. We appreciate your cooperation, but I've got to run. Needless to say, we'll be in touch."

"Certainly," Culbertson said. "As I said, you'll have our full cooperation. By the way, per your request, guards are already in place outside our security office and down by the dumpsters."

"Great. Thanks. Oh, and should your general manager ever show up," Elliot said with a slightly mischievous look on his face, "tell him I'm sorry we couldn't wait for him."

Rick McFarland was the general manager of the Kennedy Center. Mondays were sacred. They were his only day off. On this Monday, however, he got a frantic call from his deputy, who was by nature excitable.

"You need to get down here right away or they said they're gonna arrest you!"

At 2:45 p.m. McFarland pulled into the Kennedy Center's parking garage and the space reserved for its "General Manager." At that very moment, Elliot, Lake, and Young got in a black Chevy Suburban sitting out front and drove off.

Chapter Seventeen

The ringing of the phone startled Elliot. His head jerked up. He had fallen asleep.

The ballistics report on Mutairi lay open on his desk. When his 3:30 p.m. meeting got cancelled, he decided to use the free time to review the file and read all of the reports, including the preliminary forensics and autopsy reports. Jet lag and lack of sleep were, however, taking their toll on him.

"Hello, this is Jones."

"Agent Jones, this is Captain Kowalski with the Washington State Patrol Vessel and Terminal Safety Division. Do you have a minute?"

"Yes, of course. How are you?"

"I'm fine, thanks for asking. First of all, I want to thank you for everything you did out here last weekend. I've spoken to Officer Romano at length. What you did on the *Chehalis* Saturday was—well, you saved a *lot* of lives. This state owes you a debt of gratitude."

"That's very kind of you to say. Thanks. Those were some pretty tense moments. Officer Romano did a great job and those deckhands deserve a lot of credit too. Personally I wouldn't have blamed them if they had jumped overboard." The two men laughed.

"The second thing I wanted to mention is that I just got off the phone with the governor's office. She wants to meet you, thank you personally, and present you with one of the state's highest honors, the Medal of Valor. Do you plan to come back out here anytime soon?"

"Wow. I don't know what to say." Elliot truly was at a loss for words. He tried to gather his thoughts. "We don't currently have any plans to go out there, but that's partly because I was just there. You see, our daughter is a freshman at UW. I was there to visit her and to make sure she was settling in okay. My wife wanted to go, but she had a doctor's appointment she couldn't change."

"Well, please check your calendar and check with your wife. The state will pay for your transportation and lodging. I suspect the ceremony will be down in Olympia. If you've not been to Olympia before, you should check it out. It's nice."

"I certainly will, and I will check with my wife. We only have the one child—our daughter, Rachel. She's our baby. Thus, if I had to guess, my wife will want to jump on the next plane, especially if someone else is paying." The two men shared another laugh.

"Speaking of my daughter, my name is starting to appear in some of the articles reporting on Saturday, at least the ones I've seen online. I don't know what the television stations out there are doing and whether I'm mentioned."

"The ones I've seen," Kowalski offered, "have mentioned Officer Romano and interviewed passengers on board the *Chehalis* that day. But I suspect it's just a matter of time before reporters start calling you and your name gets mentioned more."

"In fact, some guy with Reuters left a message on my office line last night. I haven't returned it. I was on the plane flying back here. In any event, I'm worried about the safety of my daughter. I haven't said anything to her or my wife, and I don't plan to, at least not for the time being. I don't want to scare them. But the kind of people who would put a van loaded with explosives on a ferry are also the kind of people who might try to harm her. She is, after all, a very soft target."

"I agree. You want me to talk to campus police? I know the captain well. He's a good guy. He runs a very professional department. It's one of the largest universities in the world. Practically a city unto itself. They can step up patrols around where she lives and the campus in general. Is she in a dorm or—"

"Yes, please, she's currently in Hansee Hall, but she's thinking about moving. Listen, that would be great. I appreciate it."

"Oh, don't mention it. That's the least we can do. And obviously it's up to you and, I suppose, your wife, but you may want to say something to her. Just encourage her to be aware of her surroundings and to speak up if something doesn't look right."

"Yeah, I tend to agree with you. I just know my wife. She's going to freak out."

"I understand. I'm married myself."

"Say, ah, is there anything you can tell me about your investigation? I haven't spoken to Officer Romano since the ferry ride back to Seattle on the *Tacoma* that day. He was hoping you might have the driver of the van on video."

"As a matter of fact we do. He was wearing a baseball cap pulled down low, but he accidentally looked right into one of our cameras on the pier. Facial recognition identified him as Donald Mark, a welder and auto mechanic from Centralia, a small town halfway between Seattle and Portland. He appears to be a member of the QAnon Group down there, a real right-winger. He served two tours in Iraq as an explosive ordinance specialist in the 3rd Marine Logistics Group. He was arrested last year for assaulting his girlfriend, but since he had no priors, he was given probation.

Oh, and remember that jacket you thought he was wearing when he first boarded the ferry?"

"Yeah," Elliot said with a slight rise in his voice.

"We found that in a trash can on the *Chehalis*. It was fairly new, so it still had the store tag sown into the liner. Our detectives contacted the store and sure enough, Mark purchased it last year using his girlfriend's credit card. We were able to pull DNA samples from the hair on the jacket. They matched our guy."

"That's great news. But why did he ditch the jacket?"

"Well, he had to get off the ferry before it blew. Right?"

"Yeah," Elliot said, although he wasn't sure where Kowalski was going with this.

"So he was probably going to jump overboard when the screaming lady with the kids just happened to come along. She presented him with an opportunity to simply walk off."

"Jump off? People do that?" Elliot was a little surprised.

"Oh, hell. All the time. It's a real problem for us. Some try to kill themselves. Some are drunk and accidentally fall off. And some dumb shits do it for kicks."

"Huh. I had no idea. And that would explain why the couple on the Boston Whaler came alongside. They were going to pluck his ass out of the water had he jumped."

"Yup. So we just got one of our judges to sign a warrant for Mark's arrest. Hopefully he'll talk and ID the others in the boat. But even if he doesn't, one of my officers interviewed a guy fishing for steelhead that morning on the Duwamish River south of Pier 52. He claims a man and a woman in their late fifties went by him around a quarter to ten Saturday morning on a Boston Whaler with an Evinrude outboard. He remembers because he yelled at 'em. He thought they should have given his line more space. He described the boat in pretty good detail because he used to own a 22-foot Boston Whaler. He even recalled some of the hull numbers. We'll get 'em. It's just a matter of time."

"Well, good luck. And, Captain, if someone in your department could keep me posted, I would really appreciate it. As I said, I'm worried about my daughter."

"Of course. Happy to. And please don't forget to check your calendar and speak to Mrs. Jones. Let us know when you can get back out here. The governor is anxious to meet you. As am I. Take care. Be safe."

"Thanks. Goodbye."

Elliot put down the phone. He debated whether to call his wife. On one hand, he was anxious to tell her about the award. On the other, he dreaded expressing concern about Rachel's safety. But first he needed to take a piss.

A few minutes later as he walked back to his office from the restroom, Elliot stuck his head inside Young's office. "Do we have the final versions of the ballistic and forensic reports?

"No," Young said. "Hopefully later today. But forensics thinks they found Mutairi's coffee cup! Toxicology is looking at it now."

"Fantastic. I was afraid we'd have to dig through every landfill in northern Virginia to find it. Okay, let me know the minute you get those reports. As I said, I'm particularly interested in the origins of that slug."

Elliot walked back to his office. Just as he started to sit down, his phone rang. He didn't recognize the number. It looked like an overseas number. Who could it be? In that moment his intention to call his wife vanished, not by design, but because of preoccupation.

"Hello, this is Jones."

"Elliot Jones?" The connection was poor.

"Yes, speaking. Who is this?"

"This is Abdul Rasham in Cairo."

"Abdul. Hey, how are you? It's been a while."

Rasham was the director general of Egypt's Bureau of Homeland Security (HS), the main security agency responsible for domestic surveillance and counterterrorism in Egypt.

The other two principal security organizations in Egypt are the General Intelligence Service and the Office of Military Intelligence Services and Reconnaissance, both of which specialize in gathering foreign intelligence. The HS, also known as the National Security Agency (NSA), is the successor to Egypt's General Directorate for State Security Investigations (SSI). The SSI was widely hated and feared in Egypt. Thus, during the country's revolution in 2011, its offices throughout the country, with the exception of its headquarters off of Noubar Street in Cairo, were sacked by protestors who made off with sensitive records and other items. The HS was created two years later after the *coup d'état* that toppled Mohamed Morsi and installed General Abdel Fattah El-Sisi. Many believe the HS is essentially the old SSI operating under a new name.

"Yes, it has," Rasham said. "I'm fine. I tried to call your mobile but it wouldn't connect. Has your number changed?"

"No. But we keep our cell phones turned off in the office."

"Don't tell me you're worried about the NSA listening to you?"

Elliot returned the *volley* with his own. "No, but friends do spy on friends."

"Yes, quite right. The *Five Eyes* are always watching and listening to us." Rasham laughed.

Although Rasham spoke in jest, his comments carried a grain of truth.

Five Eyes is a cooperative intelligence alliance that monitors the electronic communications of citizens and foreign governments. This network of anglophone countries includes the United States, the United Kingdom, Canada, Australia, and New Zealand. Former NSA contractor Edward

Snowden described Five Eyes as a "supranational intelligence organization that does not answer to the known laws of its own countries." Documents leaked by Snowden revealed that while the national law of many alliance countries prohibited their intelligence services such as the CIA and NSA from spying on their own citizens, it did not prohibit an alliance partner from doing so and sharing that information with local authorities.

In several interviews during 2019 and 2020 Snowden also described how the most sophisticated intelligence services could listen not only to telephone calls, but also to surrounding, ambient communications as long as a mobile phone was switched on. He gave as one example what he called a "hot mic tool" called *Nosey Smurf* used by the UK's digital spy agency, the Government Communications Headquarters (GCHQ). This program could listen not only to ambient communications if a phone's microphone was switched on, but even if it was not by essentially turning the phone's microphone on without the user knowing it. This explained why government officials around the world deposit their cell phones in lockers and other receptacles before entering secure locations like the White House Sit Room.

"So, Abdul, to what do I owe this honor?"

"Am I on speaker?"

Elliot assured him he was not.

"Good. Well, for the past couple of days we've been tracking a Russian, Oleg Krychuk. He's what you'd probably call a *scumbag*. Kind of a tough guy. We think he's SVR. In any event, yesterday afternoon a couple of my guys followed him to a hotel here in Cairo, where he met with an American. Even though my guys had hearing-amplification devices, they couldn't quite make out everything they said. Apparently they weren't speaking English or Russian. Now here's the interesting part. First, the Russian seemed to believe that Kuwait's oil minister is dead, assassinated last Saturday at the Kennedy Center. Is that true?"

"No comment," Elliot replied.

"Well, I'll take that as a yes. But true or not, the more interesting thing is who he was with. I said he met with an American. Are you sitting down?"

"Yes. Who was he meeting with?" Elliot asked.

"Farnsworth."

"I'm sorry, you kind of broke up. Could you repeat that?"

"Farnsworth, James Farnsworth. The husband of your secretary of state!"

"Are you sure?"

"Positive. I'll send you some photos my guys took. They're kind of grainy, but you'll see. It's definitely Farnsworth. What's your e-mail address?"

Chapter Eighteen

Elliot was tired. He hadn't slept since Saturday night in Seattle. It had been a long day. He could have gone home. He probably should have gone home; however, there was much to do and little time to do it. Besides, the Kennedy Center was, loosely speaking, on his way home.

Instead of parking underneath in the garage, he again parked in front of the Kennedy Center on the Entrance Plaza. This time, however, he was in his personal car and it was late, so he pulled off to the side in a token nod to the rules and to the patrons arriving for performances by the NSO in the Concert Hall and *Shear Madness* in the Theater Lab. Notwithstanding, security made a beeline for Elliot as he approached the front doors.

"Sorry, but you can't park there."

Elliot flashed his badge. "I'm Senior Agent Elliot Jones with the DSS. I'm investigating the incident in the Opera House Saturday night. I'll only be a few minutes. If you have any concerns about my car and where it is parked, call your boss, Director Culbertson. Tell Hank that Elliot Jones is here."

With that, Elliot continued inside; although he thought to himself, *If they fuck with my car I'll kill 'em.*

Elliot walked down the Hall of Nations past patrons coming and going. The red carpet beneath his feet felt soft and thick. When he reached the Grand Foyer he glanced to his left, toward the lobby outside the Concert Hall. The smell of brewing coffee lingered in the air. Through the crowd that seemed to be moving in all directions, he could see the coffee cart. Around six people were waiting in line.

Just as he was about to dive into the crowd, he decided to check on the Opera House. Ahead of him the light from the Orrefors chandeliers gleamed off of President Kennedy's recently cleaned bust. He was glad to see the entrance to the Opera House barren and dark. Police tape was still in place, as were the guards behind the tape. Elliot was tempted to enter, but he had other priorities and time was short. So he reversed his direction and went back down to the Concert Hall.

As he did he weaved in and out of well-heeled couples, both young and old, the kind of people who donate thousands and in some cases millions of dollars to the arts every year. Elliot also narrowly avoided a collision with a young mother pushing a baby stroller. Elliot apologized to the woman, but he wondered to himself, *Who brings a stroller and baby to the symphony?*

Elliot took his place at the end of the line for Coffee Virtuoso. When it was his turn he ordered a small decaf latte and a chocolate chip cookie.

As he took his wallet out of his pocket he said to Ally, "Ms. Khalil, my name is Elliot Jones. I'm a special agent with the Diplomatic Security Service. I am in charge of the federal investigation into the events of last Saturday night. I'd like to speak with you."

Ally's eyes locked on Elliot. She had already spoken to an agent who said he was with the DSS. She wondered why they were back. Was she a suspect? Her heart raced. With a slight tremble in her voice, she said, "Well, as you can see, I'm busy right now."

Elliot sensed her fear. He knew the situation was not ideal. "I understand. But this will only take a minute."

"Okay. But give me a second. I need to work this line down."

Five minutes later Ally switched places with her assistant. She walked toward Elliot, who was finishing his cookie next to one of the glass doors that led out on to the River Terrace.

As she neared, Ally wiped her hands on a towel tucked inside a black apron that hung around her waist. "Yes, sir, now how can I help you?"

Elliot wiped cookie crumbs from his chin. "Excuse me. I have a weakness for chocolate chip cookies and yours are very good."

"Thank you."

He hoped the compliment might put her at ease and break the ice. Elliot produced his badge. "First of all, let me show you this. And let me also say at the outset that I know you have already spoken to one of my colleagues. I just have a few follow-up questions."

More out of nervousness than anything else, Ally continued to wipe her hands on her towel. "Okay."

"The woman working behind your cart right now, is she your regular assistant? Does she normally help you?"

"Yes."

"What's her name?"

"Melissa Wilson."

"Do you have any other assistants?"

"No. Melissa and I have been working together for—" She paused to think. "I think this is our fifth year together."

"Ah. Well, that answers my next question. Thanks. I can see that you get pretty busy at times. What do you do if one of you gets sick or can't make it for one reason or another?"

"We do the best we can. But, yes, the line slows and service suffers."

"What about last Saturday night? Was that different?"

"Well, as you seem to know based on your question, I asked a guy to help me during intermission."

"Yes, I do know. But before we talk about him, what happened to Ms. Wilson that night?"

"She called me on my cell as I was setting up. She said she was sick. She sounded horrible. So I told her not to worry and to feel better. It was a short call. I was busy. I didn't have much time to talk."

"Is it common for that to happen? I mean, does she often call in sick?"

"No. Melissa is very reliable. If she says she's sick, she's sick."

"Do you happen to know Ms. Wilson's middle name?"

"Yeah, I think it's Rogers."

"Okay, now about this guy who helped you Saturday night—how do you know him?"

"Well, I don't really. But I believe he's a super in *Otello*. He's been around a lot lately. I don't know how much you know about opera, but they rehearse for approximately three weeks and then there are typically seven performances spread over two weeks. So Ralph—I think that's his name— has been around a lot the past month. He usually buys at least one coffee and one snack from us every night. Nice guy. Very friendly."

"So you're here for performances *and* rehearsals?"

"Well, we try to be here for all the opera rehearsals. Not so much for the ballet or orchestra."

"Why is that?"

"Because it takes a lot of people to put on an opera. You've got the principals, the chorus, the supers, the orchestra, often dancers, and then of course all the stagehands and staff. More bodies means more customers. The orchestra and ballet have fewer bodies, so for those and some of the other venues at the Center we just set up for performances. Not rehearsals."

"That's interesting. By the way, did you say *supers*? What are—"

"Yeah. Those are what you'd probably call extras. Opera calls 'em *supers*."

"Thanks."

"Sure. Now I need to get back to work. Are you finished?"

"I just have a few more questions. You said his name was Ralph. Do you know his last name?"

"Yeah, he said it was Allen."

"Did he ever say where he was from or where he worked?"

"No, not to me. I was usually pretty busy. We never talked for very long."

"Would you say there was anything unusual about this guy? Did he say anything odd or have any distinctive marks?"

She thought for a moment. "Well, he didn't say anything odd to me. But he did have a tattoo on his arm."

"Do you recall which arm?"

"Yes, I think it was his right arm." She pointed to her wrist. "By his wrist."

"Can you describe the tattoo?"

"Actually, I asked him about it one night. He said it was an Ethiopian Coptic cross. He said he was a Coptic Christian. He said Stevie Ray Vaughn and Keith Richards both had one. Since I'd never heard of a Coptic Christian or a Coptic Christian cross, I just said 'cool'."

She shrugged her shoulders and tilted her head slightly to the right. "I didn't know what else to say."

Elliot thanked Ally for her time. She hurried back to her cart. Elliot stood for a second. He thought about interviewing Ally's assistant; however, he could see that she was busy helping customers. He decided he had inflicted enough pain on Coffee Virtuoso for one night. Besides, his wife was probably beginning to wonder if he was <u>ever</u> going to come home. Interviewing Wilson would have to wait.

He headed down the Hall of Nations and to his car. When he got about halfway a young woman with thick brown hair approached him. "Mr. Jones?"

"Yes?"

"Hi, my name is Stacey Gelman. I work for the Washington Opera Company. I was a friend of Emmy Treadwell. Do you have a moment?"

"Yes, yes of course. How can I help you?"

"Do you know Hank Culbertson? He's the director of security at—"

"Yes, I met Mr. Culbertson earlier today."

"Oh, good. 'Cause I spoke to him earlier today and he said you're investigating what happened to Emmy."

Mutairi's murder remained confidential. Elliot had to be careful. "Yes and no. Technically that investigation is being handled by the US Park Police. But my office is collaborating with them, especially the threat posed to the US secretary of state who attended the performance Saturday night."

Everything Elliot told Gelman was technically true. The killing of Mutairi and to some extent the killing of Treadwell posed a threat then and now to Secretary Farnsworth. The DSS was investigating *that* threat.

"Huh. We all heard a VIP was in attendance, but I never learned who it was. The secretary's a woman, right?"

"Yes, Lynne Farnsworth."

"Is she alright?"

"Yes. She's fine. So what can I do for you?"

"As you can imagine, everybody's been talking. I don't know how much of it is true, but some of the folks I work with are saying one of the supers might have killed Emmy. Is that true?"

"What exactly have you heard?"

"I don't want to get anybody in trouble, but Emmy was my friend so I thought you should know."

"Know what exactly?"

"We're a pretty close-knit group. A lot of us have been working for Washington Opera for many years. Most of us are unpaid volunteers, but we love it. Anyway, last month one of our supers got hurt. We needed a replacement and fast. Then, like magic, this guy named Ralph Allen showed up. I might have been the first to meet him. I think he said he was interested in being a super, or something like that. I was busy, so I sent him to see Emmy, the director of supers."

"Yes, I know."

"Well, Emmy met him and the next thing you know he's the captain of the guards in *Otello*. Emmy thought he was cute."

"Okay, but why are you telling me this?"

"Because I always felt he was a little strange, like he didn't fit in. The way he just showed up out of the blue right when we needed someone. And now he's disappeared. No one has seen or heard from him since Saturday, and we're all supposed to attend a meeting in the Concert Hall tomorrow. If he doesn't surface by tomorrow evening we're going to have to find another guard and quick."

"You said Ms. Treadwell thought he was cute. Can you describe him for me? Did he have any distinguishing marks or features?"

"Yes, he had a rather large religious symbol on the inside of his right forearm. I think he called it a Coptic cross or something. It had to be covered up before each performance."

"I see. How tall was he?"

"He was good size. Probably 6'1" or 6'2". I don't know. Maybe 220 or 230 pounds. He was a big guy with very thick, black hair."

"Anything else you remember about him? Did he ever say where he was from or where he worked?"

"I didn't really talk to him very much. Emmy told me once that his family was from Egypt. But you should check with some of the other supers. They might know more. Maybe also talk to Ally. She runs the coffee cart. He used to talk to her a lot. I think he was hot on her."

"Yes, I've spoken to Ally. Anything else you remember about him?"

She thought for a second. "Yeah. The first time I met him, like I said, I was busy. He came off of the elevator. I asked him his name. At first he said something like Ruf or Roof. I don't know. But then he quickly corrected himself and said his name was Ralph. Ralph Allen. I think he said his mom called him Roof. Anyway, I thought that was a little strange. Weird. You know?"

"Okay. Thanks. Anything else?"

"No. Not that I can think of."

"Okay. Listen, I got to run. But if you think of anything else, please give me a call. Here's my card." Elliot reached into the breast pocket of his jacket and handed her one of his business cards.

"Yes, sir. I will. Thank you."

Elliot was glad to see that his car was still there. As he walked to it he thought about what she had said.

Raouf was a fairly common name in the Arab world. In fact, he had two friends named Raouf—one from Egypt and one from Lebanon. The one from Lebanon died several years ago, but the one from Egypt was a professor at Villanova in Philly. He remembered his friend telling him that when he first came to the US people had trouble pronouncing his name, so he changed it to Ralph.

Chapter Nineteen

Young's office was on seven, the same floor that Elliot was on. Lake was on eight.

It was a little past 7:30 p.m. when Young pressed the elevator button to go down. The chime sounded and the elevator door opened. Standing there on the elevator was Lake. She still wore a crisp white blouse and black heels. However, she had exchanged the black skirt for a pair of tight-fitting black jeans and her hair was now in a ponytail pulled through the back of a light gray baseball cap that said *Guinness* across the front. Young was still wearing the clothes he had put on at the YMCA that morning.

"Hey. Do you mind"? Young asked.

She smiled. "Of course not. There's plenty of room."

"Thanks." Young pressed the door-close button. Rather than endure awkward silence, he said the first thing that popped into his head. "Do you drive or take the metro?"

"I drive. I live over in Fairlington," she said.

"Oh, nice."

"Yeah, I really like Fairlington. Everything I need is nearby and Shirlington is just on the other side of I-395. I can be to the airport or downtown in minutes. It's just not very close to the metro. How about you?"

The elevator stopped and the doors opened. They continued their conversation in the lobby.

"I live on East Linden in Alexandria. Off of Commonwealth. My place is close to the King Street metro, so I ride the subway pretty much every day. I get off at the Rosslyn Station and walk over here. But if the weather is bad, I usually grab a taxi or Uber."

"Cool."

"Yeah, the only time the metro sucks is during off-peak hours like now. The trains don't run very often. What should be a 20-minute ride can take 40 if you have to wait for a train."

"Let me give you a ride. The King Street metro is not that far out of my way."

"You sure?"

"Absolutely." She motioned with her hand. "Come on."

They took the building's garage elevator down to the second level. After walking 40 feet she said, "Here we go."

Young had always thought of himself as a car guy. His dad had bequeathed to him a 1967 Mustang with Goodyear Polyglas tires with raised white lettering and reverse chrome wheels. It was robin egg blue and in perfect condition. Young stored it in his mom's garage in San Diego. But in the DSS garage that night, he was stumped.

"Whoa. What's this?"

"It's a 1954 Jaguar XK120 drop head coupe in British racing green."

The XK120 was manufactured between 1948 and 1954. The 120 in the name referred to the car's top speed, which made it the fastest production car in the world at the time.

"I don't drive it very often. Only on nice days like today. Hop in."

She loved her toy. And if she was being honest, one of the reasons she offered him a ride home was to show it off. She inserted the small key into the ignition, which was located to the right of the tachometer on the shiny, burl wood dashboard. But before she turned the key to the right and pressed the ignition button, she dropped the top and swapped her heels out for a pair of brown driving loafers she kept in her bag.

Lake smiled. "Not a lot of room in these things. You certainly can't drive them in heels."

As they pulled out of the DSS garage, she asked him, "You hungry?"

"Yes, I'm starving."

"Why doesn't that surprise me? Men are always hungry. If it's not food, it's sex. Do you like Ethiopian food?"

"I don't know. Never had it."

"Then you're in for a treat. There's an Ethiopian restaurant near your place. It's in Old Town on King Street."

"Sounds good. Let's go," Young said.

Young was mentally revisiting Lake's reference to sex when his phone rang. It was Elliot. Young didn't tell him he was in Lake's car. He also didn't tell Lake he was talking to Elliot.

"Vic, this is Elliot Jones. You got a minute?"

"Yes, sir."

"Thanks. I'm over at the Kennedy Center. I just spoke to the young lady who runs the coffee cart. I'd like you to run a background check on her and her assistant. But it sounds like you're in a car, so I'll e-mail you their names right now."

"Yes, sir."

"Also, while you're at it, please check on every twentysomething male with a tattoo on his right arm in the Triple I Index, in particular something called an Ethiopian Coptic cross. Include in your search males with the first name of Raouf. Also search for Ralph, the Anglicized form. And please be in my office by 9:30 tomorrow. Can you tell Lake to do likewise?"

"Certainly, sir, can do."

"Great, thanks. See you tomorrow."

"Yes, sir, good night." Young put his phone back in the left breast pocket of his sport coat. "That was Jones."

"Yeah, I figured."

"He was calling from the Kennedy Center. Did you know he was going back over there tonight?"

"No. What did he want?"

"Well, first, he wants us in his office at 9:30 tomorrow. He asked me to tell you. He also wants me to run a check on the two ladies who run the coffee cart."

"Anything else?"

"Yeah. He also wants me to look for any twentysomething males in the Triple I that have a tattoo on the lower part of their right arm and are named Ralph or Raouf."

The Interstate Identification Index (aka Triple I) is a national index of state and federal criminal histories (or rap sheets) in the United States. It is maintained by the FBI at the National Crime Information Center.

"Raouf? Why Raouf? I thought his name was Ralph."

"It is. He said Ralph is the Anglicized version of Raouf."

Chapter Twenty

The US ambassador's residence in Jakarta was more of a compound than a home. In addition to a sprawling six-bedroom house that included multiple gardens and ponds, there were separate buildings for staff and security. Everything was surrounded by a twelve-foot fence with security cameras every thirty feet and Marine guards stationed at every entrance. The DSS rotated three teams of four in and out of the compound 24/7. With the secretary staying there, DSS added a fourth team and shortened their shifts from eight to six hours.

At 7:30 a.m. Jakarta time Tuesday Lynne Farnsworth's bedside alarm clock awakened her. Normally she would have arisen by 6:00 a.m. But this was her first morning in the Far East and her body was still adjusting to the time difference and jet lag. She had to be at the Climate Conference at the Shangri-La Hotel by noon. She had plenty of time to have a cup of coffee in her room, check e-mails and messages, shower, get dressed, and meet with her team.

Meanwhile Agents Faber and Payne were up and dressed. Payne was on the phone with his wife, Julia. Given the twelve-hour time difference he wanted to catch her before she went to bed and before his day started.

Both he and Faber were in the kitchen of the ambassador's residence finishing their second cup of coffee of the day. They would be ready, along with embassy security, to drive the secretary over to the hotel whenever she wanted.

Agents Condon and Abramovich stayed at the Mandarin Oriental Hotel only a few blocks from the ambassador's residence. They both had the morning off. They would meet Faber and Payne at the Shangri-La when the secretary arrived.

* * *

Abramovich was up early. After a quick breakfast and coffee he headed for the lobby. He wore slacks, a long-sleeved dress shirt, a sport coat, and loafers. He made eye contact with the doorman. "Taxi, please."

"Yes, sir," the doorman said with a Bahasa accent. He blew his whistle.

Abramovich had the taxi take him to Saint Thomas Russian Orthodox Church near the Gandaria City Mall on Syahi'I Hadzami Street. After paying the driver with rupiah he had from his last trip to Indonesia, he entered through the church's main doors. It was dark inside.

It took a second for his eyes to adjust. Once they did he bowed toward the altar and crossed himself. Even though he was not very religious, he lit a candle to the left of the doors before walking halfway down the center of the church.

On this Tuesday morning the temple was largely empty. As was customary in Orthodox churches, there were no pews or chairs, with the exception of some chairs and wooden benches along the wall for the sick and elderly. With his head lowered, Abramovich stood for a minute.

Unlike many Orthodox churches, Saint Thomas had a set of side doors that worshipers could use. When Abramovich reached those doors he quickly scanned the church. If he was being followed, his tail would be inside the church by now. He saw no one other than two elderly Indonesians sitting on chairs and a priest up near the altar.

Facing the altar, he crossed himself again and exited the church. Outside he caught another taxi on Taman Gandaria Street. This one dropped Abramovich off at Pacific Place Mall, fifteen minutes from the Russian embassy.

He took the escalator up to the second floor of the mall. His instructions were to meet a heavy-set white man outside the Levi Strauss store. On the ride up the escalator he powered down his phone. He was being careful. The man he met was not.

Anatoly Ivanov was a mid-level SVR agent recently assigned to the commercial section of the Russian embassy in Jakarta. He had never been to the mall before. He had trouble finding the store. The CIA agent following him did not.

Aaron Jensen had been to the mall many times. He first went as a teenager during his first mission to Indonesia on behalf of the Church of Jesus Christ of Latter-Day Saints. Then, during his senior year at Brigham Young University, he attended a job fair held in the Wilkenson Student Center. The recruiters were arranged more or less in alphabetical order. As he wandered the aisles looking at his phone and only occasionally glancing at the recruiters, he just happened to see the table for the CIA between the tables for Caterpillar and Cisco Systems. One of the recruiters made eye contact with Jensen. The CIA will never admit it, but it loves Mormons. They are viewed as more patriotic and trustworthy than most other Americans. Jakarta was Jensen's first and so far only overseas assignment.

As Ivanov approached, Abramovich asked him in Russian if his phone was off. If the man was not his contact, he would hesitate, confused either by the language or by the question. Ivanov responded immediately in Russian. "Yes, of course." They shook hands.

"Good morning," Abramovich said.

"Good morning. How was your flight?"

"Long, but fine. Traveling with the secretary of state has its advantages," Abramovich said with a wry smile.

"Do you think they suspect anything?" Ivanov asked.

"No, I don't."

"What about the PSS? Were you able to retrieve it?"

"I tried. After we got the secretary home that night I went back to the Kennedy Center. I got there around midnight. Using my DSS credentials, I was able to get inside the building; however, two overzealous guards stopped me from entering the Opera House. I could have forced the issue, but I didn't want to cause a scene. I thought that might do more harm than good."

Ivanov lowered his eyes as he thought to himself for a second. "Well, just because the PSS was developed in Russia does not mean Russia was behind the hit. And they certainly won't be able to trace any markings on the gun to us. You wore gloves, right?"

"Yes, of course."

Ivanov quickly changed the subject. "What has the secretary said about Mutairi?"

"Not much. She was upset and crying on the way to the hospital. But once there, she composed herself pretty quickly. I think the first person she called was her chief of staff. The second person was someone at the White House, probably the president's national security advisor. Since then she has been focused primarily on two things."

"What's that?"

"First, she's scheduled a meeting later this week with President Waskito. Apparently the US administration has run out of patience with China on the South China Sea. With one exception, they think they have everyone in the region on board with what sounds like an ultimatum. The exception is Indonesia. I heard her tell someone back in Washington yesterday that it was time to deliver some 'tough love' to Jakarta."

"I see. Do you know when she will meet with Waskito?"

"I think after lunch on Thursday."

"Okay. What's the other big thing she's been working on?"

"Well, she's under a lot of pressure to extend the Abraham Accords to at least two more Arab or Muslim-majority countries. The White House views that as critical to the president's reelection efforts and, in particular, the Jewish vote. From what I can tell their two best candidates appear to be Qatar and possibly Kuwait. At least that was the case before Saturday."

"What about Saudi Arabia?"

"Oh, I think they would *love* to get the Saudis, but they view that as a long shot. I heard her tell someone the other day that Tony Blinken was only days away from nailing down a deal between Israel and the Saudis in the fall of 2023. Then Hamas attacked Israel from Gaza. Israel retaliated. And, well, the rest is history."

"Huh. Interesting."

"Yeah. And yesterday I overheard her talking to Israel's foreign minister, Moshe Peretz. She was practically screaming at him."

"What about?"

"I didn't hear everything, but I think she was angry because Israel has authorized more settlements on the West Bank and some of Likud's coalition partners have openly questioned the need for a two-state solution to the Palestinian problem."

The Levi Strauss store was in a section of the mall where the stores were located on four levels with a spectacular, open atrium running down the middle of the mall. The atrium was visually stunning, but it wreaked havoc on acoustics. This presented Jensen with a challenge.

The closest he could get without being noticed was across the atrium and down a little from Abramovich and Ivanov, a distance of fifty or sixty feet. He faced away from them with his legs casually crossed. He wore white sneakers and leaned against the polished metal rail, pretending to look at his phone. In fact, he was listening to their conversation while at the same time transmitting it live to a computer server in Langley, Virginia.

The listening device was sewn into his baseball cap with the business end of the device under the bill. Fortunately, it was not unusual for young Indonesians to wear their baseball caps backwards. Jensen, who looked ten years younger than he was, could turn his cap around without seeming odd or out of place. It also didn't hurt that Jensen's skin was dark from years spent under the Indonesian sun. As a result, he looked like a local, especially from a distance.

In addition to the listening device, Jensen wore a camera ring on his left hand, which was extended along the mall's metal railing. Using his phone, Jensen could adjust the focus and direction of the camera.

Chapter Twenty-One

Traffic was relatively light on I-66 inside the capital beltway at 8:30 on a Monday night. By the time Elliot pulled into his garage, it was 8:50 p.m.

"Hi, honey. Man—long day," Elliot said with a sigh.

"I bet. You must be exhausted." They embraced. She kissed her husband on the cheek. "How was your flight?"

"It was okay. But it's hard to sleep on those things. They're six hours long, it's the middle of the night, but the seats don't recline enough."

"I told you. You should have taken another day of leave and flown back today."

"I know. You're right. But I was trying to save money and Adams wanted to see me this morning."

"How was Rach?"

"Great. She seems happy. She likes her classes. Seems to have made a few friends. To be honest, no red flags. I kept waiting to see some. You know how she can be—a real drama queen. But no—nothing. Everything seems fine."

"God, is that ever a relief. She's so far away. If there was a problem, I don't know what we'd do."

Elliot tried to ease her concerns. "Well, maybe being so far away from home and on her own is a good thing. No one out there is going to entertain her drama. Keep your fingers crossed."

"I guess that's all we can do. So how was Seattle? Did the weather cooperate?"

"Oh, my God. It was perfect. Clear. Crisp. I wish you could have been there. Rach was constantly saying, 'I wish Mom was here.'"

"Aaahh. That's so sweet. Bless her. Yeah, next time."

"How was your doctor's appointment Friday?"

"Fine. I saw Dr. Walters. He said the results of my stress test were fine. But he wants me to purchase one of those home kits for testing blood pressure. He said if my blood pressure continues to rise, he might put me on—I think he called it losartan."

"Boy, is that ever a relief," Elliot sighed.

"So how was work? Russ wanted to meet with you," she said more as a question than as a statement.

"Yeah. Did you hear what happened to Kuwait's oil minister?"

"Well, sort of. BBC and CNN said he's in the hospital. Something happened to him Saturday night at the Kennedy Center. The online editions of the *Washington Post* and *New York Times* suggest he may have been the victim of foul play. Then I watched a little bit of Al-Jazeera a few minutes ago. They said he's dead. What's going on?"

"Well, I can't say much right now, but Adams asked me to lead the investigation."

"Wow. Congratulations." She knew from experience not to ask too many questions about her husband's work. If he could say more, he would. So she changed the subject.

"Are you hungry? I didn't make anything. I wasn't sure when you'd be home. I just had a salad. There's a little left. I can also scramble you some eggs. Would you like that?"

"Yes, please."

Elliot's mom had died in a car accident when he was eight. His dad never remarried or even dated anyone. When it came to cooking, he did the best he could. As a result, Elliot was not a picky eater. He would eat just about anything put in front of him.

"I'm gonna go upstairs and change. I'll be right back."

"Okay. You wanna watch something on Netflix or Amazon after you eat? We could watch the latest episode of *Freely Feinstein* on Apple."

"No, sorry. I'm beat. I think I'll just eat and go to bed. But if you want to watch something, go ahead. I won't mind."

Elliot and Karen Jones had been married for thirty-two years. They would celebrate their thirty-third anniversary the following year on May 31. Karen knew her husband. He was always there for his family. He rarely missed one of Rachel's concerts or softball practices. He never forgot their anniversary or her birthday. And when they went away for the weekend or on vacation he was always fully engaged and in the moment. But when push came to shove work came first, and she accepted that. She had to. He was the breadwinner in the family and a workaholic.

In 2001 they bought their house, a four-bedroom colonial off of Hunter Mill Road in Vienna, for $645,000. At the time Elliot thought they might have paid too much. Now it was worth at least $1.4 million. With their only child away at college, they had started to think about selling it, cashing out, and renting an apartment downtown closer to Elliot's work, restaurants, the theater. But for now those thoughts were limited to quiet Sunday mornings spent drinking coffee and reading the newspaper in the living room.

Elliot sat by himself at the kitchen table and ate. It didn't take him long. He wolfed his food down. They were not the kind of manners he normally displayed, but he was tired and no one would notice.

When he finished he put his plate and utensils in the dishwasher. He rinsed out his glass and opened the refrigerator. He hoped there might be an open bottle of wine inside. Sure enough, he found a half-full bottle in the door. It was a Riesling from Germany. Ever since they had gone on a barge-and-bike cruise on the Moselle River in Germany about eight years ago, Karen had been buying Rieslings at Costco. He poured himself a glass. Instead of heading upstairs, he went to his office around the corner from the kitchen, glass of wine in hand. Karen watched. She said nothing.

They had always had a cat. Mitzi was a gray-haired tabby. This evening, like almost every evening, she was curled up in Karen's lap. If Rachel had been home, Mitzi probably would have been curled up in *her* lap. Karen hated to disturb Mitzi, but she had to go to the bathroom. Mitzi would have to move. She also wanted to check on her husband. He might be sound asleep in his chair.

She dried her hands on the towel in the powder room. As she came around the corner and Elliot came into view, her phone rang. It startled him.

"Hello? Rach! Hi, sweetie. How are you? Let me put you on speaker. Dad's right here." She put her cell phone on the desk between them.

Elliot swung around in his chair. Karen took a seat in a nearby stuffed chair. She took her Ugg slippers off and tucked her bare feet underneath her in order to get comfortable and stay warm.

"Hi, honey. How are you?" Elliot asked.

"I'm fine. How was your flight home?"

"Tiring. Hard to sleep on those red-eyes."

"Did you go home or straight to the office?"

"Rach, come on," Karen interjected. "You know your dad. What do you think?"

"Yeah, I went into the office," Elliot admitted. "Just got home. Long day. Lots going on."

"Okay, then I won't keep you. I just wanted to check on you. I called Mom's phone because I thought you might be asleep. It was great seeing you. Thanks for coming out."

"Of course. Say, how you'd do on that quiz today in biology?"

"I don't know. I thought I knew everything. Probably pretty good. The TA said he'd post scores on Friday."

"Rach, how's the dorm?" Karen asked. "You still thinking about moving?"

"Hansee Hall is fine. Great location. Pretty quiet. I don't know. I might just stay here. Moving would be a hassle. I want to focus on my classes."

Karen and Elliot smiled at each other. "Smart girl," Karen said.

"Yup, smart," Elliot echoed.

"So, Mom?"

"Yeah?"

"Did Dad tell you?"

Karen gave Elliot a quick look as if to say, *What's she talking about.* "Tell me what?"

"He's a hero. Everyone out here is talking about it."

"Talking about what?"

"Oh, my God, MOM! There was a huge bomb in a van on our ferry. Dad was the first to notice it. He and some other guys pushed the van off the back of the ferry. He probably saved my life and the lives of everyone else on board! Didn't he tell you? Dad? Come on!"

"What?" Elliot said as if pleading his innocence. "I've been a little busy. All-night flight. Straight to the office. Long day. Come on. And besides, I forgot."

"Forgot? You forgot? How do you forget something like that?" Karen exclaimed. To be honest, Karen was not angry or surprised. This was classic Elliot Jones, consumed by his work.

Inside, Elliot was kicking himself. *That was a rookie mistake, Jones! You should have stopped at being busy. No need to admit you forgot. Haven't you learned anything after 30 years of marriage? Oh, well, might as well tell them the rest. Get it over with.*

"There's actually more," Elliot sheepishly added.

"More? What do you mean, more?" Karen asked.

"Yeah, well, the governor of Washington wants to give me the Medal of Valor."

"Dad, are you serious?"

Karen piled on. "Are you joking?"

"No, I'm serious. I got a call this afternoon from the head of the Washington State Patrol. The governor wants to meet me, thank me personally, and present me with the state's Medal of Valor. He thought the ceremony would be down in Olympia. He said Olympia was nice."

"That's incredible," Karen exclaimed.

"My dad the hero," Rachel said with a mixture of sarcasm and pride.

"They'll even pay our way. Airfare and lodging included."

"You're kidding," Karen said with a big smile. "When? I'm ready."

"I don't know. We need to decide."

"What's there to decide? Let's go! Besides, I want to see Rach."

"I know you do, but I'm really busy at work, especially with this new investigation. I can't just disappear for a few days."

"When will you know?" Karen asked.

Rachel interjected, "What new investigation?"

"Oh, nothing. There was an incident at the Kennedy Center Saturday night. The secretary of state was there to attend the opera. Her guest was a high-ranking official from Kuwait. Somebody tried to kill him."

"Oh, my God."

"I can't say more. Just that it's a complicated investigation, politically sensitive, and it's chewing up a lot of my time. Say, Rach, before I forget."

"Yeah, Daddy?"

"Be extra careful until they catch the people behind the bombing. You know, be aware of your surroundings. And should you see anything odd, tell a cop. Say something. Get help. Okay?"

"Of course, I will, Dad."

"Great. Thanks. Just be smart."

"I will. Listen, I have a bunch of reading to get to tonight. Fifty pages of *Beowulf* and sixty-five of biology. I'm going to let you guys go."

"Okay, honey," Karen said. "We love you."

"Yes, love you, Rach. Good night." When it came to his daughter, Elliot had a soft side.

"Love you too. Good night." Rachel hung up.

The second Karen turned off her cell phone, she launched in to her husband. "Is Rachel in danger? What's going on? What aren't you telling me?"

"Nothin'! I'm not keeping anything from you. I just want her to be careful. You never know. People nowadays are crazy." Elliot knew his wife would react this way.

Chapter Twenty-Two

Shortly before 10:30 a.m. local time on Tuesday Lynne came downstairs. Waiting for her at the bottom of the stairs and in the residence's main dining room were approximately two dozen people, including the US ambassador to Indonesia, Heather Kim; the president's special envoy for climate, Ambassador Jim Burns; Lynne's CoS, Peter Drinker; and various State Department and embassy personnel.

They met for forty-five minutes around a large wood dining table graced in the middle with tropical flowers in a navy blue vase. After Lynne had a chance to greet Kim, Burns, and some familiar faces, Drinker began by giving the secretary a three-ring binder containing all the briefing materials she would need for the next three days.

They went over her schedule, paying special attention to a presser at 3:00 p.m. during a short break in the conference's second day and what they expected would be an aggressive intervention by Bangladesh directed at the United States during one of the plenaries.

When the meeting ended Agent Payne was waiting to speak with Lynne. He stood a respectful distance back. He spoke quietly with the distinctive accent that betrayed his East Tennessee roots.

"Ma'am, might I have a word with ya?"

"Yes, of course, but I have only a few minutes before I need to get over to the conference."

"This won't take but a minute. How 'bout we step back into the dinin' room for a tad more privacy?"

"Certainly." Lynne retraced her steps.

A few embassy and State Department personnel were chatting in the room. "Folks, can you give us a minute, please?" Lynne asked. In an instant they exited the room. She was, after all, the US secretary of state.

Payne closed the doors behind them. Lynne sat down.

"Ma'am, I wanted to tell ya that DSS wants to interview ya 'bout Saturday's incident at the Kennedy Center. They're sendin' Elliot Jones, the agent in charge of the investigation, to Jakarta along with two assistants. I've known Elliot for a long time, though I wouldn't say we're buddies or anythin' like that. Ya see, the Office of Investigations is kept mostly separate from the rest of DSS."

"What's he like?"

"Senior Agent Jones is kind of a legend at DSS. He's got a reputation for bein' tough. I first heard 'bout him on the shootin' range."

"Oh?"

"Yes ma'am. You see, we gotta keep up with our firearm skills, it's mandatory. We get tested once a year. Now, this must've been 'bout twenty-five or thirty years ago, but word started spreadin' 'bout a fella with near-perfect scores. That was Elliot Jones."

"Quite the marksman, huh?" she said in sort of a dismissive way.

"Yes, ma'am. But not just good. We're talkin' Olympics-level good."

"Oh, my goodness." Payne's mention of the Olympics got Lynne's attention.

"Yes ma'am. I believe he grew up on a farm in Illinois: good ole country boy, huntin' and fishin', that sort of thin'. Well, after high school he goes to Purdue University. The coach of the school's gun team saw him one day shootin' on the range. A year later he was captain of the team, and six years later he won a silver medal at the Olympics in Atlanta in the free-pistol competition and the gold medal in the rapid-fire competition."

"Wow. That's impressive." This time she meant it.

"I know. After college he joined the DSS, where he made quite a name for himself on more'n one occasion. For example, in 2005 he led an investigation that discovered the Chinese tryin' to bug our embassy in Beijing. And it was Jones who first pieced together the link between Al-Qaeda and them bombings in Nairobi and Dar es Salaam."

"When is he expected? As you know, I'm on a plane to Bali Friday evening for some R & R."

"Yes, ma'am. We've been in touch with the Indonesian national police—the POLRI—and with security at the Ritz Carlton Reserve in Ubud. Everythin' is set. As for Agent Jones, he's expected to arrive Friday mornin'. Given traffic, which is usually pretty bad between here and the airport, we expect 'em to arrive at the embassy around 10:00 a.m., 11:00 a.m. at the latest. That oughta give ya plenty o'time to talk with him and make it to the airport. Wheels up at six. It's a ninety-minute flight. So I expect you'll be in your room in time for a late supper."

"I assume Jones will also want to meet with you and the other members of my detail."

"Yes, ma'am. I've already told Agent Faber. I'm gonna tell Agents Condon and Abramovich when I see 'em later this mornin' at the conference."

She wasn't in a position to ignore Elliot, but she didn't mind making her feelings known. "He better not be late!"

"Yes, ma'am. Understood."

* * *

During the ride over to the conference Lynne flipped through the notebook her CoS had given her. She quickly went to the list of delegates, which was organized by country. She found the name she was looking for behind the tab for "Q."

* * *

The POLRI has a unit known as the Directorate of VIP and Important Facility Protection or PAMBOVIT. One of its principal responsibilities is to assist diplomatic missions operating in Indonesia. For a country wracked by corruption and inefficiency, the PAMBOVIT is remarkably good at its job.

The DSS advance team had been in Jakarta for a week. Working with PAMBOVIT and security at the Shangri-La Hotel, they had swept the facility, particularly the conference center, twice—once when they arrived and once that morning. They were pleased to find that security at the conference was extensive and multilayered.

Indeed some complained it was too tight—it did not permit adequate participation by civil society, including those working on climate change. Similar concerns had been expressed during every Conference of the Parties (COP) since COP 27 in Sharm El-Sheikh. On those occasions, Australia was a staunch defender of the right of civil society to be heard and to participate. In Jakarta, however, Australia was silent. The Bali nightclub bombing in 2002 had killed 202 people, including 88 Australians. The collective scars from that tragedy remained raw.

Condon and Abramovich were waiting for Lynne's motorcade at the delegate entrance to the hotel. They were joined by four members of the DSS jump team and two members of PAMBOVIT. Next to them was Indonesia's foreign minister, Taman Pritya. Faber was in the front seat of the first Suburban, which carried Ambassador Burns. Payne was in the front seat of the second Suburban, which carried Drinker and Ambassador

Kim. Lynne, alone in her limousine, was in the middle with two heavily armed DSS agents up front.

When the vehicles came to a stop, the DSS agents moved quickly into position like they had practiced a hundred times. First, Payne jumped out of the second Suburban and took up the primary security position facing the secretary's door with his right hand holding the top edge of the door and his left hand holding the handle. Faber moved with equal dispatch, although he stood next to Payne to the left of the door facing away from the secretary's limo, looking for any threats. Condon and Abramovich quickly took up positions four to five feet away from the door guarded by Payne. Finally, two members of the jump team went to Ambassador Burns's vehicle and two went to the vehicle containing Ambassador Kim and Drinker. The two PAMBOVIT officers stayed with Pritya.

All scanned the immediate area for possible threats. Faber spoke to the others using the transmitter on his left wrist. "Are we ready?"

The others responded in the affirmative.

Payne then turned to Faber. "We clear?"

Faber replied, "Clear!"

Payne opened Lynne's door. In an instant the secretary was out and walking toward Pritya. As she covered the distance between her limo and the foreign minister, Payne, Faber, Condon, and Abramovich formed what DSS calls the "close protection diamond"—Payne slightly behind and off of the secretary's left shoulder, Faber and Condon ahead and on her flanks, and Abramovich about six to eight feet in front running point.

Minister Pritya wore the traditional *batik* all Indonesians wore on important occasions. Lynne thought about wearing *batik*, but had opted instead for a light blue Givenchy suit. She thought *batik* was hideous, and besides, she was furious with the Indonesians. After first voicing support for the coalition of countries led by the United States that was opposing China's claims to the South China Sea, lately their comments and actions appeared weak-kneed.

After exchanging greetings with Pritya, Lynne made her way into the conference accompanied by her close protection detail and her CoS. Ambassadors Kim and Burns lingered with Pritya.

Once inside the vast center, Lynne walked down the carpeted main concourse past vendors selling books on climate change and the environment. Energetic young Indonesians in *batik* handed out coffee, tea, water, and light snacks. Indonesia's Ministry of Travel urged guests to take free lanyards, pens, posters, and brochures plastered with the ministry's two official tag lines—visit "*Amazing Indonesia*" and "*Beautiful Bali*."

Upon entering the grand ballroom where the plenary sessions would take place, Lynne immediately encountered the prime minister of Kuwait, Prince Jaber Al-Khalid Al-Hamad Al-Sabah.

"Your Royal Highness, it is wonderful to see you."

"Madam Secretary. What a pleasant surprise. Hello."

They gently embraced.

Lynne asked the prince, "What are you doing at the APCW? Didn't you attend the Climate Week held in Amman earlier this year?"

"No, I was unable to. I had meetings in South Africa and Luanda that week. Besides, I have meetings in Singapore on Friday, so I thought I might as well come to Jakarta for a few days and catch part of the conference. How about you? What is the US secretary of state doing at an APCW event in Jakarta?"

"I'm meeting with President Waskito tomorrow, so like you, I thought I might as well attend the conference for a few days." Lynne chose not to share with the prince the other reason she was there—US concerns with the agenda for the next COP in Doha.

"I see. Then we are both interlopers," the prince said, eliciting a momentary laugh.

Lynne smiled. "Yes. Your Royal Highness, on a serious note, please accept my deepest sympathies on the passing of my dear friend Mohammed Al-Mutairi. He was such a kind and gentle person."

Lynne assumed the prime minister knew that she had been with Mutairi when he died. Did he know Mutairi had been murdered? Perhaps not. Perhaps he believed the statement the Kuwaiti government had released. Neither of them knew at that moment that the prime minister's own government had a hand in Mutairi's death. The prince responded with aplomb and grace.

"Thank you, Madam Secretary. Your words mean a great deal to me and my country. We are so very lucky to count you and the United States as a friend."

"Thank you, Your Highness. Speaking as a friend, the United States is keen to have your government join Egypt, Jordan, Bahrain, the UAE, and the other Arab countries that have normalized their relations with Israel. Expanding the Abraham Accords to include Kuwait is an important priority of President Hansen's as he seeks reelection next fall. I hope we will have time this week to discuss this important matter."

Lynne's CoS, Drinker, observed from a distance. After a few minutes he suspected it was time to rescue her. Moving toward Lynne, he said, "Madam Secretary, sorry. But the conference—"

Lynne shot Drinker a quick glance. As she did she raised her right hand to stop him. "Peter, give me a few more minutes with the prince. Thank you."

"Of course, Madam Secretary." Drinker instantly stepped back. Standing next to him now were Agents Payne and Faber. Meanwhile, Agents Condon and Abramovich moved about the large room. As they did they were never more than forty feet from Lynne and always in eye contact with either the secretary or Agents Payne and Faber. Within the DSS this was known as the *Five-Second Rule*. An agent was never supposed to be more than five seconds away from the principal they were charged with protecting.

A few minutes later Drinker heard Lynne say, "Your Royal Highness, it was good to see you. I'm sure we'll have more time to chat this week. Will you excuse me?"

"Yes, of course. Thank you for your kind words, Your Excellency." Prince Saber shook the secretary's hand and moved on to his next set of pleasantries.

Just then the delegate from Bangladesh approached Lynne. "Secretary Farnsworth, it is good to see you. I hope you are well."

"Yes, Ambassador Hassan. I couldn't be better. How are you?"

"Splendid. Thank you for asking. I wanted to inform you that my capital has instructed me to advance a strong intervention during the plenary on Thursday. I trust you will understand my country's concerns with desertification and rising temperatures. As I'm sure you know, Bangladesh is one of the world's most climate-vulnerable countries and—"

"Ambassador Hassan, I'm sorry to interrupt, but you do not need to explain. I am fully aware of Bangladesh's situation and the United States is eager to work with your government on meaningful solutions. Indeed, these are problems we all face. Have you spoken to China regarding your concerns? As I'm sure you know, China emits more greenhouse gases than any other country. Indeed, it emits more than twice what the United States emits."

This time Drinker *knew* he should go to her rescue. "Madam Secretary, I'm sorry to interrupt, but the conference will start soon and we have several matters to discuss."

Lynne gladly accepted the offer. "Ambassador Hassan, I'm sorry. It was very good to see you. I'm sure we'll have more time to chat this week. Would you excuse me?"

"Yes, of course, Your Excellency. Thank you."

With the assistance of her CoS, Lynne found her seat around the giant circular table. In front of her assigned seat was a placard that read "Ètats-Unis" and a microphone at the end of a gooseneck stem on a black stand with a red button. She set her notebook down on the table, which was covered in white linen. She headed for the nearest ladies' room. As she did, she told Drinker, "I'll be right back. Watch my notebook."

Payne, Faber, and Condon watched. On the way to the restroom she stopped to talk to Abramovich. Apparently he said something that made her laugh. She briefly placed a hand on his shoulder as she passed. The agents could not hear what was said.

Chapter Twenty-Three

During her time in government Lynne had attended countless international conferences, summits, and ministerial gatherings, from peace talks in Africa to the annual meeting of the UN General Assembly in New York, from trade and climate conferences to arms control negotiations and territorial disputes. And, of course, there were the G7, G8, and G20 summits, not to mention the annual meetings of the World Bank and the International Monetary Fund. She had, in short, lost track of how many international conferences she had attended over the years. In the beginning she thought they were exciting—huge rooms, thousands of delegates, lots of press. Now they were routine and boring, typically lots of speeches, posturing, and communiqués followed by unfulfilled promises.

The only thing that still got her *juices* flowing was when the United States was the *demandeur*. On those occasions when the United States really wanted something and the secretary of state had to go and get it, coalitions had to be formed, actions coordinated, and joint statements agreed upon. Lynne was presently engaged in two such initiatives. First, she was scheduled to be back in Asia in a month for a meeting in Bangkok of the Association of Southeast Asian Nations (ASEAN). In close cooperation with her counterparts in Australia, South Korea, and Japan, she planned to insist that every member of ASEAN, including Indonesia, speak with one voice and tell China "no more." China's claims to parts of the South China Sea were contrary to long-settled principles of international law and further encroachment on those waters risked a coordinated military response.

Second, Lynne would be in Brussels the following month for a special meeting of the North Atlantic Treaty Organization (NATO) to consider increasingly aggressive actions by China on the moon. The United States, along with the UK, Japan, and Australia, believed China's new base in the Von Kármán Crater in the South Pole–Aitken Basin violated fundamental principles of international law, including the ban on military installations and non-civilian use of the lunar surface. Russia and India were expected to side with China. Therefore, the secretary needed every member of NATO to speak with one voice on the subject.

The regional climate conference in Jakarta was not one of those high-stakes meetings. As Lynne had told the president, the United States was mainly there to listen.

* * *

Indonesia's Ministry of Tourism sponsored a sprawling dinner around the hotel's main outdoor pool at the end of the conference's first day. It was a beautiful evening. Tiki torches illuminated lush garden pathways and gentle Balinese music serenaded everyone. Thankfully, a light breeze kept the humid Indonesian air moving.

Within seconds of arriving a young woman carrying a tray full of white wine in glasses approached Lynne. She happily took one. It was a Sauvignon blanc from California, one of her favorites.

Organizers of the event envisioned a relaxing, informal evening. Instead of everyone sitting down to a meal service, stations had been established around the pool, allowing guests to mingle while eating whatever they wanted, whenever they wanted. There was a station overflowing with crab and shrimp on ice, and another with all kinds of sashimi and sushi. There was a station stuffed with breads and rolls, and another where a smiling young man carved slices of beef to order. There was even a station for vegans that offered an assortment of fruits and vegetables, tofu, edamame, nuts, and seeds. And, of course, there was a station with assorted pastries, cakes, and other desserts.

Lynne wasn't particularly hungry; therefore, instead of filling her plate and sitting down to eat, she opted to stroll the grounds with her glass of wine under the watchful eyes of her detail. It was near the coffee and tea station that she saw Saman Khalil Al-Fhani.

"Well, there you are. I was beginning to wonder if I would see you here. How are you?"

"Good evening, Your Excellency." He kissed her gently once on both cheeks. "I am fine. How are you?"

"I am fine. Where have you been? I didn't see you at the conference today."

"I know. I just arrived. My flight from Doha was delayed."

Fhani was Qatar's industry and commerce vice minister. Normally Qatar would not send anyone to a regional climate conference for Asian and Pacific countries; however, Qatar was the chair and host of the next COP Climate Change Conference organized by the United Nations.

Fhani was sixty-six years old and single. His wife had died of ovarian cancer when she was fifty-eight. That was eight years ago.

Fhani spoke perfect English, having gone to college at the University of Michigan in Ann Arbor and to graduate school at the University of Cambridge in England. At Michigan he fell in love with American football. When time permitted, he liked to watch the Kansas City Chiefs in the (US) National Football League. Unfortunately for Fhani, time always seemed in short supply.

Lynne met Fhani at a ministerial gathering in Doha in 2001 organized by the World Trade Organization (WTO). That meeting launched the so-called "Doha Round" of global trade negotiations, which ended in abject failure fifteen years and thousands of meetings later.

Back then Lynne was still working for the Senate Finance Committee as its staff director. Fhani had the WTO portfolio in Qatar's Ministry of Finance, and the Senate Finance Committee had principal jurisdiction within Congress over US trade laws and US participation in the WTO. Over the next thirty years they saw each other one or two times a year at various international conferences. Lynne was instantly attracted to Fhani. He was a little over six feet tall with thick dark hair and equally dark eyes. That made him a virtual giant compared to her husband, who was only five feet seven inches tall, with just a hint of hair on his head. Fhani had a certain *je ne sais quoi* that made him appealing to both men and women. He was also able to move between the Arab and Western worlds with ease. He looked equally good in a flowing white *thawb* and gold trimmed *Hasawi bisht* as he did in a bespoke suit tailored by Gieves & Hawkes on Savile Row.

Aside from the occasional joke or flirt, their relationship remained strictly cordial and professional for over twenty years. That began to change when Fhani's wife died. First, they started to see each other more. Fhani seemed to always have an excuse for being in Washington. And when there, he typically made time to take Lynne to dinner or the theater. On one occasion, he even arranged for them to dine at the Inn at Little Washington, seventy miles west of DC in Washington, Virginia—the only Michelin three-star restaurant in the mid-Atlantic region.

They also started to communicate with each other the way close friends often do. While they would occasionally call each other or send e-mails, their preferred means of communication was text messaging using WhatsApp. At first it was just "How are you doing?" or "Did you see this or that movie or television show?" But as time went by, their exchanges became more intimate and meaningful. They started to talk about their aches and pains, their ups and downs. For example, when Fhani had to be hospitalized for an emergency appendectomy in 2023, Lynne called him often and had flowers delivered to his room.

And without being too obvious about it, they began to coordinate their travel schedules, which allowed them to be in the same place at the same time more often. A perfect example of this was the APCW in Jakarta. Yes, Qatar was host and chair of the next COP Climate Change Conference sponsored by the UN; however, Fhani didn't *have* to attend. He could have sent somebody else in his ministry. But he wanted to come. He wanted to see Lynne.

Standing off to the side of the coffee and tea station with wine glass in hand, Lynne asked Fhani, "So what's your schedule the rest of this week? Are you free for dinner tomorrow?"

"I'm sorry. No. I have a dinner meeting with our ambassador here and his team. What about Thursday? I should be free Thursday evening."

"Oh, Sam." Fhani's given name was Saman. Aside from his mother who was eighty-three and still lived in Al-Wakar, the small town in Qatar where Fhani grew up, Lynne was the only person who referred to him by that name. "I can't. That's the night I am speaking at the big AmCham Indonesia event at the Mandarin Oriental."

Chapter Twenty-Four

The restaurant was small, only half a dozen tables. Most of its business was for takeout. Lake and Young found a table in the back.

The menu was as worn as the tables and chairs. Recorded Ethiopian music poured endlessly from the kitchen. So did the aromas. The smell of *berbere*, a base seasoning used in many Ethiopian dishes, lingered in Young's senses. It triggered memories of the outdoor markets he'd wandered through as a Marine in Amman, Bagdad, and Kabul.

"Do you like beef or lamb?" Lake asked.

"Sure. I like 'em both," Young replied.

"What about spicy? Can you handle spicy food?"

"Yeah, up to a point."

"Okay, so I'll order for both of us. Everything comes on a big platter anyway. There are no forks or knives. You eat with your hands. You'll see."

After placing their order, Lake went to the bathroom to wash her hands. Meanwhile, Young looked at his e-mails. Elliot had sent the names to be checked. Using a secure line Young called in the background and ID checks.

When Lake returned to the table, Young leaned back in his chair with a bottle of Bud Light in his hand and asked, "So how'd you know about that poison?"

Lake laughed. "My dad was a chemistry professor at the University of Maryland. He always wanted me to follow in his footsteps. So I took AP chemistry in high school and majored in chemistry at Hopkins. We learned about poisons in my third-year toxicology class."

She took a swig of Harar, one of the most popular beers in Ethiopia. "But I wanted to be a detective or a cop."

"A cop? Why?"

"I don't know. Probably because my great grandfather was a cop of sorts. In fact, he was the very first agent to join the DSS back in 1917."

"You're kidding," Young said in amazement.

"No, not at all. Before his appointment he served on the protection details of Presidents Taft and Wilson. He was part of the team that famously escorted Germany's ambassador to the United States out of the country when we entered World War I in April 1917."

"That's incredible."

"Yeah, well, I bailed on chemistry and got a master's degree in criminology from Georgetown. What about you? What's your story?"

"I was a military brat. Dad was in the Marines. We moved every couple of years. I was always the new kid in school. It was a challenge, but Mom said it made me tough and gave me confidence. When Dad got out we were in San Diego, so we just stayed there. We lived on Coronado Island. I went to Coronado High School. Within six months of graduating I enlisted in the Marines. I spent eight years in the Marines. I loved every minute of it. And from there I joined DSS."

One of the things Lake liked best about Ethiopian food was the leftovers. Overnight all the spices and oils from the meats and vegetables would soak into the spongy bread called *injera*. Popping a plate of leftovers in the microwave for forty-five seconds the next day was her idea of heaven. But not this time. Lake was hungry, but Young's appetite was *epic*. As she watched him consume the last morsel of "special tibs" on the platter, she thought, *I bet this guy could give Joey Chestnut a run for his money eating hotdogs on July 4.*

"So, did you like it?"

"I loved it. Reminded me of Indian food."

"A lot of people say that. Did you know there are lots of Ethiopian restaurants in and around Washington?"

"No. I didn't."

"Yeah, Washington has the largest Ethiopian population in the US. Next time you're in a cab, ask the driver where he's from. I bet it's Ethiopia."

"Huh. I didn't know that either."

After dinner she dropped him off at his place on East Linden Street by the Masonic Temple and the King Street subway station. As he got out of the car he recalled what his dad had always said: "Don't shit where you eat." But he'd had a couple beers and Lake was beautiful, so he thought, *What the hell? I'll take a shot.*

"You want to come in for a cup of coffee or after-dinner drink? I have some great cognac."

"Thanks, but no. It's getting late and we need to be in Jones' office first thing in the morning."

Young studied her face for any clue. Was she interested but being cautious? Was she interested but truly concerned about the hour? Or was she simply not interested? Her blank expression gave away nothing. Young felt a sense of defeat. He tried to cover his tracks.

"Okay, maybe next time. See you tomorrow." And with that he closed the car door.

The XK120 won the 24 hours of Le Mans in 1951 and 1953. Many regard it as the first super car. Lake loved to rev the engine. The 3.4 liter straight six with Weber carbs growled like a lion when it accelerated. As Lake pulled away from the curb she made a point of accelerating. She could see Young in her rearview mirror. She watched with cool pleasure as he walked toward his front door with his head down. A smug smile spread across her face.

Chapter Twenty-Five

It was a short walk to Elliot's office. Young knocked on the door at exactly 9:30 a.m. Without looking up from his desk Elliot said, "Have a seat."

Lake took the stairs down from eight. Since Young was already there, she just walked in and sat down in the other chair next to Young. Young looked at Lake a little sheepishly. She did not reciprocate.

Elliot closed whatever he was looking at. After taking a swig of coffee, he said, "Okay, we have a lot to cover and little time. First, Vic, have we heard back from toxicology on Mutairi's paper cup?"

"Yes. It tested positive for BTX."

"And, Alice, do we have the final version of the autopsy report? If so, does it still conclude that he had BTX in his system?"

"Yes and yes," Lake said.

"Great. Please get me a copy of that report ASAP."

"Vic, what about the slug? Do we have the final version of the ballistics report? What does it say about the origins of the slug and the angle of entry?"

"We have the final version of that report and I will get you a copy this morning. As for the slug, it is just as we thought—Russian. And it came from the weapon we found backstage, which, by the way, is not a PSS-2. Rather, it's one of those new PSS-3s Alice mentioned the other day. Apparently, it's causing quite a stir with the guys at Langley and Quantico. But what really has people talking are the optics and motor on that thing. New technology. Very sophisticated. The shooter could sight the weapon using a cell phone or—"

"I've been thinking about that," Elliot interrupted. "Let's assume the shooter was in the Opera House that night. Is he or she going to sit close to Mutairi and pull the trigger? I don't think so. What if the scope, motor, or gun malfunctioned? You might accidentally shoot yourself. And I find it a little hard to believe that the shooter is going to whip out a phone while sitting next to other patrons in the darkened Opera House and then spend several minutes sighting the gun before hitting *shoot* or whatever button activated the trigger."

Elliot briefly paused before continuing. "I think the shooter was probably in the Opera House, but off to the side or in the back. Somewhere he or she could fiddle with the phone without attracting undue attention. Does that rule out backstage? In the dark? Maybe not. But I just can't see the shooter sitting in the audience. What do you think?"

With some trepidation Young offered his opinion. "I definitely agree with your second point. Missing was not an option. Therefore, it might have taken the shooter several minutes to sight the gun and make sure he or she was going to hit the target. As for your first point, I don't know. I certainly haven't studied the minds of assassins, but in my experience, soldiers will expose themselves to great danger if that is what it takes to get the job done."

Elliot grabbed his coffee mug. He leaned back in his chair and took a sip. After a moment of thought, he asked Young, "Did they find any prints on the PSS-3?"

"No. As you suspected, whoever put it there was careful. Probably wore gloves."

"And what about the rifle found backstage?"

Young realized he was doing most of the talking, so he looked at Alice. "You want to cover the rifle?"

"Sure," Alice said without hesitating. "The rifle is a custom-made .223 Remington made to look like one of the props. The .223 is popular with snipers when working in low-wind conditions at relatively close range. The bullet generally splinters on impact, which limits excess penetration that could hit nearby innocents such as the secretary of state. It was never fired, although there was a round in the chamber. As for prints, forensics found two—one set matching Emmy Treadwell and the other matching the guy who helped Ally Khalil at the coffee cart that night. We know this because Mutairi's cup had four sets of prints on it. Of course Mutairi's. Agent Payne's, who can be seen on the security tape throwing Mutairi's paper cup in the trash. Ally's. And finally, our mystery man—Ralph Allen. Oh, and the prints on the rifle and the coffee cup don't match anything in the database."

"You say *custom-made*. Do we know who made it?"

"Not yet, but we're checking."

Without hesitating Elliot asked Young, "What about the search of Triple I? Any hits on a twentysomething male with a tattoo and the name of Raouf?"

"Unfortunately, nothing," Young replied.

"So we have a name, we have prints, we have a distinguishing mark, and we even have him on video, but we in fact have nothing. Sounds like the perfect guy to assassinate someone. Finally, what about the ladies running the coffee cart? Anything on them?"

"Nothing. They're clean. No priors," Lake said.

Just then the phone on Elliot's desk rang. "Hello. This is Elliot Jones."

"Elliot, this is Carter Cleveland with the US Park Police."

"Carter, how are you? I heard you're working the Emmy Treadwell case."

Elliot looked at Young and Lake. He raised his index finger to signal the call would only take a minute and to remain seated.

"Yeah, so sad. It has all the earmarks of a professional job," said Cleveland.

"That's what *we* thought," Elliot offered. "But why does a pro kill her?"

"Well, that's why I'm calling. Russ said you're investigating the death of Mohammed Al-Mutairi."

Elliot wasn't sure how much he should acknowledge. When he had spoken to Adams the day before Mutairi's death was still confidential. It wasn't that he didn't trust Cleveland. In fact, he thought Cleveland might actually be able to help him. So he decided to play things as close to the vest as possible. Afterward he would circle back with Adams.

Elliot opted for a noncommittal response. "Go ahead."

"We've run a thorough background check on Ms. Treadwell. No priors. Nothing. As you presumably know, she was the director of what they call the supers for Kennedy Center Opera. You and I would probably call them extras. In any case, a man, Ralph Allen, was one of the supers in *Otello*."

"Yes, we know about Allen."

"What do you know?"

"Not much. He shows up—as if by magic, as one person put it—right when they needed a last-minute replacement. They make him the captain of the guards. He goes to all the rehearsals. No one seems to know where he's from or what he does, other than that his family was originally from Egypt. And within minutes of Ms. Treadwell being killed, he disappears. No one can reach him or find him. The Opera Company has an all-hands-on-deck meeting scheduled for tonight, but he's MIA."

"Did you know he has a tattoo on his right forearm? An Ethiopian Coptic cross?"

"Yes."

"Well, you might want to send some of your guys down to Belle Haven Park in Virginia. A guy with a Coptic cross tattoo on his right forearm was just found floating in the Potomac River near there face down, minus his fingertips."

"Minus what?"

"His fingertips! Someone chopped 'em off."

"Thanks, Carter. I appreciate the heads-up. I'll send some of my guys down there now."

"Okay. Listen, I gotta run. But I'll let you know if we learn anything else."

"Thanks, Carter. Goodbye."

Elliot hung up his phone. "Our boy may have just washed up along the Potomac near Belle Haven Park. According to Park Police, this person has a tattoo on the right forearm, but no fingertips."

"No what?" Young asked.

"No fingertips. Someone cut 'em off."

"Jesus," Young said.

"Yeah, well, get down there ASAP. Take someone from forensics with you. Make sure they take an iris scanner with them. Depending on how long he's been in the water, you may be able to get a usable scan. And be sure to have his DNA run through the local, state, and federal databases, including CODIS. We may get lucky and find a match."

Lake and Young stood up to leave. As they did, Elliot told them to also pack their bags.

"We're going to Jakarta. We need to interview the secretary and her detail. Return on Sunday. United has a flight leaving Dulles at 12:30 p.m.

tomorrow. Tickets and itineraries should already be in your Outlook inbox. If not, check with Ops."

Chapter Twenty-Six

The drive from Fort Meade, Maryland, to Rosslyn, Virginia, was relatively long. The drive from Langley, Virginia, to Rosslyn was not. However, on this Tuesday afternoon the latter took longer than the former. There was a bad accident on the southbound lanes of the George Washington (GW) Parkway whereas traffic on the Baltimore–Washington Parkway was unusually light. As a result, Anthony Sonsini got to the DSS offices in Rosslyn before Audrey Ackerman did.

Elliot was sitting in his office when Adams called.

"Elliot? This is Russ. Can you join me in the conference room next to my office for a few minutes?"

"Sure," Elliot replied. "When?"

"Now, if you don't mind. Sorry for the short notice."

"No problem. I'll be right up."

Elliot knocked briefly on the door before entering. Adams sat at one end of the short conference table. To his right and facing the door sat Ackerman and Sonsini. Audrey Ackerman was a career civil servant. She grew up in Chesapeake, Virginia, and attended Great Bridge High School.

Upon graduating from Georgetown with a bachelor's degree in Russian studies she joined the CIA.

Tony Sonsini was from Wilkes-Barre, Pennsylvania. Tony's grandparents on both sides of his family were Italian. He was thick and tough like his dad. He attended Syracuse on a football scholarship, but his playing days were cut short by a torn ACL and MCL. Unlike most jocks, though, he was a good student and graduated near the top of his class with a degree in computer science.

Ackerman and Sonsini rose from their seats as Adams began the introductions. "Elliot Jones, I'd like you to meet Audrey Ackerman and Tony Sonsini. Audrey works up at Langley. She heads up the Russia Bureau there. Tony is over at the NSA in Fort Meade. He focuses on Russia for Signals Intelligence. They have some intel they want to share with us."

Elliot shook their hands and sat down opposite them. "Is this about Mutairi?"

"Yes," Adams replied. "They also have information on the secretary's husband you should hear."

"Huh. It just so happens—"

Before Elliot could finish a knock came at the door. Adams' secretary stuck her head in.

"Mr. Adams, Messrs. Talbot and Levenson are here." With that she stepped back and two men in dark suits and ties entered the room.

"Oh, hi," said Adams, rising from his chair. "I'm glad you could make it. I'm Russ Adams, the director of investigations. Come in, please."

"I believe you know Audrey and Tony," Russ said more as a statement than a question.

Ackerman and Sonsini did indeed know Talbot and Levenson. As Elliot looked on, all four shook hands and greeted each other.

The room was small. Therefore, Elliot had little choice but also to greet Talbot and Levenson even though he had not been formally introduced. Adams tried to catch up.

"Elliot, this is Lance Talbot and Ori Levenson. Lance is the assistant attorney general for national security at Justice and Ori is his principal deputy. I asked them to join us because they have been advising Audrey and Tony on the matters that will be discussed today and I wanted you to get their perspective, especially as prosecutors, before you interview the secretary and her detail in Jakarta on Friday."

Looking at Ackerman and Sonsini, Adams asked, "Who wants to start?"

"It probably makes sense for me to start," Sonsini said somewhat as a question as he looked in Ackerman's direction.

"Certainly." Ackerman nodded.

Sonsini began. "I don't know how much you know about Mr. Farnsworth."

Elliot interjected, "Not much."

"Well, he and some friends run an energy trading company down in Houston called Energy Plus. They specialize in the Middle East. At the moment Farnsworth is collaborating with a Russian oil company, Rusoil, on an auction that will take place one week from today in Bagdad. All the major oil companies are participating. Apparently Iraq has discovered a ton of oil in one of its western provinces. In any event, Farnsworth has been spending a lot of time lately with a guy he believes to be an employee of Rusoil, Oleg Krychuk. In fact, Krychuk works for the SVR. Now, Lance should express his views on this, but as far as we are concerned, Farnsworth has not broken any laws, at least not yet. He's being duped. That is certain. And if this became public, it would embarrass the secretary and the White House. But at least until now, Mr. Farnsworth has not crossed any lines that we know of."

Talbot leaned forward in his chair. "Justice agrees with that assessment."

Sonsini paused. He didn't want to interrupt Talbot. Once it was apparent Talbot had said what he wanted to say, Sonsini asked Ackerman, "Audrey, do you want to say anything?"

"No, but show him the cable."

"Right. So on Sunday, October 26, Farnsworth met Krychuk at a hotel in Cairo. We don't have any photos of the meeting, but we do have a fairly complete transcript translated into English from the original Italian." Sonsini took a folder with an orange border out of a small briefcase on the floor next to his chair. The folder was marked TOP SECRET in large letters on the top and bottom. He slid it across the table to Elliot.

"Wait a minute," Elliot said. "They spoke Italian? Farnsworth knows Italian?"

"Yes," Sonsini said. "In college he spent a semester in Florence. In fact, that's where he met Secretary Farnsworth. He's been studying it for years."

Elliot placed his left hand on the folder. He was about to open it when he said, "Earlier today I got a call out of the blue from an old acquaintance in Cairo. He's the head of Egypt's homeland security. He said he has photos of Farnsworth meeting with an SVR agent. I think he said the Russian's name was Oleg something. I wrote it down. It's back in my office. In any event, he hasn't sent me anything yet."

"Was it Abdul Rasham you spoke with?" Sonsini asked.

A faint smile appeared on Elliot's face. *How did he know that?* Elliot started to ask. Then he thought better of it. He was talking to the NSA, after all. One of the Five Eyes. Elliot was willing to believe the NSA did not eavesdrop on Americans inside the United States. But a call from outside the US to a federal employee? Especially the Middle East? That was probably fair game.

Elliot simply said yes in response to the question.

If he were being honest, Sonsini would admit that he was having a little fun with Elliot. He of course knew the answer to his own question. But this was an idle diversion. He came to the central point.

"As you'll see from the transcript, Krychuk claims to know on Sunday that Mutairi was killed at the Kennedy Center on Saturday. Correct me if I'm wrong, but Mutairi's death was not made public until Monday and even then it was said he had died of a heart attack. Which begs the question, how did Krychuk know about Mutairi's fate before everyone else?"

Elliot responded. "Well, as you ponder the answer to that question, you should know that we found a Russian-made PSS-3 backstage at the Kennedy Center and ballistics matched it to the slug found in Mutairi."

"Yes, we know about the PSS," said Ackerman.

Wait a minute, Elliot thought. *How does the CIA know that?*

But before he could ask, Sonsini said to Ackerman, "Show him the cable from Jakarta."

"Sure," Ackerman said. "So, earlier today one of our agents in Jakarta followed an SVR agent assigned to the Russian embassy there to a shopping mall. He met with Steve Abramovich. As you know, Abramovich was part of the secretary's detail at the Kennedy Center that night and he is part of the secretary's detail at the UN Climate Conference."

"Yes, I do know. I also plan to interview Abramovich on Friday."

This time it was Ackerman's turn to pass Elliot a folder marked TOP SECRET, although this one had a yellow border and been assigned an additional SCI code name, SOSTAT. Elliot opened the folder.

"Here are several photos taken by our agent. You can see Abramovich on the right and the SVR agent on the left. Our guy was also able to record most of the conversation. A nearly verbatim transcript appears on the pages behind the photos. They discuss the PSS and Abramovich's attempt to retrieve it Saturday night after Mutairi was taken to the hospital and Secretary Farnsworth returned home."

Elliot quickly read the transcript. Ackerman paused to give him time. When done, Elliot offered his opinion.

"This confirms my suspicions about Abramovich. We believe the aiming of the gun was accomplished by someone on their cell phone. That would require some time. Security videos in the Opera House show Vince Faber and Roger Payne in their seats near the secretary and Mutairi when he is hit. Neither spends much time on their phone beforehand. Wally Condon and Abramovich are never seen until they help Mutairi and the secretary exit the building. I've known Condon for years. It's hard for me to imagine Wally would have anything to do with something like this. But Abramovich? I don't know him. And now this," Elliot said pointing at the transcript.

Looking mainly at Sonsini and Ackerman, Adams asked, "Why would the Russians want to kill Mutairi?"

Ackerman spoke. "Hard to say, but the Russians are facing a massive shortage of oil that is expected to get worse. The Kremlin is pulling out all the stops to address the problem. They are desperate to secure as many concessions as possible next week in Bagdad. We believe the SVR, acting through Rusoil, is bribing Iraqi officials right and left. We think they are doing the same through KyrgyzOil based in Bishkek, which will also submit one or more bids that, if successful, will benefit Moscow. The Kremlin believes their stiffest competition will come from the Kuwaitis. They believed Mutairi was central to those efforts. We disagree. Mutairi was not focused on Iraq. He was focused on increasing Kuwait's production of oil. He was taking steps to do that. My boss, Deputy Director Holcumb, briefed the president on those efforts yesterday morning. I am not at liberty to share them with you, but suffice it to say the Russians, in general, and the SVR, in particular, are wrong. The Kuwaitis do *not* have the inside track in Bagdad. And one more thing, if I may?"

"Certainly, please finish," said Adams.

"Thank you. I'll just conclude by asking if anyone seriously doubts the Kremlin's willingness to try such a stunt. Attempting to assassinate a high-ranking official of an important US ally as he sits inches from the US secretary of state in a crowded theater? Words like *audacious* seem inadequate. But look what they did to Navalny, Markov, Berezovsky, Litvinenko, Politkovskaya. I could go on."

She didn't need to. Her assertion was profound and would rattle Washington if it became more widely known—Russia had assassinated a senior official of a close US ally in Washington and in doing so threatened the life of the US secretary of state.

For a second Elliot thought about asking Ackerman or Sonsini if they had an opinion on who might want to poison Mutairi. But before he could do so Adams asked another question.

"So, as you know, Elliot is scheduled to interview the secretary and her detail in Jakarta on Friday. He and his team leave tomorrow. Assuming his source in Cairo provides the promised photos, should he show them to the secretary? And what about the photos of Abramovich in Jakarta? What do you recommend?"

"If I may," Talbot said more as a statement than a question.

"Of course," Adams replied.

Ackerman and Sonsini sat back in their chairs. Elliot listened intently.

"Thank you. Justice has no concerns with DSS showing the secretary a photo of her husband in Cairo. As noted earlier, we have no reason to believe Mr. Farnsworth has broken the law and, to be quite honest, we'd rather he didn't. So the sooner she is informed, the better. Presumably she will confront him with the news and he will cease further associations with Mr. Krychuk. Now, if he doesn't, we may be looking at violations of the Foreign Corrupt Practices Act, among other laws. But we'll cross that bridge if and when we get to it."

"It will be interesting to see how she reacts to the news," Elliot offered. "Presumably it will come as a shock."

"Yes," said Talbot. "If it doesn't, we've got way bigger problems on our hands." Everyone in the room knew what he meant.

"Now, as to Abramovich," Talbot continued, "we have to be *extremely* careful. First, he is under constant surveillance by the Agency when he is outside the United States and the FBI when he is not. And the FISA Court has issued a warrant allowing the NSA to monitor his electronic communications at all times."

Adams and Elliot said "good" at essentially the same time.

"Second, every minute he is around the secretary is a minute he could harm her. And after Saturday night, those concerns have only grown exponentially. Obviously we are also concerned about the risk Abramovich poses to national security and US foreign policy. As a member of the secretary's security detail, he is often in close proximity to her as she speaks with various world leaders and US government officials, including the president. An interagency team from Justice, the FBI, CIA, NSA, and the White House is weighing these and other concerns right now. In fact, I am scheduled to meet with them later today and brief my boss tomorrow morning."

Elliot couldn't help but ask. "If you've had these concerns, why haven't you arrested him before now or at least pulled him from her detail?"

"Fair question," Talbot said. "We were hoping he might expose other Russian agents. And until last Saturday, we put the risk of harm to the secretary at low. Unfortunately, he hasn't led us to anyone and now we have a dead Kuwaiti oil minister on our hands. Look, hindsight is 20/20. In hindsight, we *should* have arrested him. In my opinion, the only question now is where and when."

"But what can Elliot say or not say on Friday? How much of this should he disclose to the secretary?" Adams asked.

"Nothing should be said or done that might spook Abramovich. Nor should anything be said to the secretary that might cause her to change her interactions with him. For now, we want business as usual. So go easy on him during your interview."

Chapter Twenty-Seven

Elliot had a Red Top cab take him to Dulles. He was *old-school*. Young took the metro, which, thanks to the Silver Line extension completed in 2022, now serviced the airport. Lake took a Lyft.

Young got there first. In fact, he was at the United counter when Elliot arrived. They were about to head to the gate when Lake arrived. They waited for her.

Elliot used that time to call Abdul Rasham in Cairo. Young used that time to marvel at Lake from behind.

"Abdul? This is Elliot Jones. I'm at the airport so I don't have much time. Can you do me a favor?"

"Of course. What do you need?"

"I need you to see what you can find on a twentysomething male, possibly from Egypt, with the first name of Raouf. He has, or I should say *had*—as he was found dead yesterday here in Washington—a tattoo on his right forearm in the shape of an Ethiopian Coptic cross."

"A Coptic Christian? We have many Copts in Egypt. Why would someone kill him? Does this have anything to do with the assassination of Mutairi?"

"I'm sorry. I can't say. But I wouldn't ask if this wasn't *really* important."

"No problem. I understand. I'll check at once. Although it would help if you could send me a photo of him."

"Sure. I'll have someone send that to you shortly."

"Great. I'll let you know if I find anything."

"Thanks. I really appreciate it. Got to go."

* * *

Once Lake finished checking in, the three of them headed for the TSA precheck line. It was 10:30 a.m.

Flying to Jakarta from Washington on a commercial carrier was not easy. Total flight time was about twenty-three hours. In addition they would have a three-hour layover in Tokyo. The car ride into downtown Jakarta from the airport would take close to an hour. Door to door it would be a twenty-seven-hour trip. Since they would cross the international date line, they would depart Washington shortly after noon on Wednesday and arrive at the US embassy in Jakarta around the same time on Friday. That would leave approximately five hours to interview the secretary and her security detail.

United's flight to Tokyo Narita Airport departed out of gate D3. With a business-class ticket, Elliot could wait for the flight in the United Polaris Lounge across from gate D1 at Dulles. Lake and Young could not. Because Elliot wanted to talk to them, they found a quiet spot opposite gate D5. Elliot spoke first.

"Are your phones off?"

Lake and Young checked their phones. Both nodded.

"Okay, so all interviews will be in the embassy's SCIF."

Most US embassies around the world have what is called a sensitive compartmental information facility (SCIF) where highly sensitive information can be discussed without risk of disclosure or compromise.

"I'd like to meet with the secretary first and Abramovich last. I'd like at least one of you to join me. Take good notes. Alice, why don't you join me for the interview with the secretary and, Vic, you join me for the interview with Abramovich? I don't need to meet with Payne, Faber, or Condon, and I don't really care how you two divide those up. If you want to double up for one or more, go ahead. It's up to you."

Lake and Young listened intently. Both nodded.

"Now, it is crucial that we obtain a complete picture of what was said and done between the time the secretary left her house that evening and the time she returned. I am particularly interested in the location of the secretary's detail at the precise moment when Mutairi slumped in his chair. From the security tapes we have a pretty good idea of where everyone was located during intermission, especially when the secretary and Mutairi got coffee. But the inside of the Opera House is so large and the lights were dim. As a result, we do not know the exact positions of the secretary's detail during the performance. You can see Payne seated on the aisle one row behind the secretary and Faber in the seat right behind the secretary. But Condon and Abramovich are never seen on the tapes during the performance. Questions?"

Lake and Young both said "no."

"I also want to know what the secretary said once they left the Kennedy Center, especially on the way to the hospital. Was she upset? Was she calm? Did she ask questions that were appropriate to the situation? Obviously I will ask the secretary these and other questions, but I want you to ask her security detail the same questions. Okay? And one more thing."

Lowering his voice even further, Elliot said, "I have a photo taken last Sunday in Cairo. I got it from Egypt's version of the FBI. In it you can see the secretary's husband, James Farnsworth. He is meeting with a man posing as an employee of Rusoil—a Russian oil company. In fact, the man is believed to be an agent of Russia's SVR. Now, let me quickly add that we do not believe the secretary knew about this meeting and we do not believe

Mr. Farnsworth knows the true identity of the man. Nonetheless, I intend to show the secretary the photo. How she reacts to the photo will obviously be interesting."

"What's Mr. Farnsworth doing hanging out with a Russian in Cairo, especially an SVR agent?" Young asked.

"He has a company called Energy Plus. It specializes in the trading of gas and oil, especially in the Middle East. Langley believes Farnsworth has partnered with Rusoil to pursue oil drilling rights in Iraq."

"I'm not familiar with Rusoil," Young said. "Hasn't it been sanctioned like all the other Russian energy companies? I know Gazprom, Rosneft, and Lukoil have."

"No. So far Rusoil has not. But I haven't told you the most interesting part." Elliot leaned forward even more.

"The Russian knew about the assassination of Mutairi. He told Farnsworth about it. The NSA has a fairly complete transcript of the conversation. Now recall, this is Sunday, Cairo time. It would be another twenty-seven hours before Kuwait would acknowledge Mutairi's passing."

"Wait a minute," Lake exclaimed. "How did he know that?"

"Langley thinks the Russian knew because the Russians were behind it. After all, the gun was developed in Russia. The slug came from Russia."

Lake leaned back in her chair. All she could say was, "Wow."

Elliot could have revealed more. He could have shared with them the photos and recording of Abramovich's meeting in Jakarta with the SVR agent, but that would have to wait.

Chapter Twenty-Eight

Washington Opera had little choice but to delay the next performance of *Otello* and move future performances to the Concert Hall. The Opera House was closed until further notice. The Kennedy Center had to juggle performances of the NSO to accommodate the change. It was difficult, but doable.

Monday morning Washington Opera posted a notice on its website announcing the change of date and venue. The Kennedy Center did likewise on its website. No reason was given by either for the change.

Following discussions amongst the leadership of the Washington Opera Company and outside legal counsel, it was decided that more explanation was needed and the passing of Emilia Treadwell should be acknowledged. No one thought Washington Opera should comment on the condition of Mohammad Al-Mutairi.

Therefore, the following notice was posted on the Washington Opera website around 6:00 p.m. ET Monday:

UNTIL FURTHER NOTICE, FUTURE PERFORMANCES OF *OTELLO* WILL BE HELD IN THE KENNEDY CENTER'S CONCERT HALL. THE NEXT PERFORMANCE

OF *OTELLO* WILL BE ON THURSDAY, OCTOBER 30, AT 7:00 P.M. ET. THE WASHINGTON OPERA COMPANY APOLOGIZES FOR ANY INCONVENIENCE CAUSED BY THESE CHANGES.

WASHINGTON OPERA ALSO WISHES TO EXTEND ITS DEEPEST SYMPATHIES AND HEARTFELT CONDOLENCES TO THE FAMILY AND FRIENDS OF EMILIA ("EMMY") TREADWELL. EMMY WAS A CHERISHED MEMBER OF THE WASHINGTON OPERA FAMILY. HER UNTIMELY DEATH IS FELT BY US ALL.

Throughout the day on Monday Washington Opera representatives contacted all cast members and staff. With the exception of the principals performing in *Otello*, all were asked to meet in the Concert Hall at 6:00 p.m. on Tuesday for 45 minutes. Alain Bonnet was also asked to attend. During the meeting the director of *Otello* and her assistants discussed the adjustments needed to stage a performance in the Concert Hall.

At the end of the meeting Stacey Gelman pulled Alain aside. "Do you know Ralph Allen? He's a super in *Otello*. The captain of the guards."

"No. I don't think so."

"Well, no one has heard from him since Saturday. He's not answering his phone and he hasn't responded to any e-mails. We don't know if he will be here Thursday. If he doesn't show, could you fill in? His costume might be a little loose on you, but I'm sure Carl and the folks in wardrobe can take it in a little with pins and staples."

"What does the captain of the guards do?" Alain asked.

"He's only in Acts I and II. In Act I he leads the other guards across the stage and up the steps of the castle to see if Otello has returned. In Act II he protects Otello as he enters the castle. But given the circumstances, I think it will be a lot easier if we just have one of the other guards serve as the captain. That way all you need to do is follow the guy in front of you. Pretty simple, actually."

"Okay."

"Thanks, Alain. We really appreciate it. What's the best number these days to reach you? If we hear from Allen, we'll give you a call. But if we don't, can you plan to be here by four on Thursday? That should give wardrobe enough time to make last-minute adjustments to your costume."

"Sure. Happy to."

* * *

The atmosphere in the Concert Hall Thursday night was tense. Some patrons struggled to find their seats given the change of venue. Others compared rumors over what happened Saturday night in the Opera House. Still others were struck by the presence of heightened security. Plainclothes agents and uniform police officers and guards were everywhere.

No one had heard from Allen. Therefore, Alain stood backstage ready to go on. He would follow the other guards. His loose-fitting costume was held together with safety pins and clips.

As patrons settled into their seats and the houselights dimmed, the orchestra did not launch into Verdi's *Esultate* and the curtain did not rise. Instead, the general manager of the Washington Opera Company walked slowly on to the stage in front of the curtain.

"Good evening. My name is Lillian Garten. I am the general manager of the Washington Opera Company. If you are a fan of opera, like me, you know that many operas tell stories of great tragedy and great loss. Giuseppe Verdi's *Otello* is perhaps the best example of that. Last Saturday the Washington Opera Company was visited by great tragedy and great loss. Emilia Treadwell, a young woman who had been a part of our family for over fifteen years, was viciously and senselessly murdered. I speak for everyone associated with Washington Opera when I say we are heartbroken and extend our deepest sympathies to Emmy's family and friends.

Her funeral will be held on Sunday, November 2, at Parkland Memorial Gardens in Rockville, Maryland, at 1:00 p.m. Now, please sit back and enjoy Giuseppe Verdi's ... *Otello*."

Chapter Twenty-Nine

Unbeknownst to Elliot, the US embassy in Jakarta reached out to the POLRI. In hindsight, that was a good thing. Air traffic control over Jakarta that day was busy. Their flight arrived thirty-five minutes late. In addition, the lines at immigration and customs were horrendous, and traffic from the airport to downtown was as bad as anyone could remember.

When Elliot got to the top of the jetway, he was greeted by two PAMBOVIT officers and two junior Foreign Service (FS) officers from the US embassy. One of the FS officers took his carry-on luggage. Once Lake and Young joined them, they headed for immigration control. Immigration was a *zoo*—long lines of angry and tired people. However, thanks to PAMBOVIT, immigration took them less than five minutes. Since no one checked luggage, Elliot, Lake, and Young flew through customs.

Upon entering the terminal, they were instantly struck by a wall of heat and humidity. November signals the arrival of the monsoon season in Jakarta. Every day is uncomfortably wet and sticky, and temperatures rarely dip below ninety degrees Fahrenheit. This day was no different. It was pouring down rain and blazing hot.

Thankfully, they did not have to walk far. Sitting in front of the terminal at curbside was one of the embassy's black Chevy Suburbans with the air-conditioning blasting. With two blue-and-white Indonesian police cruisers in front and two in back, and sirens blaring and lights flashing, they headed off for downtown.

Young and Lake felt like VIPs as the traffic on the Sedyatmo Parkway parted for the motorcade like the Red Sea. Elliot knew better. They were not being accorded this treatment because they were VIPs. They were being accorded this treatment because the US secretary of state wanted to go on vacation.

Security around the embassy was unusually tight, but that was understandable. The compound was full of VIPs—the secretary and Ambassadors Kim and Burns, to name a few. As a result, it took Elliot and his team approximately ten minutes from the time they approached the gate to the time they were inside the building. It was 11:00 a.m. when they arrived.

* * *

During his thirty-plus years with the DSS, Elliot had met every secretary of state beginning with Warren Christopher in 1997. He had not met Secretary Farnsworth before.

After depositing his phone in a locker outside, he grabbed a chair in the embassy's SCIF. Lake sat in the chair to his right with a notepad in front of her. The room was devoid of any adornments or comforts, just a table and six chairs. After setting his briefcase down and organizing his notes, he went back out to grab a cup of coffee and a bottle of water from a nearby kitchen. As he did he asked Lake if she wanted anything.

"Yes, please. A bottle of water would be great."

At noon the door opened, preceded by a perfunctory knock. It was the secretary of state. Elliot and Lake rose from their chairs.

"Hello, Madam Secretary. My name is Elliot Jones. This is Alice Lake. We're both with DSS."

"Hello."

They shook hands.

"As you presumably know, we are investigating the unfortunate events of last Saturday at the Kennedy Center. We have a few questions we'd like to ask you."

"Certainly. I assume you know that I have a flight to catch at six this evening. On your ride in from the airport, you probably saw what traffic can be like here. Therefore, I should get on the road by five at the latest."

"Oh, that shouldn't be a problem," Elliot said. "We just have a few questions to ask you. But before we start, can I get you anything to drink?"

"No, I'm fine. Thank you. Let's get started."

"Certainly. Let's see—how about if we start with when you met Mohammed Al-Mutairi? Do you recall?"

"Ahh, well. I've known—" She caught herself speaking in the present tense. She recalibrated. "I think I met Mohammed in Paris at an OECD meeting on steel. By then I was working for the Senate Foreign Relations Committee. That was around 2002 or 2003. Thereafter, I would see him at this or that conference or meeting. We became good friends. When he'd come to Washington, Jim and I." She paused to explain. "Jim's my husband. James Farnsworth."

"Yes, I know."

"Well, as I was saying, when Mohammed would come to Washington, Jim and I would often go to dinner with him. He really liked Washington. He had friends there and I believe his sister lives up in Bethesda with her husband and two kids."

"Did you have dinner with him last weekend?"

"Who, Mohammed or my husband?"

"Sorry, I meant Mr. Mutairi."

"Yes, I did. We ate at Fiola Mare in Georgetown before heading over to the Kennedy Center."

"Did your husband join you?"

"No, he didn't. I believe he was in either Cairo or Bagdad that weekend."

"Speaking of Mr. Farnsworth, do you know where he is right now?"

"No, Mr. Jones. I'm afraid I don't."

Elliot detected a hint of irritation in her voice.

"My work keeps me busy and my husband leads a busy life. He is a principal in a small energy trading company."

"Yes, thank you." Elliot didn't want to irritate her. He wanted to keep the interview on track, so he simply said, "I am aware of that. What did you and Mr. Mutairi talk about at dinner last Saturday?"

"We discussed many things. As you may know, the president would like to extend the Abraham Accords to other Arab and Muslim-majority countries. Kuwait is one of the countries we are talking to."

"Would you say that conversation was cordial or did it get heated?"

"I wouldn't describe it as heated, but it did get intense. The emir is reluctant to join the Accords. He has a lot of questions. My job is to answer them and overcome that reluctance."

"I see. Did Mr. Mutairi seem in a good mood that night?"

"Yes. He was, as always, delightful and charming."

"Can you think of anyone who would stand to gain from his death?"

"Not really. He was a gentle man. Smart, warm—" Her voice trailed off.

"How about the Russians? Can you think of any reason they might want to see Mr. Mutairi dead?"

"The Russians? No. Not really."

"I'm sorry, Madam Secretary, but I have to ask this question."

"Go ahead."

"Were you in love with Mr. Mutairi?"

"No! Absolutely not. We were friends, that's all."

As she finished her answer Elliot leaned to his left and pulled a folder marked TOP SECRET out of his briefcase, which sat on the floor leaning against his chair. He slid the folder across the desk toward the secretary.

"Madam Secretary, please open the folder. Inside is a photograph. Do you recognize anyone in the photo?"

"Yes, I believe the man on the right is my husband."

"Madam Secretary, this photograph was taken last Sunday in Cairo. It has been reviewed by Langley and I can confirm its authenticity."

"Okay," she said, as much as a question as anything else. "Why are you showing me this? As I said, and as you presumably know, my husband spends a lot of time in that part of the world. His company, Energy Plus, specializes in the trading of oil and gas in the Middle East."

"Madam Secretary, the other man in the photo your husband is meeting with is a gentleman by the name of Oleg Krychuk. We have reason to believe Mr. Krychuk works for Russia's SVR."

Lynne looked at the photo. She was silent. It didn't take long for Elliot to realize she wasn't going to say anything.

"Has Mr. Farnsworth ever talked to you about Mr. Krychuk?"

"No. Absolutely not." That was a true statement. "My husband and I essentially live separate lives. We're both very busy." While that was also a true statement, it belied the fact that their marriage was running on fumes and they rarely spoke to each other about anything.

"Madam Secretary, have you ever heard of a Russian company called Rusoil?"

"Yes, of course."

"What do you know about the auction being conducted by Iraq on Tuesday?"

The question stopped Lynne in her tracks. Her pulse quickened. She wondered where Elliot was going with this. What did he know? Did he know she had spoken to Iraq's oil minister about the auction at least a dozen times over the past six months? She quickly collected her thoughts. *Stay calm*, she told herself.

"I'm not sure I understand your question," Lynne said. "Of course I know about the auction. I wouldn't be doing my job if I didn't. But what exactly do you want to know about it?"

"Do you know which companies are participating in the auction?"

"Well, certainly Exxon, Chevron, Total, BP. All the big ones. Are you interested in any in particular?"

"How about Rusoil? Do you know if Rusoil has submitted a bid?"

"No, I don't. But that shouldn't be too hard to find out."

"Thank you, but that won't be necessary."

She breathed a sigh of relief. He didn't ask about any other companies.

"What did you do when you got home Saturday night?"

"Wait a minute. Before we discuss Saturday night, I want to go back to this Krychuk fellow."

Elliot wasn't used to anyone wresting control of one of his interviews from him. Then again, he didn't normally interview the secretary of state. "Yes, of course."

"Do you know why my husband was meeting with this guy? I can't believe Jim would knowingly meet with a Russian agent."

"Yes, I believe I do. Mr. Krychuk has been posing as a senior executive with Rusoil. Mr. Farnsworth and his company have apparently teamed up with Rusoil to pursue opportunities in Iraq. We believe they have submitted one or more joint bids in connection with the auction on Tuesday."

"I see. Is my husband in any danger?"

"Not that we know of, but I can flip that question back to Langley if you like."

"If Jim is being duped by this guy, I want to tell him. And the sooner the better. Is there any reason why I shouldn't?"

"No, ma'am. In fact, I would encourage you to."

Lynne wrote something down on a small notepad in front of her. "Okay, where were we? Ah, you had a question about last Saturday."

"Yes, ma'am. I asked what you did when you got home Saturday night."

"I grabbed a snack out of the pantry and finished packing. It was late and my flight to Canberra left in the morning."

"Did you talk to anyone?"

"At home? No, the house was empty."

"How about on the phone or via e-mail or text?"

"Not really. Not that I recall."

"What did you do when you left the Kennedy Center? Did you go to GW Hospital with the ambulance?"

"Yes."

"Did you talk to anyone on the way to the hospital?"

"Yes."

"Who?"

"I spoke to my chief of staff, Peter Drinker."

"Anyone else?"

"Yes, I spoke to Mark Esmond. He's the president's national security advisor."

"What did you talk to Mr. Drinker about?"

"I told him about Mutairi. And that I was on the way to the hospital."

"Anything else?"

"No, not really."

"What did you talk to Mr. Esmond about?"

"Basically the same thing."

"I see. When did you learn that Mr. Mutairi had died?"

"My chief of staff called me and told me while I was on my way to Andrews the next morning."

"Madam Secretary, let's switch gears for a minute. When did you meet Steve Abramovich?"

"Well, let's see. I think I met Steve at the US embassy in Moscow. He was working there. No, wait a minute ..." Farnsworth looked away from Elliot, deep in thought. "It was actually... it wasn't at the embassy. I met Steve at a reception at the ambassador's residence in Moscow. Yeah." She paused again as if to confirm her recollection. "Technically, he was an attaché assigned to the embassy's agricultural section. In reality, he worked for the CIA. I was there as part of a CODEL led by Senator Lugar."

"Do you recall the year?"

"That must have been around 1997 or 1998. I was working for the Foreign Relations Committee by then."

"And I take it you stayed in touch with him?"

"Yes. Steve was very helpful to me on Russia-related issues. My committee was engaged on a variety of sensitive matters having to do with Russia during those years, things like Senate ratification of the START II Treaty and the multiple times Clinton and Yeltsin met. People forget, but between the summit in Vancouver in April 1993 and the talks in Helsinki in March 1997, the two presidents met in person at least six times. Steve was a great resource. Then in 1997 I became staff director and a few years later we had an opening on the committee that required someone with expertise on Russia and the former Soviet Republics. So we hired Steve. Steve and I worked together on the Committee for, oh, let's see." She counted the years in her head. "About three or four years."

"Then you left the Committee in 2004 to go work for the White House and after that State as the deputy secretary. Is that right?"

"Yes."

"And then in 2008 you went to work for McArthur & Associates?"

"That's right."

"During this time did you stay in touch with Mr. Abramovich?"

"Well, I connected with Steve often on Russia-related issues when I was at the White House and State. But at McArthur? No. Not really. I kind of lost touch with him. But when the president tapped me to be the next secretary, I was asked if I had any preferences on my security detail. I didn't until I noticed that Steve had left the Committee and joined DSS. So I told the person I was dealing with that if Steve was available, I'd like him on my detail. I thought it would be good to have a familiar face around."

"I'm curious. How did you know Mr. Abramovich had joined DSS, especially since, as you say, you had 'lost touch' with him?"

"Huh. That's a good question. You know, I think I got an e-mail from him congratulating me on my new job. And instead of it coming from Senate Finance or elsewhere, it came from a DSS e-mail address. So I wrote him back and one thing led to another."

"I see."

"Tell me, Mr. Jones, why all the questions about Steve?"

Elliot had to be very careful. What he said next might get back to Abramovich and spook him.

"It's just that I don't know him. I know Agents Payne, Faber, and Condon. Not well, but I know them. But I've never even met Mr. Abramovich."

"I see." She didn't.

"I'll be interviewing Mr. Abramovich later today and I simply wanted to gain added context and background on him from you."

The reality was that Elliot found the secretary's hiring of Abramovich suspicious. After more than twenty years Abramovich had resurfaced at DSS on the secretary's security detail? Something didn't smell right. Hence, Elliot's questions had as much to do with the secretary's intentions and state of mind as they did Abramovich's background or history. Elliot could get the latter out of Abramovich's personnel file, which he did.

"But you'll be interviewing the other members of my detail as well, won't you? At least that's what I was told."

"Yes, ma'am." Elliot didn't see the need to explain that Lake and Young would interview Faber, Payne, and Condon.

"Well, Madam Secretary, I have no further questions. Do you have any questions for me?"

"No, sir. Thank you."

"Of course. Thank you and thank you for your patience."

Chapter Thirty

By 3:45 p.m. they had finished interviewing the secretary, Payne, Faber, and Condon. Only Abramovich remained. Elliot and Young were seated in the SCIF when Abramovich entered at 3:50 p.m.

"Steve, hello. I'm Elliot. Elliot Jones."

"Hi."

They shook hands.

"Steve, this is Vic Young. He and another DSS agent, Alice Lake, are helping me with the investigation into Mr. Mutairi's death last Saturday. Have a seat."

"Thanks."

"Do you need anything? I can't offer you much. Perhaps a bottle of water?"

"No, I'm fine. Thanks."

"Okay. Then let's get started. Steve, I know you are accompanying the secretary to Bali this evening, so I'll be as brief as possible. I have your file here. I've reviewed it and I have only a few questions."

Elliot had told Young before Abramovich entered the room that he was going to go easy on him. "In time you will understand why." Young wasn't about to question Elliot's motives or methods.

Abramovich was the picture of cooperation. "Certainly. Fire away."

"It says here you worked at the US embassy in Moscow from 1997 to 2001."

"That's right."

"Do you remember when you met Secretary Farnsworth?"

"I do. Yes. It was at a reception at the ambassador's residence for a CODEL led by Senator Lugar. I believe it was shortly before Labor Day in 1997. I remember because the Senate was not in session. Secretary Farnsworth was there because she used to work for Senator Lugar and had moved to Committee staff."

"Is that the Senate Foreign Relations Committee?"

"Sorry. Yes."

"If I'm not mistaken, Russia was your first overseas assignment. Is that right?"

"Yes."

"Tell me. Why did you join the Agency?"

"I don't know. I guess because I double-majored in Russian language and Russian studies in college. It seemed like historic changes were taking place around the globe. I wanted to help my country and see the world." Abramovich shrugged his shoulders and smiled as if to say, *You know, the usual stupid-sounding reasons.*

"Then why did you leave to join the Committee in 2001?"

"Two reasons, really. First, Secretary Farnsworth said the Committee needed my expertise. I suppose that stroked my ego. And it sounded interesting to work on Capitol Hill and in Washington. You know, where all the action is. But the second reason was I got married—to a Russian—and I wanted to get her out of Russia."

"Yes, I see that in your file. Her name is Ulyana, is that right?"

"Yes. Ulyana."

"How did you meet your wife?"

"Again, it was at a reception, only this time it was at the embassy. She was working for a Russian high-tech company at the time."

"Which one?"

"It's called the Azon Group. It's still around. In fact, I think it is now one of the largest, if not *the* largest, internet companies in Russia."

"Are you still married?"

"Oh, yes. In fact, we recently celebrated our thirtieth anniversary."

"Oh, congratulations."

"Thanks."

"And you live up in Rockville. Is that right?"

"Yes, sir."

"Do you have any kids?"

"Yes, we have two daughters, ages twenty-four and twenty-six."

"How about Ulyana's family? Where do they live? Are they still in Russia or—?"

Abramovich was quick to speak. "Yes, Ulyana's parents and brother live in Moscow. I've been trying to get them out. Last year we thought we had visas for them, but Moscow refused to cooperate."

"Any idea why?"

"No, not really. Ulyana was pretty upset at the time. But she's better now."

"Does Ulyana work?"

"No, she stays home."

"What about *your* family? Where do they live?"

"I have a brother. He lives outside Detroit."

"What's he do?"

"He's a civil engineer for Wayne County."

"How about your parents? Where do they live?"

"Unfortunately, my parents are both deceased."

"Oh, I'm sorry to hear that. Yeah, both my parents are gone. It sucks."

"Yeah."

"Now, if I'm reading this right, you left the Committee and went back to the CIA in 2010. I asked you a minute ago why you left the agency to work for the Committee, so let me flip the question. Why leave the Committee to go back to the agency?"

"Well, Secretary Farnsworth had been my principal sponsor at the Committee and she left to go to the White House in 2004. Also, a position opened up at Langley in the Russia section. So I applied and got it. I stayed there until I moved to DSS in 2021."

"That was going to be my next question. Why leave the agency again and join DSS?"

"Several reasons, actually. First, it meant more money. Second, my girls were getting older and required less attention. And third, I missed travel and being on the front line. My last job at Langley was a desk job."

"I see. Okay, let's turn to the events of last Saturday night. My understanding is that the secretary met Mutairi for dinner before heading to the opera. Is that right?"

"Yes."

"Who accompanied her from her home to the restaurant?"

"Faber, Condon, Payne, and I did."

"Anyone else?"

"Well, yes. There were two DSS agents in the front of her limo."

"Did you ride with the secretary?"

"No, she rode by herself in the Cadi. I was in the lead Suburban with Condon. Agents Faber and Payne were in the trailing Suburban. DC police ran point and brought up the rear."

"How did the secretary seem that night? Calm and relaxed or uptight and agitated?"

"Oh, she seemed *very* relaxed. Talking, laughing, that sort of thing. Although during dinner their conversation seemed to get—" Abramovich paused, searching for the right word. "I wouldn't say heated, but definitely intense."

"Any idea why? Could you hear what they were talking about?"

"No, I was stationed near the front door. Condon was at the door leading to the kitchen, and Payne and Faber were near the secretary's table. So if you want to know what they talked about, you should ask either the secretary or one of those agents. They might know."

"Alright, so you drove to the Kennedy Center. Did you arrive before the performance started?"

"No, but the ushers were very nice. They let the secretary and Mutairi take their seats a few minutes late. I think anyone else sitting in the front row would have had to wait until intermission or a suitable pause in the performance."

"So the secretary sat in the front row, I believe near the middle?"

"That's right."

"Where were you and the other agents?"

"I was directly up the aisle from the secretary, near the back wall." Just as Elliot suspected. "Payne sat on the right aisle one row back from the secretary. That way he had a line of sight on her at all times. Faber sat immediately behind the secretary. And Condon sat in the front row on the other aisle. The left aisle."

"Sorry, I want to make sure I understand. Are you saying Payne was on one aisle and Condon the other?"

"That's right. Sorry if I wasn't clear."

"No, you're good. Now, everyone we've spoken to said they never heard a gunshot. What about you? Did you hear anything?"

"Nothing. Just the performers who were singing and the orchestra."

"Was it particularly loud when Mutairi was shot?"

"Well, again, I never heard a gun go off. So I can't say exactly how loud it was when he was shot. The first I knew anything was wrong was when Payne announced a Code Red. At that moment I happened to be looking to my left at a guy who had just entered through the back at the top of the other aisle, the aisle Condon was sitting on."

"Huh. Do you think we should track that guy down?" Elliot knew that would be pointless. The shooter was sitting right in front of him. He only said it to lessen any suspicions Abramovich might have.

"No. I don't think so. He was older. Probably in his early sixties. I think he was just returning to his seat from the restroom."

It was getting late and Elliot didn't want to set off alarm bells in Abramovich's head. "Okay, then. I have no further questions. Do you have any questions for me?"

"No, sir. I think I'm good. Thank you."

"Just doing my job. Thank you and thank you for your patience. Safe travels and enjoy Bali."

Abramovich chuckled. "I will. Thanks."

Chapter Thirty-One

Indonesia is a vast archipelago consisting of over 18,000 islands stretching 3,100 miles from east to west and 1,000 miles from north to south. Its vastness is exceeded only by its diversity. Indeed, the official motto of Indonesia is "*Unity in Diversity*." Thus, while Bahasa is the official language of Indonesia, in fact, 700 different languages and dialects are spoken in Indonesia. And while 40 percent of the population is Javanese, an eye-popping 1,300 different ethnic groups live in Indonesia.

Although Indonesia has the largest Muslim population of any country in the world, it is in reality a very peaceful, multi-faith country that officially recognizes six religions: Islam, Catholicism, Protestantism, Confucianism, Buddhism, and Hinduism. In many cases the dominant religion in any particular city or province depends on the island. For example, the dominant religion on Bali is Hinduism.

Bali lies roughly 750 miles east of Jakarta. Lynne's flight would take around 90 minutes. It was then a 45-minute drive from Ngurah Rai International Airport in Denpasar to the Ritz Carlton Reserve in Ubud. With luck, she would be in her room by 8:15 p.m. But first she had to get to the Soekarno Hatta International Airport outside Jakarta.

At 4:30 p.m. Secretary Farnsworth came down from her room. Her luggage had already been loaded into one of the vehicles out front. As she waited with Payne and the other members of her detail for Abramovich to make his way over to the ambassador's residence from the embassy, Lynne said goodbye to Ambassadors Kim and Burns. Both agreed that the APCW had gone well. They were less convinced that President Waskito and his government would not do or say the wrong thing regarding the South China Sea. Lynne shared their view.

"Have a great time in Bali, Madam Secretary," Kim said with a warm smile.

"Thanks, Heather. I'm looking forward to it. I haven't had a break in over fourteen months."

"I'm glad you're staying at the Ritz Carlton in Ubud. It's incredible. My husband and I celebrated our twentieth anniversary there last April."

Burns had never been to Bali, let alone the Ritz Carlton in Ubud. "Is it nice?"

"Oh, my God," Kim exclaimed. "It's literally the nicest hotel I've ever stayed at, and I've stayed at some nice ones!"

"Really?" Burns said with his voice rising.

"Yes. Do you remember the TV show *Fantasy Island*? The one where the gates to a resort open and the little guy with the heavy accent points to the sky and says 'da plane, da plane'?"

"Yeah."

"Well, that's what the Ritz in Ubud is like. They open these big gates upon arrival and you think you've entered another world. Literally a tropical paradise."

Lynne disliked the way many Americans used the word "literally" in their speech; however, she liked Kim and appreciated her enthusiasm. Therefore, she kept her views on the English language to herself, and when

Kim and Burns finished and looked at Lynne, she felt obliged to say, "I can't wait."

In point of fact, Lynne could *not* wait. At least not much longer. She looked at her watch. It was 4:45 p.m. She grabbed her purse and started to head for the front door. As she did her CoS, Peter Drinker, approached.

"Madam Secretary, may I have a word with you?"

"Of course, Peter, but make it quick."

"Certainly. I just wanted to call your attention to an article that appeared in yesterday's edition of the *Washington Post.*"

"Which one?"

"It concerns Mr. Mutairi and the incident at the Kennedy Center last Saturday. I placed a copy in your briefcase."

"No. I didn't see it. What's it say?"

"Not much. They claim an unnamed source has confirmed it was not a heart attack. Perhaps someone at the hospital spoke."

"Anything else?"

"Just that he may have been shot and that you were seated next to him."

"Okay. Well, brief Public and Legislative Affairs ASAP. They need to develop talking points and be in sync on this. And when I get back from Geneva I'll go up to the Hill and brief congressional leaders. Stage a preemptive strike. I don't want them getting all worked up and spinning out of control over this. Have Leg Affairs set up some meetings for me with Susan Murray and Les Walters. Maybe also Henry Aiken. Okay?"

"Yes, ma'am."

Senator Murray was the chairman of the Senate Foreign Relations Committee, Lynne's "home" for nearly twenty years. Senator Walters was the ranking member on Foreign Relations. Congressman Aiken was the chairman of the House Foreign Affairs Committee.

"Now, where's Steve? I wanna get going."

Fortunately, Lynne didn't have to wait long. Abramovich arrived in an embassy car ten minutes before five o'clock. He quickly stowed his gear in one of the Suburbans before consulting with the other members of his team. At 5:00 p.m. exactly the motorcade headed for the airport.

Once again PAMBOVIT acquitted itself nicely. Three blue-and-white POLRI cruisers led the way. Another three brought up the rear. Their lights and discordant two-tone sirens cut through traffic like a knife.

As usual, Lynne sat in her limousine alone in the middle of the motorcade. She used the time to call Iraq's oil minister, Hussain Karim Rashid.

Lynne met Rashid in 2010 while she was working at MA. At the time he was the deputy director general of the Basra Oil Company. In the years following he rose to become the director general (DG) of Basra Oil and thereafter the DG of the Iraqi Drilling Company before eventually becoming Iraq's oil minister in 2028.

She caught him in his office as he was about to go to lunch. "Hussain? This is Lynne Farnsworth. You got a minute? I won't take much of your time."

* * *

At the airport the motorcade turned on to a service road. As it approached a gate manned by two heavily armed guards, the motorcade slowed but never stopped. Payne had given strict instructions to PAMBOVIT that the secretary's motorcade was never under any circumstances to stop until it reached its destination.

After passing through the gate the motorcade drove on to the airport's tarmac. The secretary's blue-and-white C-32A, with the prominent "UNITED STATES OF AMERICA" cheat-line markings, sat off to the side surrounded by military and police vehicles.

The secretary of state's plane was operated by the Air Force's 1st Airlift Squadron of the 89th Airlift Wing out of Joint Base Andrews in

Camp Springs, Maryland. It was one of five C-32As operated by the Air Force. All were Boeing 757s modified for government VIP use.

The secretary's plane had a large office midway between the cockpit and the wings. Her desk was the kind one might find in a first-class railcar in Europe. A large round plaque hung on the wall behind the desk. The words "Secretary of State" were emblazoned on a blue band that stretched around the rim of the plaque. In the middle was the Great Seal of the United States. On the wall opposite the secretary's chair was a 32-inch flat-panel television. It hung above a blue-and-yellow pinstriped sofa complemented by a coffee table and two matching armchairs. All furniture was securely fastened to the floor of the plane, which was covered throughout by a plush, industrial-grade carpet in cobalt blue.

A crew of thirteen was standard. They were there to operate the plane, to get the secretary of state to his or her destination as quickly and safely as possible, whether it was for business or pleasure. They were not there to make policy, pass judgment, or make news. Therefore, they tried to be as invisible as possible.

Chapter Thirty-Two

With the help of PAMBOVIT, DSS prepositioned three heavily modified and armored vehicles at the airport in Denpasar. It wasn't what Lynne or her security detail were used to, but it would have to do.

The ride from the airport to the hotel was uneventful. Her motorcade was bookended between two blue-and-white Toyota Highlanders operated by the POLRI, with an officer on a white Yamaha XJ 990P motorcycle out front. As they raced through the Balinese countryside with emergency lights flashing, traffic stopped or moved to the side.

For once Lynne did not call anyone or work in the car. Instead she enjoyed the scenery. Ubud was a small town that sat up in the hills above the coast of Bali. The road to Ubud climbed through lush landscapes and beautiful villages dotted with Hindu temples and rice paddies.

The Ritz Carlton Reserve Mandapa in Ubud sits on the Ayung River. It is one of only a few "reserve" properties operated by Ritz Carlton anywhere in the world. The word *mandapa* means temple in Sanskrit. It doesn't take long for guests to realize that the property is aptly named.

Before they enter the hotel, guests proceed down a flagstone-covered driveway bordered by gardens, lilies, and fountains. At the entrance to the hotel they are greeted by a guard in front of a twenty-foot-high rust-colored gate trimmed in traditional Balinese aesthetics. Most guests have to wait at the gate while the guard calls the registration office for clearance. Lynne was not most guests. Her motorcade slowed at the gate but did not stop.

When her limousine finally came to a stop, eight members of the hotel's senior management, including the general manager, came out to greet Lynne. They waited patiently in a straight line as the secretary's detail took up their normal positions and scanned the immediate area for threats. When they were satisfied with what they saw, Payne opened Lynne's door. As she got out of the car the manager and his staff all placed their palms together in front of their chests and bowed. Lynne reciprocated with a slight bow at the hip.

With her security detail standing nearby in a loose diamond formation, Lynne stepped forward to shake the manager's hand.

"Hello, Madam Secretary. Welcome to the Ritz Carlton Mandapa. My name is Djunari Nurwan. I am the general manager. Before you are escorted to your villa, might I suggest you take a minute to step over here?"

He gently motioned with his right hand toward some terraced structures. "Although the sun has set, you will be able to see Mandapa."

"Yes, thank you. I would like that."

The manager led Lynne across a stone walkway up to a collection of rooms with no walls, each on a slightly different level from the next. The rooms themselves were stunning. Simple square wood columns in red hues held aloft each roof. In the rooms was a loose collection of chairs and plants on large rattan mats. Small bamboo stands were strategically placed around the rooms, each with a large white candle inside a clear glass cyclone. The combination of candlelight and the bullet lights in the ceiling cast a magical glow over the entire space. The esthetic was very Balinese— light, tropical, and tasteful. But that was just the *appetizer.*

The *main course* was what lay beneath and beyond. Standing in the top room looking out at the hotel's property, Lynne saw a series of terraced gardens, complete with rice paddies, set in a giant basin that led down to the Ayung River. Scattered throughout each terrace were hotel rooms, villas, restaurants, cocktail bars, and garden pathways illuminated by hundreds of torches.

"My goodness," she said. "This is spectacular. I can't wait to see it in daylight."

"Yes, ma'am. You are always welcome to sit here. Perhaps enjoy a hot tea or other beverage. Read a book or simply relax. Just let us know what you want. We want your stay with us to be memorable."

As Lynne stood enchanted by the view, a small Indonesian girl in a long *batik* skirt that hugged her hips approached, carrying a tray. On the tray was a tall glass of hibiscus juice and a single, lemon-scented, warm, rolled-up hand towel cradled in a curved piece of mahogany. A lone frangipani (aka plumeria alba) flower lay next to the towel.

The girl was very shy, so the general manager said to Lynne, "Perhaps you would like to clean your hands and face with a warm towel. We also would like to offer you hibiscus juice. It is very refreshing."

"Yes, thank you." Lynne unfolded the towel before gently wiping her face and hands. Then she took a single sip of the juice before putting the glass and towel back down on the tray. As she did, she made a point of looking into the girl's eyes and thanking her.

The girl blushed, bowed her head, and walked quickly away.

"Madam Secretary, would you like to see your villa?"

"Yes, please. It's been a long day."

"Of course, madam." The manager looked over at his staff and raised his right hand. "I'll get you a cart."

"Oh, I don't mind walking."

"Yes, madam, as you wish. However, it is a long way down to your villa. A cart would be much better."

He was being so polite. Lynne wasn't sure if walking was really out of the question. She decided to play it safe and take his advice.

Just then three golf carts appeared. Payne and Faber got in the first cart, with a member of the DSS advance team behind the wheel. Lynne got in the second one.

The general manager, standing a few feet back with his heels together, bowed slightly at the waist and asked Lynne, "Madam Secretary, may I show you your villa?"

Lynne instantly slid over to make room. As she did she allowed herself the tiniest of giggles. "Yes, of course. Hop in."

With the assistant manager in the front seat and Lynne and the general manager in the back seat, the cart headed down the hill. Condon and Abramovich, together with the secretary's luggage, brought up the rear.

In order to accommodate the descent, the cart path was laid out in a series of switchbacks. At each turn Lynne felt the concerns in her life fall further and further away. Although the driver of the cart was careful and drove slowly, Lynne still languished in the gentle breeze that washed over her and the tropical fragrances that lingered naturally in the air.

To her left, in the distance, she could see a collection of lights and torches. *Probably a restaurant or bar*, she thought. There would be time to check it out. In the foreground it was particularly dark. *Perhaps a rice paddy*, she surmised. The lower they got in the basin the more she began to hear the sounds of the Ayung River as it arched around the property. Beyond the river there were no lights. Just a wall of darkness. She wondered the reason. Morning light would presumably reveal the answer.

* * *

Near a small wood lamppost with the number seven on it, the carts slowed and turned right. On each side of the carts were large banana leaves and discreet low-voltage landscape lights that illuminated stepping stones set in grass that led down a short path.

"This is your villa, madam. Please watch your step," the general manager said.

As Lynne stepped out of the cart, Payne and Faber came back to assist. It was dark, but there was just enough light to see the path safely. The general manager, followed by the assistant manager, escorted Lynne and the agents to a door. Standing at the door were two DSS agents who were part of the jump team. Other than a brief "good evening," they said nothing.

In many respects, the door was like any other—doorknob, hinges, an electronic lock. But in most other respects, it was not. It did not lead into a room or any kind of building. It was instead part of a high wall that led into a nearly 4,000-square-foot villa open to the sky with a main bedroom and bathroom (with indoor and outdoor showers), an outdoor terrace, a separate living room that included a powder room, and a 20 foot by 50 foot in-ground pool. It was more a compound than a hotel room, all completely private.

As the door swung open, a very thin man in his late forties wearing a brown *batik* shirt and dark slacks greeted Lynne with a deep bow at the waist and his hands clasped in front of his chest.

"Welcome to Mandapa, Madam Secretary. My name is Angga. For the next five days I will be your *patih*."

The general manager stopped just inside the door. This was Angga's space. He would take care of the secretary and show her the room. She was in good hands. Angga was Mandapa's longest-tenured *patih* (king's assistant).

"Madam Secretary, here is your key. Unless you need anything else from me, I will leave you in Pak Angga's good hands. Please do not hesitate to call me if I can be of service to you. I can always be reached by dialing 0 on the house phone." With that, the general manager and his assistant bowed at the waist and left.

Lynne was mesmerized by her surroundings. While Payne spoke briefly to Angga and Faber spoke to the DSS agents at the door, Condon and Abramovich placed her luggage inside the main bedroom. Lynne took off her shoes and went exploring. First she walked the length of the pool, making a point of walking in the grass, which was blissfully cool to the touch. The pool lights caused the water to shimmer from its surface down to the coral blue tiles that lined its bottom and walls. She couldn't wait to take a dip.

At the end of the pool she turned and walked back through the living room that was separated from the bedroom and bathroom by an expanse of grass and stepping stones. The room was open and tastefully decorated in dark wood and rattan accents, pillows, and rugs. A fifty-two-inch flat-panel LCD TV hung on the wall.

Payne was done talking to Angga. Condon, Abramovich, and Faber were sitting in the carts. Payne waited to speak with her.

"Ma'am, I reckon you're fixin' to get settled into your room. So unless y'all need somethin', we'll head back to our rooms. We're just up by registration."

"Okay, thanks."

"The hotel was swept twice by the advance team. The most recent sweep was this mornin'. Since then your room has been sealed. So you shouldn't have any problems, but if you do, ya'll have your Tiger button and phone?"

"Yes."

Over the years DSS had tried many different panic buttons. Recently it had settled on one made by Tiger. In addition to its loud audio alarm and blinding flashlight, the button connected automatically to local cellular and Wi-Fi signals, and, most importantly, was easy to use—an important attribute considering the average age of the principals the DSS protected.

"Are both fully charged?"

"Yes, I believe so."

"Good. Please connect both to the hotel's Wi-Fi as soon's ya can. Cell strength is weak down here by the river. The Wi-Fi instructions, if ya need 'em, are on your desk."

"Okay. Thanks."

"If ya'll have any problems or need anything, just hit the button on your Tiger. One of us will call ya immediately or knock on your door. Any questions?"

"No, I think I'm good. Besides, I've got Angga here to help me. Right, Angga?" she said with a smile, looking at him.

Angga stood a respectful distance back from Lynne and Payne with his hands clasped behind his back. "Yes, madam. I am at your disposal. Just dial 1 on your hotel phone if you need anything."

Payne appreciated Angga's willingness to assist the secretary. However, he was tempted to clarify that if there was a real emergency or threat, Lynne was to press the button on her Tiger, *not* 1 on the hotel phone. He looked directly at Lynne. She could tell what he was thinking.

"I'll be fine, Roger. Thank you. Good night."

"Good night, ma'am."

Chapter Thirty-Three

Lynne was anxious to freshen up, perhaps take a shower or dip in the pool and order some dinner. It was a little after 8:00 p.m. She hadn't eaten since lunch.

Turning to Angga, she said, "I might take a shower or a dip in the pool."

"Yes, madam. Would you like me to hang up your dresses and jackets in the closet and put everything else in the drawers?"

"No, I can do that. Thank you."

"Yes, madam. Will you be needing anything else tonight?"

"No, Angga. Thank you."

"Yes, madam. Certainly."

"Oh, Angga? There *is* one more thing."

"Yes, madam?"

"Mr. Fhani will be joining me during my stay. I expect him to arrive around 10:00 p.m. tonight. Could you make sure he gets a key and show him in? And I would prefer that Mr. Payne and the other members of my security detail not be informed of Mr. Fhani's arrival. Could you see to that?"

"Yes, of course, madam. It would be my pleasure. Will there be anything else?"

"No. Thank you, Angga. Good night."

"Good night, madam."

* * *

Finally she was alone. She stood on the wooden terrace outside her bedroom, looking down the length of the pool. She took a deep breath and closed her eyes. The only sounds were the water cascading over the side of the spa in the pool, and the natural sounds of the rainforest and river.

She was tempted to take a dip in the pool, but she wanted to eat and get ready for her guest. She picked up the house phone and hit the button labeled "room service."

"Good evening. Room service. How can I help you?"

"Yes, good evening. Could I get a small serving of dim sum and a small green salad?"

"Yes, madam. What kind of dressing would you like on your salad?"

"Do you have a house vinaigrette?"

"Yes, of course, madam. Anything else? Perhaps something to drink?"

"Yes, how about a glass of Sauvignon blanc or Chenin blanc?"

"We have both, madam. We also have Chardonnay, Viognier, Pinot Grigio, and Riesling, along with a white Bordeaux and a white Burgundy by the glass that you might like. Not to mention a wide assortment of reds and champagnes."

"Thank you. I'll have a glass of Sauvignon blanc, please."

"Very well, madam. Anything else?"

"No, that will be all. Thank you."

"Please allow twenty minutes, madam."

"Thank you." She hung up the phone and checked her watch. It was 8:35 p.m. She had enough time to unpack, eat, and get ready for Fhani. But first she wanted to explore her bedroom and bathroom.

Everywhere she looked the decor emphasized dark woods and rich textiles. Ceiling lights were ensconced in designer basketry, the bathroom mirrors were accented in gold, and the walls were covered in murals that local artists took two years to complete. In the middle of the bathroom was a freestanding tub for two with raised leather headrests on each end. There was both an indoor shower that was spacious and luxurious, and a private outdoor shower set in a lush setting of flowers and palm fronds. Finally, his-and-her vessel sinks were made from solid teak wood. This wasn't a place that aspired to elegance; it *was* elegance.

* * *

She dined at a small, round mahogany table on her terrace. In the bedroom behind her the Bose stereo played classical music that gently washed over her. In front of her the pool and garden lights put on a show. It had been a long time since she had been this happy or this much at peace.

With her last bite, she took the last sip of wine. Thankfully, it was from South Africa. She hated the Sauvignon blancs produced in New Zealand in general and Marlborough in particular. More often than not she thought they tasted like fermented grapefruit juice, too fruit-forward. She much preferred a more subtle Sancerre from France or certain Sauvignon blancs from California. She was tempted to order another glass or even a bottle, but it was probably better to wait for Fhani.

It was 9:00 p.m. She was nervous. She felt like she was back in high school waiting for a date to pick her up. She needed to relax. A dip in the pool was exactly what the doctor ordered.

She looked around. She couldn't see any windows or buildings from which people could see in. She was tempted to swim *au natural*. At the last minute, she donned her bathing suit and grabbed a towel from the bathroom.

The water was heavenly, the perfect temperature. However, she resisted the temptation to swim down to the other end and back. She needed a shower. She needed to get cleaned up and ready. Besides, the chemicals in the water might be hard on her hair.

She dried off enough to keep from leaving puddles of water on the bathroom floor. She hung her suit over the edge of the tub. There was a second Bose unit in the bathroom. She had it play the same music that was on in the bedroom. Together the two units created a stereo effect that bounced off the walls of both rooms and down the short hallway between them.

Lynne had never showered outside. It sounded sinfully delicious. She grabbed her towel and walked out on to a synthetic wood floor placed over gray pea gravel. Instead of ceramic tile, she found herself surrounded by areca palms and assorted lilies and ornamental grasses.

The water fell straight down from a large waterfall showerhead. The air temperature and water temperature were nearly identical. For the first minute or two she simply stood there, with her eyes closed, letting the water caress her. If only she could stay there forever.

Eventually she lathered up her hair with special shampoo she brought from the US. She used the body wash provided by the hotel for everything else. It smelled of roses.

With her eyes closed and the water cascading over her head and ears, she did not sense his approach. He quietly approached her from behind, undressing as he walked. His clothes fell randomly across the bathroom floor.

He embraced her, reaching around her arms and chest. "Good evening, Madam Secretary," he whispered in her ear. He put his cheek next to hers and kissed it. He could taste the water on her cheek.

"Oh, Sam, you made it." Lynne turned around to face him. They kissed long and hard.

She had known his kiss before. But not like this. This felt different. She wanted this *entire* night to be different. She desperately wanted to believe he loved her.

"I'm sorry I couldn't meet you for dinner Wednesday or Thursday. As I said, I had—"

He raised his right index finger to her lips. "Shush. No need to apologize. What's important is that we are together now."

She immediately fell silent and looked into his eyes. Without saying more, he gently inserted his finger into her mouth. She closed her lips around it and slowly sucked on it, never taking her eyes off his. Now it was her turn to taste the water on his body.

Fhani was aroused. Lynne could feel his body stiffen. As much as that excited her, the thought of making love standing up in a shower scared her. She didn't want to disappoint him. She preferred to move things to the bedroom. She played for more time.

"Have you eaten anything? I had a light snack around eight."

"As a matter of fact, I'm starving. I wanted to get here as quickly as possible, so I didn't stop to eat and they didn't serve anything except crackers on the plane."

"Then let's order something. We can also order a bottle of wine. They have a nice Sauvignon blanc from South Africa. Would you like that?"

"That sounds great."

She grabbed a large white towel she had hung on a nearby hook. She wrapped it around herself.

She grabbed the in-room dining menu off of the desk. "Here's the menu. Pick something and I will call them."

Chapter Thirty-Four

By midnight the last drop of wine had been drunk and the laughing had stopped. Seated on each side of the small table on the terrace, they stared at the pool. Like a fire in winter, the pool lights captivated them. It was quiet. The stillness was occasionally punctuated by the sounds of owls and other nocturnal creatures in the forest.

Fhani reached across the table and took Lynne's hand.

"Madam Secretary," he said with a smile. "Can I interest you in something else?"

An equally broad grin graced her face. "What did you have in mind?"

"Come to bed and you'll see."

The room was dark. Brahms's *Violin Sonata No. 1 in G* serenaded them. Lynne slipped off her robe and climbed into bed. She watched Fhani as he lit a candle on the coffee table and another on the desk.

"Ohhh, aren't you the romantic one?" she said in jest.

"But of course," came his whimsical retort. "Besides, I want to see you." They both laughed.

With the mood set and the lights low, Fhani slipped off his robe and laid down next to her. He stared into her eyes.

After a long moment she asked him, "How do you do that?"

"Do what?"

"Look at me like it's for the very first time."

"I can't help it. I love you."

"Oh, Sam. I love you."

Lying on their sides, they embraced. He kissed her again and again. She raised her top leg, placing it on his hip. He reached down and pulled her knee even higher. As he did, he pressed his pelvis between her legs and rolled gently on top of her.

This is what she wanted. This is what she needed. To be loved. Passionately. Uncontrollably. Without reservation. Their bodies moved as one. In rhythm. Again and again. He did not hold back.

* * *

For the next three days they rarely ventured out. They didn't need to. They had everything they could possibly want within the four corners of the villa. And the ability to be outside, to swim, to sun, in a totally private setting, was something neither had ever experienced before. It was the epitome of elegance and luxury.

By Monday evening, however, they began to feel a little guilty. They had not explored any of the hotel's many amenities. Therefore, a little after 5:30 p.m. Lynne called Angga on the hotel's phone.

"Hello, Angga?"

"Yes, madam. How can I help you?"

"Could you please make a dinner reservation for two at 7:30 p.m. at Kubu? Preferably a table for two in one of the private bamboo 'cocoons' overlooking the river."

"Yes, of course. I'd be happy to. Will you need a cart or would you prefer to walk?"

"Is it very far?"

"No, madam. Only 130 meters. And the path is very flat and safe."

"Okay, then we will walk, at least *to* the restaurant. Depending on how much wine we drink, we may want to get a cart for the trip back," Lynne said with a slight chuckle.

"Yes, madam. As you wish. I will call the restaurant now. Will there be anything else?"

"No, Angga. Thank you."

"My pleasure. Good night."

When she hung up, Lynne pressed the button on her Tiger. Within seconds her cell phone rang.

"Hello."

"Madam Secretary, this is Roger. Did you need somethin'?"

"I just wanted to let you know I will be having dinner tonight at Kubu. Our reservation is at 7:30."

"Is Mr. Fhani gonna join ya?"

"Yes."

Payne didn't volunteer how he knew Fhani was staying with her and she didn't ask.

Chapter Thirty-Five

Their flight back to Washington was not scheduled to leave Jakarta until late Sunday. With the secretary and her detail gone and all interviews completed, they could relax. Lake and Young spent most of Saturday sightseeing. Neither had been to Jakarta before. Elliot spent the day in his hotel room, watching TV and ordering room service. When he wasn't eating or watching TV, he napped or worked. He actually enjoyed these kinds of days. They gave him a chance to rest up and catch up without anyone bothering him.

For Elliot, Sunday was another day spent inside his hotel room. Except, instead of working on the Mutairi matter, he spent much of his time searching the internet for stories about the attempt to sink the *Chehalis*. They weren't hard to find. There were thousands of them. And although he had managed during the previous week to avoid speaking to reporters, about half of the stories mentioned his name and place of work, with about half of those also mentioning Rachel and her attendance at the University of Washington.

The hotel staff members were very accommodating. Not only did they allow late checkout, they also arranged for an air-conditioned van to take them to the airport a little after 5:00 p.m. Traffic between downtown and the airport was typical—hellish. Little was said in the van. They arrived at the airport close to 7:00 p.m. Their flight to Tokyo's Narita Airport was scheduled to depart at 9:45 p.m. and arrive at 6:50 a.m. Monday. Even though they were traveling on official government passports, it took them a while to pass through security and passport control.

When they finally got to their gate, they were told their flight was delayed one hour. Fortunately or unfortunately, the delay was of little consequence to them. Young and Lake had a long layover in Tokyo. Their flight to Washington didn't leave Narita until 4:50 p.m. local time on Monday. Elliot had an even longer layover. He was meeting Karen and Rachel in Seattle. They would attend the award ceremony in Olympia on Tuesday. His flight to Seattle didn't leave Narita until 9:15 p.m. local time on Monday.

* * *

Elliot had been to Tokyo five or six times. He had passed through Narita Airport many more times on his way to places like Bangkok, Jakarta, and Singapore. He had never known it to be anything other than busy; a giant sea of people moving in all directions. It reminded him of that *Star Trek* episode where Captain Kirk, played by William Shatner, beamed down to a planet where the population had grown so much the government was desperately trying to introduce a deadly virus.

It was in the middle of a particularly busy intersection of passengers that Elliot stopped and said goodbye to Lake and Young.

"I'm going to say goodbye here. My flight to Seattle doesn't leave for another thirteen hours, so I'm going to head up to the lounge on the second floor. I believe your flight departs from gate 42 down there," he said, pointing to a nearby concourse. "Thanks for your help." He shook their hands. "Please be sure to send me your interview notes. I want to review them before they are finalized and released into the official file."

"Will do," Lake said. "And good luck with the award ceremony."

"Yeah," said Young. "That's pretty incredible. Safe travels."

Elliot thanked them both again and walked away.

Chapter Thirty-Six

November brought cool weather to the Washington metropolitan region, including Rockville, Maryland. The leaves on the trees began to embrace the colors of autumn. Those that broke free from their branches fell to the ground, eventually to be carried away by the wind.

The weather forecast Sunday called for scattered clouds but no rain. The funeral home assumed a canopy over the grave site was not necessary. By 1:00 p.m., however, a light rain began to dance on Emmy Treadwell's casket. Droplets that beaded on the shiny wood surface fell down the sides of the casket in narrow lines that disappeared as quickly as they appeared. As mourners arrived attendants did their best to dry off the white, wooden chairs with a towel. Women wearing heels struggled to walk on the wet, soft grass. The lucky ones had an arm to hold on to.

Captain Cleveland of the US Park Police attended. He was joined by two detectives responsible for investigating Emmy's murder. Upon arriving they introduced themselves to the Rockville police officers who were there to help with security and traffic.

Over 300 people attended. Most were from the Washington Opera Company and the cast of *Otello*. Others from Georgetown University and American University. Still others were friends of Emmy's family or attended high school with her.

Alain Bonnet had come alone. He debated whether to sit or stand. Alain wanted to be there. He wanted to say goodbye to his friend. But he wanted to mourn alone. So he stood back on raised ground underneath a red maple tree. As Alain looked down on Emmy's casket, the clouds, as if on cue, parted. A ray of sunshine came to rest on her casket for a brief moment. Around her casket, like a protective embrace, was a twenty-feet-deep ring of black umbrellas. The pitter-patter of the rain hitting the umbrellas was strangely soothing to all who heard it.

Emmy's dad sat in the first row, his head down, his pant legs wet from the rain. He didn't care. He was now alone in the world. He had no siblings. Both his parents were dead. He had buried his wife (and Emmy's mother) in this same cemetery a few years earlier. Now he was burying his daughter. He wanted his beautiful little girl back. No parent should ever have to bury a child.

A very patrician-looking man with flowing, silver hair and a slight build sat alone near the head of the casket under a black umbrella. He wore a long black coat. As he stood Alain could see that he was a Jesuit priest. The man walked over to where Emmy's father was sitting. He said something. Without looking up, Emmy's father nodded. The priest walked back to the head of the casket.

In a loud, clear voice that all could hear he said, "Hello, everyone. My name is Father Jeffery Wilkerson. We gather here today to lay to rest one of God's children—Emilia Anna Treadwell. Regardless of your faith or domination, I would ask that you bow your head for a moment of prayer." Everyone obliged.

Heavenly Father, we are gathered here today as friends and family of our loved one who departed from this world recently and came into your presence. Lord, it is not easy for us to sit here and eulogize our beloved, but we know that Emmy is now together with You in heaven. As we honor our loved one, let the unconditional love that you showered upon Emmy during her life fill this service. Help us to learn how to love others unconditionally like our beloved did when she was with us on earth. In Jesus' name we pray. Amen.

"I have known Harper Treadwell for over thirty years. I first met his daughter, Emmy, when she was fifteen and a sophomore in high school. Emmy loved classical music, especially opera. I can remember many Sunday afternoons after church listening to the likes of Pavarotti and Caruso with Emmy and her parents. She was so wonderfully full of life. Now I am seventy-five-years old. The vast majority of my life is behind me. Emmy Treadwell was only thirty-seven when she was senselessly and tragically killed. The vast majority of her life was in front of her. The Bible says at John 20:31 that God considers your life valuable and precious. Since life is indeed precious, I thought it fitting that I read from a poem called 'Life' by Sarojini Naidu."

Alain had been deep in thought when Father Wilkerson mentioned the poem. He knew it well. It was one of his favorites. Emmy had also liked it. Alain wondered if the priest knew that.

Father Wilkerson read the poem slowly.

Children, ye have not lived, to you it seems

Life is a lovely stalactite of dreams,

Or carnival of careless joys that leap

About your hearts like billows on the deep

In flames of amber and of amethyst.

Children, ye have not lived, ye but exist

Till some resistless hour shall rise and move

Your hearts to wake and hunger after love,

And thirst with passionate longing for the things

That burn your brows with blood-red sufferings.

Till ye have battled with great grief and fears,

And borne the conflict of dream-shattering years,

Wounded with fierce desire and worn with strife

Standing alone underneath the tree, Alain spoke the last line of the poem aloud.

"Children, ye have not lived: for this is life."

Alain wept.

Chapter Thirty-Seven

B
ob Hansen loved routine. He often quoted Darren Hardy, the author of *The Compound Effect*, who said, "A daily routine built on good habits and disciplines separates the most successful among us from everyone else." Thus, every Monday at 9:00 a.m. sharp he liked to meet with his CoS, Bob Salter, in the Oval Office. Alone. The fact that they had met for an hour up at Camp David on Saturday didn't matter.

After serving in the Senate for two terms, he had run what many believed was a brilliant presidential campaign. As a Republican, Hansen could count on seventy-three Electoral College votes from the so-called "flyover" states, the states in America's great heartland like Indiana, Kansas, and Nebraska that have, with very few exceptions, voted Republican in every presidential election since Richard Nixon in 1968. And although he wasn't particularly religious, Hansen knew how to talk about the issues that mattered to the evangelicals and others in America's "Bible belt." As a result, he could count on another eighty-five votes in the Electoral College from states like Alabama, Mississippi, Oklahoma, and Texas.

That meant his election to the presidency came down, in the end, as it had in five out of the previous six general elections, to the so-called "swing" states, in particular, those states in America's "rust belt" where glo-balization and automation had decimated the country's factory jobs and organized labor—states like Michigan, Ohio, Pennsylvania, and Wisconsin. The citizens of those states had traditionally voted Democrat in the years after World War II. These were "blue-collar" states where the typical voter believed "free trade" and trade agreements, such as the North American Free Trade Agreement and the US–Korea Free Trade Agreement, were the main cause of their job losses. Organized labor groups like the United Auto Workers and the AFL-CIO put the blame for those agreements at the feet of Republicans.

That all changed with Donald Trump in 2016. When it came to inter-national trade, Trump was more protectionist than any Democrat, includ-ing Hillary Clinton. Figuratively speaking, he stole the chapter on trade out of the Democrat's playbook and made it his own. That explained why, when Joe Biden became president in 2020, his administration did not roll back the tariffs Trump had imposed on a wide range of Chinese products or why the Biden administration did not reverse the crippling effects of Trump's policies on the WTO in Geneva, Switzerland. Trump's policies on trade were textbook Democrat. Hansen and his campaign understood this.

After Hansen's three years in office, reelection was priority num-ber one at the White House. Indeed it was the *only* priority. If he ran a smart campaign, Hansen believed only one thing stood in the way of his reelection—higher gasoline prices. Conventional wisdom was that most Americans voted with their pocketbooks. Abortion, immigration, and a variety of other social issues moved some to vote one way or the other; but for the vast majority of Americans, jobs, taxes, and the economy were the most important issues. And no single topic commanded the attention of Americans more than the price they paid for gas at the pump. It didn't matter that Americans paid about a quarter of what Europeans paid for their fuel. It didn't matter that gas prices in the United States were far below those in Japan, Korea, and most other industrialized countries. No amount of reasoning or rationale was going to change the fact that Americans loved their cars and demanded cheap fuel to operate them.

Hansen understood this and he made sure his CoS understood it. During their meeting that morning, Hansen was emphatic.

"Bob, only three presidents since Herbert Hoover have run for reelection and lost. I don't want to be the fourth. If our plans in Kuwait have fallen apart, come up with another plan and come up with it fast. The Dems will screw around with their primaries, but in the end they'll nominate McCormick. He'll beat me like an old rug if gas prices are high come Election Day. Understood?" Hansen said it more as a command than a question.

"Yes, sir. I'm meeting with Energy, the CIA, DOD, and others later this morning to identify a course of action and next steps. My goal is to give you three or four options to choose from by the end of the month."

"Good. Get it done and keep me informed! Now I've got to meet with some representatives of the Sudanese diaspora who are in town."

* * *

Salter entered the Sit Room at 11 a.m. Seated around the table were Audrey Ackerman and Sharon Holcumb from the CIA; Energy Secretary Middleton; the president's national security advisor, Mark Esmond; his director of national intelligence; his secretary of homeland security; and Collin Donovan, the deputy secretary of defense, who was joined by Brigadier General Craig Rafferty, the commander of US Special Operations Command (SOCOM), and Marlin Lackey, the undersecretary of defense for irregular warfare and counterterrorism.

Salter began by asking Middleton if he had been able to connect with Holcumb about Kuwait and Mutairi.

In his Cajun accent, Middleton said, "Yessir, I reckon I'm up to snuff."

Holcumb concurred.

"Great. Then let's get started. Do we have anyone on video or remote?"

The watch team comms officer replied through the room's speakers: "Yes, sir. We have Russell Adams, the director of investigations at DSS."

"Hello, Mr. Adams. I don't believe we've met. I'm Bob Salter, the president's chief of staff. With me today in the Situation Room are representatives from Langley, Energy, and the DOD. I don't have a lot of time this morning, so I wonder if you could brief us on the status of your investigation."

"Certainly. Let me begin by apologizing for not being able to join you in person. But my schedule—"

Salter interrupted. "No need to apologize. We understand. Now please fill us in on the status of your investigation."

"Well, our investigation is being led by one of our senior agents, Elliot Jones. Elliot and his team are flying back from Jakarta at this very moment. They were in Jakarta to interview the secretary and her security detail."

"Right. She was there for a UN Climate Conference. Correct?"

"Yes, sir. I believe she gets back to Washington on Thursday. Now, while our investigation is ongoing, we can say with a high degree of certainty that the Russians had a hand in the assassination of Mutairi. We have the slug, we have the weapon, they match, and both were made in Russia. We also have not one but two Russian agents on tape discussing the hit."

"The Russians?" Salter exclaimed. "Why would the Russians want to kill Kuwait's oil minister?"

"Last week we met with folks from the CIA and the NSA to discuss that very issue. I think I see Audrey Ackerman in the room. Audrey participated in that meeting. Perhaps she would like to respond to your question."

"Bob, if I may?" Susan Holcumb, Audrey's boss, asked.

"Yes, of course."

"Thanks. Like us, the Russians are running low on oil. The Kremlin is desperate to find more. I believe you know about the auction being conducted in Iraq tomorrow."

"Yes. I believe they discovered a huge field out in the Anbar Province."

"Right. Well, the Russians are pulling out all the stops in order to win as many concessions as possible, and that includes bribing Iraqi officials and killing Mutairi."

"But I don't understand. How does killing Mutairi increase Russia's chances of success in the auction?" Salter asked.

"It actually doesn't. Killing Mutairi served no purpose. At least not in Moscow. Mutairi was not particularly interested in Iraq's auction. He was focused on increasing Kuwait's production of oil. But the Russians believed he was the key to Kuwait's efforts and that Kuwait had the best shot at winning some of the bids. We think the Russians misread the intel. They also endangered Secretary Farnsworth's life. As I believe you know, she was sitting four inches from Mutairi in a crowded and dark theater when he was shot."

Very few things got past Bob Salter. His attention to detail was extraordinary.

"Thanks, Susan. Russ, I believe you said earlier that Russia had 'a hand' in Mutairi's death. Did anyone else?"

"This is the part of our investigation that remains ongoing. Let me separate what we know from what we don't. We know that Mutairi was poisoned. We know that—"

"Whoa, whoa. Wait a minute," Salter insisted. "Mutairi was shot *and* poisoned?"

"Yes, sir. And we know who did it, how it was done, and the type of poison used. The problem is that our suspect is dead. He washed up face down six days ago on the banks of the Potomac a few miles below Alexandria with his fingertips removed."

"So I'll ask essentially the same question I asked a minute ago. Who would want to *poison* Mutairi?"

"The short answer is we don't know. If we can identify our water-logged suspect, we may find out. We'll just have to see."

"What about Kuwait?" Salter asked. "Could they be behind this?"

As he asked the question, Salter looked around the room. Everyone knew why he asked. Salter could not, however, reveal what he was thinking to Adams—that the Kuwaitis were behind this, that they had uncovered Mutairi's plot and put a stop to it. This was Khashoggi 2.0.

"Well, sir. We just don't know. It's certainly possible. Although I can't imagine why they would want to kill one of their own."

"All right, everyone. Let's take a quick break. Mr. Adams, thank you for joining us. We'll let you go, but please keep my office informed of any developments in your investigation."

"Yes, of course. Thank you," said Adams. The video and audio connection ended.

Salter stood. He asked everyone not to go far. "We'll reconvene in ten minutes."

* * *

Once everyone was seated, Salter described the task before them.

"America is running short of oil. So are Russia and a lot of other countries. We can build more pipelines, dig more wells, but none of that will address the near-term problem we face. Now, we thought we had a line of sight to more oil and fuel in Kuwait. The death of Mohammed Al-Mutairi, Kuwait's oil minister, changed that. Hopefully our companies will do well in tomorrow's auction in Bagdad. But even if they do, the president is concerned about the price of gasoline over the next 12 months. I don't have to tell you he faces a difficult path to reelection if oil is at $150 or $175 per barrel and gas is $8 or $9 a gallon this time next year. Therefore we need to give the president options. If not Kuwait, then what? I need this group's best ideas by the end of next week, the 15th. Meet among yourselves. Put something together and get it to me by then. Needless to say, this is TS/SCI classification within your agencies. Any questions?"

Chapter Thirty-Eight

A Washington State Patrol (WSP) officer and a member of the governor's staff were waiting for Elliot when he exited customs and immigration. It was the second time he had passed through Sea-Tac Airport in the past month. The young staffer offered to help Elliot with his luggage. He politely declined. He only had one suitcase and one small backpack that contained his laptop and papers.

An unmarked WSP squad car sat out front in a loading zone. After stowing his gear in the trunk, Elliot got in the back seat. The staffer held the door for him.

The ride down to Olympia was uneventful and even though (or perhaps because) it was a Monday, it was slow. The two- to three-mile stretch through Fife and Tacoma should have taken five minutes. Instead it took nearly twenty. The WSP officer said traffic was always bad in that part of I-5. He apologized. He also apologized for the weather. The clouds hung low, as did the temperature. A steady rain fell. Needless to say, the *mountain* was <u>not</u> *out*.

Elliot slept well on the flight from Jakarta to Tokyo. On the flight from Tokyo to Seattle he spent most of his time working. As a result, he had difficulty staying awake in the car.

They dropped him off at the Red Lion Inn & Suites in Olympia at 5:00 p.m. They said a car would pick Elliot and his family up in the morning around 10:00. The award ceremony would start in the governor's office in the Capitol at around 11:00 a.m. on Tuesday.

He was excited to see Karen and Rachel. He hoped they would be excited to see him. He was not disappointed. As he unlocked the door they exploded in squeals of joy. Hugs and kisses quickly followed.

After he unpacked and freshened up, Elliot suggested they go out for dinner. Karen and Rachel breathed a sigh of relief. They were starving. They had skipped lunch. They were afraid he might be too tired to go out. They excitedly described the restaurants they were most interested in. Elliot said he didn't care. "Just pick one and let's go. I don't want to be out late."

They ate at Anthony's Homeport on the water. Unfortunately, the low clouds cut down on the views, but it was still nice to be on the water. The food was fine and the prices were reasonable. Elliot liked that. He was particularly glad to sit with his back to the wall. He didn't say anything to Karen or Rachel, but he was concerned about their safety. Thankfully his actions did not betray his thoughts. Had that happened it would have been a major buzz kill.

* * *

The Washington State Capitol campus was impressive. A collection of five buildings, including the Supreme Court and the Governor's Mansion, sat on a hill. The centerpiece, however, was the Legislative Building with its 287-foot-high dome—thought to be the tallest masonry dome in the Western Hemisphere. The capitol was where the members of the state's House of Representatives and Senate met.

Elliot and his family, escorted by two WSP officers, arrived at the capitol's north entrance close to 10:30 a.m. As they exited the van about a dozen reporters, some with TV cameras, descended. Some shouted questions. Others were there just to record the moment. Elliot did not speak and tried to avoid eye contact. Rachel and Karen found the whole experience rather exciting. Elliot did not.

The north entrance of the Legislative Building sits atop 42 steps made of granite. One of the officers noted that the number of steps was noteworthy because Washington was the forty-second state to join the Union, which it did in 1889. Inside the rotunda hung the largest bronze chandelier made by Tiffany & Co. in the world. In the center of the floor was the state seal featuring an image of George Washington in polished brass. According to some, more than 500 images of Washington appeared throughout the state capitol.

Governor Tracey Elder was incredibly gracious to Elliot and his family. So too were the Senate majority leader and the speaker of the House. Captain Kowalski was there, as were ten members of the WSP, including Officer Romano. Elliot was particularly delighted to see some of the deckhands from the *Chehalis*, including Pete Langlie. He joked with them before the ceremony began.

"I told Romano I thought you guys were frigging brave. If I had been in your shoes I think I would have jumped off the other end of the ferry."

As Governor Elder approached the lectern, Elliot asked Kowalski in a hushed voice why Romano was not receiving the same honor. "He deserves it."

"I agree," Kowalski whispered. "But the statute establishing the award expressly states that cops, firefighters, and others acting in their official capacity are not eligible."

The governor began by thanking the crew of the *Chehalis* and Officer Romano for their hard work and bravery. She then presented Elliot with one of the state's highest honors, the Medal of Valor. According to Governor

Elder, fewer than 10 people had received the award since its inception in 2015. She then asked Elliot to say a few words. The invite caught Elliot off guard. He wasn't used to that sort of thing. He did the best he could.

"Thank you, Governor, for this award, and thank you for your kind words. I am truly honored. It was a magnificent day on the *Chehalis*. The weather was perfect. You have a beautiful state. I just happened to see something, so I said something. Had it not been me, I'm sure someone else in my situation would have done the same thing. Thank you."

Kowalski looked at Romano. Both tried to hide the smirks on their faces. Both had the same thought: *No damn way. Very few people would have done the same thing. This guy's a frigging hero!*

Chapter Thirty-Nine

After the ceremony Captain Kowalski invited Elliot and his family to join him for lunch. Just as Elliot was about to accept, Karen reminded him that Rachel had classes in the morning and their flight back to Washington left at 8:00 a.m. "We should get going," Karen said. "Traffic will probably be bad."

Kowalski said he understood. "Let me at least get you a van or car to take you. Do you have your luggage with you or is it back at the hotel?"

"We've already checked out," Elliot said. "We left our things with capitol security."

"Great. Then let's get you on your way," Kowalski said.

A WSP officer walked in front. Captain Kowalski walked slightly behind with Elliot. As they walked across the rotunda, the officer stopped to explain the state seal in the floor and the giant chandelier overhead to Karen and Rachel. Elliot stood back with Kowalski. In a low voice he asked the captain about the status of his investigation. Kowalski explained that Mark remained in jail. The judge denied him bail. The couple in the Boston Whaler remained at large.

Elliot was about to ask a follow-up question when Karen came over and asked, "Isn't that interesting, honey?"

"Yeah, it sure is." He had no idea what she was talking about.

After retrieving their luggage from security they exited the capitol building through the heavy glass and metal doors on the north side. A WSP officer passed through first, followed by Karen and Rachel. Elliot started to hold the door for Kowalski, but the latter insisted that Elliot walk with his family. So Elliot released his hold on the door. As he turned to resume walking he noticed two people, a middle-aged man and woman, standing on the steps of the capitol about fifteen feet away. They didn't seem to be entering the building or leaving. Instead, they appeared to be taking pictures of the capitol and its dome like any other tourists, except at the last minute as Elliot and his family passed, the man looked directly at Elliot and snapped a photo with his phone. Was he taking a photo of Elliot because he was being escorted by police and might be somebody important or did he recognize Elliot from all the media coverage? Elliot made a mental note of their features and dress. He couldn't help but wonder if they weren't the same people on the Boston Whaler. He kept his thoughts to himself. He didn't want to scare Karen or Rachel.

The ride north to Seattle on I-5 was routine. As Karen predicted, traffic was heavy, especially through Fife and Tacoma. No one noticed the gray pickup truck that followed them. As they got closer to Seattle, Karen and Elliot debated whether to have the van drop them off at their hotel downtown or at Rachel's dormitory. They hated to say goodbye to their daughter any sooner than necessary, so they asked the driver to drop them off on the UW campus—besides, Karen wanted to see Rachel's dorm.

Hansee Hall was built in 1936. It was the oldest residence hall in continuous use on the UW campus. Covered in red brick in a Tudor Revival style and rising three-and-a-half stories, it had undergone numerous renovations and upgrades over the years. Hansee was located on the north end of the campus just off NE 45th Street. From there it was a short walk to Red

Square, the center of the campus, and to Suzzallo Library, the university's main library. It was also a short walk from Hansee to the cultural center of the university district, the street known simply as the "Ave" (*i.e.*, University Avenue).

They quickly exited I-5 onto NE 45th Street. Traffic was light. They made it across Roosevelt and University Avenues in record time. However, as they approached the entrance to the campus, they could see a line of cars at the security checkpoint. Therefore, they asked the driver to pull over. They would walk.

Elliot and Karen stored their luggage in Rachel's dorm room. They then spent two hours walking around the campus. For the first time that day they were without a police escort.

Rachel wanted to show her parents Husky Stadium and the ASUW Shell House made famous by the movie (and book) *The Boys in the Boat*. Unfortunately, both were on the south end of the campus and there wasn't enough time. She also wanted to show them the incredible view of Mount Rainier framed over the Frosh Pond (aka Drumheller Fountain), but the weather and clouds did not cooperate.

Around 4:00 p.m. they headed back to Rachel's dorm. She needed to study and Karen and Elliot were getting hungry. The hotel they were staying at downtown had a nice restaurant off of the lobby. They could eat there.

Rachel pulled out her phone and ordered a Lyft for her parents. While Karen waited outside for the car to arrive, Rachel and Elliot went upstairs to retrieve their luggage. On the way back down the elevator stopped on two. A very skinny young man got on. Rachel didn't know him. He didn't say anything. When the elevator doors opened, he stood aside to let Rachel and her dad go first. Rachel had barely taken a step when Elliot grabbed her by the arm. "Stop!"

Rachel jerked her head around. "What?" she asked as much out of surprise as anything else.

"Look! Those people your mom is talking to."

Almost instinctively, Rachel again said, "What?" She looked outside. Her mother was talking to two people, a man and a woman probably in their late fifties. Each had a small, black backpack slung over a shoulder.

"Those people were down in Olympia today. Quick, go back up to your room! Call campus police and then STAY IN YOUR ROOM! I'm going outside."

"But—"

"No *but* GODDAMN IT! GO!!" Elliot shoved Rachel back into the elevator. The young man required no encouragement. Even though he had no idea what was happening, he gladly slipped back into the elevator. Elliot reached around and pressed the button to close the door. Rachel had never seen her dad so anxious before.

Approaching the dorm's front doors, Elliot assessed the situation. The Lyft had arrived. Karen stood at the front left corner of the car. The couple stood closer to the driver. The driver appeared to be a twentysome-thing Asian male. His window was down, as was his head. He was probably looking at his phone. A constant stream of students entered and exited the building. It was a typical Tuesday afternoon and school was in session.

As soon as Elliot passed through the doors, Karen asked, "Where's Rachel? I want to say goodbye to her."

"She forgot something. She had to go back up to her room. She'll be down in a minute." Elliot stood next to the man.

Karen's natural tendency under these circumstances was to make polite small talk. So it wasn't surprising when she said to Elliot, "Honey, these folks are from Florida. They're here visiting their son, who is also a freshman."

"Nice," Elliot said. "What part of Florida?"

"We're from the southern part of Florida. Along the Gulf of Mexico."

"Oh, down around Tallahassee?"

"Yeah," the man said.

Up until that moment Elliot was not *completely* certain these people were the ones on the Capitol steps. Up until that moment Elliot was not *completely* convinced these people meant his family harm. Now all doubt vanished. These people weren't from Florida. Most people know Tallahassee is the capital of Florida and even if they don't, Tallahassee is in the far north of Florida, not the south. No resident of Florida would make that mistake. What should he do? His wife was standing right there.

"Say, aren't you the guy who stopped that bombing on the ferry? I saw your photo in the paper the other day." As he placed his backpack on the hood of the car the man said, "Can I get your autograph? I think I have a pen and paper in here."

The instant Elliot saw the butt of the gun rise from the backpack he did two things. First, he yelled as loud as he could at Karen—"RUN!!" Second, he lunged as hard as he could into the man, driving his face onto the hood of the car. Karen was caught completely off guard as was the Lyft driver, who dropped his phone.

Not surprisingly, Karen hesitated. A second earlier she had been relaxed and happy. Now she was in a state of panic and shock. Who wouldn't be under those circumstances? But when the man on the hood of the car yelled at the woman, "SHOOT HER," Karen snapped out of it.

She turned and ran as fast as she could, screaming over and over again—"Oh, God, oh, God, oh, God ..." She was hysterical. She bumped into people without apologizing. Tears swelled in her eyes and snot streamed from her nose.

At the same time, Elliot tried to hold the man down on the hood of the car with as much of his body weight and force as possible. He even pressed his face down on the man, anything to exert pressure and trap the man like a wrestler trying to pin his opponent. Meanwhile, with his left hand Elliot groped for the gun in the backpack. As he did, he could feel the man's left hand frantically doing the same thing. Once or twice they scratched each other with their fingernails.

Students and other passersby looked on in horror at what was happening on the normally peaceful campus. Shouts of "oh, my god" and "call the police" echoed off the walls of Hansee Hall. At least a dozen people stood back recording the moment on their cell phones.

The Lyft driver was also in a state of shock. A life-and-death struggle was taking place on the hood of his car! He tried to retrieve his phone from the floor of his car. He needed to call 911. But before he could, he happened to touch the pistol he kept under his seat. He had never used it. It was there for emergencies. Wasn't this an emergency? In a state of total panic and breathing rapidly, he jumped out of his car, a Smith & Wesson .44 Magnum Model 29 revolver in his right hand. His immediate attention was on the men struggling less than a foot away. What should he do? Hit them with the butt end of the gun? Shoot one of them? But which one? His quandary was resolved when he looked at the woman standing at the front of his car. She had what looked like a pistol in her hand. She was taking aim at Karen as she ran away.

The .44 Magnum is one of the most powerful handguns in the world. Clint Eastwood famously used one in his 1971 movie *Dirty Harry* and again his 1973 movie *Magnum Force*. Call it beginner's luck or divine intervention, but the Lyft driver saved Karen's life. The slug from his .44 Magnum entered the back of the lady's skull just below where the occipital and parietal bones meet. When it exited it took the woman's face with it. In fact, the force of the slug was so great that after traveling through her skull, it came within an inch of passing through one of Hansee's foot-thick concrete-and-brick walls.

There is nothing subtle about the .44 Magnum. When discharged it sounds more like a cannon than a pistol or rifle. The sound from the gun was still reverberating when Elliot lifted his head. Had Karen been shot? He had to know. In that moment, though, he gave the man beneath him an opportunity. Instead of trying to retrieve the gun from his backpack, the man pulled his left elbow back as fast and as hard as he could. He caught Elliot flush on the chin. He was out before his head hit the ground.

The man was now able to grab the gun in his backpack. He turned around. First he looked to his right. His wife, or what was left of her, lay motionless in a pool of blood. The man responsible for his son's arrest and now his wife's death was at his feet. Next he pointed his gun at the Lyft driver.

"I ain't got no fight with you," the man said quickly and out of breath. "Put your gun down and I won't hurt you."

The Lyft driver hesitated. He was completely out of his league. What should he do? Again circumstances made his decision for him.

"Put down your weapons," shouted a campus police officer. Both the Lyft driver and the man looked in the direction of the command. The Lyft driver was smart. He dropped his weapon. The man was not so smart. His first mistake was when he turned in the direction of the officer. His second mistake was when he raised his weapon to shoot.

The magazine capacity of a .40 caliber Glock is 15 rounds. Three entered the man's chest cavity before he hit the ground. But before he did, he was thrown back violently onto the hood of the car before sliding down the side of it in a river of blood. When the shooting finally stopped, the north entrance of Hansee Hall looked like a scene out of a Quentin Tarantino film.

* * *

When Elliot regained consciousness Rachel and Karen were at his side. He was still on the ground, but now he was covered in blood and surrounded by ambulances, police cruisers, police tape, and two fire trucks. The lights from all the emergency vehicles bounced off Hansee Hall and the surrounding trees like a nightclub.

An EMT checked Elliot's vitals. "How do you feel, Mr. Jones?"

Elliot ignored the question. Instead he reached for his wife and daughter. "You guys okay?"

"Yes, we're fine. But how are you?"

"I'm fine." But as he touched his jaw he amended his answer. "Except my jaw hurts like hell." He started to get up, but as soon as he did he laid back down.

"Damn, my head hurts." He couldn't help but notice that he was covered in blood. "Was I hit?"

"No, Mr. Jones. You weren't shot. That's Mr. Mark's blood. When campus police shot him, he basically fell on you. But you did take a pretty nasty blow to your head. You need to take it easy. I can give you something for your headache. Do you normally take ibuprofen for that sort of thing?"

Elliot and Karen said yes at the same time.

"Okay, here's some water. I'll get you some extra-strength ibuprofen out of the rig. If you feel good enough to sit up, go ahead. But don't stand. Wait until I get back."

As soon as the EMT departed, a police officer arrived and knelt next to Elliot. "Mr. Jones. Hello. I'm Officer Reynolds. How are you feeling?"

"Except for a bad headache, I think I'm okay. What happened after I blacked out? The last thing I remember is fighting with the guy on the hood of the car."

"Well, it appears the Lyft driver shot Mrs. Mark as she was about to shoot your wife and Officer Carlson shot Mr. Mark in self-defense."

"You say *Mark*. Were these guys related to the bomber?"

"They were his parents," the officer said.

"Geez. What about the Lyft driver? Is he okay?" Elliot asked.

"Yeah, he's fine. A little rattled, but he's fine."

Elliot turned to Karen. "Honey, we need to thank that guy. He saved your life."

Seeing Elliot turn and speak caused two dozen reporters being held back by police tape to shout Elliot's name. At least half held either a microphone or TV camera. The lights from all the cameras were blinding.

Officer Reynolds couldn't help but quip, "Mr. Jones, you make news every time you come here. First the *Chehalis* and now this."

"I can assure you, it is *not* my intention to make news."

"I'm sure. In any case, medical is going to take you down to the UW Hospital for observation and so you can get cleaned up. It's just a few blocks away. I'm going to stay here with your wife and daughter. I need to finish getting their statements and tying up some loose ends. Once all of that is done, I can bring them and your luggage down to the hospital. Sound like a plan?"

"Yes, sir. Thanks."

* * *

The hospital discharged Elliot a little after 7:00 pm. A taxi dropped all three of them off at the Hotel Monaco on 4th avenue around 7:45 pm. Luckily, Elliot and Karen were able to get Rachel a room down the hall from theirs.

At dinner they discussed what they should do. Elliot thought Rachel should finish out the fall term in Seattle and then assess possible moves. Karen wanted to pull her out now and try to transfer to George Mason or another school closer to home. In the end, they agreed it was not their decision to make. Rachel was 19. She had wanted to go to UW. Within reason, they would support whatever she wanted to do. They also agreed that Karen would extend her stay in Seattle by another day or two. She hated to leave her *baby*. Elliot wanted to do the same, but he had to get back to Washington.

Chapter Forty

There is nothing particularly remarkable about a government having more than one national security or intelligence service. The examples are legion: MI5 and MI6 in the UK, the CIA and FBI in the United States, and the FSB and SVR in Russia, to name a few.

Oftentimes one agency will take the lead on foreign intelligence and threats, and the other will focus on domestic counterintelligence. That was the case, at least on paper, in Egypt. The General Intelligence Service, often referred to as El-Mukhabarat, had primary responsibility for foreign intelligence and the HS, led by Abdul Rasham, led on domestic security.

Rasham walked out of his office in downtown Cairo around 10:00 a.m. local time. His security detail, which had been seated in chairs in the spacious outer office on the fourth floor, jumped to their feet. Rasham motioned for them to relax. He didn't need his car. He was meeting an old friend at a nearby coffee shop. He would walk.

Two minutes later Rasham exited the east gate of HS on Abd Al-Aziz Gaweash. He was surrounded by four heavily armed men, all with dark hair, dark moustaches, and dark suits.

Kuwait has numerous national security and intelligence services. The National Police is primarily responsible for domestic security. The National Guard takes the lead on foreign intelligence matters. Most of the time they cooperate with each other; however, like many government agencies around the world, they compete for budgets and the favor of their boss. In the case of Kuwait the boss was Crown Prince Sabah Al-Ahmad Al-Sabah.

Faisal Al-Ahmad Al-Khaled was the director of Kuwait's National Police. When Khaled sent Rasham an e-mail earlier in the week telling him he would be in Cairo for a few days attending a conference, Rasham suggested they meet for coffee. He thought this would not only be a good chance to catch up with Khaled, but also possibly help Elliot. He had a photo of Raouf Allen in the right breast pocket of his suit jacket.

It was a short walk to Cafe Eish on Noubar Street. It wasn't fancy. In fact, everything about it was old and cheap. To make matters worse, things were taped or stuck to the walls in a haphazard manner, like the plastic banner with cheap triangular images of the Egyptian flag that was strung across the cafe's three windows and held in place with scotch tape. Put simply, no tourist was going to find Cafe Eish on Tripadvisor or Yelp, but it served good coffee, was close to Rasham's office, and was owned and operated by a retired SSI officer.

Two members of Rasham's security detail entered the cafe first. Only two young women sat at a table by the door. They had finished their coffees and were about to leave. The men flashed them their badges and held the door for them. They left quickly without saying a word.

Rasham sat down at a small table near the back. The table felt dirty, as did the old wooden chairs. The floor looked worse, with crumpled napkins and falafel crumbs strewn about. A member of Rasham's detail ordered him a double cappuccino from the young man behind the counter. Two members of the detail took up positions at the door. The other two stood next to Rasham's table.

Just as his coffee was being set down on the table, two men in suits who looked remarkably similar to the men in Rasham's security detail opened the door. Khaled stood a few feet behind them. Luckily Rasham saw him; otherwise, guns might have been drawn.

"Faisal, come in. Please."

Instantly the competing security details parted. Rasham met Khaled in the middle of the cafe.

It had been several years since they had met in person. The greeting was warm. Rasham gently clasped Khaled's elbows. Khaled returned the gesture by grasping Rasham's arms below the elbow. Both wore big smiles. As Rasham leaned forward to kiss Khaled's left check, he said, "*as-salàmu alaykum*."

Then, as Khaled moved to kiss Rasham's right check, ending with a kiss again of the left check, he returned the greeting. "*Wa alaykumu-ssalaam*."

With the formalities satisfied, Rasham took one step back and to the side. As he did, he motioned with his right hand toward the table. "Faisal, please, have a seat. Would you like a coffee?"

"Yes, thank you. That sounds good. I'll have a black coffee, please."

Rasham motioned to the same member of his detail who had ordered his cappuccino. The man nodded and went back to the counter.

For the next fifteen minutes they discussed nothing but family, friends, and world events. On at least two occasions customers tried to enter the cafe. Each time the guards at the door gently but firmly turned them away.

When Khaled finished his coffee, Rasham asked him if he wanted another.

"No, thanks, but I would welcome some water."

"Of course." Rasham motioned to one of the men in his detail to get a water.

Rasham sensed that Khaled might need to leave soon. Therefore, he decided to broach the subject of Mutairi. He began by offering his condolences. "Faisal, I am so sorry to hear about Mohammed Al-Mutairi. May God have mercy on him."

"Yes," Khaled said, "very sad. A sudden heart attack while attending the opera in Washington."

Rasham tried his best to be gentle. He did not want to seem aggressive. In a hushed tone he said, "I must tell you, Faisal, that is not what I heard."

"What did you hear?"

"I'm sorry, but I heard he was killed. Shot while attending the opera in Washington. Someone also tried to poison him."

"Who did you hear that from?"

"I'm sorry, Faisal, I can't say. But I can tell you that the Russians know and obviously the Americans know. They know it wasn't a heart attack. Secretary Farnsworth was sitting right next to him when it happened."

In an instant the Kuwaiti's manner changed. He leaned forward and whispered. "Abdul, there are many rumors in my country."

Rasham lowered his voice even more. "What sort of rumors?"

"I can't say for sure, but there are rumors that the National Guard had a hand in this."

"Why? Why would—"

"I don't know. His Royal Highness loved Mutairi. So did the crown prince, but Mutairi was quoted in the papers saying critical things about the government. I don't know." He repeated what he was most comfortable saying. "There are lots of rumors." His voice trailed off.

"Faisal, take a look at this." Rasham showed him the photo of Raouf Allen. "Have you ever seen this person before? The Americans believe his name is Raouf. They're not sure about his family name. Perhaps Alam, Alim, Alavi, or something similar."

"I don't think so. Who is he?"

"The Americans believe this is the person who killed Mutairi."

Rasham was playing a little *fast and loose* with the facts, and he knew it. Elliot never told him Raouf killed Mutairi or even that Raouf *tried* to kill Mutairi. He simply asked Rasham if he could help identify the person in the photograph. At the same time, Rasham was no fool. He knew precisely why Elliot wanted his help.

"Can I have this?" Khaled asked. "I'd like to show it to a few of my colleagues."

"Certainly. But to be clear, the person in that photograph is dead. He was found floating in the Potomac River in Washington about one week ago."

"I see. Very interesting. Well, I have a luncheon appointment at the Four Seasons in half an hour. I need to run. It was good talking to you."

"You as well."

"I'll let you know if I learn anything about this person."

"*Shukran,*" Rasham said shaking his hand.

"*Bkhatirkon,*" Khaled replied.

"*Ma'ssalaame.*"

Chapter Forty-One

Iraq's oil minister, Hussain Rashid, entered the room at 11:00 a.m. local time on Tuesday. He was followed by eight officials from the Ministries of Oil and Interior. Four sat in chairs behind a dais to Rashid's right and four sat to his left. The man to his right carried a sealed manila envelope. Security officials assigned to the Ministry of the Interior's elite Wolf Brigade were stationed at all doors and lined the sides of the room.

Rashid looked around the room. Representatives of all the major oil and gas companies were present—BP, Chevron, Exxon, Shell, and Total, to name a few. Jim Farnsworth and Oleg Krychuk sat next to each other in the second row. To describe Farnsworth as anxious would have been an understatement.

A half dozen television cameras mounted on tripods stretched across the back of the room. Their bright lights made it difficult for the government officials to see. Once his eyes adjusted, Rashid took the envelope from the man to his right and stood behind the podium. On the front of the podium was affixed the seal of Iraq's Ministry of Oil.

In addition to being broadcast on various television and radio stations, the results were live-streamed on the ministry's website. In Bali,

Indonesia, 5,400 miles away, Lynne and Fhani monitored the results. Both had a notepad and laptop in front of them. As the leases were announced, Lynne and Fhani recorded the lease number, the winner, and the approximate size of each parcel.

It took nearly ninety minutes for all of the results to be announced. In all, Iraq awarded leases covering eighty-three percent of the new field. Rashid said a decision on whether to auction off the remaining seventeen percent would be made before the end of the year.

Chevron, Exxon, and BP did well. Each was awarded two leases. Shell and Total each won one. Japanese and Chinese companies also secured one each. However, the day's big winner was Qatar. Qatar's state-owned oil company, QatarEnergy Company, won four leases covering nearly 750 square miles, and another company based in Qatar, Qatar Gulf Oil Company, won two about half that size. To Jim's utter astonishment, Kuwait Petroleum Corporation was awarded only one lease. Russia and Kyrgyzstan? Nothing.

Once the final results were announced, Fhani and Lynne jumped for joy like schoolkids. Jim Farnsworth was devastated.

"Madam Secretary," Fhani said as he kissed her, "this calls for a toast." Her head tilted back ever so slightly as she let out a laugh that was as much a sigh of relief as it was an expression of joy. This was the perfect result.

Fhani picked up the phone. The person on the other end spoke. "Good afternoon. Room service."

"Good afternoon. Could I get a bottle of chilled Veuve Clicquot Brut and beluga caviar?"

"Yes, of course, sir. Would that be for two?"

As he spoke, Lynne slipped off her sundress and dove into the pool. Her bathing suit was hanging up in the bathroom. Fhani was distracted for a moment. "What?"

Room service repeated the question. "For two, sir?"

"Yes."

"Is that all, sir?"

"Yes, thank you." He hung up the phone.

While Lynne relaxed in the pool, Fhani retrieved a floating tray he had seen in one of the closets.

"What's that?" Lynne asked.

"You'll see."

Ten minutes later Fhani greeted the waiter at the door.

"Sir, would you like me to open the champagne for you? I'd be happy to set a table for you by the pool."

"No, thank you. That won't be necessary. I can take it from here."

"As you wish, sir. Please let room service know when you are done and we can come back to clean things up."

"Thank you."

For the next two hours they drank champagne, laughed, and ate caviar from their floating tray in the pool. Lynne couldn't remember the last time she spent that much time in the water naked!

* * *

After dinner Fhani asked Lynne where she was going to have the funds deposited.

"I don't know. I have an account at the Senate Federal Credit Union and a brokerage account with Fidelity. The account at the credit union is a joint account with Jim. So that won't work. Do you have any suggestions? It needs to be somewhere safe, secure, and private."

"Well, it's hard to beat the Swiss banks. And the most secret is probably Pictet Bank in Geneva."

"Pictet? I never heard of it."

"And they want to keep it that way," he said with a smile. "It's actually one of the oldest banks in Switzerland. Very exclusive."

"Really? Okay, I guess I can always move some or all of the funds somewhere else after the initial deposit is made. Can you help me set it up? I'm not very good with computers and technical stuff."

"Sure. But you need a personal laptop or phone to open an account. Preferably one not connected to a carrier in the United States. Your phone and laptop are linked to State."

"Yes, but I also have a personal cell phone that I use for personal calls, texts, and e-mails. It's with AT&T. Not the best service in and around Washington, but superior to all other US carriers overseas."

"It's up to you. You can use that phone, but it'd be better if you had another phone, a third one, not registered with a US carrier."

"How do I do that? Where can I get such a phone?"

"Well, I happen to have one you can use." Fhani reached into a satchel by the bed. "Here it is. It's registered to a company in the Cayman Islands. I don't use it anymore."

"You sure?"

"Absolutely. Like I said, I don't use it anymore."

"Thanks, Sam. That's very kind of you."

"Of course."

She leaned forward and kissed him on the cheek.

"You can download the Pictet app to that phone. Establish a user name and password. Give them that phone number. Then, whenever you access the account they'll send you a temporary passcode. Enter that code and you're good to go."

"Okay, but what's the number for this phone?"

"Huh. You know? I don't remember. It's been so long since I used it. Let me check. I have it written down somewhere."

"Thanks. Then let's do it," Lynne said. "And once we're finished, I'll send the bank account and routing information to my contacts in Doha."

Chapter Forty-Two

Lake and Young had left Washington in October. They arrived back in November. The weather in Washington during November could be as varied as the spots on a starling. It could be seventy-seven degrees and sunny one day and nineteen degrees and snowy the next.

The rain in Washington was light that Tuesday morning. It was so light that Young took the metro to work and walked the two blocks from the Rosslyn Metro Station to the DSS offices on North Lynn Street. The temperature was mild, a high of 64 degrees Fahrenheit by 2:00 p.m. Unfortunately for Young, he did not keep track of the weather that day and he ate lunch at his desk. Thus, when he came down the elevator at 6:30 p.m. he had every intention of repeating his morning routine, except in reverse.

He had barely taken a step out of the elevator when he realized he and Mother Nature were not on the same page. The rain was coming down in buckets and the temperature had dropped.

He stood to the side of the building's revolving doors, looking out the glass walls of the lobby. He had a raincoat in his left hand and an umbrella in his right hand. He pondered his options.

Lake exited the elevator around 6:35 p.m. As she had many times before, she turned to her right and started to walk over to the elevators that connected to the parking garage below. This night, however, she glanced to her left for no particular reason. It took a second, but she soon realized that the forlorn figure standing there looking at the downpour was Vic Young. She hesitated. Should she offer him a ride home or keep walking to her car? He was, after all, a big boy. He could order a taxi or rideshare. In that moment, however, her growing appreciation of Young surfaced. He was a nice guy. Indeed, a gentlemen. He was in great shape. Good looking. Smart. What's not to like?

She walked up behind Young. "It's only two blocks to the metro. You're not going to let a little rain stop you, are you?"

Young turned around. Lake stood there with a big smile on her face.

"Oh, hi." Young chuckled. "Yeah, it's coming down pretty hard. I was going to take the metro home. I guess I was so busy today I never really paid much attention to the weather."

"Come on. Let me give you a ride."

"No, you don't have to. I'll order an Uber."

"No, I insist."

"You sure?"

"Absolutely. Come on." Lake turned and headed for the garage elevators. Young followed.

In the garage Young asked Lake about the car she unlocked. "What's this? A Beamer?"

"Yeah, an X3. I wanted an SUV, but I also wanted something relatively small and easy to maneuver. To tell you the truth, I kind of wish I had gotten a Honda CR-V or maybe a Mazda CX-5. You pay extra for the Beamer name."

"What happened to the Jag?"

"Oh… I still have it. But there's no way I'm going to drive it in weather like this. In fact, in the five years I've had it, I don't think it has ever been driven in the rain."

* * *

She turned south on to the GW Parkway. Stretching from north of the CIA to George Washington's estate down in Mount Vernon, the Parkway hugged the Potomac River for over 25 miles.

Their conversation was light and lively. They had a lot to talk about. They had spent essentially two days together on a plane. They had spent an entire day sightseeing in Jakarta. And when they weren't on a plane or playing tourist, they were working together on the same high-profile murder investigation. It was during this period that they both came to the same realization: neither posed a professional threat to the other. Thus, while Young had initially thought Lake was trying to upstage him with her knowledge of toxins and weapons, he had come to the conclusion that she was simply smart. There was no pretense. There was no agenda. Just a beautiful, capable woman.

The rain had essentially stopped when Lake pulled up to Young's place. Young reached for the handle. "Thanks for the ride, Alice, see you tomorrow." What came next totally surprised him.

"Aren't you going to invite me up for a drink?"

"But the last—"

"But that was last time. This is this time," she said with a smile.

"Sure," Young said excitedly. "That'd be great." He couldn't believe it. Was he dreaming?

She followed him up the steps to the front door. As Young fumbled for his keys, he said to himself, *Be cool, Vic, be cool.*

He opened the door for her. She thanked him and entered. When she heard the door close behind her she wheeled around. Without hesitating she pressed her body hard against his, so hard that Young was slammed back against the door. Her kiss was voracious and open-mouthed. Lest there be any doubt about her intentions, she raised her right leg and wrapped it tightly around Young's legs. Young got the message. Using both hands, he grabbed her firm ass and pulled her hard against him.

Chapter Forty-Three

Wednesday afternoon came too soon. Lynne hated to leave Fhani, but duty called. The president wanted to meet with her in the Oval Office Saturday morning. When she inquired about the topic, she was simply told it had something to do with Russia. That could mean any number of things. She asked her CoS, Peter Drinker, to inquire.

Her C32A took off from Ngurah Rai International Airport at 1:25 p.m. on Wednesday. It disappeared into the sky over Bali before the red carpet at the base of the plane's stairs could be rolled up.

Normally she would have been joined on board by half a dozen State Department and embassy personnel, plus anywhere between five and ten members of the press corps. This trip would be different. Because she was headed back home after a long personal weekend, the press that normally followed her every move had returned to Washington on Sunday with Ambassador Burns and his team of climate specialists. So had Peter Drinker and two senior FS officers who always traveled with the secretary. Only two mid-level FS officers stationed in Jakarta, a young man and a young woman, were seated in the senior staff area of the plane in case

Lynne needed help with anything. Lynne spent most of the trip working at her desk or watching television. She only ate once at her desk.

Then somewhere over the northern reaches of Saskatchewan DSS Agent Payne knocked on the secretary's door. He was accompanied by an Air Force colonel. "Madam Secretary, I'm sorry to disturb ya. Could we have a minute?" Payne asked.

"Certainly, come in." Lynne was seated behind the desk in her office. Notepads and notebooks competed with telephones and laptops for space on the desk. As she sat back in her chair and put her reading glasses on the desk, Lynne asked, "Roger, what can I help you with?"

"Ma'am, this here's Colonel Frank Richardson, the senior officer on today's flight."

"Hello, Colonel. I don't believe we've met."

"No, ma'am. I don't believe we have. I typically travel with the vice president or the First Lady."

Payne got to the point. "Ma'am, we'll be touching down at Andrews in 'bout two hours. When we land you might see some extra security folks 'round the tarmac. There ain't no reason for you to fret. I will need you, though, to stay in your office until I come and fetch you. Colonel Richardson and a member of his team will stay with you 'til then."

"What's this all about, Roger?"

"I'm sorry, ma'am, but I can't say more. Again, the only thin' I can say is that the extra security is unrelated to any real or perceived threat to you. I expect I'll be able to explains things better after you get off."

Lynne looked at Payne and the colonel, hoping for more explanation. None was offered.

Ninety minutes later, as her plane began its descent, the secretary powered down her computer and put away her papers. After everything was stowed she sat back in her seat, tightened her seatbelt, and looked out the window. She let out a sigh.

She sat alone with only her thoughts to keep her company. It was a beautiful day in Washington. The sky was blue and the wind was out of the north. She could see the Washington Monument, the Capitol Dome, and other major landmarks in the distance. Everywhere she looked the rolling hills of Maryland and Virginia were bathed in a carpet of orange leaves and green pastures.

As the plane gently turned left over Clinton, Maryland, and began its final approach from the south, she couldn't help but think about Fhani and the magical weekend she had spent with him. They swam in waters as blue and clear as the sky she now gazed off into. She was in love. She ached to be with him. She counted the days and minutes until she could.

Her plane landed at 12:45 p.m. on Thursday. As it turned left to taxi back to hangar 5, Lynne could see Air Force One parked down to the south over by the new AF1 hangar in the corner of Andrews. Air Force Two was inside hangar 6 receiving routine service. Lined up in front of hangars 5 and 6 was an assortment of military vehicles and armored black Suburbans. Military police and other personnel stood watching as her plane came to a stop.

In the back Faber and Payne looked out their windows in silence. They knew what was coming. Condon and Abramovich did not. Condon asked Abramovich, "what's with all the security?"

"I have no idea. I was just about to ask you the same thing. Hey, Roger, do you know what's going on?" Abramovich asked.

Payne had no choice but to lie. "I'll be darned if I know. If that's a welcoming committee, it's a mighty peculiar one." He glanced at Faber for a brief moment.

Abramovich stared at the greeting party. He thought he recognized one or two faces. *Was that Agent Jones standing by the black Chevy Suburban on the left? And the man next to him—wasn't that the guy who interviewed him in Jakarta? What the hell?*

When the plane came to a stop, Payne stood to grab his gear in the overhead compartment. It was barely noticeable, but Abramovich saw it. Payne released the safety on his sidearm. Abramovich never saw Faber do the same thing a second later.

Outside, the Air Force ground crew wheeled stairs in to place at the plane's front and mid-doors. Normally, they would have used only one door, with a belt at the back to handle luggage and cargo. DSS agents in dark suits, wearing their ubiquitous aviator sunglasses, took up their usual positions at the base of the stairs and alongside the secretary's vehicle. A supervisor stood alongside the stairs watching everything. Abramovich grew increasingly concerned. Something wasn't right.

Soon the whine of the plane's engines stopped. Abramovich thought it odd that neither the cockpit door nor the door to the secretary's office had opened. Usually Secretary Farnsworth liked to be one of the first to get off. He wasn't sure what to do; therefore, out of habit more than anything else, he pulled his roller board down from the overhead compartment as he contemplated his options. As he bent to pull up its handle, a tiny bead of sweat dropped from his brow.

He was in the back of the plane where the press usually sat. Payne, Faber, and Condon were the closest to him. All were armed. Had he been discovered? If so, what should he do? Surrender? Fight? Maybe he was overreacting.

Just then one of the FS officers who had been working most of the flight in the senior staff area mid-plane came down the aisle to grab a piece of luggage from one of the overhead compartments. As she reached the press quarters at the back of the plane where Abramovich and his colleagues were standing, the plane's forward and mid-doors opened. The first person through each was an Air Force MP in full battle gear, a Sig Sauer XM5 Spear angled downward across their chests. Their hands were in dark combat gloves. Their index fingers were next to the triggers. The second person through the mid-door was Elliot Jones. Agents Young and Lake came through the forward door and took up positions outside the secretary's office.

Elliot immediately locked eyes with Abramovich, who was 20 feet away. As he did he reached for his sidearm. Unlike most DSS agents, who had switched over to the newer Sig Sauer P229 9mm, Elliot liked his old Sig 226. Over many years he had adjusted the trigger to suit his touch. However, on this occasion, he did not draw his pistol. Instead he said in a very loud voice, "Steve Abramovich, you're under arrest for the murder of Mohammad Al-Mutairi and violation of the Espionage Act. I need you to step into the aisle with your hands behind your head."

Everyone on the plane turned to see what was happening. Abramovich did not hesitate. He grabbed the only lifeline available to him—the young woman coming down the aisle. In one motion he drew his weapon and grabbed the girl. Condon was blindsided. Payne and Faber were not. They immediately drew their weapons. Abramovich shot Faber twice in the chest before he could discharge his weapon. Both slugs exited his back in a spray of blood and lodged in the plane cabin's wall. He died within seconds. Next Abramovich shot Payne. He hit Payne between his neck and left shoulder, above the heart. The impact from the slug spun Payne around, causing the round Payne fired to penetrate the plane's cabin over Abramovich's head. Payne fell to the floor in an awkward twisting motion. Blood poured from his wound onto the nearby seats and carpet. Passengers and crew screamed. Young and Lake drew their sidearms. Remarkably, Elliot did not. Instead, as he looked directly at Abramovich, he held his arms out as if to signal he was not a threat.

The last thing Talbot had stressed to Elliot before the plane came to a stop was the importance of taking Abramovich into custody. "We need to interrogate him. The White House may also want to trade him for that newspaper reporter Moscow seized last year."

Twenty minutes ago Elliot was fine with that request. Now? Not so much. Abramovich had shot two DSS agents and was holding an FS officer hostage.

Abramovich pressed his gun tight against the girl's head. A whiff of smoke floated up from the barrel. The smell of sulfur and gunpowder wafted through the cabin. The girl was screaming and twisting in Abramovich's grip. Elliot desperately wanted to tell her to be still and it would all be over.

Using the FS officer as a shield and with his gun still to her head, Abramovich ordered Condon to drop his weapon. "Kick it over here, Wally. I don't want to hurt you."

Condon complied. What Abramovich did next caught even Elliot by surprise.

"I wanna talk to the secretary. If you let me talk to her, I'll let the girl go. Otherwise, she's as good as dead."

The girl screamed uncontrollably. She pleaded for her life. Abramovich did not relent.

Elliot hesitated. Standing next to him now was an FBI agent and a second Air Force MP, weapons raised and aimed at Abramovich. Assistant AG Talbot stood in the doorway of the plane with Ori Levenson a few feet behind. Both wore ballistic vests on the outside of their dark suits.

Elliot tried to reason with Abramovich. With his arms still stretched out wide, he said, "Steve, come on. Put the gun down. Let the girl go."

Just then Payne coughed, the kind of wet cough that comes when one has bronchitis or pneumonia; however, Payne wasn't coughing up phlegm. He was coughing up his own blood, which was now collecting in his mouth and running down his chin.

"Steve, COME ON! Roger needs help or he's going to die! Let the girl go. Put down your weapon!"

"No, not until I talk to the secretary." Abramovich was getting more and more agitated.

"Steve, I can't let you do that. Not under these circumstances. I can't put her life at risk."

Abramovich pleaded. The stress in his voice was apparent. "I won't hurt her. I just want to talk to her!"

Then, from the front of the plane, came the unmistakable voice of Lynne Farnsworth. "I'm RIGHT HERE. What do you want to say to me?"

The US secretary of state stood in the aisle. No ballistics vest. No weapon. Colonel Richardson on one side, the colonel's aide on the other, and Agents Lake and Young directly in front of her with their sidearms pointed directly at Abramovich.

Abramovich and the FS officer froze, stunned by the sight of Lynne. Elliot did not take his eyes off his target. He thought about taking the shot. Instead he paused to see what would happen next.

"Madam Secretary, I won't hurt you. I promise."

Lynne shouted. "STEVE! Have you lost your mind? What are you doing?"

"I'm sorry. I never meant for this to happen." Abramovich was distraught.

"Is it true? Did *you* kill Mohammed?"

"I'm sorry. I had to. They threatened to hurt Ulyana and her parents if I didn't." Abramovich grew more rattled.

"Oh, Steve," she said with a deep sense of despair in her voice. "But why? Why would anyone want to hurt him?"

Abramovich started to cry. He was disintegrating in his own anguish. He pressed his pistol harder against the side of the girl's head. She screamed even louder. Through clenched teeth he shouted, "It's oil. It's always about oil!" Then, as if he was talking to himself, he mumbled, "In Iraq, Kuwait, and soon Suriname."

The stress of the situation was too much. Without warning the FS officer fainted. It caught Abramovich by surprise. She went limp and slumped in his arms for a brief second. But in that moment, Elliot drew his weapon and fired. It happened so quickly the MPs and others, including Condon, barely had time to react. Instinctively their knees and heads jerked down, their stomach muscles tightened, and their eyes blinked.

Elliot put two rounds precisely between Abramovich's eyes less than half an inch apart. His face exploded and a geyser of blood blew out the back of his head. He was dead in an instant. Thankfully the young FS officer never saw or felt a thing. She was passed out and lying at Abramovich's feet when the shooting stopped. Subsequent medical examination would reveal that Elliot's bullets singed the girl's hair.

"Jesus, did you see that?" Young said to Lake. "Holy shit."

As others paused in awe of what had happened, Elliot leaped forward. "MEDICS!"

His shout caused everyone else on board to spring into action. Elliot checked first on Faber. No pulse. Then he moved to Payne. The MPs were by now immediately behind him. Richardson and Young pushed the secretary back into her office.

Payne was still alive but bleeding heavily. Elliot quickly found the wound. He did the only thing he could. He shoved his index and middle fingers into the hole, desperately trying to stop the bleeding. Blood oozed over Elliot's hand and Payne's chest. Elliot screamed again for a medic.

"Hold on, Roger. Look at me. HOLD ON!!!!"

Meanwhile, Condon crouched over Faber on the other side of the aisle. Elliot shouted at him. "Wally, Payne's losing a lot of blood! I need something to stop it. A napkin. A towel. Anything!"

"Here. Try this." Condon handed Elliot the only thing he had—a white pocket square that up until that moment had provided a stylish accent to his sport coat. Elliot stuffed it in the wound.

Just then an Air Force medic knelt down next to Elliot and over Payne. Elliot slid to the side to make room. Soon two more medics bent over Payne and Faber.

Thankfully for the White House, there was no press on board to record the moment.

Chapter Forty-Four

Elliot woke up Friday with a headache. Most days he would shave, shower, get dressed, and head to the office. All before Karen had awakened. All before traffic on the Dulles Toll Road or the GW Parkway had become snarled and unforgiving. Not today, not this morning. Instead he remained a moment in the warmth of his bed, staring at the ceiling and thinking about the events of the past two weeks. The attempted bombing of the *Chehalis*. The shooting outside Rachel's dorm. The shooting on the secretary's plane. He needed three Advils and a cup of coffee.

The water on his face was cold. It felt good. He dried his face with a towel. As he hung the towel back up, he looked in the mirror. The person staring back at him was a stranger. Where had all the years gone? His normally sharp brown eyes looked weary and drawn. The gray hair, which had for many years been limited to his temples, was now advancing deeper into his thick brown hair. Even his beard was turning gray; however, he would erase that sign of aging with a razor after he had a cup of coffee.

Elliot put on his robe and a pair of slippers. He turned the bathroom light off before he eased the door open. The bedroom was still dark. Karen was still asleep. She was a wonderful woman, the mother of his child, and a faithful companion for over 30 years. He loved her very much. But if he woke her? Look out. There would be hell to pay.

Downstairs was equally quiet. The sound of a school bus picking up kids at the end of the block was the only thing that breached the silence.

Elliot made a small pot of coffee with the Cuisinart Rachel and Karen had gotten him for Christmas. As soon as he pressed the start button he grabbed the bottle of Advil out of the cupboard where Karen kept all the family's prescriptions and medicines. He didn't see a glass on the counter that looked like his, so he grabbed a new one. Karen struggled to swallow even small pills. She had a strong gag reflex. Elliot did not. Three small pills posed no challenge at all. A little water, tilt the head back, and SWOOSH. Easy.

The sun was just starting to come up. As it did, Mitzi came down the stairs. Normally she would have stayed cuddled up with Karen on the bed for at least another hour. However, Elliot had disturbed that routine. She did not make a sound. Instead she sat in the center of the kitchen staring at him. Elliot knew exactly what the cat was thinking. *What the hell are you doing? You're not supposed to be here.*

Elliot quickly flipped the channels on the TV. He also checked the internet on his phone. Nothing on yesterday's shooting at Andrews. He checked his e-mails. There it was. At midnight, the assistant secretary for diplomatic security had circulated an e-mail to everyone in DSS. Copied on the e-mail were Secretary Farnsworth, the deputy secretary of state, and the undersecretary for management. It read in part:

> Yesterday, November 6, the Diplomatic Security Service suffered a heart-breaking loss. Agent Vincent Faber was killed in the line of duty. Vince was a 20-year veteran of the DSS, having protected Secretary Farnsworth, Secretary Wilson, and numerous ambassadors and other dignitaries around the world during his illustrious career. Vince is survived by his wife, Lesley, and his sons, Nathanial and Peter.

It also saddens me to report that Agent Roger Payne was seriously injured in the same incident that took Agent Faber's life. Roger is a 25-year veteran of the DSS. Roger is being cared for at Walter Reed and is expected to make a full recovery.

As soon as arrangements for a memorial service for Agent Faber are made, I will let you know. Please stay safe.

The e-mail made no mention of Abramovich or his role in Faber's death and Payne's injuries. At first Elliot thought that was odd. But the more he thought about it, the more that made sense. This e-mail was being sent to thousands of people around the world; people who supported President Hansen and those who did not. The president's critics would have a field day if all the facts were known. It wasn't hard to imagine the headlines: *Russian Spy in Secretary's Detail. Member of Secretary's Detail Assassinates Key US Ally.* The list was potentially endless. Thus, for now, the less said the better.

* * *

Elliot entered his office a few minutes before noon, his headache a thing of the past. He hung his coat on a hook located on the back of his door and sat down at his desk. Before he could turn his computer on, his phone rang.

"Hello, Elliott Jones."

"Elliott, this is Rasham."

"Rasham, hello. Wow, what time is it there? Let's see. 8:00 p.m. on a Friday?"

"Yes. It's late, but tomorrow I'm visiting family in Aswan and Sunday I fly to Amman for meetings. So this is my only chance for the next few days to call you."

"I appreciate that. Thank you."

"Of course."

"So tell me, do you have something on our suspect?"

"Yes. Am I on speaker?"

"No. But give me a minute. I'm going to close my door." Elliot swung his door shut and plopped back down in his chair. "There," he said exhaling. "That's better. Now, what do you got for me?" Elliot took a swig of coffee from the cup he always kept on his desk.

"His name was Raouf Alam. He was born in Alexandria to a well-off family. They were disappointed when he didn't go to college. But he wanted to be a secret agent. You know, the next *James Bond*."

"Huh. So what did he—"

"He joined our El-Sa'ka Brigade after school. Have you heard of it?"

"No, sorry. I haven't."

"It's our version of your Navy SEALs. Some people call them the Thunderbolt Force."

"Is he still in that unit?"

"No, no. He left El-Sa'ka about two years ago. I spoke to his former commander. He said Alam had visions of grandeur. He wanted to become a paid assassin or maybe a bodyguard to someone famous. Make millions. But it took him the better part of two years to get his first paying client. And when he did he couldn't wait to tell his friends. According to a guy in El-Sa'ka, Alam said his first client was the government of Kuwait. He specifically mentioned Kuwait's National Guard."

Elliot said in a hushed tone what he was thinking. "I'll be damned. Well, that explains why Kuwait didn't put up a stink when they—"

"What's that?"

"Oh, nothing. Anything else?"

"Yeah, I also spoke to a friend of mine who heads up Kuwait's National Police. At first he tried to peddle the lie that Mutairi died of a heart attack. I gently pushed back. As soon as I did his whole attitude changed. I told him both the Russians *and* the Americans knew that it wasn't a heart attack. I pointed out that your secretary of state was sitting right next to Mutairi when he died."

"What did he say when you told him that?"

"He was clearly reluctant to say much. He kept repeating that there were lots of rumors floating around Kuwait. After about the second or third time he said that I pushed him to explain. I said, 'what rumors'? That's when he said rumors are circulating that the National Guard was behind this. At one point I think he even compared the hit on Mutairi to the hit on Khashoggi."

"Did he really?" Elliot said more as a rhetorical statement than an actual question.

"Yeah. Finally I asked him the obvious question—why? Why would his government want to kill Mutairi? While he definitely tried to dance around the question, he did make reference to certain comments Mutairi had apparently made recently in the press that were critical of the emir and the crown prince."

"Huh. You know that part of the world better than I do, Rasham, but are the rulers of Kuwait as ruthless as, say, the rulers of Saudi Arabia?"

"No, but these are hereditary monarchies, Elliot. In the case of Kuwait, the Al-Sabah family has ruled Kuwait for over 250 years. That's 250 years of palaces, wives, and wealth beyond your wildest imagination. Isn't it true even in the United States? People who have power want to keep it."

"Yes, you have a point there," Elliot said grudgingly.

"So that's the answer to your question."

"Rasham, listen. I really owe you. This has been extremely helpful. I have to be over to the White House in a couple of hours to brief them on my investigation. This information adds an important piece to the puzzle. Thanks."

"My pleasure. Always happy to help my American friends."

Chapter Forty-Five

Elliot knew visiting hours at Walter Reed National Medical Center in Bethesda ended at 8:00 p.m, but the briefing he and Adams had given Salter and Esmond at the White House on the Mutairi matter ran late. With no traffic it would take thirty-five minutes to get to Walter Reed. But during rush hour? On a Friday? He'd be lucky if he got there by 7:30 p.m. He was cutting it close.

He pulled up to gate 1 on Woods Road at 7:35 p.m. Thankfully the guard who looked at his DSS ID was in a good mood. He let Elliot in.

Payne was initially treated at the infirmary on Andrews. Once he was stabilized, the Air Force took him via helicopter to Walter Reed.

It took Elliot about ten minutes to park and another ten minutes to find Payne's room. As he came off the elevator, he instantly saw Condon and another man come out of a room, presumably Payne's.

"Hi, Wally."

"Hello." They shook hands.

"Elliot, this is Tom Davis. He and Roger used to work together protecting the First Lady. They're also neighbors out in Ashburn. Their kids go to the same school."

"Hi, Tom. Pleased to meet you."

"Yes, sir. Likewise." Davis had been with the DSS for fifteen years. Although this was his first time meeting Elliot, he, like most in DSS, had heard of him.

Elliot looked at Condon. "How's he doing?"

"Remarkably well. We spoke to one of the doctors. He said they're going to keep him over the weekend. But assuming no setbacks and he keeps improving, they may be able to send him home on Tuesday or Wednesday. There's a nurse in there now giving him some medicine. Say, how'd you get in so late? She told us visiting hours were over."

"I guess I got lucky at the gate."

"Yeah, well, I hope she lets you talk to him." Condon frowned as if to say *She seems pretty tough.* "Good luck."

"Thanks. Hey, before you go, does he know about Faber and Abramovich?"

"Yeah, we told him. He asked about 'em. He didn't know."

"Okay, well, I'll see you. Take it easy. Nice to meet you, Tom."

"Yes, sir. Nice to meet you."

Elliot knocked on Payne's door. The nurse attending to him turned around. "I'm sorry. Visiting hours are over."

"Yes, ma'am. My name is Elliot Jones. I am a senior agent with the Diplomatic Security Service. I shot and killed the man who shot Mr. Payne. I just need a brief word with him."

She stared at him, a bit stunned by his claim. At this point, she could go one of two ways. She could relent or insist.

"I'll only be a minute. Please."

"Okay, but I'll be back in five."

"Thank you, ma'am." As she walked out of the room, she gave Elliot a disapproving look.

Elliot knew he didn't have much time and this was not a secure room. Therefore, he stood close to Payne and spoke in a low voice. "Roger, how you doin?"

"Oh, I've been better, that's for sure. I reckon I wouldn't even be here if it hadn't been for you. Thanks for helpin' me on the plane."

"Of course. You had me worried. You lost a lot of blood."

"Yeah, the medics at Andrews done a real good job."

"I spoke to Wally in the hall. He said he told you about Faber and Abramovich."

"Yeah."

"This probably isn't a fair question, but did you ever have any concerns or suspicions about Abramovich?"

"Nah, not really. I mean, yeah, he'd been stationed in Russia and he had himself a Russian wife, but I figured if the FBI gave him the thumbs up, and the CIA and DSS cleared him for duty, who was I to question his—"

"Yeah. No, I get it."

"I just reckon what else he might've been up to. I mean, think 'bout all them conversations he must've listened to. Secretary Farnsworth's always chattin' away with them folks in London, Paris, Berlin. And don't forget 'bout the president and others at the White House. Shoot." Payne exhaled. As he did so he blew a brief whistle. "Figurin' out that mess will be a big job."

"I'm glad I don't have to do it."

"You and me both, partner." Payne said.

"Say, do you remember when the secretary and Mutairi bought those coffees at the Kennedy Center during intermission?"

"Yeah, of course."

"Well," Elliot lowered his voice even more. "We think the man working behind the coffee cart that night slipped poison into Mutairi's cup. You tossed his cup in the trash, but we found it in one of the Center's dumpsters. It tested positive for BTX."

"What's BTX?"

"A rare poison. Google it."

"I reckon that explains why he was spittin' up white foam. I noticed it when they loaded him in the rig out front that night and later when they were wheelin' him into the emergency room. But there was so much blood from the gunshot wound, ain't nobody really mentioned it."

"Yup. BTX is—"

"Y'all manage to ID the fella behind the coffee cart?" Payne asked.

"Well, yes and no. We know he was in the cast. He was one of the soldiers. They carried rifles on stage, although his was real."

"Good Lord Almighty."

"Yeah, and we think he killed that girl backstage."

"Oh, yeah, I heard 'bout that."

"We think she might have heard or seen something so he—"

Just then the nurse came back into Payne's room. As she looked at Payne's chart she said without looking up, "Okay, sorry to interrupt, but visiting hours are over. Time to go."

Elliot stopped in mid-sentence. Looking at Payne, he said, "Okay. Listen, let me know when you're feeling better. I'll fill you in on the rest. I hope you feel better soon. And say 'hi' to Julia for me."

"Thanks, will do. And thanks again for savin' my life yesterday."

Elliot thought that was a bit of an exaggeration, but he didn't want to argue with him. So before he turned to leave the room he simply said with a smile, "Sure. Any time."

The nurse stared at Elliot as he left.

Chapter Forty-Six

Until 1995, Pennsylvania Avenue in front of the White House and E Street along the South Lawn of the White House were open to traffic. Cars, trucks—it didn't matter. All could pass close to the White House and did 24/7. Two events changed all of that. First, on September 11, 1994, a 38-year-old truck driver, Frank Corder, crashed a stolen Cessna 150 on the South Lawn mere inches from the Oval Office and the Rose Garden. Then, seven months later, on April 19, 1995, Timothy McVeigh parked a rental truck full of explosives in front of the Alfred P. Murrah Federal Building in Oklahoma City, Oklahoma. The blast tore the face of the building completely off and turned well over a third of the nine-story building into rubble. One hundred and sixty-eight people died in the blast, including 19 children.

These two events caused the US Secret Service to rethink security around the White House. If the truck in Oklahoma could do that much damage, what could something similar do parked at 1600 Pennsylvania Avenue?

Today the security perimeter around the White House stretches many blocks in all directions. Traffic is no longer permitted on Pennsylvania Avenue or E Street near the White House. Guard stations that once hugged the White House were pushed out many, many blocks. Finally, when the New Executive Office Building across from the White House was renovated in 2005, a new surface-to-air missile system was installed on its roof.

Despite these changes, foreign dignitaries, especially foreign heads of state, still arrive at the White House via the Northwest Appointment Gate on Pennsylvania Avenue. Their motorcades can stretch a block or two. Streets are briefly closed to crossing traffic by DC police officers on motorcycles and in squad cars. Typically the motorcade will first pass through the security checkpoint at the corner of 17th Street and Pennsylvania Avenue. It will then proceed down Pennsylvania Avenue past Blair House before turning right on to the north lawn of the White House and eventually stopping under the famous portico.

A little after 10:00 a.m. local time on Friday, November 7, the president's national security advisor informed the Russian embassy in Washington that the president wanted to meet Ambassador Umansky in the Oval Office at 10:30 a.m. on Saturday. The ambassador's CoS was back in Moscow when the call came in. Therefore, the embassy's chief of mission called the White House back to inquire about the topic. All she was told was that the president wanted to meet the ambassador and to allow approximately 30 minutes for the meeting. No further details were provided.

Traffic in Washington on a Saturday can be bad, especially around the White House. Tourists swarm about everywhere. On this Saturday the ambassador's motorcade attracted a lot of attention as it proceeded down Wisconsin Avenue before turning left onto Pennsylvania Avenue. Tourists gawked and took pictures with their cameras and phones. DC police and uniform DSS officers did their best to keep people back and safe.

The motorcade slowed as it approached the security gate on 17th Street between the Renwick Gallery and the Old Executive Office Building. However, this was not going to be the kind of visit where the president greeted his guest underneath the north portico. Instead the motorcade was told to enter through the Southwest Appointment Gate and park on West Executive Avenue.

Waiting for him at the entrance to the West Wing underneath a gray awning was the president's national security advisor, Mark Esmond. "Good morning, Mr. Ambassador. It's good to see you. Thanks for coming in on a Saturday."

"Of course, Mr. Esmond. Russia's relationship with the United States is of the utmost importance to my government."

Esmond gave no response.

It was a short walk to the Oval Office. The ambassador was accompanied only by his embassy's chief of mission. He did not need an interpreter. He was fluent in English. Moreover, he had no reason to believe this would be a substantive or sensitive discussion that required subject-matter experts. In fact, he told his chief of mission in the car on the way over that he would not be surprised if the Americans proposed a summit between the two countries' presidents.

"It's been nearly ten years since any American president has met with our president. President Hansen has an election next year," he said. "One of the advantages that an incumbent American president often has over his rival is foreign policy and national security. A US–Russia summit in a foreign capital like Helsinki or Reykjavik, within a year of the election, would contribute to that narrative and play to those strengths." The ambassador was in for a rude awakening.

Hansen had done little to the Oval Office. Unlike many of his predecessors, he did not change the drapes, the carpets, or most of the art on the walls upon arrival. He did, however, replace the bust of Martin Luther King with a bust of Abraham Lincoln. He also took down the painting of Franklin Delano Roosevelt over the fireplace. In its place he hung a portrait of George Washington in his military uniform. Other than that, things looked pretty much the way they had for the past seven years.

Hansen particularly liked the so-called Resolute desk, which had been used by his predecessor. Indeed, nine presidents, including Kennedy and Trump, used the Resolute desk when in office. It had been a gift from Queen Victoria to President Hayes in 1880. It was said to be made from the timbers of the British ship HMS *Resolute*.

Hansen was seated behind his desk when Ambassador Umansky entered the room.

"Yuri, come in. Welcome. You know Arthur and Lynne. And this is Bob Salter, my chief of staff. Please sit down." Hansen pointed in the direction of the empty couch.

As the ambassador shook hands with Vice President Luck, Secretary Farnsworth, and the president's CoS, Hansen walked around to one of the chairs in front of the fireplace. It was November. A comforting fire burned in the hearth. Mark Esmond sat in a cane-back chair with an upholstered seat in front of the president's desk.

As soon as he sat down, Hansen's demeanor changed quickly. The pleasantries were over. As Hansen's dad used to say, it was time to explain how the cow ate the cabbage.

"Mr. Ambassador, we have a very serious matter to discuss with you. One that, if it became more widely known in the halls of Congress or the streets of America, could set the relationship between our two countries back one-hundred years." The ambassador's pulse quickened and his blood pressure rose.

"I've asked Mark to summarize what we know so far. Secretary Farnsworth may also want to add her perspective, as she has unfortunately been an eyewitness to most of these events." The ambassador was stunned. Had he not been seated, he might have fallen over. What was happening?

Over the course of the next fifteen minutes Esmond essentially repeated what Adams and Elliot had told Salter and him in a private briefing the previous evening – to wit, Abramovich was acting on behalf of Russia. Russia threatened his wife, a US citizen. Abramovich assassinated a close ally of the United States in Washington. Russia threatened, intentionally or not, the life of the US secretary of state who was seated only inches away. Abramovich killed one DSS agent and wounded another while on board the secretary's plane. Finally, he explained how US law enforcement officials had tried on Thursday to arrest Abramovich; however, he resisted, threatened an FS officer, and was killed in the process. Lynne never spoke.

The Russian ambassador sat quietly and listened. He betrayed no emotion. It was not clear if the things he was hearing came as a surprise or confirmation of what he already knew.

When Esmond finished, the president rose from his chair to say goodbye to the ambassador. Lynne and the others in the room joined him. But before the president shook the ambassador's hand, he stood inches away with his index finger resting on the ambassador's tie and his jaw firmly set.

Hansen was first and foremost a politician. Like most politicians, he could be wishy-washy. Words to a politician are like matches to a smoker. If one doesn't work, simply try another. Salter understood that. He accepted that. But what his boss said next made him proud.

"Look, our two countries have been spying on each other since the Bolsheviks came to power in 1917. Probably even before that. I get it. But if Russia ever threatens a member of my administration again, or otherwise puts one of their lives at risk, I'll treat it as a threat against me and, Mr. Ambassador, the consequences of that will be uncompromising. You understand me?"

"Yes, Mr. President. Thank you." The ambassador stepped back and lowered his eyes. He then looked sheepishly at Hansen. "I will convey your words and concerns to my capitol. Good day, sir."

* * *

Esmond escorted the ambassador and his chief of mission to the door that exited onto West Executive Avenue. No one spoke. At the door Esmond shook their hands. "Mr. Ambassador, thank you for coming." The ambassador struggled to make eye contact.

Esmond quickly returned to the Oval Office. The president had moved back behind his desk. He was talking to the vice president, Lynne, and Salter, who stood in front of the desk. Esmond stood next to the vice president.

Hansen spoke first. "How they think they could pull a stunt like that and get away with it is beyond me. The Russians are frigging crazy."

"Yes, sir," Esmond said. The others voiced or nodded agreement.

"Speaking of crazy, Mark, I want you to tell Lynne about the Kuwaitis."

"Certainly." Esmond cleared his throat. "Madam Secretary, the Russians don't know this, but we believe they were not the only ones trying to kill Mohammed Al-Mutairi. We have reason to believe the Kuwaitis did as well, although their motivation was different from the Russians."

"What are you talking about? The Kuwaitis?" Lynne was incredulous and didn't try to hide it.

"Yes, ma'am. The Russians wanted Mutairi dead because they thought, mistakenly, that he was the key to Kuwait's efforts in Iraq, especially the auction last Tuesday. He wasn't."

Lynne was not satisfied with the explanation because it did not make plain how the Russians in particular would benefit from Mutairi's death. However, she let it go because she was more interested in understanding what if any role the Kuwaitis might have had in Mutairi's death.

"But why would the Kuwaitis want to kill their own oil minister?"

"If I may, I'd like to explain the *how* before the *why.*"

"If you must." What choice did she have in the Oval Office with the president sitting there?

"Do you remember when you and Mutairi bought those coffees during intermission?"

"Yes, of course."

Well, the man who worked the coffee cart that night slipped a deadly poison into Mutairi's drink when no one was looking. Something called BTX. The hospital found traces of it in his body during the postmortem, and DSS found it in his cup, which was retrieved from the garbage."

"Is that why he was spitting up white foam?"

"Yes, ma'am. Now, the DSS investigators believe that man was named Raouf Alam. An Egyptian hired by Kuwait's National Guard. They hired him and then they killed him, presumably to silence him."

"What?" Lynne exclaimed.

"Yes, Alam was found floating in the Potomac about ten days ago. Admittedly, we don't have hard evidence tying the emir or the crown prince to either the hiring or *firing* of Mr. Amir, if I can call it that. But no one believes something of this magnitude could happen without the express approval of one or both."

"Alright. Let's assume all of that is true. Why? Why would they do something so brazen? Something so vicious—especially after the uproar surrounding Khashoggi's death?"

"The intel is split on this. Some believe it's because Mutairi was critical of the leadership. Because he was calling for unspecified changes in Kuwait. However, we believe there is another reason known only to a handful of people."

"What's that?"

Although she was the secretary of state, Lynne had not been consulted on the plan agreed to with Mutairi. No one from State had participated in the briefings or the recent meetings in the Sit Room chaired by Salter and attended by the president. The White House viewed the arrangement with Mutairi as a political matter and possibly a military matter. Only people who had a need to know had been read in. Until now, Lynne did not need to know.

The president's CoS felt the need to explain before Lynne heard more.

"Mark," Salter said, "before you answer that, if I may?"

Hansen welcomed this move by his CoS. He and Salter had discussed more than once the possibility that Lynne would not appreciate being left out of the loop. He didn't want his national security advisor to stick a rhetorical knife, however unintentional it might be, into his secretary of state and twist it.

"Certainly." Esmond pulled back.

"Thanks Mark. Madam Secretary, the president has been told by Energy, the CEA, and the CIA that the price of oil is likely to exceed $150 per barrel by the time of the election. Global production is not keeping up with global demand. The president has also been advised that the impact high oil prices will have on the price of gas at the pump and in turn the US economy, is nothing short of disastrous. Again, this is all right before the election. Now, Mutairi came to us about ten months ago with a plan to increase his country's oil production. In a nutshell, he thought a 'false flag' attack involving a few inconsequential wells in the north of Kuwait could be blamed on Iran. He thought that was particularly true after the Iranians, as you no doubt recall, staged attacks back in 2019 on the Saudi oil facilities. In any event, Mutairi thought he could get the crown prince to essentially declare a state of emergency and invite the US to help secure Kuwait's oil complex. Most importantly, that could lead, he thought, to our oil companies helping Kuwait increase its oil production. Anything that increased supply, especially supply that we would presumably have at least some access to and that further isolated Iran on the world stage, was seen as a win-win-win for us. Finally, that plan was only months, if not weeks, away from execution when Mutairi was killed."

Hansen did not hesitate to put his imprimatur on Salter's and Esmond's remarks. "Look, the press is already reporting that this wasn't a heart attack. It's just a matter of time before they start pointing fingers. When that happens, I'd rather those fingers are pointed at Russia and not

Kuwait. I don't want this episode to damage our relationship with the Al-Sabah family. They are an important ally in an important part of the world. So, Lynne, I want you to talk to the Kuwaitis. Tell them their story about a heart attack is not going to hold up. We'll do what we can to keep the press from tracing Mutairi's death back to them. But there's only so much we can do."

During the three years he had been the vice president, Arthur Luck could count on one hand the number of times he had been included in a substantive debate about policy. He regretted it but accepted it. Like most vice presidents before him, he played a limited role in the administration.

Therefore, he wasn't exactly sure why the White House asked him to meet the Russian ambassador. It wasn't like he knew Umansky particularly well. He didn't. But he was invited and he had something he wanted to say. "Mr. President, may I?"

"Yes, of course, Art."

"Thank you. I'm not sure we'll have the luxury of a choice here. The press may put Mutairi's assassination at the feet of *both* Kuwait *and* Russia. But I appreciate, just as you say, we can only do so much and it's better for us to agree on a strategy and then pursue it as best we can."

"What's your point, Art?"

"My point is this. If we try to steer this toward the Kuwaitis, we may or may not damage our relations with the emir and his family. But what we *won't* do is damage this administration, especially a year out from an election. However, if we point the press at Russia, that could entail significant blowback for us. It's not hard to imagine headlines like *Russian Spy Infiltrates Secretary of State's Security Detail.*

"Art, you're absolutely right. The safer thing for us to do would be to throw the Kuwaitis under the bus. I mean, they'd only have themselves to blame. Right? And as tempting as that may be for me personally, I've got to put the interests of the country first. US foreign policy and national security interests in the Middle East are more important than my reelection efforts."

For the second time that morning, Salter was proud of his boss.

"So, again, I want Lynne to meet with the Kuwaitis. Show them some love, Lynne, but make it *tough love*. We can't have the Kuwaitis, or anyone else for that matter, thinking they can kill their citizens on American soil with impunity. Any questions?"

Lynne was angry. She should have been consulted. But this wasn't the time or place to show it. Her response was succinct. "No questions. Understood."

"Thanks," Hansen said.

"Mr. President," Esmond asked, "if I could go back to the Russians for a minute."

"Yes, of course."

"Thank you. One of the things Abramovich said on the secretary's plane has many of us scratching our heads."

"What's that?"

"Well, I certainly wasn't going to mention it in front of the ambassador, but several people who were on the plane said Abramovich mumbled something about oil in Iraq, Kuwait, and Suriname."

"What does that mean?" Hansen asked.

"That's just it. We're not sure. Now we think he would have mentioned Iraq and Kuwait in those last moments because of the auction in Bagdad and his killing of Mutairi. But Suriname? That reference is a mystery."

"Does Suriname have oil?" Hansen asked.

"Not really," Esmond said. "In 2015 Exxon found the first of what are now around eleven billion barrels of proven crude oil reserves in Suriname's neighbor to the west—Guyana. And, of course, further west is Venezuela, which has tons of oil. But Suriname? I'm not aware of any major finds there."

"Mark, why don't you check with Energy. Ask that guy who heads the Oil and Gas Bureau. What's his name? Atwater? Rob Atwater?"

Salter corrected his boss. "Sir, I believe you are referring to Rick Atwater. He briefed you in the Sit Room the other day."

"Right. Rick. Also, I can ask Larry Middleton to check on Suriname. I'm supposed to play golf with him tomorrow."

"Yes, sir," Esmond said.

Chapter Forty-Seven

"Hello, Rick?"

"Speaking."

"Hi, this is Mark Esmond at the White House. We met in the Situation Room two weeks ago. You briefed the president on global oil markets."

"Yes of course. How are you?"

"I'm fine. Sorry to bother you so early on a Monday morning. You got a minute?"

"Certainly. What's up?"

"On Saturday the president asked me if Suriname had much oil. I told him I didn't think so. I told him about the discoveries in Guyana, and of course about the large reserves in Venezuela further west. But I wasn't aware of any large deposits in Suriname. Was I right?"

"Well, that depends on who you talk to. I can explain if you got a minute."

"You bet. In fact, I got an hour. My next meeting just got cancelled. Fill me in."

"Okay. Well, I think a dramatic transition is actually taking place down there right now. I've written several reports on it, but I'm not sure anyone ever reads those things. At least not the right people."

"What kind of transition?"

"It's really quite interesting. For starters, most people don't realize that Latin America has the second-largest proven oil reserves in the world after the Middle East. However, state-run oil companies in the region such as PEMEX in Mexico, Petroecuador in Ecuador, and PDVSA in Venezuela, have repeatedly squandered their opportunities. Each is plagued by decades of incompetence and corruption. Second, their crude is very dirty."

"I've heard that term used many times over the years. But what exactly does it mean?"

"Dirty crude is high in CO_2 emissions. It's very dense. Look, the transition to cleaner energy alternatives is underway. There's no stopping it. However, during that transition the world is still going to need oil. But in order to be competitive, that oil has to be cheap to produce with low carbon emissions. That spells trouble for Venezuela, Ecuador, Mexico, and others like them. By comparison, the CO_2 equivalent emitted per barrel from the oil discovered in Guyana in 2015 is only 10kg. The global average is 26kg."

"That sounds like a big difference."

"It is," Atwater replied. "Now, I think what happened in Guyana will soon happen in Suriname."

"Really? Why?"

"Several reasons. First, in 2023 the French company Total, in partnership with the US firm APA, announced they'd discovered some 'commercially viable' offshore fields in Suriname. Those efforts have been slow to develop, but I suspect it's just a matter of time before they do. Second, Brazil is convinced there are very large fields located along what is called the 'Equatorial Margin.'"

"Sorry, where is that?"

"Just to the east of French Guiana and Suriname. Along Brazil's northeast coast."

"Okay."

"And the Brazilians are not screwing around. They're spending billions of dollars over the next five years to explore and develop those areas."

"Huh. I didn't know."

"You're not alone. This is happening in our backyard and few in Washington are paying much attention."

"So what about Suriname?"

"Well, you got Venezuela and Guyana to the west and the Equatorial Margin to the east. And right in the middle is Suriname. It simply stands to reason."

"You say Total and APA are active in Suriname?" Esmond said as a prelude to his real question.

"Yes. So is a Dutch company, Energie Bronnen. In fact, Bronnen recently commissioned its second oil rig off the coast of Suriname."

"How about the Russians? Are they poking their nose around there?"

"Funny you should ask. Last week I spoke to a guy in Suriname who works for the state-owned oil company there—Staatsolie. He mentioned that a delegation from Moscow was in Paramaribo back in September. He said it was led by the oil minister. Apparently, he brought a bunch of Russian oil executives with him. You know—Roseneft, Rusoil, Gazprom."

"Interesting. Did he say why they were there?"

"Aside from dinners and drinks with the president, his cabinet, and some rich Russians living down there, he said they spent a lot of time meeting and traveling around the country with a Russian engineering firm, Gazneft. He said Gazneft has spent the better part of the past year in Suriname. Testing soil. Seismic imaging."

"Did he say anything else about the Russians?"

"Ahhh. No. Not really."

"You say you've written some reports on this?"

"Yes. Two to be precise. One earlier this year and one late last year."

"Are they classified?"

"No. They're public documents."

"Could you send those to me?"

"Of course. Happy to. What's your e-mail address?"

"It's mesmond@whitehouse.gov."

"Wait a minute. I'm sorry. He *did* say something else."

"No problem. What was that?"

"He mentioned a security firm that seemed to be protecting the Russians wherever they went. At first he said he didn't think anything about it. Only four or five guys. He assumed they were part of the minister's security detail. Normal stuff. But after the delegation left he happened to drive by the Gazneft offices on the outskirts of Paramaribo and he noticed quite a few trucks and men behind a newly installed fence. He couldn't tell if they were workers or security. He said he only caught a brief glimpse of them as he drove by."

"Huh. Anything else?"

"No, not that I can think of."

"Okay, well, this has been helpful. Thanks for taking the time to talk to me."

"My pleasure."

"And I look forward to reading your reports."

"They're on their way right now."

"Great. Thanks. Goodbye."

Chapter Forty-Eight

Vladimir Putin's rise to power in Russia began in 1975 when he joined the KGB. This was followed in 1990 by a mid-level position in the office of the mayor of Leningrad, where Putin was an advisor on international affairs. Then, in July 1998, his big break came when President Boris Yeltsin appointed him to be the head of the FSB.

Aside from brief stints as Russia's prime minister from 1999 to 2000 and from 2008 to 2012, Putin has ruled Russia as its president on a continuous basis with what can only be described as an *iron fist* since 2012. In April 2021 he signed into law amendments to the constitution that would allow him to serve as president until 2036.

According to the Kremlin, Putin has survived six assassination attempts during his time in office. British MI6 puts the number at closer to fifteen. The latest attempt occurred on Putin's birthday—October 7. While attending a public birthday celebration in his hometown of Saint Petersburg, two drones believed to be operated by Ukrainian special forces slammed into a reviewing stand where Putin was seated. Four people, including the deputy mayor of Saint Petersburg, were killed. The Kremlin claimed Putin escaped with only minor cuts and bruises. According to

MI6, Putin suffered a severe concussion and potentially permanent damage to his hearing. When Ambassador Umansky and Russia's foreign minister briefed Putin on Umansky's meeting at the White House earlier in the week, the president was still recovering at his winter home on the Black Sea.

The meeting took place Tuesday in the ornate Victory Room inside the Kremlin. In attendance were Umansky, his boss Foreign Minister Sergei Lagerev; Putin's CoS, Aleksander Zabolev; and the head of Russia's FSB, Maxim Smetanin. Putin participated via Kumospace.

Umansky described his meeting in the Oval Office. He tried his best to convey the anger and vitriol President Hansen had demonstrated. Everyone in the room wondered how Putin would react. They soon found out.

"Yuri," Putin asked, "you say the Americans killed one of our agents while on board the secretary's plane. Is that right?"

"Yes, sir. That is what I was told."

"Was this the SVR agent embedded in the secretary's detail?"

"I believe so, Mr. President. Yes."

Putin did not react to the news. Instead he asked his CoS, "Alek, what happened at the oil auctions in Iraq last week? I heard neither we nor the Krygs got anything. Is that right?"

"Yes, sir. That is correct."

"And what about the Kuwaitis? How did they do?"

"I believe Kuwait Petroleum Corp was awarded only one lease."

"Is that because we eliminated Mutairi or because our intel was wrong?"

"I don't know, sir."

"What does Bortaikov say?"

"I don't know, sir. I haven't spoken to him. I believe he has been on vacation most of this week and last."

"Vacation?" Putin shouted. "He hasn't been on vacation. He's been at his dacha fucking his girlfriend and drinking expensive French wine!"

No one said a word.

For the next thirty minutes they discussed, in no particular order, the troubles Russia faced. Amongst the topics discussed were Western sanctions on Russia, declining oil revenues and production, the failure to secure any oil concessions in Iraq, and damage to Russia's relationship with the United States caused by the assassination of Mutairi. A constant theme throughout the discussion was the repeated lapses in Russia's foreign intelligence.

During the discussion Russia's foreign minister did not hesitate to take rhetorical shots at the SVR. Two factors motivated him. First, he disliked Bortaikov. He thought he was a bully and a pig. Second, there was a long history of the SVR meddling in Russian foreign policy. Indeed, in an October 2026 interview with the China Media Group, Putin admitted that SVR often played a greater role in Russian foreign policy than the Foreign Ministry.

Smetanin also disliked Bortaikov, although his reasons differed from those of Lagerev. Smetanin didn't like Bortaikov because he saw him as his chief rival within the Kremlin. There was bad blood between the SVR and FSB that went back many decades. Therefore, he was perfectly willing to let Lagerev attack Bortaikov.

In fact, at one point in the discussion when he thought Lagerev was not going after Bortaikov hard enough, Smetanin told Putin, "The FSB does not believe Kuwait was ever focused on the auctions in Bagdad. Nor was it collaborating with anyone in the US regarding the auctions. If the US was collaborating behind the scenes with anyone, it was Qatar, who did very well in the auctions. Thus, we believe the killing of Mutairi was unnecessary."

"Thank you, Max," Putin said. "Listen, I have another appointment at the top of the hour. Why don't you and Alek stay on for a few more minutes? I want to talk to you privately."

"Certainly, sir," Smetanin said.

Turning to Lagerev and Umansky, Putin said, "Yuri, when do you return to Washington?"

"On Thursday, sir. I'm giving a presentation on Friday at the Center for Strategic and International Studies in Washington. Afterward, the *New York Times* is interviewing me for a piece on the current state of the US–Russia relationship."

"I hope that piece comes out before anyone connects Mutairi's death to us."

"Yes, sir."

"Alright, safe travels."

"Thank you, Mr. President." Umansky and Lagerev left the room.

Chapter Forty-Nine

Secretary Farnsworth's plane was not scheduled to leave for Geneva until 11:00 p.m. on Tuesday. Thus, when her last meeting ended at 5:30 p.m., she sent Carter Nassif, the assistant secretary for Near Eastern affairs, an e-mail telling him she was headed home and would meet him at Andrews. However, before she left the Truman Building she stuck her head in her CoS' office.

"Peter, I'm going home to finish packing and grab a bite to eat. I told Carter to meet us at Andrews. I'll see you there, okay?"

"Yes, ma'am. Do you have everything you need for your meeting with the prime minister?"

"I think so." And with that Lynne was off.

* * *

As usual, the house was quiet. No sign of Jim. Indeed, she hadn't heard from him in over a month. She was anxious to talk to him in person. She wanted to warn him about his Russian business associates. She also intended to tell him she wanted a divorce.

For the third time in the past week she sent Jim an e-mail. "We need to talk ASAP. Can't do it over the phone. Any chance you can meet me in Geneva tomorrow or Thursday? Staying at President Wilson. Let me know."

By 8:30 p.m. she was ready to go. The ride out to Andrews this time of night would take only 45 minutes. No need to rush. She might as well relax. Lynne poured herself two fingers of Dalwhinnie single malt in a tumbler and sat down in her favorite chair. She asked Alexa to play smooth jazz from Pandora.

Lynne checked her work and personal e-mails. While she had a Google e-mail account, she was an early user of AOL. Friends often gave her a hard time for using AOL for personal e-mail, as if that somehow made her a technological dinosaur. Maybe she was. She didn't care. It still worked fine.

Lynne also checked WhatsApp for any new messages. She hoped to see something from Fhani. Nothing.

Lastly, she checked her new account at Pictet, but for that she would need the phone Fhani gave her. Where was it? She rummaged through her purse. After a moment or two she found it at the bottom next to a pack of gum and a bottle of eyeglass cleaner.

It took another couple of moments for Lynne to find the app on the phone—a Gothic-looking lion raised on its hind feet against a burgundy background and the year 1805 across the bottom. She anxiously entered her account number and password. The phone buzzed when the bank sent her a six-digit passcode. She carefully entered the numbers.

There it was! Twelve million US dollars received from Ahli Bank in Qatar. Two million for every Iraqi lease won by a company based in Qatar. Life-changing money. Her body tingled with excitement.

She immediately sent Fhani a message on WhatsApp, a decision she would later regret. "Funds received. Now we can buy that chalet in Zermatt we've always talked about. ☺ Any chance you can meet me in Geneva tomorrow or Thursday? Staying at Prez Wilson."

Lynne looked at her watch. It was almost 9:30 p.m. She finished her scotch and took the empty glass into the kitchen.

* * *

Her plane touched down at Geneva's Cointrin Airport a little before 6:15 a.m. local time. Instead of taxiing to the terminal, it pulled off to the side on the north end of the airport. No sooner had the engines shut down than three large black, heavily armored Chevy Suburbans pulled alongside the plane. Three Toyota Land Cruisers belonging to the cantonal police of Geneva took up positions on the far side of the plane. Ground crew rolled stairs up to the front door of the plane.

Lynne was tired. She always found trips to Europe more tiring than trips to Asia. While travel time to Asia could and often did exceed twenty-five hours, compared to only six or seven to Europe, there was enough time on those trips to sleep, eat, *and* work. Travel time to Europe, by comparison, was just too short for much of anything. Plus, flights to Europe arrived at the start of a long day whereas flights to Asia typically arrived at the end of the day.

Lynne liked the Hotel President Wilson. In thirty-eight years she'd probably stayed there over a hundred times. Many of her colleagues urged her to stay at the Beau-Ravage or the Ritz-Carlton. They insisted those hotels were nicer than the Wilson, and they probably were. But the Wilson was familiar and comfortable to Lynne, kind of like an old pair of slippers or a favorite sweater. Besides, it was right on Lake Geneva and close to the US Mission and the WTO.

The DSS advance team had swept the Wilson twice. The most recent sweep was completed an hour before she arrived. Her room at the end of the hall on the fourth floor was ready. Two members of the DSS jump team stood outside the door and two stood near the elevator. DSS agents would also rotate in and out of the room next to the secretary's throughout her stay.

Her motorcade pulled up to the front doors of the hotel a little after 7:00 a.m. As she stepped out of the car, her DSS close protection detail formed its standard diamond formation. Nassif and Drinker followed close behind.

It was winter in Switzerland. The wind coming off the lake was cold and raw. The plane trees in front of the hotel were stripped of their leaves. In their place were large holiday ornaments twice the size of basketballs. Lynne knew the lights on the ornaments would be pretty at night. She had seen them many times before.

Pierre, the head porter, held the door for Lynne as she entered the hotel. "*Bonjour Madam Secretary. Bienvenue chez le président de l'hôtel Wilson.*"

"*Bonjour Pierre. Comment allez-vous?*"

"*Ça va bien,*" he said with a broad smile. "*Et vous?*"

"*Très bonne,*" Lynne replied in her best French accent.

The Wilson always did a nice job of decorating its lobby. Nothing too extravagant and yet always elegant. Since it was late November and the end-of-year holidays were only a few weeks away, a giant Christmas tree adorned with dozens and dozens of lavender ribbons and ornaments stood in the center of the lobby. Beautifully wrapped packages, each with a lavender bow and ribbon, surrounded the base of the tree. Along the sides of the lobby leading to the registration desk were a dozen or so smaller Christmas trees covered in faux white snow with silver-colored packages around their base.

Like many hotels in Geneva, most of the guests at any given time were from the Middle East. This explained why the Wilson had an award-winning Lebanese restaurant called Arabesque just off the lobby. It also explained why the dominate scent in the hotel was sandalwood. Arabs, particularly Arab men, loved it. Fhani loved it.

Lynne stood by the large Christmas tree and chatted with Nassif while Drinker checked them in. Her close protection detail observed from a short distance. A couple members of her detail also spoke to members of the DSS advance team who were in the lobby. When Drinker was done, Lynne suggested they meet back down in the lobby at 11:30 a.m.

Once in her room she hung a few things up in the closet and ordered a continental breakfast from room service. The butter and bread at the Wilson were to die for. She couldn't wait.

She hung up the phone and turned on the Bang & Olufsen flat-panel TV. A greeting from the hotel manager set to gentle music scrolled across the screen. Lynne took a moment to simply look out her window.

Below her the hotel's pool was covered for the winter, the lounge chairs and garden umbrellas put away. As usual, traffic along Quai Wilson was backed up, Geneva's version of morning rush hour.

Beyond the hotel and Quai Wilson the sun was starting to peek over the snow-covered Alps to the east. The sky was clear and brilliant. The sun sparkled off the lake. Were it summer this part of the lake would be full of boats by noon. Not today. It was cold and windy. She did, however, spot one hearty soul in a sailboat up by Versoix. Lynne loved Switzerland.

After breakfast she turned off the TV, brushed her teeth, and got ready to go. When she was younger, she would have avoided the traffic by walking over to the US Mission to the United Nations. Now? That was out of the question. For one thing, her security detail would have objected if she tried to walk along the lake and through Parc Mon Repos.

Her meeting with Kuwait's prime minister wasn't until 1:30 p.m. and she didn't need to be down in the lobby for another 20 minutes. She checked e-mails and messages and her makeup one last time. When she finished, she reached for her coat and scarf in the closet. As she did, her doorbell rang. Who could that be? Perhaps a member of her detail wanted to speak with her. She opened the door.

"Jim!"

"Hello, sweetheart." He leaned forward to kiss his wife on the cheek. She did not return the gesture. He couldn't help but notice.

"May I come in?"

"Of course." She stepped back to let him in. As she did, she glanced at one of the DSS agents outside the door. He returned her look with the slightest of smiles.

Jim took off his overcoat and threw it on one of the chairs. "Boy, your security detail almost didn't let me up. I had to show them my ID and do some fast talking. They were tough."

"Sorry, they're new."

"What happened to your old detail?"

"Oh, it's a long story."

"No problem. By the way, you act like you're surprised to see me."

"I am."

"Didn't you get my e-mails? You said you wanted to speak with me and that you'd be staying at the President Wilson."

"Yes, but I never heard back from you."

"You didn't?"

"No."

"Huh. I wonder what happened." Jim sat down on the bed and checked his phone. "I have the e-mails right here. Let's see. Oh, you know what? They never went through. They're still in my outbox. I wonder what happened. Sorry."

Typical Jim, Lynne thought to herself. *Stumbling and bumbling.* No point in belaboring the issue.

"Did you fly in this morning?" she asked.

"Yes. Just landed about an hour ago."

"Where'd you come from?"

"Doha."

"Business or pleasure?"

"Business. I would never go to Qatar for pleasure."

Lynne could think of many reasons to go to Doha for pleasure. For one thing, Fhani lived there.

Jim continued. "The Iraqis discovered a bunch of oil in the Anbar Province. Two weeks ago they auctioned off about eighty percent of the drilling rights."

"Yes, I know."

"Did you hear who won?"

"Only vaguely," she said. "I heard a lot of companies won, including Exxon, Chevron, BP, and Shell." Technically that was true, but she wasn't being honest with him. She knew exactly who won and who didn't. Hell, she had spent the better part of the past year lobbying the Iraqis to award as many concessions as possible to the United States and Qatar.

"Well, yes, those companies had some success, but the big winner was Qatar!"

Lynne struggled to show no reaction.

Jim continued. "Specifically, QatarEnergy and another company called Qatar Gulf. I was there to see if I could get some business from them."

Fat chance, Lynne thought to herself.

"So what did you want to talk to me about?"

"Wait a minute. Before we get into that, I need to send an e-mail to someone." Lynne sat down in the room's other chair, the one without Jim's coat draped over it. Using her phone, she sent a brief message to Nassif and Drinker.

"There. Sorry. I was just heading over to the US Mission to meet with the ambassador when you arrived. I needed to let my chief of staff and another person know that I might be a few minutes late."

"Sure. Say, you hungry? I'm starving."

"No, I already had breakfast," Lynne said pointing to the tray on the bedside table that contained the remnants of her breakfast. "Besides, I have a full schedule today. After lunch I'm meeting with Kuwait's prime minister." And, to be honest, she was hoping Fhani would show up in time for dinner.

"Okay, I understand. So what's up? What did you want to talk to me about?"

"Two things actually. First, I was recently shown a photograph of you meeting with a man in Cairo. I was told you believed the man in the photo worked for Rusoil—a Russian oil company. He doesn't. Multiple US security services believe the man you were with works for Russia's SVR."

"Are you serious?!"

"Yes."

"Jesus!!"

"Yes. Now, I've been assured that if you discontinue your contacts with this man, no charges will be brought. But if you continue to see him and, especially if you continue to do business with him, well—"

Jim quickly responded. "I understand. No need to spell it out. I didn't know he worked for the SVR."

"Good, because that's what I told them. I told them you would never knowingly associate with an agent of a foreign government, especially Russia."

"Thanks. I appreciate it."

"Of course. But to be honest, I said that as much for me as for you."

"Oh?"

"Jim, don't be thick. It would be disastrous for me and the administration if people believed the spouse of the secretary of state was palling around with Russian agents."

"Lynne, I understand. I get it. I'm not dense."

"GOOD," she said more as an exclamation point on the conversation than anything else.

"Now, what else did you want to talk about?"

She wasn't sure if now was the right time to discuss a divorce, so she put it off. At least for a few minutes.

"Jim, you have to stop pouring money into Energy Plus. You're ruining us! I want to retire at some point, but I don't see how I can. Especially if you keep throwing good money after bad."

"What are you talking about?" Jim shouted.

"Keep your voice down!" Pointing to the door she said, "they'll hear you."

"I don't care. This is bullshit."

"Well, I do care. And this is not bullshit! I see the money being withdrawn from our account. Has Energy Plus earned a dime in the past five years?"

"Yes," he said meekly. In fact, Energy Plus had been bleeding red ink for close to seven years.

Lynne was surprised by Jim's attitude. He was the one destroying their finances. Not her. *That does it!*

Jim was anxious to change the subject. "Anything else you wanna talk about?"

"Yes, I want a divorce." There, she said it.

"A what?"

"A divorce. You heard me. I want a divorce."

"But—"

"Look, we hardly see each other anymore. And I can't remember the last time we had sex. Your life is completely separate from mine. We've grown apart. The love I felt for you many years ago has vanished.

Evaporated. The only thing we share at this point is a name and a mailing address. I don't want to live the rest of my life in a pretend marriage. It's over and I think you know it. I intend to file for divorce when I get back to Washington."

While all these things were true, would she be saying them if she wasn't in love with Fhani? Maybe not. She would never know. She had said it and that was that. No going back now.

Lynne looked at her watch. "Look, I'm running late. I need to get over to the US Mission. We can continue this conversation if you want. Maybe tomorrow. Where you staying?"

Jim held both hands out to his side. "I thought I'd stay here with you."

"That's out of the question. You're not staying here. Perhaps one of the other hotels in town has a room. Now I need to go. I'm already late. Sorry."

Chapter Fifty

A ccording to the United Nations there are 193 countries in the world. Most have an embassy in Bern, the capital of Switzerland. At last count, more than 180 countries also have what are called permanent missions in Geneva that represent their interests before the United Nations and the numerous international organizations that call Geneva "home." Indeed, Geneva is home to over 40 international organizations such as the World Health Organization (WHO), the International Labour Organization, the World Intellectual Property Organization (WIPO), and the WTO. Geneva is also headquarters to over 400 nongovernmental organizations such as the Inter-Parliamentary Union, World Economic Forum, and the World Jewish Congress.

Before her meeting with Kuwait's prime minister, Lynne wanted to spend some time with the US ambassador at the US Mission to the UN and other International Organizations, Wendy Cochran; maybe have an early lunch with her.

Lynne met Cochran when she was deputy secretary of state in the Bush administration and Cochran was the chief of mission in Brussels.

When President Hansen tapped Lynne to be the secretary, one of her first calls was to Cochran to see if she was interested in serving in Geneva.

It was not unusual for Cochran to eat lunch in the Mission's cafeteria. In fact, she made a point of doing so at least once a month. She liked eating in the cafeteria and she knew it was popular with the Mission's rank and file. However, for the secretary of state to join her in the cafeteria was a rare occurrence. The room was buzzing.

They sat at a large round table in the middle of the room. Lynne, Cochran, Nassif, and Drinker were joined by the mission's deputy chief and Cochran's CoS. Lynne's security detail took turns eating at a nearby table. Few people noticed the four FBI agents eating lunch in the corner.

For Lynne the lunch was a mix of work and pleasure. On one hand, the food and company were great. On the other hand, she was able to ask a lot of questions and pick the brains of some very smart and knowledgeable people.

She asked them a lot of questions about Kuwait. She wanted to know what Kuwait was focused on in the WHO, the WTO, and WIPO. She needed to know what was important to Kuwait at this time. What did it want? Kuwait wasn't going to join the Abraham Accords for nothing. A price would have to be paid. Certainly, there would be a financial and military component to that price. That was a given. But Lynne didn't want to overlook anything else that might be of value to Kuwait. The emir was reluctant to join the Accords. She needed to find a way to overcome that reluctance that was politically palatable to Washington and Jerusalem.

After lunch Lynne and Drinker took the elevator up to the second floor. Nassif headed for the lobby to greet the prime minister.

Lynne and Drinker sat down in an empty conference room reserved for them. Coffee, tea, and water sat on a side board. At 1:40 p.m. there was a knock at the door. A young security office assigned to the Mission opened the door for the prime minister of Kuwait and his principal deputy. Nassif followed.

"Your Royal Highness, it is wonderful to see you again and so soon after Jakarta. Thank you for taking the time out of your busy schedule to see me." Lynne and the prince gently embraced.

"Thank you, Madam Secretary. It is always a pleasure to see you."

"Your Highness," Lynne said gesturing toward Nassif, "I believe you know Carter Nassif. Carter is our assistant secretary of state for Near Eastern affairs."

"Yes, of course. Mr. Nassif and I are old friends," the prince said with a broad smile, knowing full well that his words were an exaggeration, but a welcome and warm gesture for everyone in the room.

Lynne continued the introductions. "And you know my chief of staff, Peter Drinker."

"Certainly. Hello, Mr. Drinker."

"Hello, Your Royal Highness," Drinker replied.

For the next forty-five minutes they had a wide-ranging and deeply substantive discussion about Kuwait joining the Abraham Accords. When it was over, Lynne asked Prince Jaber if she could speak to him alone for a few minutes. What she needed to discuss with him she was not at liberty to share with Nassif or Drinker.

"Of course, Madam Secretary," Jaber said.

"Thank you, Your Highness."

Nassif and Drinker rose from their chairs and nodded toward the prince. They excused themselves and exited the room. The prince's deputy followed.

Once alone, Lynne spoke softly to the prince. "Your Highness, I carry a message directly from the president. First and foremost, he asked me to stress in the strongest possible terms that the United States values its long-standing and close relationship with your kingdom and the Al-Sabah family."

"Thank you, Your Excellency. As I told you in Jakarta, my country is very lucky to count you and the United States as a friend."

"Thank you, Your Highness. It is precisely this friendship, that makes what I must tell you so difficult."

"Oh?" the prince said in anticipation of what might follow.

"Yes. You see, I was sitting next to my dear friend Mohammed Al-Mutairi when he died."

"Yes, I know. That must have been difficult."

"Yes, Your Highness. But it was difficult not because he had a heart attack."

"Oh?"

"No. He was murdered. I saw the blood for my myself." She did not try to describe the effects of the poison on Mutairi. She didn't think it was necessary. The prince was not going to split hairs with her. He sat silently listening.

Lynne continued. "Your Royal Highness, my government has confirmed that agents hired by Kuwait had a hand in Mohammed's death." Again, she was not going to tell him everything. She was not going to implicate Russia. Russia's involvement in Mutairi's death was, for present purposes, irrelevant. The message she carried from the president focused exclusively on Kuwait and its involvement.

"Your Excellency, this is shocking news. I don't know what to say."

"I understand. I too was shocked when I heard it. But please let me quickly add that while my government takes very seriously all homicides that occur within its borders, and while we want all nations to know that the United States is not some sort of hunting ground for their nationals, we will do all that we can to keep this news out of the press and the public eye."

"Your Excellency, I will convey your message to my capital. But I must tell you I do not know how my government will respond to these allegations."

"That is completely understandable, Your Royal Highness. And should anyone in your government have any questions about this matter, please let me know and I will try to provide you with answers."

"Thank you."

"However, as evidenced by the fact that I asked Assistant Secretary Nassif and Mr. Drinker to leave the room, the number of people in my government who are privy to these facts is very small. Fewer than ten at this time." In fact, Lynne wasn't sure how many people in Washington knew, just that it was a small number.

When done they got up and gently embraced. The prime minister said little. Was he mad? Was he in shock or disbelief? Was this information news or confirmation of what he already suspected? She couldn't tell. He played his cards close to his vest.

Lynne, Nassif, and Drinker escorted Kuwait's prime minister and his deputy down to the Mission's main lobby. US Marines flanked the doors and the welcome desk. The prime minister's limousine and security detail could be seen through the lobby's glass walls and doors. Just inside the doors best wishes and goodbyes were exchanged. The Americans waved to the prime minister as his car drove off. Lynne's security detail stood a few feet back. Four FBI agents in dark suits that had observed Lynne during lunch stood further back along one of the lobby walls.

After Prince Jaber's limousine turned on to Rte de Pregny, Lynne said to Nassif and Drinker, "I need to use the ladies' room. Then I'd like to meet for a few minutes with both of you to compare notes and discuss next steps. Carter, you got a few minutes?"

"Certainly. I'm all yours."

"Great. I'll be right back. Peter, could you see if that conference room remains available for a few more minutes?"

"Sure."

* * *

The FBI agents tried not to attract attention. The fewer people who knew their purpose, the better. Thus, only one of them followed Lynne, Nassif, and Drinker back up to the second floor. She sat on a chair in the hallway pretending to read a magazine while they met in the conference room.

The agents didn't want to interrupt the secretary's meetings. At the same time, they couldn't act once she exited the Mission. Pursuant to the Vienna Convention on Diplomatic Relations and the US–Switzerland Host Agreement, their jurisdiction stopped at the Mission's edge. Hence, the other three agents waited near the Mission's main welcome desk.

A few minutes after 3:00 p.m. Lynne said goodbye to Nassif and Drinker outside the second floor conference room. They both had friends and colleagues in the Mission they wanted to say "hi" to. Both also had dinner plans that did not include the secretary.

Lynne had her head down when she exited the elevator. She was checking e-mails on her work phone. Her security detail was waiting for her. She finished checking her work e-mails as she approached the welcome desk. She was anxious to check her personal e-mails and messages. She hoped she had a message from Fhani. Just as she reached for her second phone in her purse, two of the FBI agents stopped her. The other two agents stood back and behind.

"Secretary Farnsworth, I am Agent Gleason with the FBI and this is Agent Webster." Both agents showed her their badges. Lynne's close protection detail shot glances at each other.

"Madam Secretary, can we step over here for a moment?" The agent pointed to the side of the lobby. "We'd like to have a word with you in private."

Lynne was speechless. What was happening? She also shot glances at her security detail. After a momentary pause she accompanied the two agents. Her security detail and the other two FBI agents stood 10-feet away. No one in the lobby seemed to notice.

"Madam Secretary, we are placing you under arrest. You have the right to remain silent. Anything you say can and will be used against you in a court of law. You have the right to an attorney. If you cannot afford one, one will be provided to you."

Lynne's head was spinning. What? Arrest? In a whisper she asked, "Why are you arresting me? What for?"

"I have the warrant right here. I can provide you with a copy. It details several alleged crimes, including accepting payments from a foreign government in violation of the Federal Bribery Act, wire fraud, and conspiracy to act as a foreign agent."

Lynne was silent. She had not known fear like this since she was a child.

"Madam Secretary, I want to explain to you what is going to happen next. I know this is unexpected and likely overwhelming. Please try to concentrate. First, we are *not* going to place handcuffs on you. We will, however, accompany you back to your hotel, where we will help you pack and check out. A plane is waiting for us at the airport. Mr. Drinker will be informed by one of my colleagues that you had to return to Washington unexpectedly. Once back in Washington US marshals will take custody of you and federal prosecutors will advise you on next steps. If you have an attorney, you will have an opportunity to call that person on the ride out to the airport. Now speaking of your phone, we will need to confiscate them. I believe you have three."

Lynne suddenly focused. They knew about the phone registered in the Cayman Islands. She shouldn't have listened to Fhani.

Agent Gleason gestured in the direction of the female FBI agent. "Madam Secretary, this is Agent Cooper. She will be at your side at all times until we hand you off to the marshals in Washington. Agent Cooper needs to take possession of your purse and anything in your pockets. Please provide those items to her at this time."

Chapter Fifty-One

General Bortaikov lived in one of the nicest and newest apartment buildings in Moscow with his wife, Polina, and his sixteen-year old son, Dmitriy. SVR agents protected the building 24/7 and provided on-demand chauffeur services day and night. By any measure, they lived a privileged life.

Like most Russian elites, Bortaikov also owned a dacha in the countryside. In fact, he owned two—one located south of the SVR campus that he and his family used, and one west of Moscow in the exclusive Rublyovka neighborhood that his mistress and other "guests" used.

Bortaikov and Polina had been married twenty-four years. In March they would celebrate their twenty-fifth anniversary. However, today was the last Sunday in November—Mother's Day. An increasingly important holiday in Russia.

As he entered the kitchen a little after 6:30 a.m., Polina handed him his first cup of coffee of the day.

"Good morning, Misha."

"Thank you. And Happy Mother's Day."

"Oh, you remembered. I thought you might forget."

"No. Of course not. What do you want to do to celebrate? What sounds good? You want me to see if I can get a reservation at Bryanskiy do Brazil?" Bryanskiy was the hottest, new restaurant in Moscow. Online reviews claimed it was the most authentic *churrascaria* outside of Brazil.

"No, I don't want to eat too much, especially a heavy meal at night. How about lunch at the Club?"

The Moskva Club was a legendary yet mysterious venue in Moscow. It was located about halfway between downtown Moscow and SVR's campus in Yasenevo. A visit there was proof of one's status. The quality of the wine and the creativity of the chef were legendary. Moreover, as a senior government official, Bortaikov enjoyed special privileges at the Club, including access to private rooms, valet parking, and a personal wine locker. On any given occasion, guests of the Club could rub elbows with ministers, TV personalities, members of the Duma, famous journalists, and provincial governors.

"Sure. Maybe Dmitriy can join us."

"That'd be great. I'll ask him when he wakes up. How about one o'clock?"

"Can we move it back a little? Say 1:30 or 1:45? I've got a meeting I need to chair that starts at noon. It shouldn't last over an hour."

"On a Sunday?"

"Yes, I'm sorry."

"Oh, Misha," she said with a sigh. "I was hoping we could have a quiet morning followed by a nice lunch."

"No, I can't. I'll meet you there at 1:45."

Polina knew it would do no good to whine or complain. The conversation was over. As far as he was concerned, she was lucky to see him at all.

Her husband was not the most attentive man in the world, nor the most romantic. Nonetheless, their marriage worked. Compared to most Russian woman, she had little to complain about.

Bortaikov finished his coffee, showered, and got dressed. At a little after 9:30 a.m. he kissed his wife on the forehead and walked out the door. It would be the last time she would see him alive.

* * *

Bortaikov's meeting at SVR finished at 1:10 p.m. Back in his office he quickly checked e-mails and text messages before slipping into his private bathroom.

As the director of the SVR, Bortaikov had access to a private elevator and a small fleet of cars stationed outside his personal entrance to the building. It was Sunday. The building was quieter than usual. This meant fewer guards and attendants standing around when he came off the elevator. The ones who were present were unknown to him. Moreover, he didn't make eye contact with any of them. Instead he quickly passed through the doors and jumped into the limousine waiting for him.

As his car pulled away from the building, two *gelikis* did as well, with one in front and one behind. Bortaikov did not notice the plain white windowless van that followed. Neither did he notice that the driver of his car and the other man in the front seat were not employed by SVR. They were instead *opers* (aka operatives) who were part of a little-known paramilitary group run by the Division of Operations against Criminal Organizations (URPO) within the FSB. So were the men in the van.

URPO enjoyed considerable autonomy within the FSB. They had their own car pool, technical support services, SWAT units, and even their own building, separate and apart from the FSB's famous headquarters in the former offices of the KGB on Lubyanka Square in Moscow.

In the beginning, URPO's mandate stopped at the Russian border and was limited to extrajudicial actions against suspected criminals. Over time, however, its reach extended beyond Russia, and included the torture and killing of anyone, anywhere, anytime.

Bortaikov loved eating at the Club. Since it was Mother's Day, he suspected the kitchen would prepare something special. A juicy steak sounded good to him. Perhaps a Porterhouse.

As his motorcade approached the turn-off for the Club, Bortaikov was deep in thought. Should he open that 2001 Leoville-Barton from Bordeaux that he had been saving or the 2016 Tignanello "Super Tuscan" in his locker?

About a half-mile past the turn Bortaikov realized what had happened. He did not immediately notice that the *geliki*s were gone and only the white van followed.

"Hey, driver. You missed the turn-off for the Club. Go back!"

The driver did not react. His face betrayed nothing. He stared straight ahead through dark sunglasses.

"Did you hear me?" Bortaikov shouted.

Not another word was spoken Instead, the man in the front passenger seat calmly turned around and pointed a 9 mm Glock 17 with a silencer on the end of it at Bortaikov's forehead. *Pffft-pffft.* Only two shots were needed. He was glad none of Bortaikov's blood or brains splattered on his freshly pressed suit or shirt.

They drove another twenty minutes to an automobile junkyard. The white van followed.

The entrance to the yard was at the end of a long, gravel road. The sign at the gate read "Moscovet Co. Ltd." Aside from the fact that the gate was open, the place appeared to be closed and abandoned. No one came out to greet them and what passed for an office was dark inside. Nonetheless, the driver of Bortaikov's car did not hesitate. He drove past the office and over to a large machine. The van stopped at the gate. Four heavily armed men in gray camouflage fatigues exited the van and stood in front of the gate.

The two men in the car got out. They said nothing. The driver threw the keys on the front seat. Neither looked back at Bortaikov, who was slumped over in the back seat in a pool of blood.

A large crane roared to life. Black smoke belched from its engine. The sound caused a flock of magpies resting in nearby trees to kick up in search of safety. The men kept walking, unfazed by the commotion.

The main boom on the crane was over forty-feet tall. A thick steel cable ran from a spindle near the cab to a large steel claw that resembled the talons on an eagle. At a height of twenty feet, the operator of the crane released the brake and let the steel claw crash into the roof of the car. The spikes on the claw tore through the car's roof. The operator then flipped a lever that caused the spikes to contract. Once the car was firmly in the claw's grasp, the operator lifted the car off the ground, swung it around, and dropped it into the large machine that was next to Bortaikov's car. The machine then proceeded to squeeze and press the car over and over again until it was the size of a small washing machine.

Then a large piston slowly and very deliberately pushed what was left of the car out of the crusher, like ground beef being squeezed through an antique meat grinder. Once the cube of metal had passed out of the crusher, a second crane with a large, round scrap magnet on the end of a steel cable picked it up and dropped it into a furnace. The temperature inside the furnace was 2,850 degrees Fahrenheit.

Meanwhile, back at the Club, Polina and Dmitriy were being shown to their table in one of the VIP-only rooms. Upon entering the room Polina immediately saw Nikolai Borovikov, his wife, and their two daughters. Borovikov was the deputy director of the SVR. They chatted for a few minutes. Borovikov asked Polina where her husband, his boss, was. She explained that he was coming from the office and would be along shortly.

Unbeknownst to Borovikov, at that very moment he was getting a promotion.

Chapter Fifty-Two

"Hello, this is Tony Sonsini."

"Tony, this is Audrey Ackerman over at Langley. You got a minute?"

"Sure. What's up?"

"Last month we got a call from the president's national security advisor. He expressed some concern about Suriname. He said he had reason to believe the Russians might be looking for oil and gas there. He asked us to check it out. Since the request had to do with Russia, it got bumped over to my office. I immediately had my guys check with our sources in Suriname. I also asked the National Reconnaissance Office if they could get some satellite time over Suriname. At first they thought they could piggyback on to regular passes over Venezuela; however, the imagery was off, so they had to request a small "retask." As you may know, those things take time, even when it is the White House that is ultimately making the ask."

"Yeah, I do. In fact, I was talking to one of our *squints* in the cafeteria last week. He said any reprogramming of a satellite, big or small, practically requires an act of Congress."

Squints is a slang term used in the intelligence community. It refers to a satellite imagery analyst (aka a photo interpreter).

Ackerman laughed at the hyperbole. "Yes, well, it took two weeks, but I now have several very interesting images that have been thoroughly vetted by our SIGNIT Office. One is of Paramaribo, the capital, and the other is of a site along the coast called Coppename. I can upload them to JWICS. Take a look at them and then let me know when you might be available to discuss. Ideally, we'd get my team and yours in the same room for an hour."

JWICS stands for Joint Worldwide Intelligence Communications System, an interagency network reserved for top secret/SCI information.

"Sure. That sounds like a plan."

"Thanks. I got a hunch my boss is going to want to brief the White House on this."

"Understood. I'll be in touch."

* * *

Salter and Esmond were the last ones to enter the Sit Room. Seated around the table were Sharon Holcumb and Audrey Ackerman from the CIA, Tony Sonsini and his boss, the deputy director of the NSA, Kiran De, and from the Department of Defense Collin Donovan, General Rafferty, and Marlin Lackey. Seated in chairs along the walls were various staffers from Defense, State, and the president's National Security Council. Also in attendance was Langston Chu, the deputy secretary of state, together with his principal deputy. Following Secretary Farnsworth's arrest, the president named Chu the acting secretary of state.

Salter began the meeting. "Alright. First of all, I want to thank everyone for coming on such short notice. I especially want to welcome Langston to this meeting. I know it's been a busy couple of weeks for him."

"Thanks, Bob," Chu said with a broad smile.

"Okay, who's going to kick things off?" Salter asked the room.

Esmond replied. "Bob, why don't I go first? I can provide some background for this discussion and then perhaps Sharon can fill us in on the Agency's investigation."

"Sounds good. Go ahead."

"Alright. Well, about a month ago the president met with Russia's ambassador in the Oval Office. After that meeting the president asked me if Suriname produced much oil. I told him I didn't think so, but I would inquire. One of the people I checked with was Rick Atwater at Energy. Rick, as some of you may know, leads the Oil and Gas Bureau there. We talked at length about Suriname. Rick said Total and APA believe there are significant reserves in Suriname. He also said a Dutch company, Energie Bronnen, has recently commissioned its second oil rig off the coast of Suriname. Rick provided me with two reports his team recently authored that look at the oil and gas industry in that part of the world. Based on my discussions with Rick and others, I asked Langley to see what they knew about Suriname in general and Russia's activities there in particular. Unless anyone has any questions, I'll stop here and yield the floor to Sharon. Sharon?"

"Thanks, Mark," Holcumb replied. "Suriname lies along the northeast corner of Latin America, between Guyana and French Guiana. It was a Dutch colony for many years, until it gained its independence in 1975. In 2015 significant oil reserves were discovered to the west of Suriname, in Guyana. Brazil is also moving to exploit oil it has found just to the east of Suriname, in what is called the Equatorial Margin. For the past year an engineering firm linked to Russian oligarch Grigori Nikolaevich has been conducting tests and collecting rock and soil samples in various parts of Suriname, particularly along the coast. We believe this firm, called Gazneft, is looking for oil and gas. Then about three months ago Russia's oil minister, Sergei Petrov, led a delegation of Russian oil and gas companies to Suriname. Representatives of all the major Russian companies attended. They spent close to a week there traveling around the country, and wining and dining Suriname's president and cabinet. During most of their time in Suriname they were accompanied by executives from Gazneft."

Holcumb paused. Speaking to faceless staffers in the Sit Room Comms Center, she asked, "Could someone please bring up the satellite photos of Paramaribo?" In an instant two photos appeared on the screens at the end of the room.

"These are satellite photos of the capital city—Paramaribo. The one on the left was taken fourteen months ago. On the right is essentially the same image, except it was taken two weeks ago. Please focus your attention on the upper-left quadrant of each image. See the difference? The facility that you see there is a compound belonging to Gazneft."

Salter asked, "Is this the only one, or does Gazneft have other facilities in Suriname?"

Holcumb answered Salter by asking the Comms Center to pull up another set of satellite photos. "Bob, these images show the coastline of Suriname. Not far from the border with Guyana. This area is called Coppename. Again, the image on the left was taken fourteen months ago. The image on the right was taken two weeks ago. The change is unmistakable. Sir, we believe Russian oil and gas companies, supported by paramilitary forces belonging to the Volga Group, are preparing to ramp up operations in the region."

"The Volga Group?" Salter asked.

"Yes, the Volga Group is sponsored by Nikolaevich," Ackerman said. "It is every bit as lethal as the Wagner Group. Using Russian military transports, including the Ilyushin IL-76, they have been bringing oil equipment and men into Suriname on a fairly regular basis since the end of November. For now, we estimate the number of paramilitary operatives at fewer than 55. However, as their ranks have grown over the past few weeks, they have become more and more aggressive. Officials at Total and APA report numerous episodes lately of harassment and vandalism of their property by men they believe belong to the Volga Group."

"Jesus," Salter exclaimed. "Anything else?"

"Just one other thing, if I may?" Kiran De said more as a statement than a question.

"Of course, Kiran. What do ya got?" Salter replied.

"Thanks. The NSA is closely monitoring communications between Suriname and Russia in general and between and amongst officials at Gazneft and the Volga Group in particular. With one exception, those communications do not add much to what you've already heard."

"Oh? What is the exception?" Salter asked.

"The exception is a series of recent communications between leaders of the Volga Group in Suriname and the Russian military base on the Island of La Orchila off the coast of Venezuela. Those comms reveal that their goal is to get as many as 200, and maybe as many as 500, Volga operatives into Suriname by the end of March. In a small country, that's a lot of men. In fact, I believe Suriname's total armed forces barely exceed 2,000."

"Fucking Russians," was all Salter could say in response. "Thanks, Kiran." Looking around the room, Salter asked again. "Anything else?"

Holcumb responded on behalf of everyone. "I think that's it for now. Obviously we are working closely with the NSA and others to monitor the situation. And to the extent there are any developments, they'll be noted in the President's PDB."

The President's Daily Brief, sometimes referred to as the President's Daily Briefing or the President's Daily Bulletin, is a top-secret document produced and given each morning to the president of the United States. It is also distributed to a small number of top-level US officials such as the national security advisor.

"Okay. Thanks, everyone. This has been helpful. I need to brief the president. He's going to want to know about this."

Chapter Fifty-Three

(10 Months Before the Election)

The young FBI agent on a six-month detail to the White House sat next to a phone in front of the fireplace in the Oval Office. President Hansen, flanked by Acting Secretary Chu on one side of the Resolute desk, and Esmond and Salter on the other, waited to pick up his phone. A White House photographer captured the moment. Many years later the FBI agent would proudly hang the photograph in her office in the main FBI building on Pennsylvania Avenue.

"This is the White House. I can connect you to the president whenever the prime minister is ready."

In The Hague, 3,800 miles away, the prime minister of the Netherlands sat in his office in the Het Torentje (the "Little Tower"). It wasn't every day that he spoke to the president of the United States, but this was important. The State Department and the White House arranged the call on very short notice.

One of the prime minister's aides replied. "Thank you. Prime Minister Geraets is on the line."

"Mister Prime Minister, I will connect you to the president of the United States now." Looking at the president, the agent said, "Go ahead, Mr. President."

Hansen hit the button that opened the line and turned on the phone's speaker. "Mr. Prime Minister, this is President Hansen. How are you?"

It wasn't Hansen's style to be so formal; however, he didn't really know Geraets. He'd only met him once at a NATO summit in Brussels, but even that was just for a few minutes.

"I'm fine, sir, thank you for asking. And thank you for taking my call on such short notice."

"Of course. It's late there," Hansen said with a slight rise in his voice. "What is it, 9:30 p.m.?"

"Yes, sir. But what I have to discuss with you cannot wait."

"I see. What is so urgent?"

"Well, sir, as you may know, my country has a very close relationship with Suriname. For over 300 years it was a colonial possession. And even after the Surinamese gained their independence in 1975, we continued to have a close relationship with them. In fact, the Netherlands is the largest investor in Suriname and we are the single largest provider of foreign aid to Suriname."

"I'm afraid we provide very little assistance to Suriname. Our priorities in Latin America and the Caribbean are Haiti, Columbia, and a handful of other countries where our assistance seeks to combat, among other things, poverty and the drug cartels."

"I understand, sir. Now, you may also know that oil was discovered in Suriname about fifteen years ago. One of our companies, Energie Bronnen, recently commissioned its second oil rig off the coast of Suriname. An American oil company, APA, and a French company, Total, are also active in Suriname. Others, including Shell, have begun operations in Suriname. In any event, starting around February of last year a Russian engineering firm, Gazneft, began looking for new oil and gas deposits in Suriname. Then in September Russia's oil minister led a delegation of Russian oil and gas companies on a week-long visit to Suriname. Since then a paramilitary group called Volga has been building its presence in Suriname. At first, they largely kept to themselves; however, beginning about two months ago they became more aggressive. Harassing Bronnen's personnel, vandalizing their equipment. I believe similar things have happened to APA and Total. Nothing too serious, until yesterday."

"What happened yesterday?" Hansen asked.

"We're still investigating, but preliminarily it looks like a supply ship operated by Bronnen got into some sort of confrontation at dockside with a group of men belonging to Volga. One thing led to another and shots were fired. Four men were killed and two were injured. All from the Dutch city of Rotterdam."

"I'm sorry to hear that."

"Thank you, Mr. President. Unfortunately, two of the casualties were brothers. I have to inform their mother in the morning. I'm not looking forward to that."

"What about the police? Is Suriname's government investigating the incident? Has anyone been arrested?"

"Mr. President, they say they are investigating, but Suriname is a small country. In fact, the smallest in Latin America. We're not optimistic that anything will be done. Besides, the Russians are believed to be bribing officials and throwing their weight around Suriname. And things are only going to get worse. NATO believes Russia is desperate to find new sources of oil and Suriname is one of its top priorities."

"Mr. Prime Minister, your comments and observations echo what my intelligence officials have been telling me about Suriname and Russia. So what do you want my government to do? Why the late-night call?"

"Mr. President, our two governments share an interest in the fair and healthy development of Suriname's energy sector. We do not need another Venezuela in Latin America."

"I agree. But—"

"Mr. President, I'm sorry to interrupt, but 4,000 miles and a large ocean separate my small country from Suriname. We need your help. The Volga Group is a cancer that is growing in Suriname. It needs to be removed. The longer we wait, the more difficult it will be and the more harm they will do to the people and institutions of Suriname."

Hansen leaned back in his chair deep in thought. He looked at Esmond and Salter. His eyes were intense and unblinking. As he turned to look at Chu, he said to Geraets, "I see."

"Mr. President, we are not asking the United States to do anything we wouldn't do. In fact, our Commando Corps has trained on many occasions with your Navy SEALs, Delta Force, Green Berets, and Army Rangers. If they would be welcome, they will assist in this operation. I just don't know how quickly they can deploy to that part of the world. I have not discussed this with our military leaders."

"Mr. Prime Minister, may I call you Ruud?"

"Yes, of course."

"Well, Ruud, please call me Walter."

"Yes, sir." Hansen ignored the continuing formality. He'd been president of the most powerful country on earth for three years. He was used to it by now.

"Ruud, I'll obviously need to consult with my military leaders. And perhaps they'll want to speak with their Dutch counterparts."

"Yes, sir, I completely understand."

"But as I think about this, I wonder if we could agree at the outset on two things."

"What is that, Mr. President, I mean Walter."

"Well, first, there can be no press conferences or any public announcement of any kind about this. I don't want to get in a shooting war with Russia over Suriname. This would have to be top secret top to bottom."

"I agree."

"Personally, I don't mind sending a signal to Putin through back-channels that he's not welcome in Suriname, but I don't want to rub his face in it."

"Yes sir, what's the other condition?"

"Americans are facing record high gas prices and Shell has more gas stations in the United States than any other company. Now, I know it has moved its headquarters to London, but I believe it still has important ties to the Netherlands. Could your office talk to Shell? I would love to see a price war at the gas pump."

"That's a *tall* ask, Walter."

"I know, but not as *tall* as the one you are making of me." Hansen looked Esmond and Salter in the eyes. They both smiled. Hansen blinked at Salter.

Unbeknownst to Geraets, Hansen had already ordered a military strike on the Volga facilities in Suriname. Preparations were well underway.

"Fair enough, Mr. President. I'll see what I can do."

Hansen wanted to return the discussion to a more formal plane, "Mr. Prime Minister, I will do the same. Anything else?"

"No, sir. I deeply appreciate your time and consideration."

"My pleasure. And perhaps we can explore the possibility of a state visit in the fall, before our elections in November. I believe it's been many years since the prime minister of the Netherlands has been to the White House."

Now Salter was grinning from ear to ear. He was observing a master politician at work. Geraets, like most political leaders in Western Europe, would *kill* for an invitation to a state visit in Washington. And it never hurt for a president, especially one running for reelection, to be seen conducting the affairs of state on a grand stage like the East Room of the White House.

Chapter Fifty-Four

Elliot liked to relax around the house on Sundays. Karen liked to get out and do something. On this Sunday, they would do a little of both. After a quiet morning spent drinking coffee and reading the paper, they had plans to visit Roger Payne and his wife Julia at their home out in Ashburn, Virginia. Elliot wanted to see how Roger was doing and Karen liked spending time with Julia.

Other than to catch a flight at Dulles, Elliot couldn't remember the last time he'd headed west out of Washington. When he and Karen first moved to Fairfax County in 1996, much of Loudoun County was cornfields and barns. Now it was part of Washington, DC's massive urban sprawl that stretched essentially from the Chesapeake Bay to the Blue Ridge Mountains.

The Paynes lived in a brick three-bedroom colonial off of Gloucester Parkway. Elliot rang the doorbell shortly after 1:00 p.m. He held a bottle of red wine in a decorative paper wine bag. Karen had a small plant in a clay pot. Julia answered the door.

"Hello, how are you? Come on. Come in. How was traffic?"

Elliot let Karen enter first. Karen gently embraced Julia. Elliot did the same.

"Oh, traffic was fine," Elliot replied. "But my goodness, how things have grown out here."

Karen wasn't surprised by the growth. She often spent time in Loudoun County, shopping at Costco in Sterling or venturing out to Purcellville and the outlet stores in Leesburg.

"I know," Julia said. "And they keep building. In fact, they're building a new high school off of Ashburn Road. When we first moved here in 1999 Loudoun County had only five high schools. Now it has 18."

"Yeah, it's amazing. So—" Looking down at the wine, he handed it to Julia. "We brought you some wine. It's a Cab from Napa. We hope you like it."

And Karen reached her arms out. "I also thought you might like this. It's rosemary." With a slightly mischievous look on her face, Karen said, "a sprig of rosemary is a great addition to a cosmo!"

"Say, that's an idea. It's five o'clock somewhere," Julia said followed by a giggle.

"So where's your husband?" Elliot asked.

"He's out back on the deck." Raising her voice, Julia called to her husband. "ROGER, Elliot and Karen are here." Pointing at sliding glass doors off of the kitchen, she told Elliot, "Go ahead, I think he has a cooler full of beers out there. Help yourself."

"Now you're talking. I don't mind if I do," Elliot said with a smile. Karen stayed inside with Julia.

It was a beautiful winter day, a bit cold, but Elliot brought a coat and Roger had one of those six-foot high propane heaters sold by the big hardware stores. It put out a surprising amount of heat.

When Payne saw Elliot come through the sliders, he started to get up. Elliot could immediately tell that Payne was not 100 percent. "No, no, don't get up." They shook hands and Payne settled back down in his chair.

"How you doin'?" Elliot asked.

"Oh, I'm alright. Still a tad sore."

"Considering you were shot through the chest less than four weeks ago, I'd say you're doing pretty well."

"Thanks. They say I should fully recover and be back at work by July or August. That seems a tad ambitious to me. I get tired easily. But I'm goin' to PT twice a week. And we've started goin' for short walks 'round the neighborhood. We'll see. How 'bout you? How you doin'? Say, you want a beer?"

"Sure, I'll take one. Thanks."

Payne pointed to a cooler siting on the deck behind Elliot. "They're over yonder. Help yourself."

"Thanks."

Elliot grabbed a Yuengling. His favorite. As he sat down next to Payne he said, "I'm fine. Been trying to take it easy. The Mutairi investigation really had me hoppin'. Still dealing with the paperwork and aftermath."

"I bet. Say, did ya manage to make it to Vince's funeral? I heard it was up in Scranton."

"Yeah, Karen and I drove up. Lousy weather the whole way. But notwithstanding the weather, lots of people attended, including Acting Secretary Chu and the undersecretary for management, Gretel Espinoza. I happened to speak to her for close to ten minutes. Very nice lady."

"How 'bout Steve's funeral? Did ya go to that?"

"No. I didn't. That would have been awkward."

"I gotcha. Say, what's the latest on Farnsworth? I heard she's out on bail awaitin' trial."

"I don't really know what's happening with her. I've been so busy."

"Yeah. Say… did the FBI interview ya? They interviewed me twice: once at Walter Reed and once here. At Walter Reed they lined the room with sound-deadenin' panels. They also had some sort of electronic devices that supposedly could interfere with any attempts to eavesdrop on the interview."

"Oh, yeah. They grilled me for close to three hours. In fact, they showed up at my house the Sunday after you were shot. I think they've interviewed everybody: Wally, Russ Adams, the two agents who were helping me—Alice Lake and Victor Young, and probably many more. Those guys are tenacious."

"They really are. Did they record your interview?"

"Of course. My dining room looked like a recording studio," Elliot said with chuckle.

"Me too. What 'bout Fhani? Did they ask ya 'bout him?"

"Who?"

"Fhani. Saman Khalil Al-Fhani. Her lover. The guy from Qatar. Don'tcha know 'bout him?"

"No, not really. They asked me about him, but I didn't have much to say. I never met him and I don't believe he ever came up during my investigation of Mutairi's death."

"Interestin'. Everybody on the detail knew 'bout him. Pretty hard not to. For a long time she tried to keep her relationship with 'em secret. But maybe startin' 'bout three or four months ago she stopped tryin' to hide it. In fact, he was with her the whole time they was in Bali."

"What about her husband? Didn't he know?"

"I doubt it. They rarely saw each other. I think that was a marriage in name only."

"Huh. I had no idea."

"Yeah, I think she really loved Fhani and wanted to be with him in part because her marriage to her husband was basically over."

"Geez. That's kind of sad."

"I'm surprised ya didn't know."

"Did Fhani love her?"

"That's a darn good question. I never did take to the fella much. I think he was just usin' her."

"How so?"

"You heard 'bout the money, didn'tcha?"

"Well, if you mean the payment she received for lobbying the Iraqis, yes. That's why they arrested her, right?"

"Yeah, but did ya hear what happen'?"

"I guess not. What?"

"So rumor has it she got $2 million for every lease Qatar snagged. Two companies in Qatar nabbed six leases altogether. That's $12 million!!"

"Damn. That's a lot of money."

"I'll say. Anyway, I ain't certain when the Qataris paid her, but the FBI arrested her at the US Mission in Geneva on a Wednesday. When they nabbed her they seized her phones and laptops. By the time she got back to Washington the following day, she was cooperatin' with them investigators. I believe it was Thursday or Friday of that week that the FBI tried to access the account holdin' the funds using either her laptop or one of her phones. Guess what they found in the account."

"What?"

"Nothin'. Nary a dime."

"Wait. What happened?"

"They don't know. One minute the money is in a Swiss bank account. The next minute it's gone."

"How do you know all this?"

"Do you know Tom Davis? He works for DSS." Pointing out his backyard Payne said, "He lives a few streets over yonder. Our kids attended school together. We catch up with Tom and his wife, Carol, every now and then. Real good folks."

"Yeah, I think I met him at Walter Reed when I went to see you. Wally introduced me."

"Oh. Huh. So the best man at his weddin' was Rob Gleason. They both went to Rutgers. Rob was the FBI agent who arrested the secretary in Geneva. Tom's been fillin' me in lately. In fact, he swung by here last night."

"So what do you think happened to the money?"

"I think Fhani took it."

"Really?"

"Yeah, Farnsworth claims the money was there 'fore she left Washington. Her phones and laptops were seized by the FBI the next day. One minute the money is in the account. The next minute, poof, it's gone."

"But how could Fhani take it?"

"Well, word is he helped her open an account with a Swiss bank. Apparently, he even gave her a phone registered in the Cayman Islands to open the account with. Lord knows what kinda back doors he might've placed on that thing? I'm tellin' ya, the guy was no good—but she loved him. Like you said, it's all very sad. Her career is ruined, her reputation is ruined, I don't think she has a lot of money, and now she'll likely spend ten or more years in jail."

"If what you're saying is true, I'd like to nail that fucker. I mean, he stole $12 million from a US citizen. Right?"

"Yeah, that's true," Payne said, his voice rising.

"Who happened to be the US secretary of state."

"Yeah, I see what you're sayin'. I 'gree." Payne could see that Elliot was getting angry.

"Granted," Elliot said, "she wasn't supposed to have that money, but it certainly wasn't his to take!"

Just then Julia appeared at the sliding glass doors. "Roger, why don't you and Elliot come in? I heated up some croissants and you can have fresh fruit with it."

"Thanks, darlin'. We'll be in directly."

Chapter Fifty-Five

The Virginia-class nuclear attack submarine USS *Alexander* (SSN-838) was nearing the end of its six-month deployment in the south Atlantic. Its crew of 132 was looking forward to 45 days in port for repairs and refurbishment when the orders were received via the ship's Satellite Information Exchange Sub-System.

The *Alexander* was to rendezvous in two days' time with the USS *Arkansas* and on board twelve Navy SEALs and their gear. The *Arkansas*, a flat-topped amphibious assault ship that normally supported helicopter missions and amphibious landing craft, would also transfer to the *Alexander* two rigid-inflatable boats (RIBs), both equipped with the Navy's latest battery-operated run-silent motors.

Like the other submarines in its class, the *Alexander* was specifically designed to support the insertion and extraction of SEALs and other underwater special operation forces (SUB SOF). For example, it had an integrated dry deck shelter (DDS) near its screws and an integrated lockout trunk (LOT) on the rear deck. Both provided underwater combatants with a floodable chamber that could equalize with sea pressure, thereby allowing so-called lock in lock out (LILO) insertions of personnel or a

SEAL delivery vehicle (SDV), such as the new Mark 14 Mod 1 via the DDS, although one of the more common ways for SUB SOF to get off a sub is in inflatable boats, like a RIB, that simply float on and float off (FOFO).

* * *

Master Chief Bradley Riddick was the assault commander. He would lead Echo Team on to the beach near the border with Guyana.

Riddick was from Brooklyn, New York. He was 37-years old. He joined the Navy right out of high school. When he was seven he stayed home from school one day to nurse a sore throat. It was September 11, 2001. He and his mom watched in horror as the Twin Towers fell.

His parents had known people who worked for Cantor Fitzgerald on the 104th floor of the North Tower. The image of people jumping out of a skyscraper because it was a better fate than burning alive never left him. He became a SEAL because he wanted to fight for people who were just trying to live their lives and make it through another day, people who had no ability to defend themselves.

"Listen up, Echo Team," Riddick barked. In an instant, everyone in the *Arkansas*' forward briefing room ceased talking.

"We're going to rendezvous with the SSN *Alexander* the day after tomorrow fifty miles off the coast of Suriname. Two of our RIBs will also be transferred, along with our gear. The *Alexander* will then take us to within a mile or two of the coast. Suriname's military capability is limited, so we are not concerned with radar or other forms of electronic detection. For the same reason, this will <u>not</u> be a LILO insertion. Instead, we'll FOFO off the back. Exfil will be the same. Our target is a compound on the beach near the border with Guyana controlled by Russian paramilitary forces belonging to the Volga Group. Mainly tents and huts. All one-story. SOCOM believes we'll encounter no more than twenty enemy hostiles, all lightly armed, but well trained. Most are former Russian special-op guys.

We'll go in under cover of darkness. We have two moonless nights coming up. We'll go in hot and dark with lasers on."

One of the older SEALs sitting in the back opened a tin of Copenhagen and put some dip between his front teeth and lip. His nickname was "Pops." Once finished, he asked Riddick, "What's our rules of engagement, sir?"

"These guys killed four employees of a Dutch oil company the week before last. They also wounded two others in an altercation on the docks. Washington doesn't want Russia to establish a permanent presence in Suriname, especially one that exploits its oil and gas sector. Our orders are to eliminate Volga and collect intel, including the hard drives on their computers. Hopefully, we can get in and out with little or no detection."

Another SEAL sitting up front, who graduated from Harvard prior to joining the Navy and whose nickname was "Brains," asked about civilians. "Do we expect any civilians in the compound, sir? If so, what should we do with 'em?"

Riddick responded. "Our orders are to eliminate Volga, not terminate everyone in the compound. Therefore, if you encounter any civilians, try not to harm them. If they pose a threat, go ahead and bind their hands and blindfold them. All others just leave them where you find them. Again, our goal is to get in and out as quietly as possible. So the less you speak English around them, the better. Any other questions?"

Another SEAL was tempted to ask if commanders had considered a kinetic option—that is, drop bombs on the compound. If the mission was to eliminate Russian paramilitaries, why not do it from a distance? Why endanger the lives of Navy SEALs? But he decided against it. For one thing, the intel on civilians was ambiguous, at best. Second, this was what he trained to do. Moreover, bombs would *scream* American. If the goal was to get in and out and not leave American fingerprints, the SEALs were the right tool for the job.

Riddick continued. "If no further questions, I'll turn it over to Lieutenant Commander Jackson who will brief you on the other aspects of the mission. Commander Jackson?"

"Good evening, men," Jackson said. "Volga is not to be underestimated. They are dangerous and ruthless. They first appeared in Suriname about four months ago. At first there was only a handful sent mainly to escort Russia's oil minister and some Russian industry executives around Suriname. At present, we believe there are between 40 and 50 enemy combatants in country. Soon we expect that number to grow to as many as 200 and possibly 500. In a country as small as Suriname, a foreign military presence of that size could be very destabilizing. They've already begun to harass and vandalize the men and equipment of Dutch, French, and American oil companies operating in Suriname. As you heard Master Chief Riddick say, they've killed four workers and wounded two more. Our orders come directly from the president. He does not want Russia to establish a presence in Suriname. He does not want Russia to do to Suriname what it did to Venezuela. That's where you come in. Now, at the same time that you are hitting the compound at the beach, Bravo Team, led by Master Chief Jason Mahal, will be hitting a Volga facility on the outskirts of the capital, Paramaribo. SOCOM believes that facility contains around 25 enemy combatants. Bravo will be supported by a squad of commandos from the Netherlands."

"Dutch commandos, sir?" Brains asked, his voice rising.

"Yes," Jackson replied. "Suriname is a former Dutch colony. The Netherlands provides Suriname with more assistance than any other country. And the four guys killed last week, as well as the two who were wounded, were all Dutch. Now, the *Arkansas* will serve as the forward operations base for this mission. MQ 9 Reaper drones will monitor both engagements from overhead. Any other questions?"

The room was silent. Their faces betrayed no fear or emotion. These were what the military called Tier 2 operatives. Hardened men. Battle tested. They were members of the Navy's elite SEAL Team Four. They had been on hundreds of missions like this in Central and South America.

Chapter Fifty-Six

Under the cover of a pitch-black night, the USS *Alexander* broke the surface of the waters off the coast of Suriname. It was 0210 hours. Two miles separated the sub from shore. On its deck, twelve members of SEAL Team Four split into two RIBs fastened to the hull. Clad in specialized gear, including ceramic body armor and state-of-the-art four tube night optical devices (NODs), and armed with silencer-suppressed Heckler & Koch 418 automatic weapons, they were ghosts on the water, their approach undetected by any watchful eyes.

As they approached the beach they made a point of avoiding the dock. Volga might have guards stationed on the dock. Instead their run-silent motors glided the RIBs on to the beach. The sound of the waves crashing against the shore acted like a muffler to prevent their detection.

The SEALs swiftly disembarked, their movements coordinated and silent. With guns up and NODs down, they quickly covered the space between the water's edge and the dense foliage that was ubiquitous. They crouched low. Their target unaware of the threat that approached.

With practiced efficiency, Riddick directed his team toward the compound's perimeter. The SEALs moved with the fluidity of shadows, their weapons at the ready. They breached the defenses with minimal distur-bance, swiftly taking down the guards stationed at key positions.

The gunfire was scarce, each shot muffled by the suppressors. Echo Team maneuvered through the compound like phantoms. In many cases their victims were still sleeping. In a few instances they rose from their beds with AKs at the ready. However, the SEALs were invisible in the dark-ness. With their NODs and infrared torches at the ends of their guns, the SEALs could see their targets perfectly. The Russians had red dots on their chests, although they didn't know it. Before long the SEALs had cleared every hut and every room with surgical precision.

Riddick led three men to secure critical intel, while others disabled communications equipment. Riddick clicked his push to talk. "Put all the hard-drives in water-tight bags." The SEALs could hear him in their ear-pieces. They operated in perfect harmony, their training and expertise evi-dent in their seamless coordination.

As the compound fell under their control, the SEALs regrouped, their mission objectives accomplished. They swiftly retreated, vanishing into the night as seamlessly as they had arrived.

Back in their RIBs the two teams headed for the pickup point. The *Alexander* slowly breached the surface, like a giant whale coming up for air. The SEALs used oars for last-minute maneuvers. When both RIBs were directly over the aft deck, the *Alexander* completed its ascent in silence and darkness.

* * *

Ten minutes before the *Alexander* first rose from the depths of the Atlantic, a dark-gray Airbus A400M descended from the clouds above Paramaribo. Its destination? A dirt airstrip twenty-five miles from the center of town. Ironically, this was the same airstrip used the previous week by Russia's air force to ferry in men and equipment belonging to the Volga Group.

The moment the plane's tires touched down on the dusty runway the crew began to lower its rear ramp. The roar of the engines was deafening. The plane spun around and came to a stop. Ready to take off back into the wind at a moment's notice.

In total darkness, Dutch commandos in two Sherpa 4X4s sporting 50-caliber mounted machine guns on top drove off the back of the plane and secured both ends of the runway.

Next the crew rolled three MD-600 Little Bird choppers down the back ramp. They quickly unfurled rotors that had been stowed during the flight. Soon the high-pitched whirl of chopper engines blended with the roar of the Airbus' engines.

At precisely 0235 hours the birds lifted off, each with four SEALs perched on bench-like seats on the outside, their weapons at the ready and their feet dangling in the wind. Secured only by a light lanyard attached to a metal rail. They traveled at treetop level. Total flight time was 8 minutes, 15 seconds. They set down 450 yards from the perimeter of the Volga facility. The SEALs would run the last quarter mile.

Once the gates of the facility were in sight, they slowed to a walk, raised their guns, and lowered their NODs. One of the SEALs put an explosive charge on the front gate. When the breach blew, they moved in on foot.

Like the Echo Team had done on the beach, Bravo cleared all the buildings of Russians in a matter of minutes. They then turned their attention to the collection of intel and the destruction of communications equipment.

While the SEALs went about their business, Mahal radioed Jackson on the *Arkansas*. "Sir, this is Team Leader Bravo. There's some equipment here. Looks new. Russian markings. You want us to leave it or blow it?"

"Any idea what kind of equipment?"

"Hard to say, sir. Brains thinks it's some sort of testing equipment. Also some serious-looking motors, sir."

"If you have extra charges, go ahead and blow it. Prefer you use delays on the fuses. I'd like you airborne before anything blows and we make too much noise."

"Yes, sir. Copy that. Over."

* * *

On board the *Arkansas* Lieutenant Commander Jackson was in constant communication with Chiefs Riddick and Mahal. He was joined in the command center by Vice Admiral Stanley Kramer, the commanding officer of SEAL Team Four, who flew in on a Chinook the night before to observe.

They and their aides watched everything on screens that streamed full-motion video transmitted down from the Reapers. Each SEAL was a small black spot on the screen. The firing of weapons looked like fireflies briefly illuminating the night. They watched as the helos kicked up a cloud of dust just outside the Volga facility near Paramaribo. The Reaper over Paramaribo stayed on station long enough to confirm the explosions, which temporarily caused the screens they were watching to white out.

Chapter Fifty-Seven

The next morning the president met with his national security team in the Sit Room. In addition to Mark Esmond, Bob Salter, and Sharon Holcumb, Hansen was joined by the secretary of defense, who was joined by General Rafferty and Undersecretary Lackey. On the video screens at the end of the room were Admiral Kramer and Lieutenant Commander Jackson, along with the commander of the *Arkansas*, Captain Leslie O'Connell. The president spoke.

"Admiral Kramer, how'd it go last night?"

"Mission accomplished, Mr. President."

"Any casualties?"

"No, sir."

"That's great news. I heard this was SEAL Team Four. Is that right?"

"Yes, sir. Commander Jackson is a member of Four. He led the operation."

Hansen welcomed the opportunity to speak to a member of SEAL Team Four. "Commander Jackson, on behalf of your nation, I want to thank you for your service."

During his thirty years in the Navy and twenty-two as a SEAL, Jackson had done some pretty incredible things. But speaking directly to the president of the United States? He couldn't wait to tell his wife.

"Thank you, Mr. President. The real work was performed by the men on the ground. We had two teams of twelve that rolled in a little past 0230 in the morning on the targets. Members of the Dutch Commando Corps provided perimeter support. At the risk of sounding smug or glib, last night was just another day at the office for SEAL Team Four."

"Well, as routine as it may have been for you and your men, I and the nation are very grateful. Again, thank you. And now I need to speak with the prime minister of the Netherlands. I'm sure he is anxiously awaiting my call."

"Yes, Mr. President. Thank you."

Kramer and O'Connell also thanked the president seconds before the screens went blank.

* * *

Sitting behind his desk in the Oval Office, Hansen prepared to call the Dutch prime minister. Esmond and Salter stood to the side, next to the president's phone. Acting Secretary Chu couldn't make it. Esmond would brief him later. An FBI agent waited for the signal to open the line.

Hansen spoke to his CoS. "Bob, I've misplaced my talking points. Perhaps I left them in the Sit Room. Could you please print out another copy for me? I pretty much know everything I want to say to him, but I'd prefer to have the TPs in front of me."

"Sure, let me go do that. I'll be right back."

"Thanks."

Back down in the Sit Room Sergeant Winston, the comms officer on duty that morning, and another member of the watch team cleaned up the room. They tossed a few empty paper coffee cups in the trash and plastic water bottles in the blue recycle bin. It was not uncommon for busy White House personnel to leave things in the Sit Room after meetings.

This morning, however, Winston couldn't help but notice a few papers on the table near where the president had sat. Before he picked them up he stole a glance. One was entitled "Talking Points for TC w/PM Geraets." The other had no visible title. Instead there were hand-written notes on a piece of yellow legal paper. In the top right-hand corner someone had drawn over and over again a round circle about the size of a dime, with a five-pointed star inside of it. Everything appeared to be in the president's handwriting.

Near the bottom of the sheet the words "no oil, no security" appeared. The phrase had been underlined twice.

Epilogue

Rachel finished the fall term at the University of Washington. She never moved out of Hansee Hall and she did not witness any more violence, although she often found herself looking over her shoulder, both literally and figuratively.

Her last exam was on December 16. She flew home on December 18. She never went back. She liked UW and she thought Seattle was beautiful, but she missed her family and friends back home. Thankfully she did well on her final exams. As a result, she was able to transfer to Georgetown in the spring. Her parents were delighted to have her back home. Georgetown would cost Elliot twice as much as UW, but that was a small price to pay for her safety and his peace of mind.

* * *

Lake and Young were married seven months later at Holy Trinity Catholic Church in Georgetown on a warm Saturday in August. Over 250 people attended, including many who served with Young in the Marines. Elliot, Karen, and Rachel were invited. The reception was held at the Fairmount Hotel on M Street NW in Washington. It went well past 1:30 a.m. Rachel had never seen her parents drink or dance so much. She had to drive them home.

* * *

For the second time in his life Jim Farnsworth narrowly escaped going to prison. Federal prosecutors did not think they had enough evidence to convict him of violating Treasury sanctions on Russia or the Foreign Corrupt Practices Act. Lynne was not so lucky. She was convicted of wire fraud, conspiracy to act as a foreign agent, conspiracy to commit bribery, and acting as an undisclosed agent of a foreign government in violation of 18 U.S.C. § 951. She was sentenced to fourteen years in prison. She spent most of her time in Alderson Federal Prison Camp in West Virginia, the same prison Martha Stewart spent time in. The funds that Qatar paid her vanished.

Lynne never filed for divorce. Instead Jim did six months after she was convicted. He shuttered Energy Plus before the divorce was made final. The company had no assets by the time the court ruled.

Jim eventually went back to Massachusetts. His career as an energy trader was over. He rented a two-bedroom apartment two miles east of I-81. He had no earned income and few assets, so he took a job as a cashier at the Yankee Candle Company south of Deerfield. It took him eight minutes to get to work. Between his social security benefits and his paycheck, he lived a comfortable, but simple life.

Eighteen months after Lynne got out of prison she suffered a massive stroke. It left her completely paralyzed on the left side. She was unable to care for herself. On her eighty-third birthday she moved into an assisted living facility north of Frederick, Maryland. Jim came to visit her once or twice a year. She never saw Fhani again.

Lynne Farnsworth died in her sleep on a Sunday morning in April. The window closest to her bed was open. Lynne had always liked the smell of jasmine in the spring. She was eighty-five years old.

* * *

Walter Hansen stunned the editorial boards and pundits when he won reelection in November. His opponent, Senator Randolph McCormick from Oregon, won the popular vote by over three million. However, he lost the all-important contest in the Electoral College. Historians will long debate the extent to which falling gas prices at the pump contributed to Hansen's victory.